THE FACILITY TOOK EVERYTHING FROM HIM, INCLUDING HIS EYES. NOW ANDREW HARKINS IS DETERMINED TO USE HIS SPECIAL ABILITIES TO EXACT REVENGE.

Doctor Andrew Harkins accepts his dream job at a cutting-edge lab, but the dream becomes a nightmare when he refuses to use unwilling human test subjects. Andrew finds himself at odds with the owner of the Facility. They take everything from him, including his eyes, but there is more to Andrew Harkins than they know. Using his unique physical abilities, he escapes the lab, but is determined to return and destroy it, along with its maniacal owner, Alain Savon. But before he can exact his revenge, he must cross a merciless desert, avoid gun runners, and elude the U.S. Military.

What People are Saying about THE MAN WITH NO EYES

"*The Man with No Eyes* is strongly character-driven with meticulous analysis of each character's mindset showing the all-important why behind their decisions and viewpoints... It is a mesmerizing tale of the heights and depths of human nature packed with insight, mystery, tension, and suspense that grasps the reader with its incredible power."—*Phil Slattery, Founder and Publisher, The Chamber Magazine*

"*The Man with No Eyes* starts with a bang and never lets up. This fast-paced, cinematic thriller has plenty to keep you reading long past your bedtime"—-*Patricia Correll, author of The Corpse Eater*

i

A woman walked toward him as he sat in a small island of shade beneath an acacia tree.

Her clothes rustled in the wind as she approached cautiously. Her slow, deliberate footsteps crunched on the sand, marking her distance with each step.

The wind swept across the desert in green, undulating lines, but when the wind struck her, it changed direction and speed abruptly. This disruption allowed Andrew to "see" her in his mind.

She spoke to him in Arabic. When he didn't answer she spoke in a broken English. "You are not spirit?"

"No."

"Soldier?" she asked.

"No."

"You look like soldier."

"Well, I took these clothes off a psychopath that fancied himself something of a soldier. But I am no soldier." Andrew shook his head.

"Spy?"

"A blind spy?" He asked, pointing to the dirty bandage around his eyes. "I'm afraid I wouldn't make a very good one. Doctor."

She stood quietly, the wind rustling her long robes and head scarf. She sighed heavily as she stared down at him.

"Medicine doctor?" she asked, there was an edge of excitement in her voice, but it faded quickly. "Who cannot see?"

"Yes."

There was a long pause while she stood before him, the weight of her decision hanging about them both. Would it be more beneficial to have him with them, or should she leave him here in the desert to die?

The wind gusted, swirling about her. The edges of her robe fluttered in the breeze, the edges snapping like tiny fireworks. Her weight shifted as the turned to look at her fellow travelers, then shifted again as she turned back to the stranger.

THE MAN WITH NO EYES

JOHN RYLAND

Moonshine Cove Publishing, LLC
Abbeville, South Carolina U.S.A.
First Moonshine Cove Edition March 2022

ISBN: 9781952439278

Library of Congress LCCN: 2022902366

About the Author

John Ryland grew up in rural Alabama and has always enjoyed a good story. After a stint in the U.S. Navy, during which he traveled extensively, he returned home and settled in Northport, Alabama where he now lives with his wife Terri and his two sons.

A published poet since 1997, his first novel wasn't published until 2020 when *Souls Harbor* was released. That was followed by *Southern Gothic*, a collection of short stories, later that same year. His novel, *Shatter*, was released in 2021. His latest work, a paranormal suspense novel entitled *Peripheral*, was released in 2022. He has published short stories in literary journals, anthologies, and magazines from coast to coast, including *Bewildering Stories, The Writers' Magazine (UK), Otherwise Engaged, The Eldritch Journal, Hell Bound Books, The Chamber Magazine*, and others.

You can stay up to date with all things pertaining to the author at his website https://gspressbooks.com and by following him on social media.

https://gspressbooks.com

THE MAN
WITH NO
EYES

Prologue

It's like drowning only worse, Andrew thought as the heat pressed against his face, washing over him in one continuous scorching wave. It took a conscious effort not to fixate on it, but it was impossible to ignore.

It was everywhere, it was everything. It hung on the dry air and rose from the loose sand that crunched underfoot. It pressed in from every direction, surrounding his body like water at the bottom of a pool. The one notable difference being that it was a thousand times more miserable.

His mind groped for the words of an old song about the desert being an ocean. Or was the ocean a desert? Maybe. Or was the desert an ocean? He shook his head, momentarily considering raising his recall function, but decided against it. He needed to conserve his energy. Normally his memory was excellent, but he'd lowered all non-essential bodily functions and devoted the energy to life support systems.

Andrew dismissed the thoughts about the song. It wasn't important right now. What was important was surviving the heat.

He took in a deep breath and blew it out slowly, stopping himself from obsessing over the heat, again. There was a part of him, however, that was glad he couldn't see the sand stretching to the horizon in every direction. The psychological effect would be difficult to overcome. But then again, if he could see, he might not be here to begin with.

He had further to go than he'd come, and the idea that he'd both underestimated the desert and overestimated his own abilities was beginning to take hold, despite his best efforts to fight it. Stumbling through the desert all night and most of another day, he was no closer to freedom than when he first left the Facility.

He let out an angry grunt as the name entered his mind. The Facility. The place he used to work at had a long, official-sounding name, but no one ever used it. In his years there he never heard it called anything else, even when they were courting him to join their work. "Please come and tour the Facility." "We have the most advanced equipment here at the Facility." "You will love it here at the Facility."

In retrospect, he could see that the subtle isolation was all part of a carefully crafted plan. Even when he'd been flown in on the company helicopter, a retro-fitted Blackhawk, it had been at night. It was all to keep the exact location as secret as possible. Not that he would have noticed anyway, with all the champaign and the smoke they were blowing up his ass.

Rumors always abound in medical offices and this one was no exception. The one that was beginning to haunt him was the one claiming it was a thousand miles from anywhere. A thousand miles of rough, unforgiving, desert between him and anyone that could, or would, help him. A thousand miles patrolled only by a merciless sun and a few desert creatures that managed to eke out a living in such a desolate place. A thousand miles of nowhere, of nothing.

Maybe that's why it was so easy to escape...

Despite coming to the same conclusion multiple times, he diverted his thoughts to doing the math of his survival. Again. It was an exercise in futility because of the variables, but it was better than thinking about the heat.

Assuming a twenty minutes per mile average walking speed and a continuous pace, it would take him nearly fourteen days to walk a thousand miles. He had been walking almost twenty-four hours, barely seventy-five miles, but he had rested twice already. So much for the continuous pace. Each break was about an hour, so that was a minus of six miles. Nine hundred thirty-four to go, give or take the life of one man.

Of course, that was all dependent upon finding water. If that didn't happen, he would be dead, and all the math would be moot anyway.

Unless... his mind reminded him. That was what he was counting on. Unless he did find water. Another rumor was of an oasis. Having never left the grounds, he'd never actually seen it, but there were a few hushed rumors floating around the Facility.

But then again, there were the other "unlesses" to consider. Unless he came upon a desert snake and got bitten. Or a scorpion, or a spider. Or some other God-forsaken creature that lived in this hellhole. Unless he tripped and fell and broke a leg.

Unless they came after him.

If they did come after him, he wouldn't be hard to find. Footprints in the sand would be easy to follow, and a man stumbling along with his eyes wrapped in dirty gauze, wearing the blue-green scrubs of a surgeon didn't exactly blend in with the environment. He was far enough away for the Facilities' chopper to find him in about five minutes.

Andrew shook his head at the thought but kept walking. It would be a depressing thought for the average man, but he was not an average man. He was a special man with special abilities, which was why the Facility wanted him to begin with.

In his old life, he was considered a genius. At the Facility he was just another cog in the works. With an IQ that hovered around the high 160s, depending on the day and the test, coupled with his abilities, he was as much a subject as he was a contributor. They paid him for his surgical prowess, but they wanted him for his abilities.

His ability to control every system of his body almost down to a cellular level was a physiological anomaly. He could isolate and contain any pathogen. He could use his body's own faculties to heal himself at an accelerated rate. His mind held vast reservoirs of visual records from almost everything he'd ever seen. His memory was a vault. He was a unique man to say the least. This ability had countless medical possibilities, making him invaluable to the scientists at the Facility.

It was also the only reason he even considered escaping.

The Facility was also a special place with special abilities, the most prevalent of which was to not get bogged down by ethics or basic human rights.

Life there was an experience in duality. If you did what they wanted the world was your oyster. You'd be fed the finest food and housed in the lap of luxury. They had the money and clout to satisfy every whim, except hard drugs. If you wanted beautiful women, you got beautiful women. If you wanted a little boy, you got a little boy. And when you were done, they would take care of any messes that arose.

If you didn't do what they wanted, your life would be an agonizing hell. If you crossed them, your son would end up one of the little boys requested. If your wife were nice looking, like his was, she would end up one of the special requests. And you would watch and listen to every second of it while your coworkers lived out their twisted fantasies.

So often the thing about great minds was that great perversion and savagery lay tucked neatly in the folds of genius. Remove normal societal restraints and the ugly comes to the surface quickly.

The hard truth was that the Facility had ways of getting what they wanted. The part they left out of the recruitment brochure was that working there was a life-long commitment whether you liked it or not. It was like that old commercial about the roaches. How long you stayed was up to you. Their secrets had to be kept at all costs.

The head of the Facility, Alain Savon, was a sadistic lunatic. The only thing he liked better than satisfying his sexual perversions was the power that he wielded with an iron fist. Savon didn't like to be told no, and he never lost. He understood how to motivate people to do what he wanted. By sugar or by salt, he always got what he wanted. Always. Savon was a master of mind games and ruthlessly efficient in everything he did.

As far as Andrew could tell, he was the first person to tell Savon no, and he'd paid a great price for it. His foolishly noble efforts had gained him nothing and cost him his family. After being forced to watch as his wife and son were brutalized and murdered, Savon ordered that his eyes be surgically removed to ensure that the last thing he ever saw was the effects of defying his orders.

Andrew plodded along at a steady pace, his body on autopilot since his escape, navigating the gently undulating sand with ease. His body temperature was elevated enough to cause a bit of perspiration to cool it, but not enough to hasten dehydration. All other functions except his sense of smell were diminished to preserve energy.

Topping a small rise, he paused and ran a hand over his short hair. He had grown it half an inch since leaving the Facility to shield his head from the sun. It was still hot, but better than the shaved head he'd left the Facility with.

He put his sweaty palm to his mouth. The salt and moisture immediately soaked into the dryness of his tongue, igniting the cracked tissue. He swept his head swept from side to side, surveying the landscape with his available senses.

The wind was blowing out of the east, represented in his mind by a series of long, neon green vector arrows. It was a trick he'd learned at the Facility from an old man who'd lost his sight in a house fire as a youth. The green arrows always denoted the wind. The varying pitch and speed painted a picture of the vastness of the land before him as the arrows moved across the uneven sand. Different shades of yellow and orange represented the sound of everything else, blue was the color of favor, and red always meant danger. His visualization techniques were still a work in process, and a far cry from that of his friend, but his abilities and determination were strengthening them with each passing day.

There was a faint smell in the air that was different from yesterday. Flowers? Vegetation? Water? It was hard to be sure, but something had changed.

Increasing his pace slightly, he corrected his direction and started off with the wind in his face. It was probably his last chance. Another day without water would push him into dangerous territory. Even a man with his abilities had limitations.

The first time Daniel Souter saw the doctor, creeping in on his hands and knees in the twilight, he mistook him for a desert animal. The shape paused, looked around, listened, then crept closer, repeating the process until he was at the edge of the oasis.

Souter remained motionless, waiting. When he realized the shape was a man, he smiled knowingly. The doctor had arrived.

The thin, streamlined goggles affixed to his face were set to FLIR, forward looking infrared, allowing him his secret observation. Sitting against the trunk of a desert palm in his usual dark green military-style cargo pants and khaki shirt, he would be hard to spot even if the man coming towards him had sight.

That was his job, to be undetected and to notice things that average people missed. He was head of security at the premier medical research facility on the Arabian Peninsula and thusly not very well liked, but that was okay. In truth, he relished the fact that people disliked him. They disliked him because they feared him. It felt good to be feared instead of being afraid. Finally.

Unlike the good doctor, who was slowly making his way toward him, he was born blind and had remained so until Alain Savon had given him his sight at the age of eighteen. So many things had changed since then, but he never forgot the gift he'd received. When a man gives you sight, you remain loyal to him no matter what.

He becomes your personal Jesus.

Souter watched the doctor make his way to the edge of the small oasis, just like he knew he would. There was nowhere else to go, they were in the middle of the desert. If the doctor was a genius like they said he was, he wasn't much of one. He'd just been outsmarted by a high school drop-out.

Hiding just behind a small palm, the doctor waited and cocked his head to listen for any sign of danger. He turned his face to the source of the water and drew in a deep breath through his nose.

After another short hesitation, he scrambled into the small clearing and approached the water. Reaching down, he scooped up a palm full and tested it, waiting a full five minutes to check the effects of it in his mouth before swallowing it.

Souter watched and waited. The doctor was disciplined, there was no denying that. He didn't have a personal issue with Doctor Harkins himself. He was just doing his job and the doctor was just another one of the arrogant men who walked around like they were better than everyone else; just another rich man who would walk past a blind kid begging on the street without even noticing.

On second thought, maybe this is personal, Souter thought as his jaw clenched tighter.

Satisfied with the water, Andrew lowered his face to the pool's surface and drank heartily before washing his face and wetting his short hair, now almost a full inch longer than when he'd left the Facility. Sitting up with a sigh of relief, his hand went out and began exploring the area. He found a large boulder near the water's edge and ran a hand along the stone. Leaning against it, he slid down onto the sand with a tired sigh.

Inside the goggles Souter's eyes moved to the heads-up display at the edge of his field of vision, focusing on the small icon of an eye in the upper right corner. The goggles transitioned from infrared to plain vision.

Looking at Andrew Harkins, Souter considered the irony of the situation. He was looking at a man with his own eyes. It had to be the first time in history that a man's eyes looked back at him while resting in another man's head, albeit aided by a pair of fancy goggles.

Instead of simply blinding the doctor, Savon had ordered a lengthy surgery to remove Andrew Harkin's eyes. He then had them implanted in him. It made sense to not waste such a valuable commodity.

When the bandages came off everyone marveled at the miracle of the event, but all he knew was that he could finally see color.

The goggles were the realization of a dream for Alain Savon and a shining achievement for the Facility. The addition of human eyes improved his vision dramatically. Before, with the old goggles that Savon had attached to his face so many years ago, his vision was a field of varying shades of gray generated by the processors in the goggles. Those images were then passed to his optic nerves, allowing him to "see." It was a limited sight with no real details, but for a boy who knew only darkness, it was heaven. He couldn't begin to understand the technology, but he didn't care. The results spoke for themselves.

The ability, and willingness, to do the things they did, was what made the Facility great, and he was proud to be a small part of it. They were leaps and bounds ahead of anyone in biotronics, medical implantation, and human/computer integration. They were the pinnacle of success and the envy of the world and charged top dollar for their technology.

Souter sat motionless, barely breathing, with his finger on the trigger of the nine-millimeter on his lap. He could kill the doctor at any moment without him ever knowing who had done it. If he was intently listening, he might hear a finger gently squeeze the trigger an instant before he died, but he wasn't listening intently. He was resting.

Besides, his orders were to bring the good doctor back alive. He could still be of service to the Facility.

He knew the doctor would be tired by the time he got to the oasis, and probably a little scared, although he'd never admit it. He would also be in pain. He could control his reactions to it, but it would still be there.

The doctor's breathing slowly relaxed; his chest rising and falling in a perfect monotonous rhythm as he sat quietly in the coming darkness, listening, smelling, and feeling the air for movement.

Waiting and watching, Souter could feel his legs beginning to stiffen as he sat motionless. The air was cooling quickly as the night grew darker. He would need to move soon or risk the chance of his legs falling asleep. Of course, the slightest movement would alert the doctor, but that was going to happen anyway. It didn't make sense to wait until his limbs went numb. He needed to get things moving along.

"Hello, doctor," Souter said calmly.

Andrew moved quickly, spinning around to face the voice, a rock clenched in his fist. "I knew it was you," he said angrily. Andrew crept back slightly, kneeling behind the boulder.

"Did you now?"

"I could smell you from a hundred yards. Don't forget that I know who you are, you stinking bastard."

"I guess you do," Souter conceded with a half-hearted chuckle. "You look good to have come so far across the desert."

"Go to hell. I'm not going back there." Every sound Souter made shot toward him as a red arrow, pinpointing his location.

"Don't be so angry at me. You knew the punishment for insubordination would be severe."

"Go to hell. Anyone who enjoys being Savon's lap dog deserves everything he gets," Andrew said, suppressing his anger as he calculated the man's position and distance.

He knew full well that Souter was the recipient of the eyes that Savon had stolen from him. Many of his nights since had been spent plotting his revenge, but he never expected the chance to come so soon.

Andrew listened carefully, taking in the noise Souter made. His breaths were coming in quick, forced pants through his nose, faster than an average man at rest. The scent of his body was strong. He was nervous.

Andrew smiled, but kept his attention focused on the man sitting less than twenty feet from him. He would only get one chance. Souter was a ruthless man. If he missed, he'd be shot and probably killed. Savon would probably be mad, but that wouldn't make him any less dead.

"So how long have you been Savon's pet, Souter? It's rumored that he raised you. Did he?"

"I don't see where that is any of your concern, Doctor. Just surrender peaceably and we can all be home in just a few hours."

"I'm not going anywhere, Souter, and you know it. Why don't you run back to Savon's lap and let him pet your head, give you an 'attaboy' for trying so hard."

Andrew's thoughts went momentarily to his friend, Nickodem Peterson, a world-renowned biotech engineer despite being blind for most of his life. The man taught him a great many things in the months after Savon took his eyes, the most important of which was how to see without his eyes. Peterson's friendship drug him kicking and screaming from the depths of depression and gave him a new mission in life, revenge. Everything since had been devoted to that end.

Many times he'd been struck by a tennis ball thrown by his friend before he learned to listen to the subtle disturbances in the air and use it to triangulate sound. The first time he caught one they celebrated with a glass of cognac. Success had never tasted so sweet, until today.

"I don't know why you have to be so difficult. All you had to do was follow orders and—." A rock the size of a baseball sailed through the air, striking the lens of his goggles before Souter could react.

A gunshot rang out as Andrew ducked behind his cover, then scurried through the undergrowth.

Souter rolled to his right and tried to stand, immediately realizing the error of his waiting. His legs were stiff and uncooperative. Cursing his own arrogance, he struggled to his feet.

Looking through the shattered lens of his goggles, he swept the area quickly to find the doctor but saw only the same empty scene he'd been looking at for hours. Now, however, there was a kaleidoscope effect showing multiple images at different angles. Switching to infrared he swept his head frantically back and forth looking for a heat signature, but the effect was the same. It would be next to impossible to catch the doctor alive now.

A knot tightened in his stomach as he thought of reporting to Savon that he'd failed. He couldn't do that. He'd have to tell him the doctor never showed and that he'd broken the goggles in a fall.

Disappointing Savon wasn't an option.

Two-thirds of the way through his sweep, he heard the rustle of palm fronds to his right. Spinning on legs that still refused to work properly, he lost his balance and went to a knee. He fired two shots at what might have been the heat signature of a man's torso. The fragmented glass lens made it impossible to tell exactly what he was seeing. Screaming, he fired another shot in frustration.

Andrew stood motionless, now behind Souter, holding a large rock above his head. He waited as Souter fired two shots at the scrub shirt he threw into his field of vision, and then another one in the general direction. Souter was frustrated and angry. That was good.

The sound of the glass lens of the goggles shattering told him he'd hit his target. It would be difficult to see, but not impossible. He still had to be very careful. Being hit by a stroke of dumb luck could still be fatal.

The new version of the goggles was his own doing, intended to interface with the wearer's optic nerves, and he knew their weakness. Although the monolithic glass provided a better, unobstructed view, damaging it would corrupt the entire sight path instead of just one lens. He was glad they'd opted to go with a simple glass for the prototype, in the later versions, the rock wouldn't have even scratched the lens.

Moving silently, holding his breath as to not alert the man of his presence, Andrew stayed just out of his field of vision as Souter turned. Going undetected wasn't hard. Souter was almost in a panic, breathing heavily and grunting in frustration. Andrew did, however, need him to speak to give him an accurate target. He had time to wait, but not a lot. The rock he now held over his head was already getting heavy.

Souter swept the area in front of him through his broken viewfinder and tried to stand again, but his right leg was still mostly numb and refused to cooperate.

"Look, Doc, I never meant you any harm," he said, watching for any movement, ready to fire. "When they decided to punish you, they were going to do it anyway. I was as much a victim as—"

Andrew brought the rock down against the man's head with all his strength. It struck with a sickening thud. The sound of the bones breaking vibrated inside his own mind as warm blood splattered across his bare chest. Hefting the rock again, just in case, he listened as the body fell limply to the ground. The wetness on the rock that hadn't been there before told him he wouldn't need it again. Lowering it, he tossed it aside and knelt beside the man he'd just killed.

His hands fell on the body along the man's waist as the last involuntary spasms passed through Daniel Souter. Andrew grimaced and slowly moved over the body. Souter's clothes were better suited for desert travel, that was good. They were also more or less the same size, that was better. The doctor placed two fingers alongside Souter's neck, checking for a pulse that he knew wouldn't be there.

Sitting back with a sigh of relief, Andrew stared down at the body. Not seeing it, but rather absorbing what he had just done. He'd killed a man with his own two hands. A bad man, yes, but another human being none the less.

Somewhere deep inside, the man he used to be, already mortally wounded, died a quiet death. The man who had taken the Hippocratic Oath to do no harm was gone. He was someone else now. Who that man was, he wasn't quite sure, not yet.

Two thoughts entered his mind almost simultaneously, pushing out any remorse he might have dwelt on. One was that he couldn't stay here. They'd eventually come looking for Souter, and for him. The second thought was one he'd had many times while contemplating his revenge.

He was taking back what was his.

Leaning over the body, he rolled the man's head to face upwards. Allowing his hands to wash over the goggles, his fingertips probed angrily around the seams where they attached to the man's face.

Stitches still lined the intersection of man and machine. In time his face would have healed and grown to the artificial skin that lined the goggles. Given enough time his invention would have blended seamlessly with the wearer. They would always look like low profile goggles, but the integration would be sleek and smooth.

Gripping the goggles in his hands, he paused momentarily, preparing himself for the task at hand. He drew in a deep breath and exhaled slowly, making sure of his grip. He took another deep breath and snatched as hard as he could.

The goggles broke free from Souter's face with a sickening, tearing sound. In the silence of the desert it sounded like something akin to ripping duct tape, only more violent. He laid the goggles carefully aside and turned his attention back the body. He still had work to do and wanted to finish before he lost his nerve.

Major Townley snapped to attention as General Michaels entered the room in a brisk walk. The scowl on his face said that he wasn't happy. He rounded his desk and sat in the plush leather chair before taking off his hat and running a hand over his gray, thinning hair.

"Well, lemme have it," he said, looking over the wide desk at his subordinate.

"Yes sir," the Major began nervously. Being the bearer of bad news was never a good position to be in. "We haven't really found out much about the doctor. We ran the picture they sent us through the database. His name is Andrew Harkins, he's a surgeon, a pretty good one apparently, at Mercy General just outside Philadelphia. He's married to Samantha Walls Harkins, thirty-seven. One kid, a son, Lane Thomas Harkins, six years old. As far as anyone knows they just disappeared four years ago. No sign of them since, well, until our friends in the desert found him. The coordinates are in the report, but it was just north of the Yemini border in Saudi. The group that found him was on a night training mission."

The General leafed through the report, shaking his head, and grunting at the news. "He's just some run of the mill surgeon who disappears for nearly four damned years and ends up in middle of the freaking Saudi desert?"

"We're in touch with the Saudi ambassador to see if he had a work visa. Nothing yet on that, sir."

"How in the hell is that possible? Freaking bureaucrats. Shit. Any involvement with any of the known terrorist cells?"

"No sir, intelligence has been all over his life, social media, friends, extended family. There's nothing to indicate any involvement whatsoever. Like I said, he and his family more or less disappeared and have been radio silent since then. No tax returns. No contact with family, friends, nobody."

"No indication that he was a player, for anybody? Not even us?" the general asked.

"Nothing at all, sir. CIA, FBI, Secret Service, Intelligence all claim not to know him."

"They would. What about MI-6? Russians? The Israelis?"

"Nothing, sir."

"The fucking circus? Boy Scouts? Anything?"

"Sorry, sir. Nothing."

"Then how in the hell does an American doctor end up in the middle of the desert, blind as a bat, and carrying..." the General looked over the file laid out before him. "A pair of fucking eyeballs! What kind of bat crap crazy shit is that?"

"I'm not sure, sir. We're still gathering information. Right now we don't know if he was dropped there, or if he was wandering the desert. They did say there were no signs of a wheeled vehicle anywhere near him when they found him. There were footprints, but they couldn't follow them far. The wind, sir. As far as they could discern, he walked to where they found him."

"What is near there?"

The major shook his head. "Nothing within walking distance."

The general shook his head. "Nearly forty years in now, Major. Forty years, and this is the weirdest shit I've ever seen. What the hell do you think happened to the poor fool?"

"I don't know, sir. Obviously, something awful. It's too bad we won't get a chance to ask him."

"That's what has Washington in a tizzy. How the hell does a blind man escape anybody? And in the condition that he was in, dehydrated, half starved?"

"That part is still a little disjointed, sir. Apparently, the person who examined him thought he was dead. The report said he wasn't breathing, and they couldn't register a pulse. They more or less sat him aside and started making calls to find out what to do with the dead body of an American civilian. Naturally, they were a little nervous about the whole situation. And things are a little unsettled over there, to say the least. Sir."

"Nothing on the family?" The general asked, closing the file.

"Nothing out of the ordinary. They're looking at all know relatives, but so far nothing."

The general pursed his lips and shook his head again, lost in thought. "Well," he began with a sigh. "At least it was some friendlies who found him. Hopefully, he wasn't into too much deep shit in Yemen. That's all we need right now."

"Well, sir, if he was it looks like they handled it. If he pissed some people off, I'd say they got their revenge."

"You never know, Major. There's a lot of crazy folks running around that part of the world."

"I'd hate to think you could do worse to a man than cut out his eyes, stick them in his pocket and leave him in the middle of the desert."

"Is that what you think happened?" the General asked. "He was just wandering around the open desert and dropped dead?"

"Pretty much all that makes sense, given the circumstances. But apparently, he wasn't as dead as they thought."

"Apparently. I'd like to find out just what happened and who the hell he is."

"Me too," the Major agreed. "I'm sure we aren't alone in that either. I've been getting calls all day about this guy."

"Of course this is all quiet. The last thing we need is an American running around stirring the pot over there. Or getting himself taken hostage and having his damned head cut off on the evening news."

"Yes. Will that be all, sir?"

"Yes, Major, that's all." As the Major left the room, the General leaned forward, propping his elbows on his desk and rubbed his temples. Looking down at the file, his eyes went to the smiling face of Andrew Harkins. In his late thirties with a head full of brown hair and two rows of perfect teeth, he hardly looked the part of an international terrorists. Maybe an agent, but even that was probably a stretch.

"Who the hell are you, Andrew Harkins?" he asked. "And what in the hell happened to you?"

One

The smell of the goats came drifting across the sand first, then the sound of them, then the sound of children. Following shortly after that was the sharp tones of women's voices speaking in Arabic. There were three women and either three or four children. The erratic movement of the goats made them harder to count, but there weren't many. Less than a dozen.

They were traveling from his right to left, talking casually among themselves and laughing quietly, then the whole procession suddenly stopped on a small rise about a hundred yards away. There was some discussion, then they started off again, giving him a wide berth. The conversation continued quietly, then there was a heated discussion among the adults. The small group continued, and one woman walked toward him as he sat in a small island of shade beneath an acacia tree.

Her clothes rustled in the wind as she approached cautiously. Her slow, deliberate footsteps crunched on the sand, marking her distance with each step.

The wind swept across the desert in green, undulating lines, but when the wind struck her, it changed direction and speed abruptly. This disruption allowed him to "see" her in his mind. After striking the woman, the lines that appeared in his mind changed color as well. They changed from green to blue.

The color of favor.

She spoke to him first in Arabic. When he didn't answer she spoke in a broken English. "You are not spirit?"

"I am not," he said with a shrug. "But if I were that is exactly what I'd say."

"You are not spirit?" she asked again, confused by his poor attempt at humor.

"No."

"Soldier?" she asked.

"No."

"You look like soldier."

"Well, I took these clothes off a psychopath that fancied himself something of a soldier. But I am no soldier." Andrew shook his head.

"Spy?"

"A blind spy?" he asked, pointing to the dirty bandage around his eyes. "I'm afraid I wouldn't make a very good one."

She stood quietly, the wind rustling her long robes and head scarf. In the back of his mind the word bourka came to him, but he corrected himself. Arabas was the term for the long, flowing gowns the women wore in this area. She sighed heavily as she stared down at him.

The wind brought her scent to him. The light smell of a flower mingled with the musky tone of her warm skin surprised and pleased him.

"No spirit?" she asked again, shifting her weight.

"No spirit. Doctor."

"A doctor?" she asked, there was an edge of excitement in her voice, but it faded quickly. "Who cannot see?"

"Yes, doctor. And yes, I am blind. The second answer leaves the first in question, I know, but whaddya gonna do?"

"Medicine doctor?"

"Yes. Ophthalmologist, by trade, specializing in retinology. Of course that makes my current condition even more ironic, but again..." Andrew shrugged and gave her a narrow smile.

There was a long pause while she stood before him, the weight of her decision hanging about them both. Would it be more beneficial to have him with them, or should she leave him here to die?

The wind gusted, swirling about her. The edges of her robe fluttered in the breeze, the edges snapping like tiny fireworks. Her weight shifted as she turned to look at her fellow travelers, then shifted again as she turned back to the stranger.

"You may call me Malika," she finally said after a long contemplation. Water sloshed in the small canteen when it hit the ground between his feet.

"Come."

Andrew grabbed the canteen and followed the sound of the wind swirling around her as she walked away.

"We must go."

The woman's voice was pleasant and soft, but insistent. She didn't speak to him often, and her English was heavy with her native middle eastern accent, but Andrew found it strangely comforting when she did.

Andrew sat up from the thin blanket laid on the sand beneath the makeshift tent. With a yawn, he began his daily chore of taking stock of his surroundings.

Somewhere close by a few children were playing, three of them. Two boys and a girl. They were the ones traveling with their small troop when they first found him.

The four men who joined the group the day after he met Malika were off to his right, discussing something in a language he couldn't discern. The tone of their voices hinted at a certain casualness, but the speed of their language suggested an urgency he didn't like.

Two of the women were talking quietly among themselves. They wanted to leave him to die when Malika found him and hadn't warmed to his presence at all.

This was his fourth day with the group and each morning he awoke with a sense of surprise that he'd survived the night. There was no way to tell who they were, or who they were affiliated with, if anybody. They might have been the Taliban for all he knew, but that seemed doubtful. Every day was an exercise in suspense, but at least he was alive. For now.

Outside the tent, the tiny group began packing up and moving about with a sense of purpose. Goats were bleating, the children were complaining, and the men didn't sound happy. Malika said that they had to go, but not why. The why wasn't important. What was important was that Malika said they had to go, and people listened to her.

The doctor stood and smoothed the robes that he'd slept in. He slipped a piece of loose fabric over his head and snugged the length of rope Malika had fashioned for him onto his head to hold it in place. Between a natural reaction to the sun and the melatonin he was encouraging to the surface, he was sure that his skin was dark enough to pass himself off as a local. In the clothes Malika had given him to wear, he'd be hard to pick out of a crowd, which was probably her intent.

He scratched the new growth of beard on his chin and took a moment to access his body. Everything was within acceptable levels except the pain behind his eyes. Rubbing his temples, he concentrated on his pain receptors, calming them until all that remained was a dull throbbing. He'd done his own post-op care and healed the wounds, but the phantom pain would not leave him alone.

He moved toward the flow of fresh air coming in through the tent's open flap. Reaching out with a hand, he found the rough fabric and stood as he exited the tent. The sun was up, and it was already getting hot. The goats continued their protests over being wrangled, but all other conversation ceased immediately. All the eyes of the camp were on him.

"We must go." It was Malika's voice again from a few feet away.

"Why?" he asked, walking toward her voice.

"Unfriendlies."

Andrew's stomach sank. She didn't need to say more.

Throughout a long day of walking, Andrew mentally logged the changes in the terrain. The loose, gritty sand slowly gave way to a more compacted, rocky soil littered with small patches of vegetation. The wind whistled through the dried branches, alerting him of their presence. Keeping pace with Malika wasn't easy, but he'd done well enough to only draw one frustrated sigh from her.

In the monotony of the walk, he allowed his mind to wander and failed to detect Malika's movements as she sidestepped obstacles. He tripped over a small bush of thorns and suffered several stab wounds on his right shin. She paused long enough for him to get up, then continued walking.

The mood of the troupe rose as they walked deeper into the new terrain. Spirits lifted, and he even heard a few bouts of quiet laughter while they were taking a midday break.

The winds had also changed, coming now in short, swirling bursts and were slightly cooler, almost creeping out of the 'miserable' range. The sounds of the chatter took on a hollow, echoing tone that could only mean one thing. Their south-by-southeast track had taken them across the high desert of northern Yemen and to the foothills of a mountainous region.

It was a long way from the Facility, but at least they would find relative safety among the rocks and vegetation. The fact that they hadn't encountered any "unfriendlies" didn't mean they weren't there. It meant that Malika had led them in the right direction.

When the decision to stop for the night came, they'd only just begun to meet the slopes of a mountain. Malika deposited him on a small outcropping a few yards from the group and joined the other women as they began to make camp. It wasn't long before the smell of savory meat, seasoned with unfamiliar spices filled his nostrils, reminding him how hungry he was.

He could do little but sit and wait. And think.

"Many people who can see are blind to so many things." Nicoderm Peterson's words echoed in Andrew's head as he sat patiently, listening to his senses.

His auditory acuity and his sense of smell had dramatically improved, far surpassing that of an average man. The nerve endings all over his body could now be activated at will, alerting him to the slightest changes in wind direction, and the most subtle of vibrations in the air around him. It still took a great deal of concentration, but even that was lessening with each day.

He turned to face Malika as she approached. She had a tough, musky smell to her that wasn't completely unpleasant, but there was also a softer undertone of a light, flowery scent that intrigued him. It might have been easily masked by the food she was delivering if he hadn't followed her closely for four days. Her smell was imprinted on his mind, and he'd only recently come to realize that he liked having it there.

The time since he'd lost his wife and son felt like years. The months that he'd languished at the Facility were fueled by rage, but the long nights he'd spent alone in the desert had allowed a certain healing to start.

"Hello, Malika," he said, offering a smile as she drew closer. "Something smells delicious."

"Eat." She took his hand abruptly and shoved a smooth, wooden bowl in it.

"Thank you." He devoured the dish of heavily seasoned meat and rice while she sat a few feet away in silence. When he began to wipe the bowl with the flat bread provided, she stood. After finishing the flat bread, he was given a flask of warm water to wash it down with.

"Enough?" she asked flatly.

Andrew nodded. Sometimes she spoke abruptly to him, other times her voice held a soft, lilting hint of playfulness. He assumed the difference was whether people were watching, or within earshot.

"You sit and rest. I will be back soon."

"What? Wait," he said, almost pleading. He trusted her, but not the rest of the group.

"You will be fine. No one will bring harm to you. Stay and rest."

"Wait." He reached out and took her arm, drawing a surprised gasp from Malika. "I'm sorry." He released her and showed her his palms. "I'm sorry."

She stood in silence for a moment, watching him, before she spoke again. "I must get water."

"I can help," he offered.

"No time. The night is almost upon us. And..." she trailed off.

Andrew nodded. He knew enough about the local culture to know that it wouldn't be right for her to venture off with him alone without being chaperoned. He gave a reluctant nod of understanding and sat quietly, listening to her make her way in the opposite direction of the group. He pulled the headdress off and ran a hand through his sweaty hair, admonishing himself for allowing his fear to show in front of Malika.

He waited long enough for her to put some distance between them, then slid off the rock and kneeled in the path. His hand met a hard-packed, well-worn path. He took a few tentative steps in the direction Malika had gone and leaned against a large boulder, trying to look as casual as possible. The men in the group were locked in what sounded like an important conversation. Beyond them, there was the sound of children laughing as they moved about quickly on the dry earth while the women, now busy with preparations for the night, murmured quietly among themselves.

No one was paying any attention to him at all. His presence had become an afterthought as the tiny group settled in for the night. Turning his face to the west, he could feel the last vestiges of daylight as the sun slowly sank toward the horizon.

The uneasiness that had plagued his mind since Malika had uttered the word, "unfriendlies" was still there. Dusk would be a good time for an attack, when everyone would be eating and relaxing after a long day. People tended to congregate as night fell, whether for safety or to ward off the loneliness of the desert, and that made them an easy target. Especially with no lookout.

Andrew took a few more tentative steps, striking his foot on a loose stone in the path. He felt around for a stick to use as a sweeper but found nothing. If he were going to make it up the mountain, he'd have to do it the hard way.

Taking a few more steps, he leaned against another boulder, this time on the mountain side of the narrow path. His hand found a large outcropping and he ducked into it, hiding from the group while he listened for any sign that they'd noticed him missing from his perch.

When none came, he began his slow trek up the mountain. Mapping the terrain and the slope of the ascent with his feet, he made considerable progress before tripping over another loose stone in the middle of a switchback and tumbling to the ground.

He rolled onto his back and sat up, cursing. The wind was swirling and seemed to be coming from every direction in a confusing mass of eddies and gusts. Of course, it wouldn't be as easy as he hoped.

Hauling himself back up, he paused to listen. There was a strange noise in the distance. He couldn't determine what it was, but it hadn't been there before.

He made it past a few more switchbacks, hugging the mountain side of the path before his ears finally deciphered what the sound was. It was mechanical and although a considerable distance away, it was moving in their direction. Out of habit, he looked in the direction of the sound before shaking his head in frustration. In his mind, he cursed the Facility once again and fresh anger rose in his chest.

Turning back to the path he hurried up the mountain at a faster pace than he wanted, ignoring the small stones that stabbed at the bottom of his feet through the thin sandals and the sharp edges of the boulders that sliced into the palms of his hands. He had to get to Malika; to warn her.

Pausing at a bend in the path, holding onto the dry branch of a small tree, he listened to the sound as it made its way across the desert. It moved from left to right over a considerable distance, maybe miles, before turning and making its way back from right to left. It would be impossible for a land vehicle to cover such ground. That meant it had to be an aircraft. A helicopter.

"It's a grid search," he whispered. "Dammit!" He turned and rushed along the path, his heart thundering in his chest. Were they looking for him, or just border crossers? Was it the Facility, or the Yemeni military? Whoever they were, they were looking hard for someone and that was never good.

The wind gusted, sending echoes through his mind as the green arrows before his eyes began to overlap. He was moving too fast, and the swirling wind wasn't helping.

Staggering forward with his hand extended at chest level, Andrew struck an overhanging rock in mid-stride. The jagged edges of the rock dug into his forehead, opening a gash that immediately sent a wave of blood onto the thin strip of cloth that covered his eyes.

He fell back, catching himself with his left hand as he hit the ground hard. Something inside his wrist gave way and he growled in pain. Sitting up, he pulled it to his chest as his free hand went to his forehead. Blood flowed freely across his fingers from the three-inch gash. He ushered clotting agents to the wound, but he didn't have time to stop the bleeding completely.

"Dammit!" he cursed again, crawling to the edge of the path.

"Why are you here?"

Malika's voice was full of urgency and frustration as she sat her heavy load on the path and came to his side. The resentment in her voice was echoed in her hurried movements.

"Can you walk?" she asked.

"Not very fast, I'm afraid."

"We must warn the others. Unfriendlies." She hooked an arm beneath his, hauling him up from the ground with a strength that surprised him.

"There is no time. We will never make it. It's a helicopter. It's getting too close."

"We must warn the others," she insisted. "My children."

Andrew faced Malika, grabbing her by the shoulders despite the pain in his wrist. "We have to take cover. Are we exposed up here?"

"My children!" she insisted again.

"Stop," he said through clenched teeth, the pain in his wrist howling as she struggled against him. "If you want to save them then help me."

"What can we do from here?" she asked. "A blind man and a woman against a helicopter?"

Andrew shook her, sensing her panic. "Stop it! Now answer me. Are we exposed?"

"Yes. There are rocks and a few shrubs, there is nothing else," she answered reluctantly.

"Okay, listen. You have to help me." He looked in the direction of the helicopter. "Can you see it yet?"

"Barely. It is about a kilometer away, and it is dark now. I can see lights."

"Does it have a searchlight on?"

"No."

"Probably got FLIR. That is worse." He wiped the blood from his face with the back of his hand. "Can you see the camp below?"

"I must go to the edge. You stay." She pushed him against a large boulder and walked away. The sound of the helicopter was getting closer as the search narrowed. Their group was probably taking a well-known path, which meant anyone familiar with the area would know where to look.

There was still a chance of escape, but it was slim.

Malika returned and told him that there was no fire.

"Can you get me into a position next to the edge directly above the camp?"

"It is too dangerous. You cannot make it there."

"It's dark now, isn't it?" he asked.

"Yes but—"

"Then neither of us can see very well. If you want to save your children, then help me. How much moonlight is there?"

"Some. There is less than half a moon."

"C'mon." He extended his hand to her. "We don't have much time." If it's not too late already, he added to himself.

After a few low passes, drawing closer to the base of the mountain each time, the helicopter slowed and hovered above the path they'd taken between two small rises. It turned slowly in the pale moonlight, training its gun on the base of the mountain.

Above, Andrew half crawled over the loose stone lining the edge of the path. He slipped once, sending a cascade of small stones down the hillside, but Malika's strong hand grabbed the back of his tunic and stopped his slide. They sat motionless in the dark, waiting to see if he'd given away their position.

"Not much further. Maybe five meters," Malika told him, yelling to be heard over the propeller noise.

Moving closer to the edge, wind from the helicopter washed a cloud of dust up the side of the mountain and into his face. It tasted dry and powdery, as old as the hillside it had been ground from. His plan was foolhardy and close to impossible, but it was all he had. At least the dust storm kicked up by the prop wash would help hide the group beneath them.

"The camp is below. The edge is a meter from your feet."

"Good, now we need—" The helicopter's fifty-caliber machine gun ripped through the night with unexpected ferocity, sending them diving for cover. Malika began wailing for her children and praying loudly.

"Stop!" he yelled. As he pulled Malika into a sitting position the guns fell silent. "They heard the chopper and took cover. They had to have heard it."

Malika was sobbing openly and praying loudly in Arabic as she began to rock back and forth.

"Stop it!" Andrew yelled. Grabbing her by the shoulders, he shook her violently to no avail. "Stop it, damn you!" he screamed and slapped her hard.

There was a quick shift beneath his grasp, then the cold steel of a blade pressed against his throat.

"Easy. No. Stop." he said, releasing her. "If you kill me, we all will die on this God-forsaken hell hole of a mountain."

The pressure against the knife lessened and then left his throat. "If you ever touch me again, I will kill you."

"Fine. Fine. I'm sorry. We need stones. Small enough to throw, but not too small. Hurry." He held his hands apart to approximate the size but didn't know if she saw him or not.

Andrew slid closer to the edge of the mountain, finding himself on a small ledge barely big enough for them both. Getting onto his knees, he concentrated on the helicopter. The echo from the mountain made it hard to be exact, but he put it about a hundred yards away and less than fifty feet below. Too far for his plan to work.

In his mind green arrows radiated from a central source, first falling, then curving and coming back up in a gentle arc before returning to the place where they had started. The result was a series of rotating circles surrounding the unseen helicopter. In his mind, it resembled a Slinky wrapped in a circle so that both ends touched. As the aircraft slid gracefully back and forth the circles followed, reacting to the terrain beneath them.

Suddenly, the helicopter closed the distance by half and spun to the right, zeroing in on movement. A short burst of gunfire followed, then the helicopter returned its attention to the camp. Another short burst of gunfire rang out, appearing to him as a rapid succession of overlapping red arrows.

From below, he heard the painful bleats of a dying goat just as Malika returned with a load of stones. She pushed them out to him carefully, still sobbing over the loss of her family.

Andrew allowed his hands to quickly wash over the stones, deciding on two that were slightly larger than a football. Lifting one, he rose on unsteady legs and listened. The helicopter maintained its close position as the occupants no doubt studied the shadows for life.

"Searchlight," Malika warned from behind him as she sought the cover of a small shrub. "On the camp."

The infrared was getting too much interference from the prop wash to be effective. Good, Andrew thought, calculating the distance. It would still be a long throw, even with the helicopter fifty feet beneath them, but it would be his only chance. The pilot wouldn't dare draw closer to the mountain.

When he yelled for Malika, she crawled out onto the ledge without hesitation. He cradled the rock in his good arm and held out the back of his tunic to her. She clutched it with both hands and sat down on the ground.

Turning, he listened again for the helicopter's exact position. He concentrated on the sound of the motor, shutting out the propeller noise. In the dark center of the rotating circles, a small red swirl began to form in his vision.

Raising the rock above his head, he spared one last nod to Malika. She wrapped the end of his tunic around one hand and placed the other over it.

Taking a step forward, he heaved the rock toward the swirling red arrow with a grunt, summoning all the strength he could muster. The tips of his sandals found the edge of the outcropping and his weight began to shift forward just as he released the stone.

As his body tipped over the edge of the cliff, he felt himself being pulled backward. He quickly grabbed the second stone and threw it after the first.

Malika yanked hard against the end of his tunic, pulling him to the ground on top of her. They lay motionless in the dark and listened to the helicopter.

The first stone struck the propellers close to the edge of the central rotor, wedging momentarily between them. The helicopter wavered, but the pilot corrected. The second stone struck one of the propellers near the end, but shattered, sending pieces flying in every direction.

The helicopter came back to a steady hover for a second but then began to shudder as the pilot pulled back from the mountain.

The sound of the propellers changed as the delicate balance of the rotors shifted. Malika flinched in Andrew's arms when the helicopter lurched upwards, sweeping the searchlight over them as the pilot struggled to control the aircraft.

The pilot fought the controls as the unbalanced blade began to shake the entire fuselage. It pitched to one side, then the other before finally going into a flat spin and crashing into the ground less than half a kilometer away.

Malika let out a cheer as she sat up. When the light from the fireball washed over them, her tear-streaked face was smiling. Looking back to the bleeding man beside her, she put a hand on his chest.

"Thank you," she said, but her reverie faded quickly as the thought of her family returned. They'd crashed the helicopter and had survived, but were they the only ones left to celebrate?

Andrew sat up with a groan. Despite the screaming pain in his head and wrist, he smiled.

"Go," he said to her. "See who has survived."

"You are hurt."

"Go. Send help if there is any to send."

Malika stood and tore a strip of cloth from the bottom of her arabas and pushed it against his head. "You stay. I will come back."

Andrew nodded and replaced her hand with his against the cloth covering his wound. "Go," he said again and laid back on the ground. He'd lost a lot of blood and his wrist hurt like hell, but he'd have to take care of himself for now.

Lying in the darkness, he heard Malika rush past as she went to see if her family was dead or alive. The roaring fire from the helicopter released another small explosion and he smiled.

He'd ridden in that same helicopter once before and he knew who it belonged to. A slight pang of guilt for Ross, the pilot, swam into his mind. Ross wasn't a bad guy to hang out with and he was one hell of a poker player, but he was loyal to Savon and tonight, that meant one of them had to die.

He was just glad that it hadn't been him. Or Malika.

Two

The blanket was warm and heavy, comforting. The room was silent, but there were muffled voices outside speaking in Arabic. Further away, several goats were being ushered from one place to another by two young boys, their voices coming gently to his ears. The air was cooler here. Not cold, but better than the intense heat of the desert.

Sliding his left hand from under the covers, he found a solid, smooth wall next to the narrow bed he was laying on. He was in a house or some other permanent structure. There was a smell of smoke and of a meal, but both were faint. The scent of his own, sweaty, unwashed body was stronger.

Flexing his hand, he discovered that a tight bandage had been applied. Raising it to his forehead, he found another bandage there too, along with a fresh wrap over his eyes.

The last thing he remembered was laying on the jagged rocks on the side of a mountain, listening to the roaring fire of a crashed helicopter, and trying to stop the blood flow to the open wound on his forehead.

A slight smile snuck across his lips as the memory of defeating the Facility's helicopter came back to him. It had to have been Devine intervention, or one hell of a lucky throw. Andrew longed to see the look on Savon's face when he got the news, but he was also thankful for the miles between them. Alain Savon would be crazy with anger and someone around him would pay dearly.

"I'll kill you one day. I swear to you I will," had been his last words to Savon before being dragged away. Savon was sitting behind his giant, mahogany desk with a smug look on his face as he gave the orders. He probably wasn't feeling so smug now. Already he'd lost Souter and Ross, as well as his favorite toy. No. He wouldn't be so smug now, but he would be pissed and that would ensure that he'd come looking for him again. He also wouldn't mind killing everyone around him to get him back, if only to torture him to death. At least if he were caught now, he wouldn't have to look at that smug face again.

Andrew pushed the blankets down and sat up, swinging his legs over the edge of the bed. He sat quietly, taking an internal survey, for several minutes. His wrist ached beneath the bandage, which had been applied very tightly. He had a mild headache, but that was to be expected. He needed to drink, eat, and relieve himself, other than that he was within acceptable limits, health-wise at least.

There was a soft scrape of wood on hard-packed earth, then another as a door opened and closed. Outside a young female voice ran from the hut, speaking excitedly in Arabic as she went. A minute later, the door opened again.

"You are awake."

Andrew smiled as Malika's voice filled his ears. It sounded lighter than usual, almost holding a smile in it somewhere.

"That I am," he replied, stifling a yawn. "How long was I out?"

"One day and the morning."

"How is everyone?" he asked.

"A few scratches and wounds. They will survive."

Andrew smiled. "Good. Glad your kids are okay."

Her abaya rustled about her body as she moved quickly across the room, leaving the door open behind her. There was a clinking of metal, and the sound of liquid being poured. Her legs moved again, brushing against the fabric of her clothes as she moved, and she was standing in front of him. A warm hand reached out and took his, leading it to a metal cup.

"Drink," she said.

The water was cool and sweet as it went down his throat, washing away the dryness. He drank the entire cup and held it out before him. "Thank you."

"Hungry?" she asked, moving away.

"Very, but first, I need to use the bathroom."

Malika moved in her usual, purposeful way to the door. She called out to someone, then returned to her station across the room. After a moment, a young boy showed up at the door smelling of youthful exuberance and breathing heavily. She spoke to the boy, and he entered the house, coming to him.

"Raheb will escort you to the place where you can relieve yourself and back to here," she said. She said something in Arabic that sounded like a warning, and the boy took the doctor by the arm. "I prepare you food. Go now."

After consuming the largest meal he could remember eating in what felt like months, Andrew leaned back against the wall of the house. The stonework was smooth and cool and the milk she offered with his meal was soft and sweet. A perfect complement to the wild, gamy meat and rice.

"Do you know who they are?" Malika asked. She was sitting to his left and slightly below him, either on the floor or a short stool.

"Do you?" he asked, swirling the milk in the tin cup.

"They were not soldiers."

"No, not in the normal sense."

"The helicopter was American," she paused. "I think."

"Yep. It was a Blackhawk. An older model, but definitely American."

"They are looking for you?"

"Yes. And they found us."

"But you stopped them. For that I thank you."

Andrew sighed. "I wouldn't thank me if I were you. They were looking for me. If you'd have left me under that tree in the desert, your family wouldn't have been in danger."

"Danger is everywhere. It is no stranger to us."

Andrew opened his mouth and tossed the last of the bread into it. As much as he appreciated her not leaving him to die, he was a threat to her and her children. As much as he needed her help, he knew that Savon wouldn't stop looking, and wouldn't miss again.

"Danger from these people is wherever I go."

"There are many paths through these mountains. Many places to hide. Many places to live."

Andrew shook his head. It was an interesting idea, but he knew he couldn't do that. That would mean forgetting what happened; what Savon did to him and his family. He wouldn't.

"In a few days, I will be healed. I should go then."

"No." Malika stood. "You will be needed here. You are a doctor, No?"

"I am a doctor. I also cannot see." He held up his left hand. "My wrist is broken, or severely sprained, and I've recently suffered a blunt force trauma to the head."

"Your hand is not broken. You can use it. Your head will be clear by tomorrow."

"Even so, I wouldn't say I was qualified to do any type of medical work."

Andrew shrugged. She was right on both accounts. "If you are a doctor, you are a doctor. Do you not have memory of what to do?"

Andrew shook his head. "It's not that. I can't see. A lot of what a doctor does is visual. I need to see a patient to properly diagnose them."

Malika rose but did not speak. Her breath came and went in a steady rhythm as she stared at him. Finally, she turned and walked to the door, then paused. "Rest now. I will come back later to see after you."

Andrew sighed as he laid back on the cot. Was he a prisoner here? What would they do if he just got up and walked away? Did it matter? He didn't know where he was, and his last attempt at navigating the mountain had not gone so well.

Drawing the cover back over him, he relaxed into the coarse fabric of the bed. He wouldn't be in any condition to go anywhere for a few days. There was no need to press the issue. Yet.

Drawing his concentration to himself, he began to "see" his left wrist in his mind as he raised it before him. Malika was right. It wasn't broken. He'd just used it as an excuse. It wasn't that he didn't want to help the people in this village, he just didn't want to get too comfortable here.

Inside his body red blood cells began to race to the site of the injury, immediately beginning to create collagen. Little by little granulation tissue began to form on the strained ligaments strengthening them and repairing the damage.

Lowering his wrist to the bed gently, he allowed his body to heal itself. Now, he just needed to rest and give it the time it needed. In a few hours, his wrist would be done, and he could work on closing his head wound. According to Malika it had been superficial, but he needed to heal it quickly to avoid infection.

When the first hints of sleep began to pull on him, bolstered by his full belly, he didn't resist. Drifting closer and closer to sleep, he heard Malika talking outside the house. Her voice came to him like a lullaby, soft and low, and he found it strangely reassuring. A smile crept across his face as he finally dropped off into a deep sleep.

The water was cool and refreshing, sweet on his tongue. Andrew licked his lips, allowing the water to trickle into his mouth.

"You sleep hard."

Andrew flinched in the bed, coming awake suddenly to the sound of Malika's gentle laugh.

"Did I frighten you?" she asked, the laugh still in her voice.

"No," he replied quickly. She didn't frighten him as much as she did catch him in the middle of a dream that he'd rather not discuss, especially with her. He shifted himself beneath the covers and tried to sit up but found a firm hand on his chest.

"Lay down," she insisted. She dipped the towel into the bucket of water and wrung it slightly. "I must begin cleaning your wounds."

"I can do it."

"Perhaps so, but as you said, much of being a doctor is seeing. And you cannot see."

"I can manage."

"Like you managed to find a tree in the desert?" she asked, dabbing the wound on his forehead, the bandage already removed.

Andrew chuckled. "I came a long way to find that tree."

"I am sure." Malika continued to clean the wound on his forehead. "There aren't many trees in that part of the desert."

"Tell me about it."

"It is because the desert is so dry that—"

"No. It's just a figure of speech. You don't actually have to tell me about it."

"Oh." She rinsed the towel and continued to clean the wound on his forehead.

Andrew relaxed, allowing her to take care of him. He told himself that it was the culture for the women to take care of the men, but part of him enjoyed her touch. She was gentle and easy as she washed the dirt and dried blood from the laceration, cleaning the cloth often.

A low hum filled his ears as she went about her work of cleaning and redressing the wound. Her voice was soft and melodious, like a mother singing to her children to sleep. This side of her was a sharp contrast to the tough, determined edge she had in the desert. When the men argued with her, her voice was strong and commanding. It left little doubt who was in charge.

"Anything I know?" he asked quietly.

"Oh, no," she said with a laugh. "It's an old tribal song my grandmother used to sing to me." She finished the bandage on his head and reached for the wrap that covered his eyes.

"Don't." Andrew put his hands on hers.

She took his hands in hers and lowered them to his chest. "I have seen worse."

"Maybe so, but..." his voice trailed off. He'd never seen the effects of having his eyes removed, and something deep inside him didn't want Malika to see them either.

"I have known nothing but war. I have seen men burned to death, torn in half by mines and bullets."

"But they weren't me."

42

"Are you so different from other men?" she asked, continuing to remove the bandage.

Andrew resigned himself to her care, somewhat deflated by her comment though he wasn't sure why. Who was she to him but a means to an end? Who was he to her but...? His mind couldn't answer the question. What was he to her? Why did she save him? It was because he was a doctor, but what could he do? His eyes weren't damaged. If they were, he could heal them. They were gone, there was nothing he could do about that.

Malika washed his eyelids, moving gently across the depression where his eyes would have been. She had long been curious as to what his face looked like beneath the bandage. There was a rugged handsomeness to him, but also a vulnerability. She caught herself staring at him, then moved quickly to apply a new wrap. She then took his left hand in hers and removed the bandage carefully. Turning his wrist gently from side to side, examining it carefully. Her brow furrowed and her eyes went to his face.

The weight of her stare was heavy as it fell on him. His wrist was now fully healed, and she was wondering how.

"Your wounds, they heal quickly," she said, laying his wrist on his chest as she moved away. "Very quickly."

There was an unease in her voice. She would have more questions than he had answers. He raised his hand and motioned for her to return to his bedside.

She took another step back.

"Look, I am no sorcerer or anything. No magic. Nothing. I've always just healed quickly."

"The wound on your head is almost gone, and your wrist." She muttered something in Arabic as she took a few more steps back from him.

"Yes. Please. Let me explain." He waited for her to return to the seat by his bed. When she didn't, he sat up. "Look. I was born with the ability to heal myself. I know it sounds like voodoo or something, but it's just a physiological trait that I have."

"No magic?" she asked tentatively.

"Not even close. I could explain it all, but it's very complicated and tedious. Quite boring, really. Just know that I can do things your average Joe can't. No magic, no voodoo, no spells, just efficient use of the properties of the human body that normally go unused. If I were magic, I would have eyeballs, now wouldn't I?" He reached out and found the stool she'd been sitting on, patting it gently. "Please come and sit."

Malika's clothes rustled as she gathered the front of her abaya and took a few steps toward him. Her breaths were coming in fast, uneasy pants. She was nervous.

No, she is afraid, he told himself. Of you. The thought brought an ache to his chest.

"I will not harm you or anyone in this camp. I promise."

She took a few steps toward him and stopped. "There is much about you that is strange. The way you move without seeing, the way you have healed."

"I did save us from the helicopter, didn't I? I'm the same man now as then." This brought her all the way to the stool. She sat, but didn't settle in.

"Who are you?"

"Look, Malika, I owe you a debt. You saved me from the desert. Why, I don't know, but you did. You brought me here for some reason, at no slight risk to yourself and your family, so why don't we concentrate on that?"

Malika sat quietly, staring at him, trying to convince herself that he wasn't a spirit. She swallowed hard then opened her mouth to speak, only to close it again. Her breathing was slowing some, bringing a smile to his lips.

"I am blind, and I will be blind for the rest of my life probably." Andrew sat on the cot, facing her though he couldn't see her. "The men who did this to me are bad men. Really bad men."

"Why?" she asked quietly.

"Because I wouldn't do the things that they wanted me to do." He didn't tell her he'd been doing things, bad things, for them for years before he finally grew a conscience and refused. He didn't tell her about the surgeries performed on unsuspecting patients, many of whom were probably her own people, or about the screams he still heard in the night.

"Things?" she asked.

Andrew waved his hand in the air in front of him slowly, allowing Malika to take it in hers. "I'm no angel. But every man has a line he will not cross. The men who did this; the men in the helicopter; the men who will come looking for me; they don't like to hear the word 'no'. There is not a line that they won't cross."

Malika drew in a deep breath and exhaled slowly. "In this world, there are no angels." She patted his hand and laid it back on his lap. Standing, she turned and looked back at him. "You will wear bandages for more days, so you do not make the people fear you. If they become afraid, they will kill you." She turned and exited the house quickly, leaving him to his thoughts.

"Okay." Andrew held the bowl and water flask out before him after devouring the small midday meal.

Raheb, the young boy who had been assigned the unenviable task of escorting him wherever he needed to go, rushed to him, and took them from his hands.

"Now we go."

"But, of course," Andrew replied jovially as if he had a choice. Malika had already informed him that he would be fed and then brought to her father's house. Beyond that, she had said little else to him since she'd discovered his healed wounds the day before.

A small, but strong hand grabbed his elbow and urged him from the cot. "We go." The boy obviously resented his chore.

Andrew allowed himself to be led from the house. Outside the sun was bright and warm, despite the coolness of the wind. As he shuffled across the dirt, being led by the boy, his mind tried to decipher how long he'd been away from the Facility. Piecing his travels together, and allowing for the time he lost while unconscious, it couldn't have been more than a month.

He sighed heavily. Just a month? It already felt like a lifetime ago. "Here."

Andrew slowed as the pressure on his elbow was released. Where was here?

"I am here."

Andrew corrected his course slightly and walked toward Malika's voice. When he reached her, she took his elbow and led him into a building.

The air was thick and warm, full of the scent of men, and of sickness. A muffled conversation started between two men, but Malika hissed at them, and all fell silent.

"Father," she began. "The doctor is here."

The room remained silent, then a horse whisper came to his ears. An old man, Andrew thought. An old sick man and I'm supposed to save him. Shit.

Malika urged him deeper into the room. His elbow brushed against the tunic of another man and the stranger shrank from him. Walking carefully, he made his way toward the whisper.

"This is my father, Abd-El-Kader. He is our leader, dearly loved." She reached out and took her father's hand, stroking it gently.

Andrew listened for a response from the old man, but none came. His breathing was shallow and unsteady. A smell rose from the bed that he knew immediately. Infection. He sighed heavily and turned to Malika.

"My father has been shot. He needs a doctor."

"Malika..." he began, unsure of what to say next. If he said no, would he be taken out and shot? If he tried to save the man, which he wasn't going to do, and failed, would he also be shot? "May I speak to you, alone?"

"No talk. Can you save him?"

Andrew could hear the desperation in her voice. He was her last chance. All her hopes had been pinned on him, however unfair that was. In his heart, he wanted to say yes. Yes, he could save the old man. Yes, everything would be all right, but his mind was screaming no.

There was no way he could save this man. Even in a top-notch hospital, and with his sight, the chances were slim. Infection had set in and there were no antibiotics.

"Look. He needs a hospital. Medicines. IV's. We have nothing." A low rumble swept across the group of men, drawing another hiss from Malika.

"Everyone out!" she said. "We must prepare for operation." The men slowly filed out, complaining among themselves as they went.

"Are they gone?" Andrew asked as the room fell quiet again.

"Yes. You, me, and Raheb, are here. And my father."

"Malika, I cannot help him."

"Yes, you can. You are doctor, no?"

"I'm blind!" Andrew reached out and found Malika's shoulder. "How can I see? How can I operate? My best advice is to make him comfortable until...." he lowered his voice, "until he dies."

"No."

Andrew ran a hand over his hair and let out a frustrated sigh. There was no way this couldn't end badly, for both him and the patient.

"You heal," Malika whispered, drawing close to his ear. "You heal him."

"That's not how this works. I can only 'heal' myself. I would have to do surgery on him."

"Then do your surgery."

"Look, this isn't my field. I haven't scrubbed in on abdominal surgery in forever. Since I was an intern. It's been years."

"Do you forget how to be a doctor?"

"No." He let out a frustrated groan. "We need medicines."

"We have some medicines." Malika pulled from his grasp and hurried across the room. She came back to him with a small, metal box in her hands. "We bought these this morning from a caravan. Medicines. American medicines."

Andrew moaned as he rubbed his temples. "Fine. What are they?" He heard Malika open the box and begin to rifle through the plastic pill bottles.

"I cannot read them," she said.

"Why? is there no label on them?"

"I do not read American. Raheb. You try."

The boy joined them. Picking up one bottle, he looked at the label. He fumbled over the name several times and gave up, complaining to his mother in Arabic.

"Try to spell them."

"Okay," the boy answered reluctantly, embarrassed by his ignorance in front of the doctor.

"It's okay. I have trouble sometimes too. Let's take this one bottle at a time. I'll help as soon as I recognize the name." Andrew shook his head. If Malika had left him under that tree, he'd be dead by now and none of this would be happening.

Three

Despite the arguments against it and a long list of reasons why he shouldn't be doing it, Andrew found himself preparing for surgery. At his behest, Malika had already crushed a huge dose of dicloxacillin, an antibiotic that wasn't even allowed in the United States anymore- and somehow gotten it down the semi-conscious patient's throat without strangling him.

The best route, explained in painstaking detail to Malika, would be to allow the antibiotics to work for a few days before the surgery, but she wouldn't hear of it. To her, getting the bullet out of her father's abdomen was priority one. He didn't agree. Surgery on a man in his condition went against every canon of medicine he'd ever learned. The bullet wasn't what was killing him now.

Washing his hands in water heated over an open fire, with a soap that smelled of lye, he found himself going through the procedure in his mind. Of course, he'd done countless surgeries on eyes, but this was a whole different ballgame. He even removed a foreign object or two in his time at Mercy General just north of Philadelphia, but never a bullet, and certainly not while blind. It was a doomed prospect, but one he had little choice undertaking.

He dried his hands on a rough towel that Raheb produced and turned, hands in the air in front of him. In the real world, a scrub tech would be waiting with sterile gloves, but nothing about this felt real.

"Okay," he said and drew in a deep breath. He exhaled slowly and moved toward the bed. "Do not touch my hands. If you must guide me do so with my elbow and tell me first."

He waited by the bed while Malika washed her own hands. When she joined him, he could smell the light, flowery scent again. It was faint but sweet and he liked the smell of it.

"I am here," she said softly. She touched his elbow gently and guided his hand to the wound. "There. The hole is not very big."

"That's the thing about bullets. They go in small and come out big."

"This one did not come out."

Andrew nodded as he put his hands on the man's abdomen, relying more on his sense of feel than her description. The wound was swollen and warm to the touch. Without proper x-rays, he had no way of knowing how deep or even what angle the bullet had taken.

He found the opening in the old man's belly and slowly inserted his pinky finger, allowing the tissue to guide him. The patient let out a low groan but remained still.

"Looks like a slightly downward angle from the left to right, mid-section of the lower left quadrant. Tissue is warm and spongy. The projectile is deeper than two inches. Penetration of the abdominal cavity is likely."

"What?" Malika asked, confused.

"Old habit. Kinda talking my way through things. Back home I worked at a teaching hospital. Usually had students watching and listening." He pulled his finger from the wound, producing a wet, sucking noise. A low moan escaped Malika as she stood beside him.

"Knife," he said, holding his hand out. "If you think that's bad, you're in for a long afternoon, sweetheart." Sliding his fingers across the patient, he found the midline of his abdomen and prepared to cut.

"That is not where the bullet went in," Malika informed him, her voice full of urgency.

Andrew smiled. "Thank you," he said. "I'm blind, but I'm still a doctor."

"I know that. But you cannot see. I did not want you to cut-"

"The reason I cut here is because there are no major arteries to hit. It is how it's done."

"Oh. Okay," she replied sheepishly.

Cutting with deliberate slowness, he sliced through the skin and fat on the man's belly, probing with his fingers with each cut. In his heart he knew he was violating the first oath of medicine to "do no harm" but it wasn't his decision. His only solace was that the patient was going to die anyway. He might as well save himself in the process and satisfy the mild curiosity he had about whether he could actually do it. It would be challenging under any conditions, but if he could make a go of it, there might be hope for his career in the real world. If he ever made it back.

"There should be a pair of scissors in the suture kit. I need them."

When she placed them in his hand, he detected a slight tremble. Now that her father's life was at least partially in her own hands, some of the pressure was also on her. Using the scissors, he worked slowly and methodically through the muscular layer while Malika wiped blood and maintained the opening the best she could.

"Remember, if you see any major bleeders, let me know. We'll have to tie them off."

"How much is bad?"

"If I hit a gusher, you'll know."

When he finally made it to the old man's abdominal wall, his fingers felt around until he found the bullet's entry point.

"Okay," he said to Malika. "So far, it's been mostly superficial. Once I open his abdominal cavity it'll be serious. It's going to look and smell unlike anything you've probably ever witnessed. Are you ready?"

"I told you I've been raised in a war zone, Doctor," she replied. "I am no flower to wilt in the sun."

"Well, I need you to hold this incision open. I will need to go deeper." He felt her hands slide over his and take hold of the sides of the opening. "You will have to hold it for a while, maybe a very long time."

"Then that is what I will do."

"It may sound bad, but at this point, you have to forget about this being your father. There will be no time for sentimentalism."

"Will you do a surgery or a talk?"

Andrew shook his head, the corners of his mouth hiding a smile as he slid the knife carefully between Malika's hands, opening the abdominal wall with one slice. Malika let out another groan as the smell of infection and feces wafted upwards in a warm cloud, drowning out the familiar metallic scent of blood.

"The bowel has been perforated," he said flatly.

"What does that mean?"

"It means his chances went down, slim as they were, and that you'll be holding that position for a long time." Sliding his fingers into the patient's bowels, he searched the area for the metal, hoping the projectile hadn't fragmented.

Sighing heavily and pushed his hands deeper into the man's body until his wrist was laying against Malika's as she held her father's muscle and fat out of the way. He probed deeper with his fingers, sliding his hand gently along the bowl, searching the area carefully for any sign of a foreign body. In his mind, he visualized the area, the twists and turns, the trajectory and plane of the organs.

Just as his hand was making a turn in the large intestine and starting to probe in the opposite direction, the tip of his finger drug across something hard. Stopping, he went back and pushed deeper. His fingertips closed around the metal projectile, and he slowly pulled it from the man's body.

"Is that the bullet?" Malika asked.

"That it is," he said with a triumphant smile. "That's what all the fuss has been about." He dropped the metal onto the blanket covering the man's lower body and went back to work.

"That was the easy part. Now we must check the bowels in the whole area. Here," he took her hand and pushed it further into the surgical site. You've got to hold this too."

He felt her fingers take the pressure off his as she grasped the abdominal wall and held it open for him to work. Standing so closely he could hear her short, measured breaths. Stripped to a tee shirt, he could feel the warmth of her skin against his arm. Despite the intensity of the situation, he admitted to himself that being this close to a woman felt nice.

"I'm going to need lots of clean water and those clean cloths I had you cut up."

Malika said something in Arabic over her shoulder and Raheb showed up with a metal basin and the cloths. He deposited them on the edge of the bed and retreated hastily to his chair by the door.

Andrew dipped one of the cloths, roughly cut to the size of a four-by-four gauze pad and began to wash the bowel as he slid his hands over it.

"Watch carefully for anything seeping out."

"Yes, you said that already."

After moving several inches with the cloth Malika stopped him. Andrew wiped the area clean and felt with his fingertips, finding the tear. It wasn't large, but any bowel perforation was too big. Picking up the suture kit he prepared before the surgery began, he sewed the tear closed, wiped it clean again, and asked Malika if it was leaking.

"I don't think it is."

"That'll have to do. Cut it for me."

Andrew laid the back of his forearm against the old man's chest. The heartbeat was weak, but it was present, and his chest rose and fell slightly. He was still alive.

Andrew drew in a deep breath and went back to work. The old man had been sedated with as many of the painkillers as he dared to give. They made him sleep, but it was not as reliable as sedation. If he woke up now and began to resist, he would surely die.

Moving forward along the bowl at a painfully slow pace, Andrew saw the procedure in his mind as he went. Remembering birthdays and anniversaries had always given him trouble, but his surgical training was second nature to him. Every procedure he'd scrubbed in on during his surgical rotations as an intern was as fresh in his mind as the when he'd performed them.

"How are you doing?" he asked quietly, sensing the desperation that had settled on Malika. The nervous sweat he smelled on her told him that she hadn't expected such an invasive surgery.

"I am good," Malika answered.

"You know it's okay not to be okay?"

"I do not know what you mean."

Andrew smiled. "Never mind. It's not important."

"I am okay," she insisted. "I am stronger than you think."

"I didn't mean that." Andrew gently traced the bowel, wiping it clean and allowing Malika to look at each section as he went. "I know you're strong. And quick with a blade."

Malika chuckled. "I am sorry about that. It was habit, I guess you say."

"It's all good." Andrew paused and examined the intestine carefully. "Look here."

Malika leaned in closer to him. "Yes, a small cut."

The scent of her chased away the smell of her father's blood and an unexpected desire to kiss her swept over him like a breeze. He didn't know what she looked like, but he liked her smell and her voice. Surely, he thought, she must be beautiful.

"Will you fix this one?"

"Yeah. Yes. Every tear we find must be repaired." Andrew admonished himself as he tied the stitch. His wife had been dead for less than six months. How could he even think of another woman? Especially while holding her father's guts in his hands.

Refocusing on the task at hand, he continued the work of tracking and repairing the damage done by the bullet.

"Luckily for him, and us too I suppose, it was a small caliber shell, and it didn't fragment."

"There are many guns here. Some are old and in bad repair. They said my father did not know he was shot until he saw the blood."

"Is that why you were in the desert? Looking for someone to help?"

"Yes. I do not usually travel to get supplies, but I felt I needed to this time. And I found you."

"Lucky you," Andrew said with a laugh. "A blind doctor, half dead from dehydration."

"You say 'a blind doctor', but it is better than no doctor." She fell silent as Andrew found and repaired another small tear. "But I could say why were you in the desert as well? No?"

"You could ask anything you want."

"Why were you so far in the desert?" she asked.

"I was running away from some bad guys, and I must have taken a wrong turn."

"Or perhaps a right one."

Andrew felt her move closer to him, ever so slightly. He turned to Malika, their faces inches apart. The part of him that wanted to kiss her was glad that she didn't pull away. He imagined dark, soulful eyes searching his face as the weight of her stare fell on him.

When Raheb stirred suddenly in his chair behind them, she did move away as much as she could. When she spoke to him in Arabic, her voice sounded shaky and nervous, like she'd been caught doing something she shouldn't be doing.

Andrew smiled, wishing he could see her face, to see if she were blushing.

"Okay," he said as he pulled his hands from the man's abdominal cavity. "I need to wash my hands and we need to soak up some of the blood and irrigate the site. Pack it with some of the pads and we will stretch our backs for a moment. We'll have to work our way out, cleaning and suturing as best we can. That'll take a while."

"Are we not finished?" Malika asked tiredly.

"Not even close, but we will need to hurry. I'm sure he's losing a lot of blood."

Back at work after the brief respite, Andrew and Malika cleaned the opening in her father's abdomen with wet cloths and sutured his visceral peritoneum together, holding his organs in place. He held the incision open with one hand, freeing her to clean the area before sewing the abdominal wall together.

"Good," he said. Make sure it's as clean as you can. How are we on four by fours?"

"Four by fours?" she asked.

"The cloth," he explained. "We will still need many."

"We have many and Raheb can get more as we need them."

"Good. How's it looking?"

"There is a lot of blood, but it is slowing some. I need to get there," Malika leaned in closer, reaching for a pool of blood near his right hand.

As she pressed her body closer to him, her breast touched the back of his arm. It wasn't large, but not small either. It was firm against his skin, and he liked it. His body reacted quickly, but he hurriedly shut off the rush of adrenalin and slowed the blood flow to his groin.

Admonishing himself again, he sighed, trying to focus on the operation. Still, his thoughts lingered on the presence of her breast against him, if only momentarily. Coupled with the smell of her and the softness of her voice, he couldn't completely remove the thought from his mind.

"Okay." He cleared his throat, slightly embarrassed. "We work our way through a few layers of tissue, fascia, muscles, subcutaneous tissue, and close him up. We'll make it home for a late supper."

He turned toward Malika, sure that she was looking at him, and smiled. When she gave no response, he went back to work, sparing the sutures as often as possible. He erred on the side of caution on the interior sutures and now they were running short. Despite knowing there was little chance the old man would survive, he found himself hoping for the best, if only for Malika's sake.

By the time Andrew finished packing the external wound with cloths and covering it with a larger towel, the room had cooled with the setting sun. Malika was working by lamplight, he by his usual darkness.

He groaned tiredly and stepped back from the bed, stretching his back. "I can't make any promises," he said, washing his hands in the fresh basin of hot water, "but it is done. We will need to change the packing and clean the wound often until we're sure the infection isn't going to kill him. And keep it covered. I don't want flies feeding off the wound, and they will."

"Yes. I've seen this."

"Keep up with the antibiotics."

"Anything else?"

"If your people have a such thing as prayer warriors, I'd suggest you get them in here and keep them in here. That might be all that saves him."

Andrew found another towel by the basin and dried his hands, stepping aside while the boy brought clean water for Malika.

"I cannot thank you enough."

"Don't thank me yet." He offered Malika the towel. "You do realize how grave his condition is, don't you? What I did just made it worse, to be perfectly honest," he added in a whisper.

Malika took the towel from his hand. "You do not have to whisper. Raheb has gone. But yes. I do know that my father may yet die."

Malika turned to step around him but stopped when he moved in front of her. His hand went out and found her arm. "Can I ask you something?"

"Yes."

"Where is your husband?"

"My husband is dead."

Guided by the sound of her voice, Andrew leaned in and pressed his lips to hers. Surprised, she gasped quietly as her body tensed. She stood motionless until he pulled back, then snatched her arm free of his grasp.

"For that, I should kill you," she said.

Andrew braced himself for a slap, or worse, the knife she carried. Neither came.

"But I will not because you help my father to try to save him," she finally said, her voice now softer.

"Thank you for not killing me. Look, I'm sorry."

"I think you are not sorry."

"I am not," he said with a smile. "But thanks for not killing me all the same."

"I will see to it that you are taken to the river to clean and that you get something to eat."

"Will you bring it? I'd like it if you did."

"I will see to it."

Her clothes brush against him as she pushed past, leaving her scent to linger in the air after her departure. He took a deep breath and exhaled as his smile widened.

"We go." The voice was that of a different young boy. He approached Andrew but did not touch him. "We go to clean you."

The fire crackled noisily while the people around it talked among themselves in their native tongue. Malika was off to his right, talking to one small group. The rise and fall of her voice sounded as if she were telling a story, and the slight laugh at the end told him it had a happy ending.

Sitting on a small blanket on the ground, alone, he smiled. She was working the room. It wasn't something every woman could do. That was good because the more well-liked Malika was, the more well-liked he would be by association. In the long run, it wouldn't matter but in the short term it might.

It was more pleasant being here by the fire with the people than stuck in his hut, even if he had no idea what they were saying. The long nights alone in the desert had brought him a new appreciation for human companionship. He followed Malika's voice as it traveled around the fire, stopping to talk to many of the people.

After his bath and hot meal, he was ushered out here and told to sit by the fire. The people had all congregated slowly, as if they were expecting something; like they were here to see a show. Perhaps, he thought, they just didn't want to be alone. Like him.

Malika's voice was growing closer as she made her way around the circle. A few feet away an old woman spoke to her, and Malika answered with a few words that made the old woman laugh. She laughed with the old woman for a moment, then made her way to his blanket.

"May I join you, doctor?"

"Why of course." Andrew swept his hand across the blanket welcomingly. "You are quite the crowd pleaser."

"Sometimes it is easy to make people happy. What are a few kind words in the time of things?"

"I couldn't agree more." Andrew shrugged. "What does *'rejulin belau yunen'* mean?"

Malika snickered at his poor interpretation of her language. "Why do you ask?"

"I've heard several people say it. Does it apply to me?"

"It means 'the man with no eyes', so I think yes."

Andrew nodded. "I guess they've noticed."

Malika chuckled again. "The whole village has. Yes. But they have never seen a man such as yourself who does the things you do."

"So, what's all the commotion for? Is it a party for me?"

"Everyone is happy. My group has brought back many things that were needed. My father is their leader. People thought he would be dead by now. Now people think he will live because there is a doctor here. They are happy."

"Will they be happy if he dies from sepsis?"

"I do not know, but if he dies now, then he will die. They will be sad, but they will get beyond it."

"What difference does it make?"

Malika sighed. "These are, *we are* simple people, Doctor. We do not ask why God does the things he does, but we accept it. My people, and many others, live with very little to celebrate. Life is hard, but we survive. To live in a way that would seem poor to you, would feel rich to us. A few supplies and the presence of a doctor is enough to bring joy to us. We thank God for what he has given us. It may sound foolish to you, but it is who we are."

"Doesn't sound foolish to me at all. Actually, I admire the strength and perseverance of your people."

"Does that mean you will want to stay here with us? A doctor would be welcomed."

Andrew turned his head to Malika. Was there a thin air of want that he hadn't heard before?

"Does it mean you want me to stay?" he asked with a smile.

"You are doctor; who would not want a doctor in their own village?"

"I mean besides that."

"I don't know what you ask."

"If I weren't a doctor, would you want me to stay here?"

"If you were not a doctor you would not be here," she answered as she stood.

"Great," Andrew replied, his smile disappearing. "Look, can you point me in the direction of my hut. I'm feeling kinda tired and I want to go to bed. Not a lot of good conversation out here."

"Have I offended you?" she asked.

"No, Malika, you have not offended me. I guess I just ask too many questions without being prepared for the answers."

"You ask questions that I do not know how to answer," she told him. She sighed before turning and walking away quickly.

By the time one of the boys touched his shoulder and told him to get up, she was on the other side of the fire talking to another group of people.

The mood in the village was high, but his own spirit was suddenly tired and deflated. Despite his attempts toward the contrary, Malika had not warmed to him at all. He hoped his kiss would stir something within her, but she obviously wanted nothing to do with him and her admission that if he weren't a doctor, she would have left him to die in the desert was a stark reminder of that. He made up his mind to prepare for his departure from the village as soon as he could. He was healed now, there was no reason to stay any longer.

Four

Andrew awoke suddenly with a sense of a heavy weight being applied to his chest. His first inclination was that he was having a heart attack, but as his mind cartwheeled toward consciousness, he became aware of the presence of another person's body on top of him.

A strong hand clamped over his mouth, and he reacted instinctively. Adrenaline surged through his veins, preparing him for a fight-or-flight scenario as his mind groped for an explanation. He thrust his hips upward and to his left while his hands gripped the shoulders of his assailant.

"Shh."

His body went limp at the sound of Malika's voice.

"What?" he asked as she removed her hand from his mouth.

"Be quiet," she whispered.

"What time is it? What are you doing here?"

"You are right. You ask too many questions." Her hands clawed at his robe, pulling it up and over his head. "But you do not wait for answers."

Climbing back on top of him, she pressed her naked body against his and found his mouth with hers in a hungry, frantic kiss.

"I like this answer."

"Stop talking, please."

Her body reacted to his touch, breaking out in goosebumps beneath his fingertips as his hands moved across her shoulders and down her back. A shudder ran through her body, and she moaned lightly.

His hands found her round, full butt and he grasped it as she lowered her lips to his. His mind rejoiced as his hands took in every curve of her body; the taste of her mouth on his; the light scent she possessed and the strong, musky scent of her arousal; the firmness of her breasts, and the strength in her arms as she embraced him.

When she moved above him, he felt the warmth of her breasts against his skin, her erect nipples brushing across his chest. Situating her hips, she guided him into her body, moving slowly until they were fully connected.

The quiet moan she released into the darkness thundered in his ears, bringing a smile to his face. For an instant, he wished he could see her, then changed his mind. His blindness had opened a new world of feelings, sounds, and smells that only enhanced the moment. There was so much more to enjoy that his sight had taken from him. A preoccupation with looks had diminished his other senses, costing him so much.

Malika leaned forward, their bodies coupled, and pressed herself against him. When she slowly began to move her hips, it was Andrew's turn to moan.

His hands roamed over her body and found her breasts, firm and fuller than expected. Massaging gently, his fingers drew their exquisite shape in his mind. When she moved slightly forward, he opened his lips and took one of her hard nipples into his mouth. Her body tensed and her strong thighs clenched firmly against his body. A low groan of pleasure escaped her soft lips as another shudder ran through her, sending more goose pimples across her skin in a pattern that followed his gentle caress.

As Malika moved over him, her hands gripping and holding him, Andrew began to lose himself in the moment. It felt good to not be "on alert." To not have to listen and be in tune with the world as a matter of self-defense. Being in tune with a beautiful, naked woman was much more pleasurable. The ever-present desire for revenge, the hatred, the anger, even his sadness, all subsided while her body, heated with passion, connected with his.

Their bodies moved in unison as she took his lead and allowed her body to be lowered to the bed beneath them, never losing the coupling. Now over her, Andrew pressed his lips to hers. Moving slowly, he began to make love to her. When his mouth ranged across her cheek and found her supple neck, the smell of her freshly washed hair flooded his mind. He inhaled deeply, imprinting the scent in his memory even deeper than before.

Everything about Malika aroused him, especially the short, natural fingernails that dug into his back as she clung to him, moving her body to meet his. She arched her back off the bed as one of his hands found her breasts and the other wove its way into her hair. Andrew directed his kisses to the base of her neck and across her upper chest.

Malika gripped him tightly with her thighs and clutched his back as another shudder of pleasure rippled through her. Her body shook slightly, and she embraced him tighter, drawing him to her.

"Please don't stop," she whispered into his ear.

"I have no intention to."

Deep in the night in the village of Sayf Alsalam, loosely translated in English as "Sword of Peace," a watchful pair of eyes trained themselves on the door of the hut that Malika had entered over two hours ago. No lamp had been lit and all had been quiet since.

A cigarette's ember glowed red, then faded in the darkness as the watcher waited in the shadows. All that could be gained was information, but sometimes information was as valuable as gold. Particularly if it was the right information, or information about the right person.

A figure moved in the night, approaching the watcher, joining him in the shadows. He spoke briefly, then moved on, leaving the watcher with a smile. One brief statement, "Abd El-Kader is dead," coupled with this new-found knowledge could change everything.

Everything.

As Andrew swam toward consciousness, he became aware that he was smiling. The smell of Malika's body was still as fresh on his skin as the memory was on his mind. Making love to Malika had been unlike anything he'd ever experienced. When she left him deep in the night, he was exhausted and completely satisfied.

Pushing up onto an elbow, he listened to the village outside. The voices moved quickly as they passed his hut. Animals were being moved about and made their resentment known. Not too far away a group of four, maybe five men were arguing. Further up the dirt track that transected the village there was the unmistakable sound of wailing.

"Shit," he said aloud, swinging his feet over the edge of the bed. Slipping his thobe over his head, he stood and found his sandals. Something major had happened and a sickening feeling in his stomach told him that it was his patient.

Dammit. I should have stayed with him longer.

Hurrying across the room, one hand extended before him, he scolded himself again for not staying with the patient. So many things could go wrong directly after surgery, especially the one he performed yesterday. Hell, he didn't even check in on the man before going to bed.

No, but you found time to bang the hell out of his daughter. Andrew froze, his thoughts turning to Malika. How would she take it? What should he do? How should he react? Of course he should console her, but in what capacity. They'd slept together, but what did that mean now? Were they a couple? Would her culture dictate that they were? Did she want them to be? Did he?

Continuing to the door, Andrew slowly pushed against the rough sawn wood. As the door opened slightly, the noise level went up. There were women wailing in the direction of the house where he did the surgery. One of the men in the argument to his left raised his voice and said something emphatically, slamming his fist onto his open palm. The other men went quiet, yielding to the loud one.

Andrew stood in the doorway, trying to formulate a plan. He wanted to find Malika, but that would be impossible in the bustling village. She would probably be in her father's house, but she might not. A sense of helplessness tried to creep into his mind, but he fought it off. A wave of guilt rushed in to fill the void. Had he done as much as he could? Had he missed something while distracted by Malika's closeness? Drawing in a deep breath, he dismissed the guilt as well.

A sense of danger replaced the guilt. He wasn't an expert on tribal happenings, but he knew enough to know that when a leader died, the transition could be tumultuous to say the least. Where did this leave Malika, being a woman? And where did it leave him, being an outsider?

Men arguing before the dead was laid to rest wasn't a good sign. The sound of hurried footfalls nearby caught his attention. They were light, with a short stride. Probably one of his "minders." He stepped back, allowing the door to close, and waited.

The door swung open as soon as it closed. Raheb spoke to him in Arabic, then sighed in frustration. He stepped inside and allowed the door to close behind him.

"Our leader has died," he said.

"I figured as much."

"You stay inside. Malika says for you to use the pot for pissing. Wait for everything else."

"Where is she? Is she okay?"

"She is fine. Much to do. Jinaza must be done before the sun has gone. Women weeping and crying. You stay here. I bring food."

"What happened?" Andrew asked.

"I do not know. Just that he is dead. Malika says there may be trouble and to bring you this."

The boy took his hand and laid a cold piece of metal in it. A gun? Andrew's heart leaped into his throat. Why would he need a gun?

"You stay in. Do not go outside until someone gets you. I will bring food." The boy turned to leave, but Andrew grabbed his arm.

"What happened?"

"He was shot and died. You are the doctor. Do you not know?"

"I do," Andrew admitted. "I do know." The bullet wasn't what killed the old man. The infection and the surgery had done that.

"Use pail, do not leave, I bring food, Malika will see you." Raheb turned and exited the door hurriedly.

Andrew sighed and ran one hand through his hair while the other clutched the gun. It was a small weapon with a short barrel. Probably a

.38 caliber revolver. At close range it would get the job done, but it only held six shots. He examined the cylinder, spinning it slowly with his fingertips, counting the shells. One was missing.

Make that five shots, he thought, dropping it into the pocket on the side of his tunic. He stood in the middle of the room and shook his head. Things had gone from complicated and uncomfortable to complicated and dangerous.

Andrew sat in the front corner of the house on a small stool and waited. A boy he didn't know brought him a morning meal of dates and one piece of flat bread smeared with oil and a spice he didn't recognize, but that had been hours ago.

He found and used the latrine bucket, paced the floor to map the house, and practiced drawing the gun from his pocket. From where he sat, he could get the jump on anyone who burst into the room. He would be able to get a few shots off before ducking for cover behind the small bed, which he'd pulled away from the wall.

While he waited, he listened. The morning activity had shifted to the other end of the village, nearer to the Kader house. Women still passed by, singing, or crying, or both. The little activity that took place near his door still had more of a sense of urgency to it than before.

The more he thought about it, putting the pieces of the puzzle together, the more uneasy he became. This was a small village and the leader just died. Given Malika's prominent role there probably wasn't a male descendant to take over, or even a husband through marriage. That would leave the tribe in the awkward position of having to choose a new leader. If they didn't act quickly, one would rise up and take the position, by force if necessary.

Malika was in an impossible position. She would have to bury her father, solidify her base, and fend off any upstarts all at once if she were to have any chance at being the leader. Of course, it might not be a position that a woman could attain under any circumstances, which again would complicate things further. The matter of his presence was another situation entirely. The fact that Malika had brought an outside man into the village who might have had a hand in her father's death would surely rouse suspicion.

There would be rumors that she planned to marry him, thereby affording an outsider a place in succession. That would not go over well, and it would put a bullseye on Malika's back for anyone who had their eye on the position.

Andrew's hand went to the gun in his pocket, suddenly more appreciative of its presence. It might keep him safe temporarily, but what about Malika?

In the short time he knew Malika, he'd heard her be tough, when she argued with the men in the desert- and tender- when they made love. He'd also noticed her humility when she went to gather water for the whole group that night in the desert. She was smart, resilient, resourceful, and probably beautiful. What else could anyone ask for in a leader?

That they be a man.

Andrew sighed and leaned his head against the wall. His body had been on alert all day and he was getting tired. He would need to diminish his senses and rest. He would be more susceptible to surprise, but only as much as an average man.

Retreating within himself, he went through his daily checks, adjusting where needed. He lowered his heart and respiration rate slightly. Leaving his hearing acuity at a high level, he allowed his sense of smell to return to baseline. Finally, he lowered his pericolic activity. The dates were already beginning to work on his digestive track and the last thing he wanted to do was poop in the bucket.

The sound of the wooden door scrubbing on the dirt alerted him to someone's presence. He reached into his pocket and drew the gun. Raising it before him, he aimed toward the door and waited. It would take a few seconds for his guest's eyes to adjust to the dim light of the room, he just hoped it was enough time to determine if they were friend or foe.

Two soft footfalls floated to his ears as the person entered the room and stopped, probably looking for him. He gripped the gun and applied pressure to the trigger.

"You must be careful not to shoot the wrong person."

The tension fled his body at the sound of Malika's voice.

"Well, you're the one who gave a blind man a gun."

"I thought it might be needed. And might be yet."

"I'm sorry about your father. I did the best I could." He wanted to go to her and take her in his arms but didn't. The typical morning after awkwardness was compounded a thousand times by their current situation.

"It was not you who killed him," she finally said with a tired sigh.

Malika crossed the room and sat a bowl of food and a flask on his bed. The light, sweet smell that she usually wore was absent, replaced by the scent of nervous sweat. Her voice was solemn and low. She was sad and worried. The urge to take her in his arms and console her rose up in his chest again but he fought it.

"How are you holding up? I know this is a difficult time."

"I will be fine."

Andrew stood and joined her. He searched for and found her hand. "Can I help in any way?"

Malika sighed again. "Things may change quickly in the village. You must be ready to leave. Neither of us may be safe by the time the sun rises."

"What has happened? Besides your father's passing I mean."

"My house girl sat up with him last night. When I awoke this morning, she was missing, and my father was dead."

"Do you think she did something?"

"No. She is very loyal to me. I believe she will be found dead. Men are searching for her. Also, my father had blood in his eyes."

"Blood?" Andrew asked.

"Yes, his eyes were red with blood."

"Petechiae? Really?" Andrew rubbed his face with his free hand. "Do you know what one of the main causes for that is?"

"I do not, but they were not red last night."

"Your father might have been murdered. Suffocated or strangled."

Malika groaned as he confirmed her suspicions. "I thought as much." She pulled away from him and walked the length of the room and back. "Things are not good. There will be a challenge for the leadership, of course. I cannot be the leader and since I have no husband...."

"That's about what I figured."

"But many people are still loyal to my father's house. We may be safe. I do not know. I have a distant uncle that is away. He has been sent for. If they find him, we will have to leave quickly."

Andrew reached out and found her shoulders, drawing her closer to him. "Malika, I will help you all I can, but if I'm a hinderance to your escape you must promise me that you will abandon me and save yourself."

"You are a fool. They will cut you into pieces long before you die."

"Maybe so, but at least I'll know you're safe."

"Because we were together, you are now loyal to me?"

"Maybe, but I probably was before that."

"Do you know that I may soon be a woman with nothing? I may have to leave with what I can carry. I will be a wanderer."

"So what? I don't care."

"Are you in love with me, Doctor?"

Andrew shrugged then leaned in and pressed his lips to hers. "I don't know exactly what I am, but I'm something."

"Then you are a bigger fool than I thought." There was a gladness to her voice that belied her words as she stepped back from his reach. "You must eat and drink. Get ready to leave quickly. I will come for you." She went quickly to the door but stopped. "I will not leave you. I promise." She stepped out the door and closed it firmly behind her.

Andrew stood in the middle of the room, breathing in the close, warm air still tinged with the faint smell of Malika's body. It reminded him of the smell she had when she'd left him only a few hours ago and a smile crept across his lips, but it was short lived.

The sound of boys arguing a short distance from the house snatched him back to the harsh reality that now surrounded him. The group, four or five boys, were locked in a heated verbal confrontation. Angry sounding words flew from everyone and then he heard the unmistakable sound of flesh against flesh as one boy struck another.

The voice of an older man burst onto the scene and scolded the boys before sending them one by one in different directions. He held one of the boys back and they conversed for a moment, then he too was sent on his way.

"Damn," Andrew said, rubbing an itch on his forehead where the wound had been. "Even the kids are taking sides." The situation was probably more tense than Malika had let on. He'd heard plenty about the various factions of middle eastern countries fighting, but the inter-tribal politics never got much airtime back home. He imagined Malika arguing with the villagers, pleading her case with the elders, or just begging for their safety, and shook his head.

Another wave of guilt washed over him, this one telling him that he should be out there with her, but what could he do? He wouldn't be able to find her, he couldn't speak the language, and he was an outsider. Most of the people were suspicious of him to begin with, and more than a few probably blamed him for the death of their leader. If he wandered outside, he could incite any sort of situation that would many matters worse. Malika asked him to stay here, safe, where she could find him. If he wandered off and got lost it would jeopardize whatever plan she already had in place.

He let out a frustrated sigh and shuffled back to his corner. He took the gun out of his pocket and was about to sit again when the door opened quickly behind him. Spinning, the gun already held in front of him, he waited for a sign to fire.

"No. Please. It is me," the boy's voice pleaded. It was Raheb.

Andrew lowered the gun and smiled. "Sorry, kiddo. I'm kinda on edge."

"Everyone is angry today." Raheb dropped a canvas bag to the floor. "Malika said you will need this. Be ready."

Andrew heard the door open and close quickly, and he was alone again. He pocketed the gun and went to find whatever the boy had left. After a few steps, his foot struck something on the floor. He picked it up, recognizing it as the canvas pack he'd stolen from the army camp after he'd been taken to when the soldiers found him in the desert.

Pulling the flap open, his hand went inside. The clothes he'd taken off Souter were there, as well as two flasks of water, and Souter's boots. At the bottom of the bag he found a broken pair of goggles and a small bag tied at the top. Everything he had when Malika found him beneath the tree was there. She'd somehow managed to save everything.

He went to the cot and dropped the bag on it. He pulled the tunic over his head and dressed quickly in the clothes provided, shoving the gun into the hip pocket of the pants. Kicking off the sandals, he sat and slid his feet into Souter's socks before donning the boots. The tall, leather boots would make a hasty retreat a lot easier, and probably save him a twisted ankle.

He was tying his right boot when the door burst open again. Before he could draw his gun, he heard Malika's voice asking if he was ready to go.

He tied his boot and shoved his robe and sandals into the bag. "I am now."

"Good." He heard her cross the room to the back wall. "Because we are out of time."

Malika drug a small table away from the wall and rounded it. Running her hand along the wall, she found a seam in the stonework. Gathering the hem of her abaya, she raised it to her hips, revealing a tan pair of loose-fitting military style pants. Putting her back to the wall along the seam, she raised her booted foot and kicked backwards against the wall. The stones moved, but only slightly. She kicked again, harder this time and a small hole, just big enough for an adult to slide through, opened in the wall.

"We must go," she said and squatted next to the hole. Andrew hurriedly came to the sound of her voice, running into the table and knocking it over. "Come," she added impatiently.

Andrew found the hole in the wall and slipped through it behind Malika. When he stood, he heard her reenter the hole, then the sound of the table being dragged. She was covering their escape route.

She took his hand and led him away from the house quickly.

"We will go down to the river," she said, gripping his hand. She pulled him over the edge of steep incline without hesitation. The small, loose rock beneath his feet shifted like large gravel, giving way easily with each step. Struggling to stay upright, he found himself leaning backwards, keeping one hand on the steep bank as they proceeded. He half-slid and stumbled all the way down the hill while Malika pulled him relentlessly.

When they reached the bottom, she paused to catch her breath and to survey the area.

"We are on the floor of the wadi," she told him. "There are many trees and shrubs. We will have cover, but we must be careful. Many people come to the water and the shade. Some are bandits and will kill us both."

"Why don't we get in the river?" he asked.

"We may have to, but I prefer not." She looked back up the slope they'd just traversed. "No one knows we are gone, which is good."

"Will they care?" Andrew asked, picking dirt from beneath his fingernails.

"Perhaps not, but when my uncle arrives, he will care a great deal."

"Why?"

"We must go." She grabbed his hand and pulled him into the trees, proceeding more carefully now.

"Why would he care?" Andrew asked again.

"Because he is a sick and twisted man." She ducked a group of palm fronds, holding them out of his path. "He will force me to marry him."

Five

Andrew sat by the small fire, idly prodding the embers with a stick. He stared at the fire, watching an array of red, yellow, and orange arrows dancing upwards from the heat source in front of him. Their movements, reminiscent of seaweed moving on the current, lulled him into a trance-like state while his mind replayed the events of their hectic day.

There were so many questions and so few answers. Malika had been quiet and hurried all day, but that was understandable. Her world had just been turned upside down.

His mind wanted to think about the feel of Malika's body; to the eagerness of her lovemaking, but he wouldn't allow it. Instead he sent his mind to the Facility, where his wife and son had been murdered. He was forced to watch, his hands and feet strapped to the wall, while several men had their way with Samantha. Savon had been the last, brutalizing her unmercifully until he finally slit her throat. He continued to rape her while she bled out in front of him.

There was a mission he'd sworn to see through, he couldn't abandon that for the sake of being with Malika. Or could he? Should he? A fight with the Facility surely would end with him dead, and probably Malika as well. But he would need help and so far, she was one of the few people on this whole damned peninsula that didn't want him dead. He hadn't a clue where he was or where the Facility was. Would she help him, or would she abandon him?

"If you stare into the fire, you will have nightmares."

Andrew jumped, startled by the sound of Malika's voice, dropping the stick.

"Luckily, I'm blind so..."

He heard her pause in front of him. "You are very worried."

Andrew drew in a deep breath and exhaled slowly. "Aren't you?"

Malika spread a blanket on the ground and sat on it. "Sit with me?"

Andrew made his way to the blanket and sat down beside her with a groan. Sitting idle, his body had begun to stiffen after a day of walking.

"Why are you bothered so?" she asked, pulling his legs toward her so that she could unlace his boots.

"You don't have to do that."

Malika swatted his hand away. "I do not have to do anything I do not want."

Andrew resigned himself to allow her the labor. "I just have a lot of questions."

Malika nodded her head and smiled. "I am sure you do. As do I."

"Will they come after us?"

Malika pulled one boot from Andrew's foot and set about unlacing the other. "They might. I do not know."

"Fair enough." Andrew thought for a moment. "Did you run away because of your uncle or was there another reason?"

"There were many reasons." She unlaced his boot and pulled it off, setting it aside with the other. "I am very upset. My father was near death and my village prayed for him. I said that we needed a doctor instead of prayer, so I went to find a doctor. I found you. I thought that you were the answer to my family's prayers. I made you do surgery, but my father has died. I wonder if I had greater faith would he still be alive."

"He was probably killed, although I don't know how much longer he would have lived anyway, to be honest. I don't think there is any amount of faith that could have saved him."

"You do not believe in faith?"

"Faith isn't what I don't believe in. I have seen things that no man should have to see."

"As have I, but if we have no faith in anything then what is the purpose for living?"

"I can think of several things. Revenge comes to mind."

Malika nodded. "Revenge," she said with a grunt of disgust.

"Sometimes you cling to the only thing you have left."

"Perhaps." After a pause she added, "Is that what you are doing with me?"

"To be honest, I don't know. I don't think it is." Andrew rubbed his beard. "Is that what you are doing?"

"You ask the same question I give you the same answer."

"Fair enough. Anyway, it wasn't a lack of faith that killed your father."

"Perhaps. But the person responsible for his death will go unpunished, or maybe even be the leader of my village. And I am here, in the wilderness with you."

Andrew put a hand on her shoulder. "I know. I'm sure it is hard. And there are your kids..."

"They are not my children. They are children of people who have died in wars, but I have come to have great care for them. They had no family, so I brought them into my father's house."

"Whether they're biologically yours or not, you were raising them. That makes them your kids."

Malika sighed. "Maybe. They will be fine. I have found places for them."

Andrew could hear the sadness and worry in her voice, and he wished for some way to console her. On the morning of her father's death she'd managed to find places for the orphans she cared for and take care of a blind man. Now she was a woman adrift. Every ounce of his being wanted to fix that for her, but he didn't know how.

"If they come after us, will you fight them?" he finally asked.

"Yes. To the death. I cannot return to the village if my uncle is the leader." Malika sighed. "Even if he isn't, I am now but a woman with no home. It is a difficult position to be in here in my country."

Andrew listened as an uncomfortable silence fell over them. Malika was restless, shifting her weight and pulling at her clothes. Her respirations were up, and he could feel her unease.

"May I ask you about your eyes?" she asked hesitantly.

Andrew shrugged. "I don't see why not."

"How do you do the things you do without seeing?"

Andrew smiled. "It's complicated, but basically, through my other abilities. I was able to fine tune my senses. My hearing, my sense of smell. I can feel vibrations in the air."

"Yet you did not know that I was coming up the hill."

Andrew shrugged. "It's kinda like I have to turn things on and off. I was lost in thought."

"Then why not leave them on?"

"It's very tiring, actually. Some things aren't bad, hearing for example. But others are quite taxing on the body. And the mind."

"I see." Malika nodded as she pulled her knees to her and wrapped her arms around them. "You are a very smart man, I am sure."

Andrew sighed. "I don't know. Some may say so. I've never really thought about it."

Malika rested her chin on her knees and stared out over the dark wadi. "What color were they?"

"What? My eyes?" Andrew smiled again. "They were green."

"I have not seen many people with green eyes. I am glad you did not say blue."

"What's wrong with blue eyes?"

Malika shrugged. "Nothing. If you are American or English. I have seen many blue eyes. Soldiers. I have decided that I do not like blue eyes."

"I guess no one could fault you for that. I have to ask you something. Did you intend to marry me so that I could be the ruler of your village?"

"That is the question of a fool."

"And that is not an answer."

"The answer is no. My plan was to marry you so that I could be ruler of my village. You would have been allowed to wear the robe."

Andrew laughed. "What if I said no?"

"You are a fool." Malika let out a soft chuckle. "I am not sitting in the desert by myself, am I?"

"What does that have to do with anything?"

"You would not have said no."

"I might have."

Malika laughed again and gave him a playful nudge. "I have a question for you."

"Shoot. I'm an open book at this point."

"You ask me if I will fight if they come. My questions is that if they come will you fight?"

Andrew smiled and turned his face to her, taking her hands in his. "It seems to me that we're in this hole together. I will fight who you fight."

The tension in her body suddenly released. "Thank you," she answered in a whisper.

Malika lay on her back beside Andrew, their bodies covered by a thin blanket. The fire had burned down to embers and the cool of the night was settling on them. The cache of supplies she'd placed beneath a small outcropping nearby the day after Abd El-Kader was shot, now proved invaluable. She loved the tiny village, but her father had raised her to be prepared, and she was glad for it.

She looked over at Andrew. He'd grown quiet some time ago and his breathing slowed to a steady rhythm. Everything that she'd learned about him told her that he was a good man; an honorable man, and she found herself hoping that he wasn't fooling her. He hadn't found her candor off-putting, or her strength threatening, but quite the opposite. He seemed to enjoy her decisiveness and ability to take charge. He was a strong confident man and probably wanted a strong, confident woman. At least she hoped he would.

But to what end?

Sighing, she looked up at the night sky. The lack of a moon would favor their escape, but she was thankful not to be here alone on such a dark night.

Her eyes trailed over the countless stars in the sky above her. The desert sky was a beautiful sight that she never grew tired of seeing. She'd been taught the constellations, the planets, and the names of many celestial bodies as a child, but it hadn't interested her. Enjoying the simple beauty without confounding it with complicated names seemed a much better way to appreciate the heavens. Staring up at the stars, spread so far and wide in the sky, her mind went back to the question of her own fate.

Her life hadn't turned out anything like she'd dreamed as a little girl staring at these same stars. All she ever wanted was a husband that was good to her, a few children, and a pleasant life. Tonight, she had none of those things and was now an outcast from her own village. She had nothing but a few supplies and the man sleeping beside her.

When Andrew coughed in his sleep and rolled towards her, his arm tucked beneath his head, she looked at him and smiled. What was it about him that drew her to him that day in the desert? When she saw him from afar, her heart fluttered briefly. The other women dismissed him as either a deserter or a crazy man left in the desert to die, but she knew differently.

Somehow, she knew.

A pang of guilt crawled into her chest, reminding her of the lies that she'd told him. Would he think differently about her if he knew the truth? No other man wanted her. A small tear formed in the corner of her eye and then escaped. Why would it make so much difference? She was still the same person. She was still the same woman that he eagerly made love to. She was the same woman that he admitted his feelings to in the village.

Dismissing the bad thoughts, she slid closer to Andrew, turning her back to him. His body was warm and welcoming. When she gently pushed her body against his, an arm slid around her and drew her closer. He mumbled something incoherent into her hair and fell silent again. The strength in his grip felt good as she lay in his embrace. It was the embrace of a man who wanted her to be beside him, with him. She smiled contentedly and closed her eyes.

Alain Savon stood on the expansive balcony of his living quarters, bathed in the faint glow of light spilling through the wall of glass behind him. The building that housed his home was sleek and clean, with graceful curving architecture designed by the best draftsmen in Dubai and built by the most skilled craftsmen in the world. It was loosely referred to as "the science building" because no one lived in it except him. It was used mostly for data analysis and storage and housed the robotics lab. At night he usually had the entire building to himself, which was also by design.

His eyes looked out over the dark land before him, his face stoic, locked in a stare at nothing. Neatly trimmed white hair dancing gently in the same cool breeze that rippled his linen shirt. It was always better when all was dark and quiet. There were no decisions to make, no excuses to hear. No failures, no successes. The desert just was, and that pleased him. It was eternal, immortal, everlasting. Everything that he wanted to be. The desert gave nothing and asked nothing in return. Whether you lived or died in the desert was up to you and your ability to adapt. Either way the desert would be the same tomorrow.

He preferred the lone vantage of his balcony over all the statues and artwork in his home; more than the marble tiles and the Egyptian cotton sheets; more than all the expensive liquors and high-end accommodations. He owned them all. They were his and his alone, but they brought him little joy. They were all part of the facade he'd built to destroy his old life.

His brow furrowed momentarily as his thoughts returned to his childhood, and to the beatings he'd taken for so many years. His drunken father beat him, his black nanny beat him, the other kids at school beat him. Every adult in his life had beaten him at one time or another, especially the teachers at the elite boarding school his father forced him to attend. Growing up in Johannesburg, South Africa was never as easy for him as it was the other "white" children.

Savon's hand clenched the cool steel of the railing as he thought of Master Helensburgh. He was a fat, sadistic bastard who genuinely enjoyed the punishment that he doled out among the boys. He liked to keep boys after class and spank their bare bottoms with his ruler until they were beet red and swollen. Any minor infraction would draw his ire. Afterwards he would console them, telling them it was for their own good while he rubbed soothing balm all over their naked ass.

Everyone hated him but dared not cross him, or any of the administrators. Most of the boys, like him, had been threatened with the notion of having to attend the local public school. As privileged whites amid apartheid they wouldn't last a week before one of the locals slit their throats, or so they'd been taught.

Snatched quickly from his thoughts as footfalls approached along the balcony, his hand slid beneath his shirt and gripped the handle of the knife he kept in a thin belly scabbard. As the footfalls approached from the shadows his hand shot out, bringing the point of the four-inch blade to rest just against the throat of the intruder.

The messenger gasped, stopping suddenly. He swallowed hard as his wide eyes stared back at Savon.

"I thought I told you not to bother me," Savon said, his eyes still looking over the desert.

The man, dressed in khaki slacks and a white shirt, swallowed hard. "S-Sir," he began, being careful not to move. "I thought you might want to read the nightly report."

"I will read it in the morning."

"Y-yessir. S-sorry sir."

"Tell me Bailey," Savon began quietly, "Are you afraid that I might kill you?"

"Yes sir. Very much."

Savon smiled at the desert and then at the trembling man at the tip of his blade. "I just might," he said as he stared into his employee's eyes, enjoying the fear emanating from them.

"But not tonight," he finally said. He retracted the blade and watched as Bailey rubbed his neck. "What is so damned special about this report, Bailey? What makes it different than the other hundred you have brought me lately?"

"One of the scouts, sir, one of the scouts finally tracked down Abd El-Kader."

Savon's left eyebrow rose slightly, his interest piqued. "That is good news. I'm glad I didn't kill you."

"Well," Bailey began hesitantly. "Not as good as we hoped. He's dead."

Savon sighed and looked back out over the desert, fighting the urge to lash out, to kill anything he could get his hands on. He stood motionless for a long time, tracing the implications of the news he'd just gotten. It was a setback, but not a major one. Still, a setback of any kind was unacceptable.

"How?" he finally asked.

"He was shot. Either raiders or a fight among themselves. We don't know yet."

Savon shook his head. "It's a pity someone else killed him before I could."

"The interesting part, sir, if you'll excuse me, is that the word is that a doctor did surgery on him and removed the bullet."

"A doctor?"

"Yes sir. I'm trying to confirm things. The village is in a bit of a skirmish right now. They've not settled on a new leader and apparently there are several options, one of which may be a woman named Malika, or something. She is the old man's daughter, apparently."

Savon shook his head. "Savages." He sighed and spared Bailey a glance. "Is there anything else? Why are you still here?"

"Well, sir, like I said these are preliminary reports and nothing has been confirmed, but the rumor is that the doctor who did the surgery was blind."

Savon looked around. "Kader's village isn't far from where we lost that Blackhawk is it?"

"No sir. A couple klicks up and through the mountain. We've only just found it."

"When is our new helicopter due for delivery?"

"Day after tomorrow. There was a hold up with the delivery."

Savon sighed again, releasing his frustration to the wind. "Damned crooks. We're overpaying for it already."

"Yessir, but there's not much we can do about it, is there? Suppliers are hard to come by with the new president over there. They're cracking down a bit."

Savon pursed his lips as he slid the blade of the knife along the railing, watching as the sharp edge of the stainless-steel blade scratched the surface of the metal. The sound of steel on steel comforted him, but not enough to soothe his anger. Bailey, like most men, was lazy and gave up too easily. He was afraid and weak, and he hated him for it.

"Never say that to me again, Bailey. There is always something that can be done in the face of incompetence and greed."

"Yessir, I didn't mean to imply— "

"Shut up." Savon looked back out over the desert as his employee complied immediately. He took in a long breath of the cool air and closed his eyes. His mind leapt back to his school days, to the last day Master Helensburgh ever spanked his bare bottom.

Instead of complying with the order to drop his knickers, he had calmly sharpened his pencil. Of course, the teacher was irate, but he kept calm, executing his plan perfectly. When he finally approached the desk, his master raised the thick ruler to hit him, but the bastard never got the chance. Instead, what he got was a keenly sharpened pencil in his bulging stomach almost up to the eraser and a promise that the next one would be in his brain via his eye socket.

"Bailey," Savon said quietly, a pleasant smile coming to his lips.

"Yessir."

"When the helicopter gets here have the pilot killed and ship his fucking head back to our supplier. And take twenty thousand off the price. I don't think they will try to cheat me again."

"Yes sir. Will there be anything else, sir?"

Savon looked at the knife for a moment before moving the index finger to the point. He twisted the blade slowly until a small drop of blood formed around the shiny steel. Removing his finger, he looked at the blood for a moment before smearing it with his thumb.

"Yes. Send up the bothersome bitch that caused such a stir yesterday. The young one. I think it's time we met."

82

"Yes sir. Right away." Bailey backed up a few paces before turning and scurrying off along the balcony.

Savon looked at his own blood, then turned his attention back to the desert. Doctor Andrew Hawkins was out there somewhere. He was out there with his arrogant smile and his holier-than-thou attitude, doing free surgeries on old men and being noble. What a pathetic waste of his talents.

The wind picked up momentarily, blowing into his face. Savon smiled. It was going to be a cold night in the desert. Of course, the good doctor wouldn't still be in the village. As an outsider he'd be an easy target for the savages during an uprising. He was out there, probably alone, and unprepared, and maybe even wishing he were back here in his warm bed with his pretty little wife.

He glanced briefly over his shoulder when the sound of a knock drifted through the open doors behind him. His package had arrived. He returned his gaze to the desert, his smile gone. Tomorrow, he thought. Tomorrow, the hunt begins in earnest.

Six

The light filtering through the sheer curtains behind her head framed golden hair in a halo, personifying her perfect existence as a wife and mother. Her thin lips were turned up slightly at the edges as she hummed intermittently while she rinsed the dishes in the farmhouse sink, a surprise during the kitchen remodel that had brought her way more joy than a sink should have.

Her thin, athletic frame moved with grace and ease as she rinsed each dish and loaded it into the dishwasher. Her nature wasn't hurried or begrudging of the labor but seemed perfectly content to serve and provide for her family in the ways she knew they needed.

Andrew, frozen by the perfectness of the quiet moment, stood in the doorway and watched his wife, soaking in every ounce of her beauty and peace. Pride swelled in his heart for her, not because she was doing the dishes, but because she loved her family so much that she didn't mind doing the dishes, even if it was his turn.

She was a gentle soul who tried to see the best in every situation and every person; the kind of woman who would stop and give money to panhandlers no matter how hurried they were. She was more comfortable in their country home than at any formal event he dragged her to. She always went, dressed perfectly, looked beautiful, and made the social rounds with a smile, but she never really liked it.

Everyone loved Samantha more than they did him. People liked him, people tolerated him because of who he was, but they adored her. At least once at every social function someone would always remind him that he was a lucky man, and he always agreed. He figured himself to be one of the luckiest men in the world.

While he watched from his unseen perch, his son, Lane, came running into the kitchen holding a small, still creature in his tiny hands.

He was in a panic as he explained to his mother that he'd rescued the chipmunk from their cat.

Samantha wiped her hands on a dish towel and took the thing from her son, wrapping it in the cloth. Kneeling, she looked at it with her son, examining the wounds on the wet fur carefully.

"Can you save it, mom?" Lane asked, tears already running down his cheeks.

"I don't know, sweetness," she replied, using the nickname she always called him. "It looks like old Chester got him pretty good. He's hurt badly."

"But you gotta save him, mom. You have to."

"Look, why don't we sit here and just let it rest. Maybe that's all it needs."

She sank to the floor and crossed her legs, holding the towel with one hand and her son with the other. The two of them looked at the chipmunk for a while in silence.

"It sure is pretty," she finally whispered. "I've never seen one this close before."

"It's beautiful. That's why we have to save it, mom. Because it's so pretty."

She let out a quiet sigh, knowing the creature wasn't going to make it. The old tom cat was nothing if not an effective killing machine.

"It is beautiful, sweetness." She stroked its fur gently with her thumb. "But I don't know if it's going to survive this."

"Stupid old Chester. He's so old and mean. Why would he kill something so pretty? It's not fair."

Samantha pulled her son close while they sat on the kitchen floor watching the chipmunk's sides rise and fall with each labored breath. She stroked her son's hair lovingly and waited for the inevitable.

"Is he dead?" Lane asked tearfully when it stopped breathing.

"I'm afraid so," she whispered, wrapping it in the cloth.

"I don't know why beautiful things have to die and ugly things like Chester get to live."

"I don't either, sweetness. But it's not our decision to make. We just have to make the best of whatever happens."

"But I loved it."

Samantha smiled as she wiped a tear from her own cheek. "I know. But you know what?"

"What?" he asked, his face shoved against her side.

"Just because it's gone doesn't mean you have to stop loving it. Listen, baby, things like this will happen from time to time, but we can't let our hearts turn cold because of it. We've got to keep on loving, and praying, and being who we are."

"I guess."

"Now look. We got to hold a chipmunk. They'd never let us hold them in the wild. We got to see it up close and really see how beautiful they are. Usually they're just scurrying by so fast we can barely see them."

She sighed again and wiped another tear from her cheek.

"But why did it have to die?" he asked again.

"Sometimes things die, baby. Even beautiful things. We're only on this earth for a certain amount of time- how much we don't know. That's why it's important to enjoy life and not fret about things that don't really matter. Like this little guy. We've probably seen him fleeting about a hundred times. He had a good life. Looks like he's gotten quite fat eating your daddy's birdseed."

The two shared a quiet, tearful chuckle.

"And even though Chester finally got him, you rescued him, and he got to spend his last few minutes inside the house, wrapped in a warm cloth, getting petted on and seen after. I'd bet he was very comfortable, all thanks to you."

Lane thought about his mother's words while he stared at the still lump beneath the cloth in her hand. "Can I see it again?"

"Sure."

The boy watched intently as his mother removed the cloth. "It's still beautiful, even though it's dead."

"It is. Beauty never dies, sweetness. It will be beautiful forever."

"Can we bury it so Chester can't eat him?"

"We surely can, baby. Let's go out back and find a spot. We can even toss in a handful of birdseed. Bet that'll make him happy."

Andrew watched as his wife and son exited the kitchen through the mudroom, laughing at how mad Andrew always got when the squirrels and other animals robbed his bird feeder.

Andrew awoke with a start, the sound of a screen door slamming echoing in his mind. Sitting upright in a panic, his breaths coming in short, fast gasps, he turned his head from side to side, looking for his wife. Her name hung on the tip of his tongue.

His hands went to his eyes and found the bandage, bringing him fully out of the dream. His fingers examined the wet spots on the bandages. Had he been crying?

"Are you okay?" Malika asked as she sat up, clutching the blanket over her bare chest.

"Yeah. Um. Yes. I'm fine." Andrew pulled his knees up and propped his elbows on them. His hands rubbed his face, again feeling the wet spots on the bandage. He tried to slow the pounding in his chest, but it continued to race. He had a similar reaction when he tried to lower his respiration.

In his mind he could still hear Samantha's words, "Beautiful things never die. They stay beautiful forever."

"Bad dream?" Malika asked, rubbing his back.

"I guess you could say that." Andrew clutched his head in his hands and concentrated. This time his heart rate did begin to slow. As it slowed his respirations dropped on their own, but an overpowering sense of guilt began to wash over him. The dream had been so vivid, so real that he felt like he was reliving the moment. It was one of the most precious interactions between two human beings that he'd ever witnessed, and it had sustained him many nights in the desert when he began to wonder if all hope was lost.

"Sometimes the good memories hurt more than the bad ones." Malika laid her head on the back of his shoulder and rubbed his arm gently.

Andrew laid his hand atop hers. "Sometimes they both suck."

"Yes. I know."

"Is the sun up yet? What time is it?"

"The sun is just beginning to break the horizon."

Andrew's hand went to the beard that covered his face. Now several inches long, it would rival that of any local man.

"Can we spare the time to talk over breakfast?" he asked.

Malika sighed quietly. "There is no need to talk about the past unless you feel that you need to. Or want to."

"Aren't you curious?"

"I learned as a child to be content with what I have." She snaked an arm around his waist and gave him a squeeze. "The past is full of ghosts that haunt us, Andrew. The future is full of spirits that entice us with hopes that may never come true. If today is all we have, I prefer to enjoy it."

Andrew sat in silence, pondering her words, and taking in the moment. Her skin was warm and inviting against his. Her breath was hot on his bare back as she rested her face against him. The desert hillside that stretched out in front of and below them was silent, except for a small bird that chirped inquisitively a few yards to his left as it fluttered between the small, dried shrubs. The first winds of the day raced across the cool sand to meet him just as the sun's rays fell upon his face.

The third day of their escape had begun.

Last night they crossed the river at a shallow point just before dusk and camped on the western bank. When Malika informed him that she was going to bathe and invited him, he eagerly agreed. Under the cover of a darkened sky, they had bathed each other in the river. Unhurried and without speaking, they washed every inch of each other's bodies in a sensual encounter that far surpassed anything he'd ever experienced.

Afterwards they made slow, passionate love on a blanket out in the open, unashamed of their nakedness. As he lay beneath the stars with Malika in his arms, her head on his chest, he realized that his feelings for her were more than a dependence, more than a physical desire or primal lust. An unspoken bond of pain had found them and lashed them together in ways he didn't fully understand yet. All he knew was that their relationship was symbiotic. Neither of them had anyone else to turn to and being together made them both stronger.

Andrew allowed the dopamine and oxytocin to flow in his brain, triggered by the memory of the emotional bonding with Malika, to assuage the quilt that plagued him. When he finally took a deep breath and released it slowly, he felt much better.

"So, what is the plan?" he asked.

"Plan?"

"We've been traveling in a southerly course, and last night we crossed the river, presumably to head southwest. Where are we going?"

Malika smiled, impressed. "You want to go back to the place that hurt you, no?"

"I do." Andrew put his hand over hers again. "But you don't have to go. It is a very dangerous place and it's not your fight."

Andrew listened to her response while they sat in silence. Her breathing increased slightly but he couldn't tell if she was offended or angry.

"How do you not know that it is not my fight as well? I have lived here my whole life. Much longer than you."

"There are many things I don't know about you, Malika."

"That is true, and perhaps that is best."

"Maybe so. For now."

"We will get dressed and eat, then we will move. It is not safe here. We are exposed for anyone to see us, and the sun is up. If you wish to continue this talk, we will find shelter and I can tell you everything about my past as if we were schoolgirls."

He felt the blanket fall to the ground as Malika stood, leaving Andrew to wish he could see her naked body in the light of day. Her feisty response brought a smile to his face as he stroked his beard again. The sounds of her getting dressed told him that she'd determined their course for the day. There would be no "schoolgirl" talk this morning, leaving him a mystery to entertain himself with while they walked.

He found his pants and pulled them onto his legs as he sat. "Where are we going?"

"Minwakh," she said flatly. "It is a town about thirty kilometers from here. It will be a safe place to stay. If you want to go back to that place, I think you will need more supplies than a small gun and five bullets. We can find supplies there."

"How do you know this?"

Andrew heard her sigh and felt the weight of her stare.

"Okay. Okay. Can't I ask you anything?"

"You may ask me anything you like," she told him. "Whether I answer or not is something else."

Andrew listened to her stride away, down the hill toward the river, and shook his head. Standing as he pulled his pants up, he looked in the direction she'd gone. There would come a time when he would have to insist on answers to his questions, but that time wasn't now. Malika was right. If he went back to the Facility, he would definitely need more than a thirty-eight-caliber pistol and a few bullets.

He found his shirt hanging on a nearby bush and shook it out, making sure nothing had taken refuge in it during the night. He had it half on when he first heard the helicopters in the distance.

"Malika," he yelled. "Helicopters! Take cover."

The faint thumping of the rotors grew louder by the second. They were moving fast and headed right for them. He kicked dirt over the dying embers of their fire and grabbed the blanket from the ground to eliminate any trace of their presence.

Malika joined him, grabbing the few remaining items strewn over the camp, and took his hand, dragging him behind her. When they neared the large cluster of rocks, she could already hear the helicopters herself but dared not spare a moment to look back at them.

She shoved Andrew to the ground and dove behind the rocks with him, covering them both with the blanket. "Be still!"

Andrew sat motionless, listening to the sounds of her hurried breaths as two helicopters approached. He felt sure they hadn't been seen, but they wouldn't know for sure until they passed, or opened fire on them.

He held his breath as the sound grew louder, echoing off the river and the surrounding mountains. The two helicopters sounded like a dozen as they approached, drowning out everything else but the rhythmic thump of the rotors. In his mind he could see them spinning, rotating above the fuselage with mechanical precision.

Malika's arms found him as the helicopters entered the valley, following the river, and embraced him tightly as they drew closer. She pressed her face to his shoulder when the sound became deafening as they passed overhead, so low that the prop wash rippled the blanket above them.

But as quickly as they had arrived, they left the area. Flying one behind the other, they crossed over them without so much as a waiver. Andrew drew back the cover and turned his face in their direction.

"They were in a hurry," Malika said. "Luck is with us."

Andrew pursed his lips as he listened to them thunder up the valley. They gained altitude quickly to clear the pass, then dropped beyond the hills, their sound fading almost instantly.

"I don't know about that," he said, shaking his head.

"They were military, no?" she asked. Pulling the blanket from Andrew, she wrapped it around her naked body.

"Yep. Just like the other one. Judging by the direction they were going and the hurry they were in, I'd say that one of them was a replacement for Savon's helicopter I dropped the other day."

"But it must cost a fortune."

"I'm sure, but they've got a fortune to spend." Andrew sighed. Malika's uncle had been an immediate threat, but the further they got from the village, the less of a threat he would be. The Facility, however, had a much longer reach. If there was any doubt that he had to kill

Savon it vanished with the helicopters. He wouldn't stop until one of them was dead.

"What do they do there?" she asked. "That they have so much money?"

"It's complicated," Andrew said. "Get dressed. Let's pack up and get moving. I'll tell you walking. Right now, your uncle is the least of our worries."

Alain Savon strolled out of his bedroom comfortable in his nudity, pausing to accept a cup of tea from a dark-skinned teenage girl who was likewise completely naked.

"May I wash?" she asked timidly, her eyes on the floor.

He answered with a dismissive wave, allowing the girl to retreat into the bedroom, the welts along her lower back and buttocks still swollen from the night before.

Sipping his tea, he walked to the wall of glass that looked out over the eastern desert. His eyes immediately fell on the two small dots in the clear blue sky and a smile crept to his lips. His package had arrived.

Standing before the windows unashamed, he watched as the two helicopters approached the compound. The lead helicopter slowed considerably and took up a defensive position, hovering a hundred feet off the ground well beyond the perimeter. The second made its way toward the compound. It hovered briefly, then crossed over the thick stone wall before ultimately coming to rest on the landing pad.

Alain watched through the windshield as the pilots went through the checklist before shutting the machine down. The propellers slowed, and the pilot opened his door. He hopped out cautiously, a hand on the gun strapped to his hip. After accessing the situation, he gave his co-pilot a wave and the man quickly joined him.

By the time the prop wash began to settle down, two men in khaki slacks and white shirts were rolling a cart out of the main building. On the cart was a large wooden crate full of crisp American cash.

Savon stared at the box. He wanted to kill both men and keep the helicopter and the cash, but he needed a supplier, as much as he hated to admit it. Besides, if he killed them both there would be no one to deliver his message.

A smile crept to his lips as he watched the two pilots leave the landing pad to meet his men with the cart. The two airmen looked around nervously, their hands still on their weapons as they met his men in the middle of the expansive yard.

The men exchanged unheard pleasantries that seemed to relax the pilots some, evidenced by the pilot's hand leaving his gun to shake Bailey's. The crate was opened, and all four men stared at the stacks of bills within. The man beside Bailey made a comment that caused all four to laugh.

Savon smiled.

When the pilot turned to the helicopter hovering outside the wall and gave him a series of hand signals, Savon's eyes diverted to the Blackhawk still in the air. It slowly descended and landed beyond the wall. From his height, he could still see the propellers. They never stopped turning.

"Now," he whispered aloud over his cup.

As if on cue the two men on the ground moved quickly, catching the airmen off guard. Bailey produced a pistol and shot the pilot between the eyes while the second man grabbed the co-pilot. He had the man subdued and his weapon removed before the pilot hit the ground.

The co-pilot struggled but couldn't break free of the grip that kept his arm held high and his neck pinned forward. Bailey pointed the gun at him and issued an unheard warning. The man stopped struggling, no doubt learning that he wasn't going to be killed unless he did something stupid.

Bailey waved to the main building. A man dressed in a dingy white tunic ran to the scene carrying a large knife. He paused to get his commands from Bailey, then went to the dead body lying on the sand.

Savon sipped his tea, watching the scene unfold as planned. The man with the knife grabbed the pilot by his flight helmet and tilted his head back. With the knife hovering over the dead pilot's throat, he spoke to the co-pilot briefly and then laughed. The co-pilot didn't laugh with him, but he did close his eyes.

The metal of the blade cast off a glint of sunlight as it moved to the pilot's neck. Wielded masterfully, the blade sank into the flesh and disappeared. With a few flicks of his wrist the wielder of the knife cut through the pilot's spine and severed his head in a process that took less than five seconds.

Savon smiled, shaking his head slightly. The savagery of some of the people in this country never ceased to amaze him, but he did admire their efficiency.

Lifting the head triumphantly, the man laughed while blood drained from the open veins in the pilot's neck, staining the sand next to him a dark crimson. Standing, he walked over to the crate. Opening it with the knife, he tossed the head onto the stack of money and pointed the tip of his knife at the co-pilot. His words made the man's eyes grow wide with fear.

Savon smiled again and took another sip of tea.

The largest of the three men released his hold and pushed the co-pilot to the ground next to his now headless pilot. His face contorted with fear and disgust as he scurried from it quickly and pushed himself up. He looked at the three men now walking back to the main building, then looked around the compound. His eyes found the open gate and he stared at it for a moment. Confused and afraid, he took a few steps toward the gate, then stopped and took a few steps toward the money. He looked at his headless counterpart and turned back to the gate.

Stopping suddenly, he turned and ran back to the cart. He grabbed it and drug it across the sand toward the gate, sparing his pilot one last look as he passed.

Savon's heart began to race as the moment of truth neared. The Blackhawk was armed and could level the compound, but would it? He was counting on his supplier's greed and banking on the fact that he wouldn't. Either way, there was nothing he could do now. He sipped his tea and waited.

The co-pilot cleared the gate with the cart and began signaling wildly at the helicopter. A man dressed in fatigues jumped out of the door carrying a military rifle and ran to him. Together, they pulled the cart across the loose sand. The co-pilot was screaming wildly at his partner as they labored with the heavy cart. When they neared the helicopter, a second man leaped out and helped load the crate into the door. All three men jumped in and closed the door as the pilot cycled up the rotors.

The heavy machine lifted slowly, kicking up a swirling plume of sand.

Savon watched intently as the fuselage slowly rose above the wall. He knew the crate of cash was worth more than one pilot, but he also knew what he'd do if the situation were reversed. He stood motionless, cup in hand, and stared through the windshield. He was sure the pilot could see him.

The Blackhawk hovered for several minutes, while the pilot undoubtedly radioed his boss for instructions. Savon stood naked before them and sipped his tea. Either he would win, and the helicopter would fly away, or he would die. To him, one was as good as the other.

When the helicopter finally waivered and began to turn, Alain Savon smiled. He'd won. Again.

Seven

"We will camp here."

"Why?" Andrew stopped behind Malika, his face turned toward the sounds of life in the distance. "Sounds like a party."

"That is why we will wait."

Malika's voice was further away now, to his left and toward the side of the mountain of sandstone they'd just circumvented. She was already unpacking and making camp.

"Might be fun," he said with a smile.

"And we might be killed." She paused for a moment. "Come, sit down and rest."

Following the sound of her voice, he joined her alongside the hill. He found a boulder at the base of the mountain flat enough to sit on and dropped his pack with a sigh. Due to Malika's pace through the desert, over-cautious in his opinion, it took them two days to get to the city. Now she wanted to wait outside the gates.

"If you grow up in Yemen you know how dangerous this can be. It is a chance to kill many people at once. Death stalks everyone here."

Andrew sighed and turned toward the sounds of music. "Is it really a party if there's not a chance of somebody dying?" he asked with a chuckle.

"You make joke. This is not the United States, Andrew. People are not what they seem. It is dangerous. We may die any moment. It is no joke when you see the ones you love die because they speak different from someone else."

Andrew cringed at the pain in her voice. "I'm sorry. It was a dumb joke."

Malika walked up to him and kissed his lips. "Do not apologize for your ignorance. You are a fool, that is why you need me with you." She tugged playfully at his beard, and stepped back quickly, narrowly evading his hands as they grabbed for her waist.

"You should be tired after a long walk today."

"You'd think so," Andrew replied with a grin.

"Well, I am tired, and we need to eat. And rest."

Andrew sat in silence, listening to the festivities less than a mile away, and thought about what Malika said. It made sense. Even back home he'd heard about the sectarian violence in Yemen, and everyone had heard of the bombing of the *USS Cole*. If a group of men could attack a United States naval vessel, a small wedding party would be nothing. The depth of his ignorance began to sink in as he considered the daunting task of passing himself off as a local when they entered the city.

His beard and skin color would pass the test, but his accent was still present in the words Malika had taught him. Mastering the nuances of the language was difficult, even for him. If they became separated somehow, he would be lost, and an easy target. He drew in a deep breath and did his best to calm his newfound apprehension.

"Come. We will eat and get some rest here among the rocks. We will be safe enough."

Andrew slid off the rock and followed the sound of her meal preparation. His hands found the opening of a group of boulders, following them to the blanket Malika had laid out.

"Will you answer some questions tonight?" he asked quietly.

"Do you not trust me?" she asked, tossing herbs into a small cooking pot.

"I do, that is why I must remove any doubt. Surely you realize what a predicament I'm in?"

"Predicament?" she asked.

"Yes, the situation; the potential danger. I'm blind and I must depend on you. That makes me nervous."

"Ah," Malika nodded. "If you must know things to trust me, I will tell you."

"Are you some sort of operative? Like a spy or something?"

Malika laughed. "A spy? For who would I spy? I am an ignorant peasant."

Andrew shrugged, feeling silly. "You're neither of those."

"Okay. I'm just a peasant."

"I don't know. It's just that you're not a typical woman, especially for this neck of the woods."

"So, you would like it better if I wear the burka and bow to you? Shall I wash your feet?"

"Not at all." Irritation was high in her voice. "You're just, just..." he struggled for the right words. "Well, you're kind of a badass."

"My ass is bad?" she asked with a suspicious laugh.

"No," he said laughing himself. "Your ass is great. You can kick butt. You're tough, strong."

"Ah," she said, placing the pot on the small fire she'd built near the opening of the enclave. "I am no spy. You watch too many American television shows. I am a poor woman with no husband. In this place, I would be better off a goat."

Andrew shrugged again. "Fair enough." He scratched his beard and leaned against one of the stones. "What happened to your husband? A war?"

"No war. He was stabbed to death."

"They ever catch the guy?" Andrew asked.

"No guy." Malika paused and drew in a deep breath. "It was me."

"What?" Andrew sat up, shocked by the ease with which she'd confessed to murder.

"It is a long story, but he was cruel and mean. Like many, my marriage was made by my parents. I was fifteen and he was as old as I am now. He took me on our wedding night and almost every night after. One night he and a friend smoked too much hashish, and he wanted to give me to his friend. I refused. He beat me and I cut his liver out."

Andrew's jaw dropped as he sat in silence, processing what Malika had said.

"I ate it with beans and some wine," she added.

Andrew's mind staggered forward, trying to make sense of what she was saying, hoping that the translation was throwing her off.

Malika laughed and threw a pebble at him. "It is a joke. From a movie. You have seen it, no?"

Andrew laughed, still confused. "What part is a joke?"

"I did not eat his liver, and I do not drink wine, but the rest is true. Do you think I am a terrible woman now?"

"No." Andrew rubbed his face. "Kinda scary just a little bit, but not a bad woman."

"Because of this, no man wants to be with me. That is why I am old woman with no husband."

"Maybe they are afraid of you."

"Are you afraid of me now?"

"To be honest I've always been a little afraid of you," Andrew said with a laugh.

"Do not beat me and I will not stab you." Malika approached Andrew and placed a small bowl in his hand. "Okay?"

"It's a deal."

"Any more questions?" she asked, pouring the remains of the pot into her own bowl.

"I was going to ask if it came to it would you be able to kill a man, but I think you already answered that question."

Malika sat beside Andrew on the blanket. "Now may I ask you a question?"

"Anything."

"Your dream the days past it was about your wife, no?"

"It was." Andrew ate slowly, anticipating her next question.

"Do you still love her?" Malika asked quietly.

"I do, I suppose. It's not like we were divorced or anything. She was taken from me."

"I see."

There was a sadness in her voice that hurt. He could feel her shrink a little as she sat beside him. He wished that he'd lied.

"I guess a part of me will always love her. But she is gone. A man cannot love a ghost."

The two sat in silence, eating as darkness crept across the desert. Andrew didn't feel like eating but forced the meal down. He needed the calories after walking all day. When he'd cleaned the bowl with a piece of flatbread and eaten it, he sat his bowl down. Finding Malika's face, he gently turned it to face him.

"Malika, I'm going to be completely honest with you. I think you're amazing. I like being with you. I want to be next to you. I want to feel you and smell you and to know you are close to me." Andrew brushed a lock of hair from her face.

"When you first approached me, your color was blue. It means that you're good. You're a good woman Malika, and any man with half a brain would be glad to have your attention."

"Thank you," she said softly, her gaze falling to her hands. "Sometimes I think I have been alone too long and do not know how to be a woman with a man."

Andrew lifted her face to his, cradling it in his hand as he bent in and kissed her lips. "You're doing just fine."

Andrew sat against the low stone wall a short distance from the house that Malika had just entered, second-guessing their plan. Dressed in a dirty robe and sandals, he waited quietly, hoping to draw little attention to himself.

The wall at his back was made of sun-dried mud bricks and rose to his standing height. He'd already walked the length of it and made a mental map of the area. The wall ran along the street for roughly forty steps on either side of the house before making a ninety-degree turn toward the back of the estate. The wall provided privacy and security, ensuring that the only easy way in was through the front door, which was probably guarded.

After half an hour of sitting he heard the rustle of clothes stop before him. A coin fell to the ground between his outstretched legs. The gracious man said something in Arabic, then walked away. He waited a moment, then felt along the ground for the coin. He stretched all the way to his ankles, his hand gently patting every square inch of the brick-paved sidewalk but found nothing.

He thought he heard the whisper of another, smaller person pass, but couldn't be sure. If it were someone, they'd taken the coin very swiftly and quietly. Whoever it was knew what they were doing.

Leaning back against the wall, he waited. There was a game afoot. He didn't care about the money, but it would keep his mind occupied while he waited for Malika. A few moments later he heard another coin hit the ground before him. If he were right, the thief would strike quickly. This time he would be ready for them.

A smile crept to his face as the sound of soft footfalls approached. They shuffled quietly on the rough surfaces of the bricks. As the feet neared him, he heard a tunic rustle and crumple as the thief bent, hand extended.

Moving quickly, he grabbed the small wrist and snatched the person down beside him, pinning him against the wall with his arm.

"La tuthurc," he said, telling the person not to move.

The thin body struggling beneath his arm complied only when it became obvious that he was caught. The thief was a young boy, ten or eleven years old.

Andrew found the coin and held it before the boy. "Want this?" he asked quietly in English.

The boy tried to grab it, but Andrew snatched it back quickly, increasing the pressure against the boy's chest.

"You can have it, but I need a favor."

The boy answered in Arabic, his voice a mixture of fear and wonder.

"Yes, I speak English. Do not tell anyone." He put a finger to his lips and smiled. "Shhh."

The boy spoke Arabic, but Andrew shook his head.

"All I want you to do is jump this wall and take a look around and tell me what it's like inside." Andrew pointed to his own eyes, then to the boys, then made a gesture of going up and over the wall.

The boy replied in excited Arabic and laughed.

It was a risky move in the first place, but now the boy was refusing. He could break away and run to the house, alerting them to his presence and his proposition. He had to gain the boy's allegiance quickly and there were only two ways to do it. Fear or money. Andrew chose money.

He reached into the pocket of his tunic and pulled out a larger coin. Malika had given all her money to him to hold, fearing being robbed by the man she was going to meet. When he held the coin up, the boy's gasp told him he'd get what he wanted.

Andrew pointed to his own eyes and shook his head, then pointed to the boys and nodded yes.

The boy answered in Arabic and nodded. Andrew smiled and held out his hand. The boy's tiny hand slid into his and they shook. He released the boy and sat back against the wall, coin in hand and waited. He listened to the sound of the boy going over the wall and hoped that he hadn't just gotten the kid killed.

Sitting on an ornate rug, Malika accepted the cup of tea from the servant and smiled. The man she came to see was very rich and very dangerous. The dance they did was a cautious one. She had made deals with him before, on her father's behalf, but this was the first time she'd been inside his home.

Sipping the hot tea patiently, she looked around the room, larger than her father's whole house. It was furnished with handsome, modern furniture and beautiful pieces of art. Her eyes fell on one painting depicting a reclining nude woman, her face blurred completely. She was laid out on an expensive-looking bed, a half-eaten apple clutched in one hand.

"Do you like that one?"

The words, spoken in Arabic, startled Malika causing her to spill a few drops of the tea on her lap. The host, known to her only as Abdullah, was an unusually tall man with broad shoulders and a neatly trimmed beard. If not for the fact that he was a loathsome human being, she'd have thought him handsome. As it was, she very nearly despised him.

"This one is new," he said, walking to the painting. "I commissioned it by an artist when I was in Paris last summer." He stopped in front of the painting and clasped his hands behind his back.

Malika watched him carefully. Standing over six feet tall, he was an imposing figure. Dressed in a deep orange, embroidered kurta, and crème pants, he looked like a man who would enjoy fine art, but she knew that if things went wrong, he also wouldn't hesitate to slit her throat and watch her bleed to death on his expensive rug.

"It is a depiction of Eve, from the Christian bible. Have you read it?"

"I have not, nor do I intend to," she answered in Arabic, careful not to slip into English. She made a mental note of the necessity of teaching Andrew more of her language.

"She is nude to show the power of her persuasion," he continued, ignoring Malika's comment. "And her face is blurred to not identify her as one woman, but to impart upon all who gaze upon it the wisdom that any woman could be the one who tempts us unto evil, pulling us away from Allah, blessed be his name."

"Some might think it strange," she began, "that such a noble gentleman as yourself would have a Christian painting."

He turned to her with a smile. "I do not care what people think." He walked to the window overlooking the street, his hands still clasped behind him. "These people are swine. Ignorant little swine. They lack even a rudimentary knowledge of anything but their own day-to-day survival. Art, literature, culture, it is all lost on them."

Malika remained silent, her eyes following him around the room. She watched him stare out the window, framed by thick maroon drapes tied back with gold-colored ropes.

"But you did not come here to discuss art, did you Malika?"

"I did not."

Turning to her, he bowed slightly. "Forgive my disrespect. My condolences on the death of your father. I always enjoyed doing business with him."

"And we, you. Thank you for your kind words."

"News travels fast across the desert, Malika. I had news of your father's death within two days of his passing."

"I do not doubt it. A man such as yourself must have resources beyond my comprehension."

Abdallah sighed deeply, his mood darkening. "I usually do not do business with women. You understand that don't you?"

"I do," Malika answered and took a sip of tea. "But I hoped you might make an exception."

"Ah," he said, nodding.

"My father used you exclusively to supply our village. A certain amount of loyalty would not be out of the question. Just this once."

"Loyalty?" he asked with a laugh. "A man is a fool who spreads his loyalty too thin."

Malika stared into his face, searching for a clue to what he was thinking. She found nothing but a blank stare.

"My enemies are your enemies, Abdullah. Surely that would count for something."

He approached her with a smile. "Enemies? You?" he asked, rubbing the back of his fingers along her cheek. "Such a pretty flower as you surely cannot have enemies."

"I do," she said, never taking her eyes off his. "As do you."

"Malika, Malika, Malika," he began, turning from her. "I will admit that you are brave, and strong, for a woman, and I have no doubt you could, and would, kill a man, but you have come to the wrong man for help."

Malika sat her tea down and stood, smoothing the front of her abaya. "I have traveled many miles from my village just to see you because I believe you to be an honest man with whom I could do business. If that is not so, I will take my business elsewhere."

"Elsewhere?" he asked with a laugh. "Where else?"

"I have my sources, Abdullah. I come to you because you were honest with my father if perhaps asking too high a price for your help." Malika crossed her arms and leveled her gaze at him. Insulting his prices would be enough for him to kill her.

A wry smile slid across his lips. "I am a businessman, Malika. I must do what profits me."

"As must I."

Abdulla held her gaze for a moment, then walked back to the painting. "The world has changed since we were youths, Malika. So many wars. So many outsiders here in our beloved land."

"Outsiders are who I intend to rid our lands of."

"Really? That strikes me as odd. My sources tell me that you have been traveling with an outsider. An American doctor no less."

Malika struggled to contain her surprise. How had he found out? How much did he know?

"Do you not deny it?" Abdullah asked.

"Would it matter? You have your sources, and you believe them. Could I say anything that you would believe?"

Abdullah walked to her again, staring into her eyes. "Probably not."

"Then our business is done." She turned to leave, but he grabbed her arm, jerking her back around to face him.

"Our business is done when I say it is done."

"Take your hands off me," she demanded, struggling against his strong grasp. She raised her right hand to slap him, but he grabbed it as well.

"You come here, a woman, and try to do business with me. I should kill you."

"Then kill me, you thief."

Abdullah laughed and shook his head. "Your father always said you were high-spirited. I must admit that I like that sometimes." He released her left hand and slapped her across the face.

Malika's head rocked to the side, her cheek stinging painfully.

"Is this how you treat women, you animal?" she asked through clenched teeth.

"It is how I treat whores." Abdullah shoved her toward the couch under the window at the end of the room. He watched Malika stagger, then fall to the ground. Following her quickly, he slapped her headdress off and grabbed a handful of hair.

The back of her head exploded with pain as he pulled her across the ornate carpet. She knew what he was going to do and promised herself she wouldn't let him. Even if he killed her.

Abdulla tossed her onto the couch on her back and looked down at her. "Tell me, whore, how many times have you laid with this American doctor. Ten times? Twenty?"

Malika got her hand up to deflect another slap, but a second followed and struck her cheek again sending daggers of pain through her body. Abdullah was strong and put all his righteous indignation into each blow.

A tear rolled down her cheek and she quickly wiped it away, not wanting him to gain any satisfaction from it. She tried to stand, but a hand covered her chest and shoved her back to the couch, ripping the front of her abaya in the process.

She quickly gathered the sides of the rip, pulling them back together as she spat at him. For that, she garnered another powerful slap. Her head slammed into the back of the couch, striking the dark mahogany wood that lined it. Stars exploded behind her eyes, and she felt herself beginning to fade.

"I will keep you, Malika, and I will make you my toy for a while. And when I am done, I will dispose of you like the whore that you are." He forced a knee between her legs and knelt over her, holding her hands above her head. "And I will enjoy every minute of it."

A metallic click filled the room. Abdullah froze as the barrel of a gun pressed against the back of his head.

"Will you enjoy having your brains blown all over the street outside that window?"

"Andrew," Malika gasped in English.

"My finger has this trigger pulled halfway down. If you so much as flinch it will go off and you will die."

"My men will kill you before you leave my house," Abdullah answered in English.

"Maybe so, but you'll never know it. Now, let her go."

Abdullah released Malika and she wriggled out from under him. She stood and hurried to Andrew, who handed her a gun from his pocket.

"I should kill you myself, you bastard." Malika hit him across the face with the gun and watched him collapse onto the couch.

"Wait, there is no need for all this. Okay, I make deal with you," Abdullah said in English as he rubbed his face. He drew his hand away and saw blood. His eyes went to Malika and narrowed. "The last woman to hit me and live to see the sunset was my mother."

"And she should have hit you more, perhaps you would not have grown into such a swine." Malika's eyes narrowed as she stared down the barrel of the gun at him.

"Now what?" Andrew asked. "Time is of the essence."

"Yes, Malika. Now what do you do? You have me, but you are in my house. You cannot escape."

"Your faith in your guards might be overstated. A blind man made his way over your fence and into your house," Andrew said with a grin. "I've already taken one of them out and I have his gun."

Abdullah shrugged. "Perhaps," he began in English, looking at Andrew. "But will you get out?"

It was Andrew's turn to shrug. "Whether we do or not you will never know it. The first sign of trouble and we shoot you. You'll be dead before either of us."

"Doctor, you watch too many television shows. This will never work. It's impossible. You are blind. How could you possibly expect to get away? The cowboy and the girl will not ride off into the sunset together. You are a fool and she..."

Andrew shoved Malika to the ground and dove in the opposite direction as a series of gunshots rang out from the doorway behind them, shattering the windows above the couch. He rose to a knee and fired two shots, hitting the guard in the chest with both. When he heard the dead weight of his body hit the ground he turned back to their prisoner.

"You're the second person to tell me I watch too much television," He crossed the room and helped Malika to her feet. "Frankly, it's a bit of a stereotype that I don't like."

"We must go," Malika said.

Andrew sighed. The sounds of panic were already rising from the street. A crowd was gathering quickly. Inside the house, men's voices shouting in Arabic were quickly drawing closer to the door. Within seconds the room would be full of guards armed and ready to attack.

"Get him up and tie his hands behind him," she told Malika, "And hurry."

Andrew turned his attention to the open doorway, where the sound of footfalls stopped suddenly. He fired a shot, striking the ornate wooden trim next to the guard's head, forcing them to take cover. The two men called out in Arabic, but before Abdullah could answer Andrew turned and drove his fist into his mouth.

"Shut up," he said. "One word and I'll kill you."

Abdullah gathered the blood in his mouth and spat it onto the floor. "I will enjoy killing you slowly, American."

"Get in line, asshole."

Malika yanked Abdullah's hands behind him and bound them with a cord snatched from a lamp. She told him to shut up in Arabic.

"We're going to have to take him with us, at least 'till we get away."

"Is that wise?" Malika asked, watching the doorway around Abdullah's shoulder. She fired a shot when one of the men peeped around the casing.

"You got another plan?" Andrew asked, joining her behind Abdulla. "Tell them to move back?" Andrew nudged Abdullah with the barrel of his gun. "And she'll know what you say, so don't be as stupid as you have been so far."

Abdullah shouted something toward the doorway and Malika confirmed his orders for the men to get back.

"Good boy. Now let's move. We'll go the way I came in." Andrew nudged Abdullah forward with his gun. "Stay close. They won't risk shooting the boss."

Using Abdullah as a shield, they slowly worked their way out of the room, side sidestepping the body of the dead guard. Andrew allowed his heart to race, flooding his body with endorphins. That would help him keep his senses on high alert. He would need all of them and a little luck to ever feel the sun on his face again.

As they neared a door, Abdullah began talking to his men in Arabic. Malika laid the gun against his cheek, and he went quiet again. She told his men that all they wanted to do was go away and that they wouldn't kill any of them unless they tried to stop them.

"Here." Sliding his hand along the wall, Andrew found the second door. "Make sure it's clear." He took Abdullah's hands from Malika, freeing her to check the garage. She opened the door and swept her gun quickly across the room.

"No one." Together they backed the large frame of Abdullah through the door and closed it behind them.

"Anything you can drive?" Andrew asked.

Malika surveyed the garage, allowing her eyes to wash over the half dozen expensive cars with a sigh. "I've only driven an automobile one time, briefly," she confessed.

Andrew groaned and Abdulla laughed, drawing a jab in the ribs with Andrew's gun. "Shut up, asshole."

"I see a motorcycle," Malika said enthusiastically.

"Can you drive one of those?" Andrew asked.

"No. But my father told me it was like riding a donkey, or a camel. Just keep your balance."

Andrew sighed again and rubbed his forehead. He gave Abdulla a shake. "What kind is it?"

"A Kawasaki," he said smugly. "It belongs to the house boy."

"Is it a dirt bike or street bike?" Andrew asked.

"It is a dirt bike, but it is probably low on fuel. The house boy is an idiot."

Andrew motioned for Malika to check it. She skirted a tan Rolls Royce and headed for the bike.

"Why couldn't you just sell her the stuff? Would that have been so hard?"

Abdullah shrugged. "To be honest," he began in English, "I was going to, then I decided to fuck her instead."

"Well, that didn't work out so good for you, now did it?"

"You have not yet made it out of my house. I have hope that I will still have a chance."

"You're going to get fucked alright, just not how you like it."

Abdullah laughed. "How do you know what I like?"

Andrew sighed heavily and waited for Malika to return.

"I ask you, Doctor, is it worth it to risk your life for a woman like that? She is a peasant from a tiny village. She has nothing, just like her father."

"Do you need to ask? I'm here. That should answer your dumbass question." He shoved Abdullah against the wall hard. "Now shut your stinking mouth."

"It is full of fuel, I think," Malika informed Andrew upon her return.

"Empty, huh?" Andrew asked, pushing Abdullah against the wall again.

"Perhaps I made a mistake," Abdullah said with a smile. Andrew hit him in the back of the head with his gun and stepped back, allowing him to fall to the ground.

"Now what?" Malika asked.

"Let's get him into one of the cars," Andrew said, already dragging the body across the polished floor. Together they hefted him into the trunk of a Maserati, then bound his feet and gagged him.

"Watch the door," Andrew said as Malika led him to the motorcycle.

It opened a peep and Malika fired a shot into the door jamb, throwing splinters into the man's face. He cursed in Arabic and slammed the door.

Andrew ran his hands along the side of the motorcycle, finding the kick start and the foot knob used to shift gears. He had no doubt that he could drive it, having grown up riding dirt bikes. Whether Malika could or not was doubtful.

"Okay, look. I can drive this thing, but you'll have to steer."

"I will do my best," she promised.

"You will probably have to shoot a few times too."

"Of course."

Hiking his robe to his waist, Andrew mounted the cycle, thankful for the decision to wear his pants beneath it. Malika followed suit, sitting in front of Andrew. He kick-started the machine and together they walked the bike to the garage door and hit the button to open it.

The door rolled smoothly upwards on its channels, quiet enough to allow Andrew the opportunity to access the situation beyond it. The bustle on the street was a cacophony of sounds, but none of them were gunfire.

As the door rose high enough to give them clearance, he gave the engine gas and they rolled beneath it. The brick-paved driveway was clear, but the back alley was thronged with people.

Malika, now steering on her own, yelled at the people to move as they wove unsteadily into the lane. She swerved to miss a cart and the back wheel slid beneath them. Andrew put his foot down to prevent a skid.

"You cannot steer too suddenly," he yelled.

"I cannot help it. Slow down."

As the sound of gunshots rang out, people scattered, giving them a free path, and the guards an easy target. Andrew throttled the engine up and they sped down the alley. The first shots had been to clear the crowd, but the ones that came next ricocheted off the stonework on the wall next to them.

"We gotta go." Andrew fired his two remaining shots over his shoulder. Dropping the spent gun, he grabbed the handlebars with both hands. Malika put her hands over his, steering with him as she directed them around the corner at the end of the street.

"One hundred meters straight and we will be close to the market," she yelled over her shoulder.

Andrew laughed aloud. "I never thought we'd make it."

"We haven't yet."

Halfway down the lane, a large wooden gate swung open, covering most of the road.

"Stop!" Malika yelled, pushing the handlebars hard to the left against Andrew's attempts to keep them straight. She pushed back hard against him, dislodging his hands, and turned the bike hard to the left. When the bike skid beneath them, Andrew put his foot out to catch them, but it was too late. The hot muffler slammed into his calf as the bike laid over, sliding along the cobblestone roadway.

He clutched Malika's waist as they struck the road, tumbling together several times before coming to a stop next to the high stone wall. Andrew's head struck something hard, and everything began to fade.

Before he could react, hands were all over him. One pair grabbed his arms and two more grabbed his legs. He was hoisted into the air and quickly carried away. Pain cried out from his lower left leg, but his thoughts were only for Malika. Had she survived the crash?

Fading quickly, he heard hurried footsteps and muffled voices. Then the sound of the motorcycle thundered in his ears. It roared down the hill and he smiled. At least she'd gotten away.

Eight

"Well, it's all shit if you ask me."

Diana rubbed her forehead and pushed a hand through her dark hair with a sigh. "I don't like it either, but we're in a bit of a situation."

"That asshole better pay us more for this."

"He said he'd 'make it worth our efforts,' Either way, we're stuck here for a few days, and we've got to come up with a plan."

"I've got a plan, how about we say fuck Savon and get the hell out of here while we can."

Diana shrugged. "I can't say I haven't considered that as well." She sighed again and rose. Going to the window, she peered out at the bustling street below. "Abdullah controls this town. Any one of those people down there could rat us out to him. If that happens, he will overrun this house and we will all be dead." She turned and looked at her counterpart, watching him puff the pipe clenched between his teeth. "Must you do that in here?"

"I don't have to, but I want to."

She rolled her eyes and sat on the windowsill. "There are more complications."

"Great. Just what we need."

"Savon said one of his informants reported some strangers in town. Several of them."

"So. It's a big city, in this part of the world at least. Probably a lot of people coming and going. Where the hell else is there to go in this shit hole place?"

"Well, considering that the target is an American, he suggested that we may also have some people who are friendly to the Americans here also."

"Great. Savage natives and now stinking Americans. It's not worth it. I want out. It's all going to shit."

"There is no 'out' now, you idiot. Trust me, you don't want to make an enemy of Alain Savon. He's the real deal, so I've heard."

Richard Covington put his pipe back in his mouth and sank into the wingback chair. "Well," he began, taking the pipe out of his mouth and saluting her with it. "We'd better get on with it then. The drugs will be wearing off soon and they'll be waking up."

Andrew burst into consciousness with a sudden jolt. In his dream, he was back in the Facility, but it wasn't his wife being raped. It was Malika, and Abdulla was the abuser. In his mind, he saw a man with an absurdly long beard and a dark face laughing loudly and unceasingly. Finally, he screamed as loud as he could, hoping to drown out the laughing, but it didn't work. Malika sat up from the table, her hair in disarray, and began to scream back at him. A long tongue slithered out between her rotten teeth and flickered at him. Just as he opened his mouth to scream again, his mind couldn't take it anymore and threw him out.

He tried to sit up but was met with a firm hand that pushed him back down on the bed.

"Here, here, good man. You mustn't move just yet."

Andrew's mind groped at the voice, trying to make sense of it. The words sounded British, but the accent sounded exaggerated. The scent of pipe tobacco drifted from his clothes and there was a slight smell of liquor on his breath.

"How is he?"

This voice, a woman, had a slight British accent but was more neutral, and more believable. What was she doing in Abdullah's house? And why was the British man here? He laid back on the bed with a groan as a fresh round of pain coursed through his head.

"You've taken quite a nasty tumble, sir. You hit your head. I believe you have been concussed. Please lie still."

Andrew opened his mouth to speak but closed it. His tongue was dry and tasted like chalk.

He mustered the strength to raise one hand halfway to his mouth to mime drinking from a glass.

"The man must be positively parched. Be a dear and fetch us some water, would you Diana."

Andrew ran his tongue over his dry lips and sank back into the bed. When a soft, feminine hand placed a cool glass of water in his, he drank it eagerly and held it out for more.

"Mustn't over do it." the man said, taking the glass from him. "Better now?"

Andrew nodded and managed to croak out Malika's name.

"Ah, yes. Your companion. She's quite all right, I assure you. Quite all right indeed."

Andrew cleared his throat and asked for more water. After he finished the glass, he handed it back and gingerly pushed himself up in the bed. The woman who arranged his pillow had a gentle touch and smelled of rich, flowery perfume.

"Where is Malika?" Andrew asked. "Can I see her?"

"I don't suppose you can see anything, my good man."

Andrew's hands went to his face, finding the bandage gone.

"Yes, we've given you a thorough once over. Other than a rather nasty bump on the head and a serious burn on your left leg you are right as rain. But I suppose that is enough. Of course, with the exception of being blind."

"Who are you?" Andrew asked, suspicious anger rising in his chest. His head erupted in a fresh wave of pain as he looked around. "And where is Malika? Did she get away?"

"I'm sorry, but no. She did not escape either. She suffered several bumps and bruises, most of which are well on their way to being healed. It seems that you took the noble route and shielded her from the brunt of the trauma."

Andrew rubbed his temples. "I feel like I've been hit by a car."

"You came close, but you'll be all right soon enough." The man stood. "Come dear, and let's let him rest."

"I don't want to rest. I want to see Malika. To talk to her."

"All in good time, all in good time. We'll bring you some supper shortly. I suggest you use the time to rest. I'm afraid that's the best we can do for you at the moment."

Andrew felt a man's hand pat his shoulder and listened as they both left the room. When the door closed, he sank into the comfortable bed. He was in no position to argue. His head was pounding, and his thoughts were drifting in and out of a thick fog. He couldn't go anywhere now if he had the chance.

Everything in his mind was out of kilter, as if he were seeing it through a veil. He tried to do an internal check to find out if he'd been drugged but couldn't keep his mind in one place. Clearing his mind had to be his first priority, everything else would have to wait. Even Malika.

The coolness of the water on his lips slowly pulled Andrew out of a deep sleep. It was refreshing and sweet in his mouth, better than anything he'd ever tasted. And there was that smell. What was it? Faint, yet herbal and thick. He knew the scent but couldn't remember where he'd smelled it before. Still semi-conscious, he smiled and let out a quiet moan. The sweet water and the delightful smell were a beautiful combination for his bleary senses.

"It is good to see that you are waking today."

The woman's voice exploded in his head, reminding him who the scent belonged to. "Malika," he said with a wide smile.

"You had us worried."

Andrew pushed up on an elbow facing her. When she moved closer, he pulled her to him and kissed her despite the pain that ricocheted around his head with each movement.

"I thought you got away," he said when the kiss finally ended.

"I did not. But I would not have left you anyway."

"I remember us crashing, vaguely, then I could have sworn I heard the motorcycle race off." Andrew gingerly ran a hand over his hair, wincing in pain.

"Yes," Malika began. The courtyard door to this house opened and we were going too fast to stop. We crashed and both fell. The people grabbed us, and someone jumped on the motorcycle and drove away, giving Abdullah's men someone to follow."

Andrew shook his head. "It's all so strange. It happened so fast. Who are these people?"

"Professor Covington owns the home. The woman is his nurse. Diana. She is very nice to me."

"Why did they rescue us?" Andrew pushed himself into a sitting position and cleared his throat. "Is there anything to drink?"

Malika put a glass in his hand, and he drank all of it. "They are not friends of Abdullah."

Andrew shrugged. "Seems like a lot to risk for some strangers. God, my head hurts."

Malika patted his hand. "Be glad that we are not dead. Do not worry yourself more. For now, we are safe and well. You must heal."

Andrew sighed. "I'm glad that you're here. I feel much better already."

Malika lifted his hand and kissed it. "I was so worried."

"I'll be fine," Andrew said, patting her hand. In his mind, Andrew found a thread and began to pick at it. Things were not adding up. Why would an English professor and a nurse even be here? The British were hated as much as the Americans. And why get involved at all? It was a huge risk going against a thug like Abdullah.

"Do you feel up to a light meal?" Malika asked, pulling him back from his thoughts.

"I'm starving, and I've got to pee, very soon."

Malika laughed. "I am sure. You have been asleep for days."

Andrew shifted his weight on the couch, testing the pressure of the stiff springs beneath the thin padding. He ran a hand across the fabric, taking in the closeness of the threads. It wasn't a local piece.

Sitting in the study awaiting the promised evening meal of mutton and potatoes, he surveyed the room. There was a faint odor of old books, pipe tobacco, and a citrus smell. His fingers went to the wooden armrest next to him. Lifting them to his nose, he confirmed the presence of furniture polish.

A house worker passed by the open doorway. Their pants legs rubbed together as they walked, coming to him in a series of quick, jagged yellow lines. The room fell silent again as he waited for Malika to return from the bathroom.

In the back of his mind, a nagging suspicion persisted, and he decided to try to learn more at supper. A few well-timed questions would tell him all he needed to know.

"Andrew, are you ready?"

He smiled and stood as Malika crossed the room. "You are beautiful," he said, taking her in his arms.

"You do not know this," she said with a laugh in her voice as she adjusted the new wrap covering his eyes.

"I know it as sure as I'm standing here." He kissed her lips and hugged her to him, wincing as the sudden movement sent a bolt of pain through his head.

"Thank you," she said smiling. "Does your head still hurt?"

"Not too bad. It'll be okay soon enough." He leaned in and kissed her lips.

"Let us go in and eat. We can kiss later, but now I am hungry."

Andrew tightened his grip on her waist and put his mouth to her ear. "Do me a favor. I'm going to ask the professor some specific questions. Watch his reactions carefully. I'm not buying this whole act. There is something odd going on."

"Why are you talking quietly?"

"I don't trust them."

Malika put her hand against his face, stroking his cheek with her thumb. "I will do as you ask, but please do not disrespect this man. You may be wrong, and they have risked much to help us."

"Maybe." Andrey took her hand and smiled. "Maybe not."

"I say there, you're looking much better this evening."

Andrew nodded to his host and smiled. "I feel much better, thank you." The truth was that he still had moments of dizziness and wanted to sleep more than he should, but the professor didn't need to know that.

A young man who had a slight scent of body odor took his arm and led him around the table, sitting him to the host's left and across from Malika. The nurse, Diana, sat at the end of the small table, opposite the professor.

"We owe you a debt of thanks." Malika sat down and slipped her foot out of her sandal and moved it to Andrew's.

"Don't speak of it, my dear lady. It has been a pleasure to have such ravishing beauty in the house."

"Malika tells me..." Andrew paused as the waiter placed his meal in front of him. The scent of the meat enveloped him, distracting him momentarily. "That you have a beautiful home. I want to personally thank you for your hospitality."

"Think nothing of it, my good man. Anything I can do to confound that savage Abdullah and his ilk. They are a blight on this lovely city."

Andrew picked up his utensils and began to eat. The meat was tender, and the flavor erupted within his mouth, reminding him that he hadn't eaten a meal in days.

"I took the liberty of choosing a light wine with dinner. I hope that doesn't offend you, Malika."

"Not at all, but the water will be fine with me."

Andrew smiled and accepted the wine. "My compliments to the chef. The mutton is delicious."

"I'm glad you approve. I'll let the chef know you enjoyed it."

"So tell me, Professor, do you live here full-time?"

The professor laughed. "Oh no. I come here from time to time, mostly this time of year to escape the rain and fog of London."

Andrew nodded. "You live in London? I've heard it's a nice place to be from."

"London, like most larger cities, has its advantages and disadvantages I suppose."

Andrew forked another lump of meat into his mouth and chewed slowly.

"How about yourself?" The professor asked. "You are definitely not a local."

It was Andrew's turn to laugh. "What gave it away?" he asked. "No, I'm from America. Just outside Philly."

"Is that close to New York?" Malika asked, suddenly realizing that she'd never asked where in America he was from.

"Sometimes it's too close, sometimes not close enough."

"Strange to find another English-speaking chap over here, so to speak."

Andrew nodded as he chewed his food. "I was thinking the same thing. What brings you to this part of the world, Professor?"

"I teach Middle Eastern studies at the University of Oxford. I have a bit of a heavy chest so for me to come here is both professional and medical, I must admit. The air in London isn't what it once was."

"The dry air is helpful," Diana added.

Andrew nodded, touching Malika's foot under the table. "Thus, the need for a nurse as a traveling companion, I suppose."

"Right-o, my good man."

"Well, as much as we have appreciated all you have done for us, I think we will be on our way in the morning." Again, Andrew brushed his foot against Malika's. "If it's all the same to you."

The professor sighed. "I wouldn't recommend that. You see, Abdullah has every exit to the city being watched. His men are looking for you both. I'm afraid our little diversion didn't work as well as I'd hoped."

"Is that so?" Andrew asked. He took another bite and chewed on it as he thought.

"Yes," Diana added. "I saw it for myself this morning. They aren't stopping anyone, just watching. And they have guns."

"So, you see, my good man. It would not be prudent for you to leave the safety of this house just now," the professor added. "Relax and enjoy some wine."

Andrew lifted his glass to his nose and took a long sniff before swirling the wine a few times and downing the contents in one gulp. He sat the glass back down on the table hard, his fist wrapped around the stem.

Malika jumped, letting out a quite yelp, and he apologized. The table was sound enough to break the wine glass if it came down to it. If he had to fight, he'd go for the professor first, grab him and go for the carotid artery running alongside his neck. He'd be incapacitated and then he'd have to deal with the woman. If Malika didn't already have her subdued.

"Forgive me for saying so, Professor, but I think you're full of shit." Andrew turned to face the professor with a smile.

"Andrew," Malika gasped, her foot tapping against his leg.

"It's quite all right, my lady. He's taken quite a blow to the head. Certain outbursts are to be expected."

Andrew turned to Diana, then to the professor, showing them his smile. "My head is fine, and I think you know it. So is my leg. It's healed nicely. But you probably know that too."

"How in the world would I know that?" Professor Covington asked indignantly as he stood. "Your behavior is quite reprehensible, sir. While I am willing to allow certain grievances due to your recent injury, I do not have to accept being insulted in my own home." He removed the napkin tucked into the collar of his shirt and threw it onto his plate before storming out of the room.

"You have anything?" Andrew asked, turning to Diana.

She chuckled and shook her head. "I do not. I know you haven't eaten well lately, so finish your meals. Afterwards, if you would do the pleasure of meeting the Professor and myself in the study it would be greatly appreciated and, I believe, quite informative."

"I would be delighted," Andrew said, releasing his grip on the wine glass. "It's delicious and would be a crime to waste it."

"Very well." She nodded to them and left the room quickly.

"What are you doing?" Malika asked once they were alone.

"I told you something was off. Their story doesn't add up. We'll soon get to the bottom of this."

"What do we do now?"

"Now," he said with a smile. "We eat."

The professor was leaning against the towering bookshelf in the study holding a small glass of brandy in his hand when Malika and Andrew entered.

"Please, do come in."

"Thank you." Andrew followed Malika to the same sofa he'd waited on before the meal. "Wine and brandy. I'm impressed, Professor. In a country whose religious practices prohibit the consumption of alcohol, you seem to have quite a stash."

"I must admit that I'm quite impressed with you. Your senses are extraordinary."

Andrew nodded but said nothing, instead he took Malika's hand in his and relaxed on the couch.

"As I'm sure you're aware, Yemen is a country in strife. Many things happen here that do not always follow religious disciplines. If one has the means and the position, nothing is out of reach."

"Ah, money and power, power, and money. It's the same everywhere. Isn't it?"

"You are correct, sir," the professor said with a smile.

"Gentlemen," Diana spoke up, curtailing the small talk, "As you stated at dinner, Mister Harkins, you have found some inconsistencies with our story. Even going as far as to say we were, 'full of shit,' I believe it was."

Andrew smiled. "My apologies for my rudeness, but I felt it necessary to prove my point."

"I commend you on your astuteness," the professor began before tossing back the drink. "What exactly gave us away?"

"Your accent is terrible, professor. It's like a cartoon, to be honest."

"I told you so, Diana." He crossed the room to where she was sitting. "The top brass thought it would be a sort of 'hiding in plain sight' type thing. Bloody idiots."

"It would probably work on the locals," Andrew said with a shrug. "No disrespect," he added, patting Malika's hand.

"I did not know anything was wrong," she admitted with a shrug.

"What we're about to tell you could get us killed, so we must insist on your discretion," Diana began. "You see, we're with MI-6. This whole cover is to help us surveil certain bad players in this region. As you know Britain has had a long and storied presence in Yemen."

"In the south," Malika added. "And even there you were not welcome."

"That is true, but it is what it is. There is nothing we can do about the past." Diana sighed. "I've only been here a short time. Please do not hold that against me personally. We are not proud of the things that have happened here."

Malika grunted, giving Andrew's hand a gentle squeeze.

"What the hell does MI-6 want with us?" Andrew asked. "And please, cut the crap. We're willing to fight our way out of this house if we have to."

The professor cleared his throat. "Very well," he began, the heavy accent gone. "We have heard a lot about a blind American who works for a secretive facility located in the southern Saudi desert. Reports have been coming in with all sorts of fantastic tales attributed to you, sir. You've aroused the attention of American and British Intelligence. We want to know who you are and what your intentions are."

"Fair enough," Andrew said with a shrug. "I'm just a blind American surgeon who escaped a hell hole usually referred to as The Facility run by Alain Savon. He's a sadistic maniac and I intend to kill him."

"Are you an American spy?" Covington asked.

"Not even close."

"What can you tell us about this facility?" Diana asked.

"Anything you want. I'd be happy to write you a detailed report. Let me start with this, imagine your most horrifying nightmares were true; your most depraved, unethical medical practices. All true."

"We've spoken with the Saudis. They say it is an international biotech company."

"It may be, on paper, but they have free reign to do whatever they want and experiment on whomever they want. They don't seek volunteers if you know what I mean."

"Did you not willingly travel to Saudi to work for them?" Diana asked.

"I did. They offered a fortune, and I was excited by the research."

"And now you want to kill the man who runs it?" Covington asked. "Why?"

Andrew pulled the bandage from his head, revealing the sunken indentations where his eyes used to be. "He did this to me, and more, a hell of a lot more."

Professor Covington grunted. "Understandable, to say the least."

"Are you working for anyone else?" Diana asked. "The Israelis perhaps?"

Malika's hand tensed slightly beneath his and Andrew patted it gently. "Nope. Just plain old revenge. I'm just a man. That's it."

"If only it were that simple, Doctor."

"Why were you at the house of Abdulla Safadi?"

"He is a gun supplier," Malika said. "My father has bought weapons from him in the past. That is why we were there."

"I take it the deal didn't go well," Covington said.

"He is a dog and a thief. So, no."

Professor Covington went to the liquor cabinet and poured himself another drink. He rejoined Diana, sitting on the edge of the desk beside her with a sigh.

"We may be in a position to help you." He tossed back the second glass of brandy and grimaced. "But, of course, it will have to get approval from the top brass, so to speak."

"Help?" Malika asked.

"Yes, you see, MI-6 isn't particularly keen on this place, or Mister Savon. We have had many reports, unsubstantiated until now, about this place. It is one of those places that quietly makes a name for itself, but a bad name. It wouldn't be a negative if things were to go awry for them that put them out of business."

"You do realize that the chance of success is pretty low. They'll probably shoot me on sight."

"Come now, don't sell yourself short."

"I'm just being a realist. This place isn't a playground. It's a secure facility with guards and security systems."

"I'm sure you're quite right, Mr. Harkins, but from what we've heard, you are no ordinary man."

"He is not," Malika said with a smile. "He can do anything."

"Except drive a motorcycle," Diana added, a wry smile creeping across her face.

"Come now, Diana. That was a bit harsh. We are prepared, if possible, to give you transport that will allow you to get close to this facility. Of course, we cannot deliver you to the gate. With international protocol being what it is, and such. You understand."

"I'll tell you what. You talk to your people, and we'll discuss it. Tomorrow we can come to some sort of agreement. But you two have got to drop the crap. I have to trust you if we're going to do this."

"And we, you," Diana replied. "We have found ourselves in a very delicate position, to say the least. The situation is still somewhat fluid, and volatile."

"You guys should be used to that type thing," Andrew said with a chuckle.

"Does one ever truly get used to one's own life hanging in the balance of a few decisions here and there?"

Malika's back stiffened. "My entire country lives like this every day, but it is often the decisions of others that determine our fate."

"Again, I am sorry for how things have turned out, dear. But it wasn't us."

Andrew cleared his throat as an awkward silence fell over the room. "I guess we have some sort of tentative deal them."

"I suppose we do," Diana agreed, her sentiment echoed by the professor.

Andrew stood and extended his hand. The man he knew as Professor Covington shook it.

"I hope we can work together against a common foe."

Andrew gripped the smaller, smoother hand in his. "I do too," he said, pulling him close. "Because if you screw us over, I will kill you myself and it won't be quick."

"As promised," Diana said, opening the door that led to the garage and waving them through.

Malika descended the steps. Andrew followed her closely, his hand on her shoulder.

"I will leave you two to discuss things openly," Diana said, her hand on the door. "I hope this will prove to you that we can be trusted."

After she closed the door, Andrew stopped Malika. "Tell me what the vehicle is."

"It is the color of the sand, with two doors, four big wheels. I have seen soldiers in these before, but in larger ones."

"Humvee," Andrew said nodding. "Not armored though. Probably a scout. That doesn't matter. We don't need it to be armored, we just need it to get us out of the city."

"There are weapons on a table." Malika took his elbow and pointed him toward the table.

Andrew went to the table and allowed his hands to wash over the weaponry. "Nice," he said, hefting one of the tactical vests. "Good spread."

"Yes, there are the machine guns, and..." she opened a metal case, "and plenty of ammunition. Some looking glasses, for me I think."

"I'm sure," Andrew said with a laugh as his tension eased. Since the encounter outing their hosts as imposters, he'd expected an attack at every moment. The past two days had left him tired and edgy.

His hand found a nine-millimeter pistol, kicking out the clip to make sure it was loaded. He reloaded the clip and shoved the pistol down the back of his pants.

"Do you believe them now?" Malika asked.

"Well, they're definitely connected to someone to amass so much stuff in two days. The question still remains of who they are connected to."

Andrew shook his head and mouthed the word "No." They had discussed the possibility of being spied upon with hidden listening devices. He still didn't trust them.

"It sure looks like they've held up their end of the bargain," he said aloud while shaking his head side to side.

"I am glad they do not like our enemies," Malika said, barely containing a smile.

"Me too. Now I don't have to slit their throats."

"That is good. They are nice people. And they did save us from Abdullah, the pig."

They both turned as the door opened again. The people they knew as Diana and the Professor walked down the steps casually and joined them. They were dressed in unmarked desert fatigues and black boots, each carrying a side arm on their hip.

"I trust this is sufficient," Covington said with a smile. "On such short notice, we had to pull some strings to get this here."

"I think this will be fine," Andrew told him.

"Surely you appreciate the position we are in here, Mister Harkins."

"It's Doctor Harkins," Andrew replied.

"Forgive me," Covington said. "Doctor Harkins. But, as I was saying, it is imperative that after we get out of the city, no one knows about this cache of weapons or where you acquired them. If that were to happen it might be an embarrassment to The Crown. As you might suspect, any and all identifying markings have been removed."

"Don't worry. We'll tell them we got it from Abdullah." Andrew laughed. "Maybe send some heat his way."

"That would be appreciated," Diana said. "As we've already told you, the exits to the city are still being watched. Even if they weren't, this vehicle would draw considerable attention from many players in the area. Bad players. Abdullah isn't your only worry. Unfortunately, desert travel necessitates such a vehicle."

"I will agree with you there." Andrew put his hand on Malika's shoulder. "I guess we'd better load this stuff and leave. It'll be daylight in a few hours. And, as much as we've enjoyed the hospitality, we're ready to get the hell out of this town."

The cool metal dug into Andrew's back as he sat in the back seat of the Humvee, but he found it more reassuring than painful. The air was thick with tension and the two agents' voices betrayed the calm nature they were trying hard to portray. Their respiration rates were up, and their movements were quick and unnatural.

Andrew listened as the professor climbed into the driver's seat in front of him. The springs of the machine squeaked momentarily under his weight as he shifted into place. In the predawn quiet, the rustle of their new fatigues was almost deafening.

When Malika climbed into the vehicle and sat beside him, she placed a hand on his leg and squeezed, the signal that no one else had joined the foursome.

Turning to face them from the front passenger seat, Diana said, "Are you two sure you want to go through with this?"

"Is there another way?" Malika asked.

"I suppose there isn't." Diana turned and nodded to the professor.

The engine came to life with a deafening roar inside the garage, flooding Andrew's senses. He grimaced, making the necessary adjustments.

Malika began to pat his leg, signaling that the door was opening, and an unknown situation was coming. Leaning forward slightly to get a better view out the windshield, Malika stared into the sliver of darkness afforded her as the door rose. When it opened and they began to roll forward, she squeezed his leg again. All clear.

"So far so good," she said. No one answered.

The vehicle lumbered out of the garage and across the courtyard as the outer gate opened slowly. Three of the four occupants of the vehicle looked around nervously. The street was deserted, just as they'd hoped.

The Humvee lurched forward and made a right turn, barely clearing the wall that encircled the courtyard. Once on the street, the professor accelerated down the hill toward the market entrance to the city. If things went as planned, they'd drive through the empty market and out the city walls, but Andrew doubted things would go smoothly. He and Malika were prepared for a fight.

As the tires thumped their way over the cobblestone road, Andrew reached behind him and quietly slipped the pistol out of his waistband. He slid it beneath his leg in the darkness and smiled when Malika gave his leg a gentle squeeze. No one had noticed.

"If they stop us, please stay quiet," Diana said.

"They are looking for you two, not us. If you remain quiet and still, perhaps they will not notice you in the dark."

"If we stop, they'll kill us all and take the vehicle," Andrew said. He leaned forward and patted Covington on the shoulder. "Cheerio, my good man. Run their arses over," he said in a poor British accent.

Covington glanced back at Malika as she laughed. "I don't think any of this is funny."

"We'll either make it or we'll die my good man. Right now, I'd say it's up to you." Andrew turned to Malika and whispered loud enough to be overheard, "We'll see if British men have grown any balls after all these years."

"Shut up!" Diana snapped. "Stay quiet or I'll kill you both myself."

Andrew leaned back in his seat and raised his hands without saying a word as the Humvee reached the bottom of the hill and crept past the closed shops of the market. They rolled across the large, open space that would be filled with daily shoppers in just a few hours. The vehicle slowed and began a left turn.

Andrew tensed as Malika began to pat his leg. With her fingers, she tapped the inside of his thigh twice, then used her thumb to indicate that there were two men on her side. The knot in his stomach tightened as the vehicle began to slow. He opened his mouth to speak, but Malika moved her hand to his chest, urging him to be quiet. They were already too close.

Andrew silently cursed as the vehicle rolled to a stop, its brakes squealing in the eerie silence. His hand found the gun beneath his thigh and gripped it tightly as Arabic voices approached the driver's side of the truck.

One man questioned the driver while the others kept their distance. The professor answered in very good Arabic and the guard's voice calmed some. He added something, and the guard laughed.

Andrew sat motionless, the sound of his own heart threatening to drown out the voices of the men right in front of him. He slowed his breathing and raised his auditory function. He wasn't worried about the guard at the driver's window. As long as he kept rambling, he could take care of him with one shot. It was the other three guards that had him nervous. He moved his leg slightly, asking Malika where they were.

She moved her hand high on his thigh and patted it once, then slid it toward his knee and pressed twice with her thumb.

Andrew sighed quietly. The guard on the left was behind them, and the two on the right were ahead. Scattering was a wise move on their part. It would make it hard to kill them all if something went wrong.

When the vehicle finally began to roll again, he allowed his hand to relax slowly. As bad as he hated to admit it, the Professor's way had worked. Malika's hand slid from his leg as she too relaxed.

The vehicle had just begun to gain speed when the air exploded with men shouting in Arabic. The truck came to an abrupt halt. Malika's hand quickly grabbed his leg again, squeezing the inside twice in rapid succession while her thumb slid on top of his knee and tapped it twice.

The guard that had talked to the professor was snatching on the door lever and shouting excitedly. Picking up his gun, Andrew leaned forward and fired two shots. The first struck the guard in the face and the second found his neck, spraying blood through the open window. Shots rang out from every direction, from both inside and outside the vehicle.

Andrew tuned in to another voice and prepared to fire. A bullet struck the outer wall of the vehicle next to his face. He squeezed off two rounds and pulled his head back from the opening. "Go, dammit!" he screamed as a hail of bullets struck the Humvee. "Go!"

The vehicle jerked forward quickly, throwing him back into the seat. There was more gunfire from outside the vehicle, behind them and to the right, but a single shot from the front passenger seat silenced the last guard.

Everyone sat in silence with the sound of the engine roaring in their ears as the Humvee rumbled over the rough terrain. Driving without headlights, Covington saw the large boulder at the last minute and swerved to miss it. The vehicle leaned sharply, tossing Malika into Andrew's lap. He wrapped his arms around her and held her tightly, fearing a rollover.

The driver's side rear fender wall slammed into the rock with a metallic crunch, but Covington didn't let off the accelerator. The large wheels powered them up and over the edge of the obstruction and pushed them onward.

"Damn," Andrew said with a laugh, bouncing in the back seat, still clutching Malika in his arms. "You drive as bad as I do."

"And I can see about as much as you too," Covington quipped, steering them sharply around another rocky crag.

"If that's the case then God help us."

Nine

The desert wind swirled around boulders that protruded from the earth surrounding their camp. In his mind, Andrew watched the green arrows move and spiral around the large stones, but he wasn't interested in the wind. His mind was full of questions.

Although they drove northwest through the night and most of the day, they'd only managed to put just under a hundred miles between them and the city of Minwakh. The terrain was rough, and the road only existed in short sections. The path they'd chosen was better suited for footed pack animals and slow-moving caravans than a powerful Humvee.

The one bright spot was that Abdullah's men weren't following them. That in and of itself felt very suspicious and too convenient. They had to know it was he and Malika that had escaped, and after their encounter, there was little doubt that a man like Abdullah was very forgiving.

Why wouldn't they give chase? Had someone cut a deal with Abdullah? If so, who?

The sound of Malika's labors brought Andrew out of his thoughts. "What are you doing?" he asked. "Need any help?"

"I am capable of making camp," she told him, slightly winded. "I will be done soon, and we can eat."

"Are you sure you don't need my help?"

"I am sure."

Andrew shrugged, glad to have her by his side. She was a good woman, a strong woman, and he knew he would have died in the desert if not for her. Still, he didn't want her to think him weak, or crippled.

He did, however, have his limitations. Accepting them was not easy.

He walked to another boulder, holding onto it as he approached the steep grade. At the bottom of the hill, less than fifty yards away, the professor and his nurse sat in their camp. When Malika suggested that they not sleep near the campfire as Diana and her companion were doing, he agreed heartily. The more time he spent with them, the surer he was that they were lying. The more distance between them the better.

Quiet voices mingled with the crackling of the fire and made their way up the hillside. Each of the voices was stationary. They were settling in for the night. The breeze brought the smell of a meal warmed over the fire and his stomach growled.

He pursed his lips, listening to the idle chatter from below. The professor was complaining about the aches and pains he'd gotten from driving and Diana was being polite, replying sympathetically from time to time, though there was a hint of disdain in her voice.

"We are ready."

Andrew made his way toward Malika's voice and sat on the blanket she'd spread on the ground.

"It's like a picnic down there."

"They are fools to have such a big fire. It will burn out quickly, and if it does not it will lead anyone within twenty kilometers right to them. There are always bandits in the desert."

"I know." He accepted a cold piece of flatbread coated on one side with oil and cheese and took a bite. "It's not mutton and potatoes."

"It is fine." Malika sat down beside him. "Do you think they lie to us?"

"Yes," he answered quietly.

"They did not want us to have our own camp."

"I'm sure they wanted to keep an eye on us. There are so many things that are just off." Andrew shook his head, chewing on the bread.

"What things?"

"I don't know," he began over a mouthful of bread. "The Humvee for starters. It's American. The steering wheel is on the opposite side than an Englishman would be used to, and the professor didn't even mention it."

"I did not notice that." She nudged him with a canteen of water.

133

Andrew accepted it and washed his food down. "And the professor said he taught at the 'University of Oxford,' That's not how it's usually spoken. Most people say, 'Oxford University,' It's a very prestigious school."

"I see. They told lies about who they were once. And he told the guard that he was 'Out for a night drive with his woman' at the city gate."

"I knew something was odd about all that. I'd have just run the bastards over."

"Who are they?"

"I don't know, but they're not British Intelligence."

"They look like Americans or English. Maybe."

"I know. You told me. That's what bothers me. There is no real military presence in Yemen outside of the coast."

"There is fighting in the west."

"Okay. Other than that, it's probably a thousand miles from a base of some sort."

"Then who do they work for?" she asked, chewing her own bread.

"Not the British and not the American government. There is only one place where one might find Westerners in this part of the world."

Malika gasped.

"Yep," Andrew replied, nodding. "That's why Abdullah's men didn't kill us and aren't following us."

"Would it not be easier to let them drive us closer to where we want to go? To, how you say, play along?"

"I suspect now that we've gotten this far away from any cities, they'll drop the pretenses. I think the only reason they didn't jump us or drug us before now is that they thought they might need us to help them fight their way out of the city. Now, it's almost a guarantee that they'll either ambush us in the night or first thing in the morning."

"Then we must act first, before they do."

Andrew nodded. "That's exactly what I was thinking."

The dark figure crept slowly up the mountain like a shadow, aided by the new moon and the darkened sky. The creeper clutched the dull black metal of a gun close, waiting for the chance to fire.

Moving with deliberate slowness, Diana placed each foot carefully above the other, aware that if the good doctor were awake, he'd hear her approach and ruin everything. The briefing had been informative, but hard to believe. He was sharp-minded, there was no denying that. He'd seen through their first cover quickly, but as far as she could tell, had bought the backup plan.

Dislodged by her step, a rock rolled down the hill gathering speed and taking others with it. Diana froze, waiting for the cascade to end. With the slight breeze, she could barely hear it, surely no man as far away as the doctor could. He was smart, not super-human.

She started up the hill again, listening for any signs of life from the camp. In her mind, she cursed Malika for protesting the fire so much. The whole affair could have been over and done with by now. The good doctor and his Arab whore would be bound and tossed in the back of the truck, and they could be on their way back to collect their reward.

Pulling herself around the face of a towering boulder, she paused to catch her breath. They'd chosen the rocky outcropping as a camp to block the wind, she never imagined anyone would climb atop it.

Their camp had to be close. She'd heard their pillow talk from her own camp and then had to endure the sounds of their lovemaking for over an hour. Afterwards they'd grown quiet while she was forced to lie awake and wait, not allowing herself to fall asleep.

Diana rubbed her eyes with the back of her free hand, cursing the desert sand. Easily moved by the wind, it always found its way into your eyes, your mouth, and even into your crotch if you stayed long enough. Why anyone would choose to live in such an environment was beyond reason.

Pushing off the rock, she crept forward, feeling her way as much as seeing it. Her hand met another rock, standing upright before her. She paused again. The wide surface of the boulder would be a good place from which to spring an ambush. Her body tensed expectantly, but nothing happened.

She bent and found a small stone between her feet. Readying her gun, she tossed the rock softly, landing it just beyond the edge of the boulder. Her eyes peered into the darkness, seeing nothing. Drawing in a silent breath, she picked up another stone and tossed it further. In the darkness, it struck another rock and bounced back, rolling back toward her. Still, nothing happened.

She sighed and took a few tentative steps up the hill. Switching the pistol to her left hand, she felt her way along the smooth face of the boulder with her right. Finding the edge, she took another step up the incline. Clearing the edge of the boulder, she pulled herself up the hill with a quiet grunt.

The edges of the thick, flat rock dug into Andrew's hands as he swung, putting his weight behind it. It met Diana square in the face, producing a wet splat as the cartilage in her nose gave way beneath the force.

Staggered by the force of the swing, he dropped the rock and went to a knee. Pushing himself up, his hand fell on cold steel, and he picked it up. Shoving Diana's gun into his thigh pocket, he stood in the darkness and listened.

"Sorry old girl," Andrew whispered. The sound of Diana's body tumbling down the hill ripped through the quiet darkness. The sound of her body coming to rest against something solid swept up the hill and Andrew grimaced. In the back of his mind, he regretted what he'd done, but he told himself that she worked for the Facility and probably deserved that and more. At the very least she would have killed him if it came to it.

Turning toward the camp, he dusted his hands and headed back. For him, the near-total darkness wasn't an obstacle, but he knew Malika would struggle. Fortunately, so would the man he knew as Professor Covington.

As he neared the camp, Andrew knelt and did his best to impersonate the sound of the night bird that Malika had taught him. It wasn't as close as he wanted, but it would fool Covington. The man didn't seem overly bright.

When she repeated the sound, he followed it to her position at the far edge of the tiny plateau they'd chosen for a camp. She laid a hand on his chest as he joined her, issuing a whispered "Shhh." They sat motionless in silence and waited for the wind to gust.

"There," Malika whispered, her lips almost touching his ear. "There was a small red light."

Andrew smiled and shook his head, taking pleasure in knowing that he was right. Covington was an idiot. He was blind and wouldn't be able to see the light, but Malika wasn't. Malika nudged him forward and they crept closer to the edge of the hill, taking up positions on either side of a narrow opening between two jagged boulders. If Covington came this way, he'd be dead before he knew what hit him. With the woman taken care of, they could just shoot him.

Malika reached across the opening and nudged him again. When the wind picked up, she whispered "Light." Joining him on his side of the opening, she took his hand and held it in hers, palm up. She stabbed her finger in two places, side by side, near his wrist, then once near the base of his fingers.

Andrew sat in silence, listening to the night. Malika's breathing was low and easy, barely decipherable above the sound of the wind. Her hand was warm and comforting as it held his, bringing a smile to his face. He was thinking how remarkable she was when her finger made the indications of their position again but noted the third position was close, near the center of his palm. With his free hand ,he rubbed her back to calm her, though he knew she didn't need it. If there was any way possible, he would spare her the task of killing Covington. She didn't need his blood on her hands. This was his fight.

After a few more moments of waiting, Andrew felt Malika make the same indications on his palm. All three points were as they were the last time. Covington had stopped. But why? If their ambush were coordinated, Diana would have beaten him to their camp badly.

Andrew shook his head again, reminding himself that the man was a fool.

Growing impatient, Andrew grunted quietly when Malika made the same three indications on his palm. Covington still hadn't moved. Had he chickened out? Was he a coward as well as a fool? Andrew drew in a deep breath and exhaled slowly. This wasn't good. The sun would be up in a few hours, and they would lose the cover of darkness.

Taking Malika's hand in his, he indicated their positions as well as Covington's, then he laid his finger on the position representing himself and drug it along her palm, making a semi-circle that led to Covington's position.

She grabbed his hand, holding it tightly. "No," she whispered.

Andrew pulled free of her grasp and reached down to the ground. Finding a small, round pebble, he placed it in the palm of her hand and closed her fingers around it.

"In about ten minutes throw it down toward the light. I should be close enough to hear it," he said.

"It's too dangerous."

Andrew put his hands on her shoulders and pulled her toward him. Leaning in, he kissed her quickly then was gone.

Shaking her head as she mumbled a prayer under her breath, she looked back down the hill just in time to see the small red light shine faintly, then go out. The wind gusted, blowing hair across her face. She pushed it aside as she peered into the darkness, but the wind promptly swept it across her face again. Closing her eyes, she said a prayer for Andrew. She opened them in time to catch a glimpse of the red light once again. It was still where it had been. Her fist tightened around the pebble, and she waited.

Andrew increased the blood flow to his legs, clearing the lactic acid building in his muscles as he crouched in the darkness. The trip down the side of the hill was slow and tedious, but if his calculations were correct, he would be close to Covington's position.

Pausing, he listened but heard nothing but the gentle hum of the wind moving between the stones. He took a long, slow breath in through his nose, but smelled nothing on the desert wind. His expectation of easily finding Covington vanished, replaced by the nagging sensation that he'd been duped. He had to be close to the position Malika had indicated, but there was no sign of the man.

Moving forward slowly in a crouch, he strained his senses. The hope that Covington had fallen and killed himself briefly fluttered through his mind, but he dismissed it immediately. He would have heard something, and if he were close by, he would be able to smell the soap that he'd been using. Having been cooped up in the vehicle with him for so long, he'd recognize the scent easily.

A faint sound floated to his ears, and he stopped. It was a very light mechanical "click," like the internal working of an electronic device. Waiting in the darkness, listening to the gentle wind, he began to count.

As the numbers crept to and passed three hundred seconds, he began to wonder if he'd imagined the sound; if he wanted to hear something, anything, so badly that his mind had made it up. No, he told himself. I heard it. Something's there.

At the count of three hundred eighty-five, he heard it again, from the same place as before. He sighed quietly in both relief and frustration. There was something there, but he couldn't tell what. Lowering himself onto a rough mound of dirt, he rested his leg muscles and allowed the mental count to start over.

Alone, he waited patiently and allowed his mind to count. Each second ticked by with agonizing slowness, allowing his sense of unease to grow. Each second that he was away from Malika, the more anxious he became. He wanted to backtrack and go to her; to make sure she was safe but forced himself to wait. He had to be sure.

The time had already passed when Malika should have thrown the pebble. He wanted to believe that it was simply that her count was off, but his mind refused the excuse. Something was wrong.

As his mental clock neared three hundred eighty, he listened carefully, both wanting to hear the sound again, and not. At the same instant that his mind told him that three hundred eighty- five seconds had elapsed, he heard the sound again.

"Dammit!" he thought as he started up the incline. The light must have been placed on a timer and left as a distraction. Covington could be anywhere. More importantly, he could be in their camp.

Sacrificing stealth for speed, he clambered up the rocky hillside, each step sending a cascade of loose dirt and rocks rolling back down the hill. Fighting to maintain his footing, he reached out, cutting his hand on the sharp edge of a ragged stone. He grimaced in pain but continued to climb, determined to reach Malika before Covington.

As he drew near the camp, winded and battered, a failure smell hung in the air. He stopped in his tracks and listened. The scent of Covington's soap was strong, but the wind swirled among the boulders making it difficult to pinpoint his exact location.

Andrew ducked behind a tower of stone and made the same bird call as before. When no reply came after a minute had passed, he repeated it.

"Be careful, Doctor, there are many things in the desert that eat little birdies."

Andrew's stomach clenched. If Covington was here, where was Malika?

"Why don't you come and join us, eh?" Covington said with a laugh, dropping the pretense of a British accent.

"If you leave now, perhaps we will let you live." Andrew's hand went to the gun in his waistband as he listened for any sign of Malika.

Covington laughed again. "That's very noble of you, but I think I'll hang around a bit."

"Suit yourself, Professor," Andrew crept slowly to the other side of the boulder, "But I don't think you'll see your beloved England again." Crouching, Andrew scurried along the ridge to another collection of rocks large enough to allow him cover.

Again, Covington laughed. "Screw the Queen. I'm not stinking British."

"You don't say," Andrew said with a laugh of his own. He moved back to the larger boulder. "But you were so convincing."

"And you're full of it."

Following the mental map that he'd made earlier, Andrew moved to another outcropping, closer to their camp. "I guess you know your partner is dead?" Andrew asked before moving again.

"I don't care. She was a real ballbuster anyway. I would probably have killed her myself."

Andrew leaned against the rock face, his senses on alert as he listened for Malika. "Tell me then, who the hell are you?"

"Now why would I do that?"

Covington's voice was coming from the same place each time he answered, tightening the knot in Andrew's stomach further. For a man to expose himself, he would have to have one hell of a shield. A shield that would keep him from shooting.

"I know what you're doing, Doctor," Covington told him.

"And what is that?" Andrew asked.

"You're triangulating the sound of my voice by asking questions from different places. I suspect the wind and the slight reverberations caused by all these stones must be making things difficult for you."

"I'm doing just fine. Don't you worry about me," Andrew told him.

"You just keep playing games. The Eastern sky is already beginning to lighten. In an hour you won't have the cover of darkness."

"In an hour you'll be dead."

Covington laughed loudly. "I seriously doubt that. You see, I've got a little insurance."

Andrew clenched his teeth angrily and cursed himself for leaving Malika alone. "Do you now?"

"I do. That sweet little tart of yours."

"Malika," Andrew called.

"Oh, she's a little indisposed at the moment. You see, Doctor, not very long after you left her up here all alone, I got my hands on her."

"I doubt that."

"Really, let's see. Her tits are a good handful, but nothing more." Covington laughed. "I got my hands all over her."

Andrew took a deep breath, calming his anger before it could boil over.

"What? Nothing to say. Now let's see. She smells good too. A little like somebody just screwed a flower bush and worked up a good lather."

Andrew moved to another position further away from Covington.

"You got awfully quiet. What's wrong, Doctor? You don't like it that I've got your little cactus flower? That I've fucked her while you were creeping around looking for my flashlight?"

Andrew gritted his teeth as Covington's laugh resonated through the boulders. "You must have a short fuse then. I wasn't gone that long." Andrew replied. "I still say you're full of crap, though. Whoever you are."

Covington fired a shot in Andrew's direction as he scurried between boulders. He laughed and added, "Oh, I forgot to tell you that I have night vision glasses. Guess I don't have to wait 'till morning to kill you."

"If that was your best shot, I don't really feel too worried."

"I could always put a bullet in your girl's head. It would be hard to miss from point-blank range. Savon said to bring her back alive, but I don't think he'd get his ass in too big a wad when I bring you in."

Andrew's laugh didn't sound convincing even to himself. "I don't think you have her."

"You just shut up and listen." Covington kneeled next to Malika's limp body and slapped her cheeks hard. "Wake up, bitch."

Andrew listened from the safety of his perch, fighting the urge to rush out and shoot until he or Covington were dead. The sound of the slaps angered him, but it was Malika's weak moan that pushed him to the breaking point.

"Okay, damn you. Stop hitting her. You have her. Now what?"

"You come out into the open and throw down that nine mil you got, and we can talk."

"How do I know you won't kill her anyway?" Andrew asked.

"You don't."

"Then go to hell." Andrew stepped from behind the rocks and fired two shots over Covington's head.

"You are a maniac," Covington yelled. "You're going to kill her yourself."

"I'd rather blow her brains out than let you take her back there."

Covington hauled Malika off the ground and held her in front of him. "Wake up, you stupid bitch," he griped, jostling her. She moaned and lifted her head momentarily, then went limp in his arms again.

"Look, I will let the girl go if you give yourself up. I don't want to have to carry her down the hill anyway. She's not exactly a little thing, as I'm sure you know."

"I don't believe you. If Savon wants us both you won't go back with just me."

"Savon isn't here. I'll tell him what I want." Covington gave Malika a hard jerk to wake her.

"Okay, you win. Just let her go."

"I will, as soon as you're out here and you put these cuffs on yourself."

"If you hurt her, I will kill you. You know that, right?"

"Look, doc, I don't have a beef with you. I don't even know who you are or what you did. The whole thing seemed like a lot of crap to go through, but I was hired to do a job and I'm going to do it one way or the other."

Andrew sighed and shook his head, convinced that there was only one way to save Malika. "Okay, look, I'm coming out. Don't shoot."

"I said I wouldn't. The boss wants you alive. Make sure I see you throw that gun out."

"Okay. Here."

Watching through his night vision goggles, Covington saw the object fly from behind the rocks and land in the sand. The cool, blue, narrow end gave way to a curved handle that shone with a red heat signature.

"Good. You're smarter than I thought." Covington jostled Malika again. "Come on out and join the party."

Andrew stepped into the clearing with his hands clasped behind his head. "You can let her go. I'm giving up."

Covington pointed the gun at Andrew and smiled. "When you're all buttoned up with these cuffs. The drugs will wear off soon enough. She'll wake up after we're gone."

"If I find out you've hurt her, I'll—"

"Sure. You'll kill me. We've been through all that. She's fine. Outside helping myself to a few feels, I haven't hurt her. Can't blame me for that, though." He let out a malicious laugh.

"You're a sick bastard. I'll bet you fit right in with Savon and the rest of those lunatics."

"Well, there are perks." Covington switched his gun to the hand holding Malika and produced a pair of handcuffs, tossing them toward Andrew. He then quickly grabbed the gun with his free hand and pointed it at him. "Put them on."

"Let her go."

"Put the cuffs on. Don't try to be a hero. Just put the cuffs on and..."

Covington smiled when Andrew's hands came down from behind his head, then the white flash of a gunshot filled his night vision goggles. His hand clenched on the gun, sending a wild shot into the night as the bullet tore through the right side of his neck.

Andrew ran toward the sound of two bodies hitting the ground. His heart wanted to check on Malika, but he knew that he had to secure Covington in case his shot hadn't hit its mark cleanly.

The smell of warm, fresh blood told him instantly that he'd hit something, but it was the sound of Covington's gurgling that told him who he'd shot.

He knelt next to the man and laid a hand on his chest. Covington's heart was racing, but it would do no good. It was pumping blood onto the desert sand. He sat in silence, his hand on the man's chest. As the first light of morning crept over the horizon the life slowly drained from the man he knew as Professor Covington.

Ten

The shade created by stringing their blankets between boulders offered little relief from the heat. It was makeshift, but it wouldn't have to last long. Just until Malika was able to travel.

The heat radiated from the sand just a few feet away, reflecting onto him as he faced the desert. A warm breeze swept across the land and provided a momentary respite from the relentless heat. It was only a movement of hot air, but it was better than the stillness of the hilltop.

Malika moaned in her sleep, and he turned to her. She stirred, then settled again. Whatever drug Covington had injected her with was powerful, already lasting over six hours. He'd checked her vital signs three times already. They were within acceptable limits, so there was nothing to do but let it wear off.

Containing his urge to vacate the area hadn't been easy, but leaving Malika wasn't an option and he couldn't carry her with him. If he took the Humvee, they'd be a sitting duck in the desert. Anyone who came looking for their two now-dead agents would spot him from miles away. It wasn't a very practical vehicle for the area anyway. He would be relegated to the lowlands and whatever road he could find, making him easier to spot.

And, of course, there was always his lack of sight that would make driving impossible.

In the end, he amassed as much weaponry, food, and water as thought they could carry and retreated to the tiny, stone fortress to guard Malika. There was nothing to do but wait and think, neither of which he wanted to do.

He wiped sweat from his forehead and scratched the long growth of beard on his face. All of this had been his own fault, all of it. He'd once had a great job in a perfectly fine hospital, a beautiful wife, an amazing son, nice house, and a near-perfect existence, but he gave it all up and moved his family to the Facility.

Why? he asked himself. Was it really the lure of cutting-edge technology? Some magnanimous attempt to make the world a better place, or was it the money? Was it the idea of not being encumbered by ethics complaints and malpractice lawsuits? Doctors didn't have to worry about malpractice at the Facility. If something went wrong, you just tried again on someone else. What did it matter? It was all in the name of scientific and medical progress. They were saving the world.

Lies. All lies. He'd believed them because he wanted to believe them.

Andrew sighed heavily, running his hand through his hair. Was he just as bad as they were? When all was said and done, was he just another animal like Savon? He'd gotten his family tortured, raped, and killed. Now Malika, another woman who cared for him, lay unconscious, drugged by one of Savon's hired henchmen. She could have just as easily been killed. Hell, he could have shot her himself.

Eager to escape the torture of his own thoughts, Andrew crawled from beneath the cover and into the furnace of the midday sun. The heat fell on his body immediately, swallowing him completely. Turning toward the west, he faced the desert. He knew what was out there: mile after mile of relentless heat and dry, scorched earth. Beyond that, the Facility and Alain Savon.

The enormity of what lay before him suddenly felt very heavy. The Facility might be a hundred miles away or two hundred. They would have to make the trek on foot across the wasteland of open desert. If they somehow survived that, there was Savon's fortress to conquer, then the man himself.

Andrew sighed and ran both hands over his sweaty hair, clasping his fingers behind his head as he stared out at the desert.

A small part of him floated to the surface that he didn't want to admit existed. In that tiny corner of his mind, he wanted to take Malika and run away; to recreate what he'd once had with Samantha and to live the rest of his miserable life making love to her and pretend none of this ever happened. She would be a good companion. She would work to please him, and to pleasure him. They could be happy.

But would they be safe? Could he ever truly be happy knowing what had happened? Knowing what they had done to his family? Could he, as a man, live with himself knowing that he'd just let that happen without exacting any revenge?

He rubbed his forehead forcefully and began to pace.

Would destroying Savon make him happy? It wouldn't bring his wife and son back, but it might save him and Malika from a lifetime of worry, of wondering if or when Savon would come for them. It would prevent a lifetime of looking over his shoulder; of being suspicious of every package, of every new person that they met. It might even end the dreams of Samantha and Lane's screams and Savon's heathenistic laugh as he killed them.

Andrew ran his hands through his hair as he paced, suddenly unable to be still. He needed to move but he was stuck on this damned hill.

He knew Alain Savon well. He was a textbook psychopath and a sadist. He enjoyed exercising his power over others and used it to inflict pain on them, which he enjoyed even more. The physical, emotional, and sexual pain of his subjects excited him because he hated everyone. To Alain Savon, everyone else was inferior to him in every way and deserved to be punished for it.

Savon was a man that no one ever said no to twice. He'd never give up. He'd never let them go. They couldn't go far enough away. If it took it, he would walk into a nursing home in America, or a hospital in Prague and stab an ice pick in his ear and spend the rest of his hellish life smiling, knowing that he'd won. For him, everything was about power and winning.

Andrew turned back to the shade as Malika mumbled in her sleep. She had a chance to be safe, but not if she was with him. Savon had his sources, but she could blend into another town, change her name and her story, and probably escape the consequence of caring for him.

She could have a real life with a real husband and live a normal, happy life for many years. She could grow old slowly, with grandkids at her knee, and only think about the blind American she'd once known on rare occasions.

She could move on and be normal. The question that plagued him was did he care for her enough to make that happen. Did he love her? Was that what this was, or was it just a desire to be coupled to someone, anyone? Was he using Malika as a surrogate for his dead wife?

His mind paraded several psychological and physiological answers, but none of them fit. The truth was that he didn't know what he felt about her other than that he wanted to be with her. For now, that would have to be enough.

Andrew bent and found a rock on the ground. He threw it into the desert with a loud scream as his frustration and anger overcame him. The desert, with its heat and sand and wind, was inescapable. It compounded everything, making it almost impossible to think clearly.

"I hate you," he screamed. He scrambled for another rock and threw it, then another. Screaming each time he sent a rock into the unseen land around him.

His hands found another rock, larger than the others, and ripped it from the sand. Hefting it over his head, he smashed it onto one of the boulders with a loud grunt.

"You God-forsaken hell hole!"

He dropped to his knees and ran a hand over his hair. He hated indecision, he hated the desert, he hated the futility of his hope for revenge, but what he hated most was Alain Savon. All of this was blood was on Savon's hands. All the deaths, all the violence was a poisonous tree whose roots grew from that damned lab of his.

When Malika stirred again, he sighed heavily and shook his head. Rising, he went to the shade and sat by her side. His hand found her tangle of hair and pulled it from her face.

His mind and his heart began a silent war as he sat by Malika. His heart wanted to stop resisting and let himself love her, if it came to that, but his mind told him it was too soon. His heart wanted to be in love again, to laugh and enjoy her, but his mind reminded him that Savon would never stop looking for him. His heart wanted to live with her in some tropical paradise forever, but his mind reminded him that he was in the middle of a desert and would probably die here.

Leaning back against one of the boulders that held up the shade, he prepared to rest. He was tired of thinking. He just wanted to sleep.

Malika plodded along angrily as she worked her way along the mountain path. She had hardly spoken to Andrew since the morning meal, when he suggested that she go back to her village and not travel with him any longer. He hadn't said as much, but she was sure it was some foolish noble effort to spare her any danger. The notion angered her as much as his suggestion that they part ways. She didn't need a man to save her, let alone a blind man who didn't even know where he was or which way to go.

The sound of Andrew's grunt brought a smile to her face. In her anger she decided to leave him to his own devices as he followed her through the hills. It would show him how much he needed her. By the time darkness fell he would change his mind.

The smile faded as she considered another reason that he might not want her to go with him. The fact that Covington had gotten the jump on her back at the camp was an embarrassment. She couldn't completely shake the nagging suspicion that she'd let Andrew down. She was supposed to be his watch, his eyes, and she'd ended up a liability.

Was he wrong to leave her behind because of that? Another such lapse could end up getting them both killed, or worse. But he needed her, she knew he did. But how? How much and in what ways did he need her? There was a passion between them, especially when they made love, but was it real? Did he love her at all? If he did love her, how could he leave her?

Malika looked back over her shoulder, watching Andrew struggle to keep up beneath the weight of the heavy pack. She sighed and shook her head as guilt began to creep into her heart.

"Do you need a rest?" she asked.

"I'm fine." He took another step and slipped on a patch of loose stones on the path. He quickly righted himself and smiled. "See, right as rain."

"I see." Malika resisted the urge to go to him. "We are nearing the wadi that will lead us to my village. We will stop when we get there and make camp."

"Good, good," Andrew replied. "You're probably tired."

Malika shook her head as she turned and began walking again, adjusting the strap of the rifle that hung against her back. "Try to keep up."

Her uncle would surely be in the village by now. Her presence there would only stir loyalties and cause friction. She would be forced to marry him to keep the peace and be sentenced to a life of subjugation and control. She would be forced to please him in any way he chose, and any refusal would mean swift punishment. Her life would be a living hell, and if she did as Andrew wanted it would be all his fault.

For her there were only two paths: one with Andrew or death. What did it matter if she were killed with Andrew or if she died at her own hand without him? Would he change his mind if she told him this? Probably not. He was a man and he had made up his mind what was best for her. This American was not so different from every other man she'd ever known.

Malika wiped a tear from her cheek. Just when she thought her miserable life would improve, the rug was being pulled from beneath her. Did he not understand that being with him and being loved and care for, however briefly, would let her die a happy woman? Did he not care what hell he was asking her to accept without him?

"No," she said aloud, stopping suddenly.

Andrew, laboring in the heat as he hurried along the path, slammed into her back, almost toppling them both.

"You gotta tell me when you stop."

"I do not have to do anything you say."

"What?" Andrew asked, confused by the sharpness of her tone.

"You tell me to go to my village and marry my uncle and be his slave and live the rest of my life in misery, wondering if you are dead or alive. Hoping that you may come back someday while I bear children for a swine of a man. Fearing every day that he may kill me and hoping most days that he would. My life would not be a life worth having, and you say go and do this so that you are safe. You say you don't trust me because I have failed you at the camp and the professor stuck me with drugs and captured me. You think I am a weak woman who deserves to be forced to cook and clean and have babies and satisfy the lusts of a man I hate, because I am not good enough to come with you. I say no. No! No to all of this."

Andrew took a step back, shocked by her outburst. "Look, Malika, I just—"

"No. You look. I am strong. I am good woman to you. I make love to you, and I try to please you. I lead you and I help you. I save you from the desert when you are close to death. I fight my village when they want to kill you. I feed you. All this I do for you, and you want to send me away."

"It's not that I want you to—"

"You want this, you want that. You want. Do you ask me what I want? When we lay together and speak of the sky and the stars, do you pretend that you love me, or do you pretend now that you do not?"

Andrew approached her. "Look, Malika, you know how I feel about you. I—"

"You are a fool!" she said, tearing from his hands as he tried to grasp her shoulders. "You cannot cross the desert by yourself. You will die and be eaten by the birds. They will peck out your eyes!"

"Too late for that."

She shook her head as she stared at the sweaty wrap around his head. "Well, you know what I mean."

Andrew shook his head with a half laugh. "Are you going to let me talk?"

"I do not want to hear you." Malika walked away, then stopped. She spun and returned to him. "You think that you know what is best for me. You do not. I have grown to a woman and have only met you. You did not help me do this. I do this myself."

"At least I know what you've been thinking about all day," Andrew said shrugging the pack higher onto his shoulders.

"You are a fool, Andrew. If you want to die alone in the desert then do so, but do not expect me to go to my village and marry my uncle. I will follow the sun until it goes dark before I do that."

Malika turned and stormed off down the path.

"Malika," he called after her. "You know I care for you." A smile broke out on his face when he heard her stop and turn around. The sound of her footfalls grew louder as she walked quickly back to him.

"You say you care for me," she began as she approached him. "I say that you are still a fool." The smile on his face fueled her anger as she marched toward him.

Andrew opened his arms toward her. "Come on. Don't be angry."

Clenching her teeth, she leaned into the punch, driving her fist into his stomach. "You do not tell me what to do," she said again and walked away. "I will make camp. You can join me if you want. I do not care."

Caught off guard by the punch, Andrew went to a knee, doubled over at the waist. He coughed and spat on the ground. After taking several deep breaths to regain his composure, he listened for Malika. She was noisily making her way down the path, muttering in Arabic.

Andrew struggled to his feet and set off after her, one hand still clutching his stomach. Shaking his head, he smiled. She was definitely one hell of a woman, and he was going to need her when he went against Savon.

"You know," Andrew said approaching Malika as she prepared their campsite, "You didn't have to leave me out there to prove your point." He heard her stop for a moment, presumably glaring at him, then continued her work.

"You know I need you, don't you?" He shrugged the pack off and dropped it to the ground. Again she paused, then returned to her work

152

without speaking to him. He sat down and leaned against the canvas pack arming sweat from his brow.

"You don't know what the people at this place are capable of. It's beyond human conception. It's..." he trailed off, shaking his head. "I just wanted to spare you the danger of being subjected to the psychotic whims of Savon. He's a sadist."

Malika grunted contemptibly as she worked.

"You know," he finally said after a long silence, "The only reason you were able to hit me is because I didn't think I had to be on guard against you."

Kneeling beside a fledgling fire, Malika looked back at him for a long time.

"I should not have hit you," she finally said. "You are a cripple."

"Really?" Andrew asked. "Now we're name calling. That's conducive to rational conversation."

Malika sighed as she fed the fire then sat back on her heels. "You speak of me as if I am an American house mother. Is that how you think of me?"

"No."

"I have watched people fight over the same rocks and sand my whole life. Because a man offended another man's grandfather, I must hate them. If a woman is taken to marry, I must hate her as well, and her children, and their children. Because of this I have seen boys shot in the face when they should be playing games and dreaming of what they will be when they become men. I have seen villages blown to rubble. I have watched babies die because of what their grandfather said before they were born. I know that you are hurt in your heart because what they did to your wife and son. I know this. But I have seen ten times that number of people I love die in countless wars with countless people. You are not only person to suffer, Andrew."

"I know, Malika, and I only wanted to spare you from watching another person you care about die."

Malika stared at him, allowing a tear to spill down her cheek, as she thought about his words. He simply wanted to spare her the pain of seeing him die. Her shoulders drooped. "I am sorry, Andrew. I have behaved badly with you."

"All I wanted was for you to be safe."

"I know that." She stood and walked to him. "But you cannot keep me safe by sending me to an unsafe place. My village is as dangerous for me as this place is for you."

"I know that, now." He took her hands and pulled her down to him. "I just couldn't imagine going through that again. Subjecting you to that same fate."

"My place is beside you. My fate has already been written."

Andrew took her in his arms and kissed the top of her head. "I think both of ours has been."

Major Townley stood at parade rest, his hands clasped in the small of his back, and watched General Michaels, the head of Middle Eastern Affairs, read the report. The General held the thin file in one hand while the other drummed a pencil against his desk.

"God damn it," he moaned, tossing the paper to his desk as he leaned back in his chair.

"I'm sorry, sir. Not very good news."

"No, Major, not at all." The General rubbed his face then shook his head. "I don't see how all this is possible."

"Well, sir," Townley began nervously, "Our people and several Saudi operatives were in place but missed them by a matter of minutes. They were supposed to go in just before dawn, but the final go was held up by a snafu."

"A snafu?" the General yelled. "Situation normal, all fucked up? This whole situation is one big snafu, Major."

"Yessir. I'm sorry, sir. These joint task force things are often problematic at best."

"It's not your fault." The general propped his elbow on the desk and rubbed his mouth again. "I just don't see how one American doctor with no proper training can evade us, the Saudi's and a freaking gun running piece of shit like Abdullah."

"It's quite frustrating, sir, to say the least. At least our team was able to cut Abdullah's men off and prevent them from getting the group."

"Sometimes I wonder if it wouldn't have been better to just let them kill the whole lot of 'em."

"Sir, the Canadians wouldn't think so. Their people would have been killed and that would have opened another can of worms. So to speak, sir."

"What were they even doing there in the first place?"

"The Canadian consultant hasn't answered our inquiries into that, sir."

The general scratched his gray hair and sighed heavily. "Damned politicians."

"It is a delicate balance, sir."

"Major, this whole thing could blow up and blow shit on a lot of faces that don't like having shit blown on them."

"I know, we're doing our best, sir."

"Looks like he picked up a traveling companion," the General said, waving a hand at the file. "Do we even know who it is?"

"Yessir. Malika Kader. Her father was the leader of a small mountain village. We're compiling a report on that, sir. Not much to tell except that he's dead and a distant uncle has assumed a tenuous leadership of the group."

"Our guy kill him too?" the general asked, his brow furrowing deeply as he looked at the file.

"Not directly. The old man was shot in a skirmish with a rival clan. The good doctor apparently did surgery to remove the bullet."

"You're shitting me? A blind surgeon removing a bullet in the middle of the freaking wilderness?"

"Yessir. The old man died though."

"You think?" the general asked, his voice rising slightly. He shook his head and lowered his voice. "Some of this might be above your pay grade, Major, but this guy is stirring pots that powerful people don't want stirred." He waved his hand over the report. "A Blackhawk helicopter being taken down is a big enough problem. Three minor terrorist cells are claiming credit for that. And now people are asking what the hell a U.S. helicopter was even doing that far east. Hell, I don't know how to answer that!"

"We're looking into that, sir. It looks like the Saudi's sold it to a South African firm that guards the United Assembly when they travel. The paperwork appears to have been in order, sir. They "lost" it shortly after delivery."

"Lost it my ass. These idiots beg equipment from us then sell it to the highest bidder." The general rubbed his face with both hands.

Major Townley paused to wipe sweat from his brow. "It was an early model, though, and the technology had been removed, including most the weapons systems. It had a fifty-cal. machine gun, navigation, FLIR, but no missile launch capability."

"I'm sure that'll be of comfort to the poor bastards that these assholes didn't like, Major." He looked back down at the report, shaking his head. "Four Yemini guards and two Canadian civilians dead. Who the hell is this guy?"

"The Saudi's did get the Humvee back, sir."

The general waved the comment off dismissively. "They're a dime a dozen, Major. Who the hell doesn't have one by now? And there is no sign of the doctor and his guide?"

"There are reports, sir, that she may not just be his guide."

The general shook his head and let out a frustrated laugh. "Perfect. This guy's running around getting native tail all over northern Yemen while the whole country is going to shit. Downing helicopters and killing assholes left and right and we can't find either of them." The general ran a hand through his hair. "He's probably getting more ass than a private on leave."

"I don't know about that sir, but everyone knows that the Canadians weren't civilians. Intel hints at the possibility of them being bounty hunters."

"By all rights, they were civilians, Major. It's enough for the press to blow up a shit storm."

"If I may sir?" the major asked. He waited for a nod from the general, then continued. "As much as we can discern, the two Canadians left their homes about two months ago. Recruited by the same biotech firm as Doctor Hawkins. They were in Jordon for a while. We have it on reliable sources that they only recently left there."

"What the hell is this place? Get me all the info we have on it. I want everything on every-damned-body who has ever worked there. I don't care if it's a rumor started by an Arab camel trader. I want it."

"I took the liberty, sir. I've got people on it and should have it on your desk within the hour."

"Good." The general nodded. "What the hell is it about this guy, Major? You think he's some kind of James Bond type or something?"

"I don't know, sir. He's very smart, a talented surgeon, and apparently very resourceful."

"And he's blind, Major. Don't forget that on his dating profile you're writing there."

"Yessir," Townley answered, deflated. "Will there be anything else, sir?"

"No. No, just get me that report as soon as you can."

"Yessir." The Major came to attention and saluted before turning and walking toward the door. He stopped and turned back around. "If I may, sir?"

"What?"

"I was talking to intel and they might have a plan to help us find this guy."

"Well, Major, you gonna spill it before I have an aneurysm or wait for the new guy?"

"Sir, it involves a covert tracking system. Basically, they can put a microchip in anything and deliver it where they will find it."

"How the hell do you propose we do that? We can't even find the guy now."

"Well, sir, there is a way. I will get you the report, but..." The major produced a small medicine bottle, shaking its contents before handing the bottle to the General. "I think it's got a good chance. We just need to find the right situation."

"Rehydration tablets? What the hell is that? Salt pills?"

"Mostly inert stuff, sir. They made them for this type of situation. Each pill has a microchip in it. When consumed, the stomach acid dissolves the outer shell, and the device becomes active. It will remain in the digestive track for up to forty-eight hours before becoming inactive."

"Have these been used before?" the general asked, opening the bottle and peering inside.

"They wouldn't confirm or deny that sir. You'll need to authorize them, since the doctor is an American citizen."

The general sighed and sat the bottle down on his desk. "Let's get that report ready, Major. I'll make some calls."

"Yessir." The Major saluted again and left the room quickly.

Alone behind his desk, the general rubbed his eyes for a long time, preparing himself for the telephone call he was about to make. He grabbed the receiver with an angry fist and raised it to his ear.

"Get me the Riyadh Air Base in Saudi." The General began drumming the pencil again while he waited for the connection. "Yes, Connect me to Colonel Dyer in Middle Eastern Affairs. Immediately." The phone clicked in his ear several times while he waited.

"Colonel Dyer's office. How may I help you?"

"This is General Thomas Michaels, Middle eastern Affairs, Pentagon. I need to speak to Dyer."

"I'm sorry, sir. Colonel Dyer isn't in his office. It's the middle of the night, sir."

"Well you wake his ass up and tell him to call me asap. Got it?"

"Yessir. I will relay the message myself."

General Michaels dropped the phone back into its cradle and rubbed his hand back and forth across his mouth. If they didn't get a handle on this situation son, things were going to get ugly.

Pushing up from his desk, he went to the modest, but well stocked liquor cabinet in the corner. He dropped two cubes of ice into a tumbler and washed them with bourbon. The whole situation could still be contained, they just had to find the son of a bitch.

He went back to his desk, drink in hand, and picked up the bottle of pills. He shook his head then drained the glass.

Eleven

Traveling at night to escape the hundred plus degree heat, they stopped mid-morning to construct a makeshift tent. It was primitive, fashioned from sleeping bags scavenged from the Humvee, but it shielded them from the merciless sun. Built on the leeward side of a dune, it also provided a small measure of relief from the heat as well.

Andrew checked the tie on the last short pole, taken from the valley before they left, and ducked beneath the cover.

"It's already boiling out there."

Malika agreed as she slathered the last of the goat cheese on two pieces of flatbread. She offered him one as she took a bite of hers. "Hungry?"

"Are you doing okay?" Andrew asked, stripping his shirt off.

"I am good," she answered quietly. "How far do you think we are?"

Andrew shook his head as he pulled a canteen of water from his pack. He handed it to Malika and accepted the bread. "Well, it's our third day since leaving the valley. You found me, what, three days out?"

"The middle of the fourth day's walk from my village."

Andrew took the canteen back from Malika and drank just enough to wash his bread down. He was slightly dehydrated, but not critically. With the water supply they'd gathered before leaving the river near Malika's village, he would be fine. What worried him most was having a heat stroke. He'd intentionally lowered his kidney function and his sweat output to preserve his bodily fluid, but that left him susceptible to the heat.

Malika, with no such abilities, was sweating profusely and her scent was strong.

"I can't be certain of knowing how far I walked, or even what direction. I have a general notion that I've kept up with, but nothing is certain. After I left the Facility, I went to a nearby oasis. That was about a day and a half walk away. Then I walked northeast. I passed out and was in some military base when I woke up. It wasn't American. That's the part that could throw a wrench into the works. I don't know how far they traveled." Andrew took a bite of bread and chewed as he thought. "They thought I was dead. In the middle of the night, I escaped them and began walking East. Then you found me."

Malika chewed on the bread as her eyes scanned the desert before her. "It will be done according to God's plan."

"I hope your god is on our side, me being what I am." Andrew said as he laid back beside her. He took another bite of bread and settled himself into the sand beneath the blanket.

"God is not on anyone's side."

"Pity. We could use some help."

"You must believe in something, Andrew."

"I believe in you," he said with a smile. Taking her hand, he tried to pull her back with him.

"It is too hot, and we are dirty," she said, pulling away. "Eat your food and rest."

"Yes ma'am," Andrew replied with a laugh. He took another bite of the bread, still smiling as he chewed it. Picking up the canteen, he nudged her arm with it. "You should finish this one. You'll be no help if you drop dead."

Malika took the canteen and drank. She felt guilty but knew she needed it. She was drinking more than Andrew, a lot more, but he was right. They probably had three days of water, four if they stretched it. After that ,they wouldn't last long in the desert.

"I think tonight we should..." Andrew stopped talking and sat up abruptly. Cocking his head to one side, he listened to the growing rumble in the distance. After a few seconds, Malika heard it as well and looked at Andrew, her eyes wide with fear.

"What is it?" she asked.

Andrew opened his mouth to answer, but the roar swept across them like a wave. Malika threw herself on the blanket, covering her head. Andrew's hand went to the gun beside him as it began to vibrate beneath the roar of the jets as they passed overhead.

"Why are airplanes here?" Malika asked as the sound began to subside.

Andrew shrugged. "Whatever they were doing, they were in a hurry." He shook his head as he laid back on the blanket again.

"Do you think they were looking for us?"

"If they were, they can stop looking. They found us. Either way, it wasn't Savon. He's got the money and clout to get his nasty hands on an outdated helicopter, but not a jet. Definitely not two of them."

"Were they American?"

Andrew shrugged. "No way to tell, really." He thought for a minute. "We must be well into Saudi. Maybe they're just patrols."

"Perhaps."

Andrew made himself relax despite his apprehension. During the entire time he'd spent at the Facility and since his escape, he'd never so much as heard a fighter jet in the distance. Something had changed, but what? He was still an American citizen, but would they spend the time and effort looking for him? Was there any reason they would even know about him? His mind began to search for answers as his tired body relaxed.

By the time he fell asleep ten minutes later, he still hadn't found any.

"I'm tired of talking. You talk for a while," Malika said throwing her hand in the air and letting it drop.

"That kinda defeats the purpose," Andrew replied. The small rise punctuated with large boulders gave way to a rock-strewn lowland. "I can't follow my own voice. That would be the blind leading the blind."

Malika listened as Andrew laughed at his own joke and shook her head. "This gun is making enough noise. Besides, the path is mostly clear. There are pillars of rock to our right and left. We are in a small valley between them, a kilometer wide. You will be fine."

"Fine then." Andrew shrugged the heavy pack up on his back. He didn't need Malika to talk to follow her, but the sound of her voice was a pleasant distraction from the misery of the heat. "I've been thinking. The jets that we heard earlier, they could be Saudi. They could be American. I don't know. They were not on routine patrol, I'm sure. I do think they were looking for something. I don't know if it was me, or us, but it's possible. The soldiers that found me must have been coalition forces. They were Saudi nationals, I think. They were excited that I was an American. One of them kept saying *'al-hatef,'*"

"That is 'call' or 'telephone,' Depending on how you use it."

"I gathered as much. So, they called the Americans, I guess."

"But why would they care?" Malika asked, swiping a stone out of their path with her foot.

"We're sort of particular about that kind of stuff. Americans don't like it when another American is killed in a foreign country."

"Then perhaps they should stay at home."

Andrew absorbed the weight of her comment and sighed heavily. "I'm not disagreeing with you. But the average citizen doesn't know much about what happens. Hell, I couldn't promise that I could point to Yemen on a map five years ago."

Malika marched on quietly.

"Do you hate us?" Andrew asked.

"I do not suppose I do. Most of the fighting is in the west, but war comes to everyone in time. I love my country. I know that you have not seen it, but there is much beauty here. Sometimes it is difficult to find."

The sadness in Malika's voice sank into his heart as he followed her. "I'm sorry for what has happened to your country."

"It is not only outsiders who have destroyed our country. We have done that ourselves for many years." Malika stopped with a heavy sigh and turned to face him. "One day when I was a young girl, a man came into my village. He was almost dead from thirst and hunger. Everyone was excited. It was the first outsider I had ever seen. He was in our village for two days. My father found out he was Sunni. He begged for mercy and explained that he'd been outcast by his tribe for not wanting to raid another village."

"That was noble and brave if you ask me."

"My father had him shot as a coward and a spy."

"Ouch," Andrew said, following as Malika began to walk again.

"I remember when they were leading him out of the village, everyone was there to watch." Malika shook her head. "You must think us barbaric."

"Not at all, well, a little. Maybe. But it wasn't that long ago that we did virtually the same thing. Public hangings were quite the spectacle in America once upon a time."

"We stood in a line. Most people spat on him as they led him past. I did not. I remember feeling sorry for him and wondering what he had done. He looked like us, spoke like us, walked, and talked like us. But my father said he was to be shot and he was."

"That's gotta be tough on a kid," Andrew said quietly.

"In my country, a child grows up quickly."

"That may be the saddest part of all this."

"Perhaps so," she sighed. Malika walked along in silence, navigating by the rising sliver of the moon. "I do not want my children to grow up so quickly."

"I don't either," Andrew agreed, a sad smile coming to his lips. He followed Malika through the flatland. Leaving her to her thoughts, he listened to the gentle rattle of the gun that hung over her shoulder. It came to his ears in a series of gentle clicks as metal met metal in a steady rhythm. When she stepped with her left foot the gun made a soft thump as it gently struck her hip, when she stepped with her right, pieces within the gun met with a metallic "click."

Lost in his own philosophical thoughts, Andrew didn't hear the distant rumble. His senses lulled into an almost trance-like state by the silence and the rhythm of the footfalls, his ears didn't pick up the sound until seconds before Malika.

He called to her and stopped. "Where can we hide?" he asked. The words were barely out of his mouth when he felt her strong hand on his arm, pulling him to the left, in the direction of the roar.

"Hurry."

Andrew stumbled over a small bush. His arms flailed wildly, reaching for her as he fell. Sensing the loss of balance, he put out his hands, just catching himself before the weight of the heavy pack sent him face-first to the ground.

Two strong hands ripped him from the ground and hauled him up, half dragging him toward the cover as the roar of the jets filled his ears. He felt himself pressed against the rocky face of the rise as the two jets passed overhead, just a few hundred feet above the ground.

Malika pushed him along the rock face, abandoning caution. Within seconds he felt himself wedged painfully in a narrow opening.

"Do you think they saw us?" Malika asked breathlessly, pressing herself against him.

"Hard to say. They were low. In the dark probably not, but if they had..." Andrew paused and listened for a moment. "They're turning."

"Will they fire at us?' she asked, the fear rising in her voice.

"I sure hope not. If they do, we're dead ducks."

"Should we fire at them?" she asked.

"No." Andrew shook his head. "If we do it will probably make them shoot back."

The sound of the jets rounded them in a wide arc before heading straight for them again.

Malika clung to him. Burying her face in his shoulder she began to pray in Arabic.

Andrew tuned his senses to her voice, wanting it to be the last thing he heard if the jets did fire on them. He knew one strike would be enough to kill them. They could fire a few missiles at the rockface and never slow down. They'd be dead before the jets were out of earshot.

As the roar drew closer, drowning out Malika's prayers, Andrew felt her body tense against his. If this was their last seconds on earth, at least they were together.

A quick yelp escaped Malika as a small rock, shaken loose by the jets passing by overhead, struck her on the head.

"It's okay," Andrew said. "They've passed."

Malika clung to him desperately as tears began to flow down her cheeks.

"We're okay," Andrew told her again, urging her out of the crevasse. "We're okay. C'mon."

Malika stumbled out of the fissure and leaned against the rock face, wiping tears from her cheeks. Andrew wrapped her in an embrace.

"I am sorry," she said.

"You have nothing to be sorry about."

"You must think me a tender as a house woman."

"It's housewife, and you're wrong on both accounts." Andrew stroked her hair. "To cry is not a sign of weakness."

"I am tired and worried," she said, regaining her composure. "I do not want us to die in the desert."

"You are perfect, and strong, and brave, and beautiful."

"Again you say I am beautiful, but you cannot see me."

"I don't have to see you," he told her, putting a hand against her cheek. He bent and kissed her lips.

She allowed the kiss to linger, then pushed him back. "We must be moving. It is not safe here."

"Okay," Andrew said with a smile.

Malika gave him a quick kiss on the lips. "Better that we do not die on the side of this hill." She bent and picked up the gun that she dropped in her rush to get them to cover. Smiling as she slung it over her shoulder, she touched his face.

"We'll be fine," he said.

"You do not know that," she said turning from him.

"It's okay that you got upset," Andrew said teasingly as she walked away.

"I did not get upset," she called over her shoulder. "Come, before you fall again."

"That's real funny," Andrew laughed as he set off after her. "Make fun of the blind guy."

"Perhaps you can follow the sound of my laughing," she called back to him.

"Right behind you."

The shadow of the Sikorsky UH-60 Blackhawk raced along the ground, slipping over the undulating sand beneath the airship as it descended quickly. The pilot pushed the helicopter in fast then throttled back, sitting the craft down less than fifty yards from the coordinates on his screen. This wasn't his first special ops mission, but it sounded like the easiest. The whole thing was pretty cut and dry. Move in quickly, extract the American doctor, and get the hell out. He'd been advised that the doctor might have a female traveling companion, but she was to be left behind.

Before the weight of the gunship came fully to rest on the sand beneath it, the eight-man tactical team was out and sprinting forward of the aircraft. Looking at his co-pilot through the dark screen of his helmet, the pilot gave a thumbs up.

"In and out," he said into the microphone. "Quicker than a cheap whore house."

"I hope so," the co-pilot replied, his voice not as confident. He turned back to the windshield and watched the extraction team sprint across the sand toward the edge of a precipice.

Following the signal from the team leader, the group split into two groups of four as they neared the ledge. Six of the men disappeared over the rim and two took up defensive positions with weapons at the ready, their eyes scanning in every direction.

Two of the six remaining men pulled up just short of the makeshift tent, also taking up defensive positions while the remaining men converged on the battered sleeping bag protruding from the side of the hill.

"U.S. Army!" The team leader yelled as he closed in on the tent. The man next to him grabbed the edge of the sleeping bag and snatched it free, sending an avalanche of sand onto the blanket below, as the men opposite him rushed forward.

All four men stood silent; their weapons trained on the empty blanket before them.

"What the hell?" one of them said over the intercom.

"Be advised that the camp is clear. There is no one present." The team leader motioned for his men to scan the area and stepped onto the blanket. He picked up the pack and weighed it in his hand. "The good doctor has been humping some heavy shit."

"I thought he was humping a native."

"Knock it off, Johnson." The team leader shook his head but couldn't help grinning as he unzipped the bag and dumped it onto the blanket. With his foot, he examined the contents. "Looks like two small handguns, some ammo for what looks like an M-16, 'bout fifty rounds present, two empty canteens- both civilian. Little bit of bread and..." he bent and picked up a small cloth bag.

"Let's see what this is. Maybe contraband," he began with a grin as he untied the string around the top of the bag. Spreading the bag open, he peered inside. "What the hell?" he asked, turning the bag upside down. "Two brownish gray, mostly rounded balls of dried up..." He tossed the bag and its contents quickly to the ground.

"What is it?" his teammate asked with a laugh. "You jumped like your old lady just handed you a pregnancy test."

"They look like freaking dried-up eyeballs!"

"You're shitting me." The soldier pushed past his commander and knelt on the blanket, gathering the objects. "Shit! That's what they look like." He turned to his team leader, holding the blobs in front of his face shield.

"Here's looking at you, kid," he said with a laugh.

"Knock it the hell off!" the team leader commanded, taking a step back. "Quit messing around, Johnson. You sick freak."

Johnson stood, rolling the eyes around in his hand like marbles. "Can I keep 'em?" he asked, still laughing. "It's always handy to have an extra set of eyes."

"Hell no." The Sargent shook his head as he turned away. "Check out those rocks over there. They didn't go far without their gear. Not in this heat." His eyes went to the two rock formations rising out of the sand a hundred yards away. The one to the right was small and would be easily searched. The one on the left had a towering rock face and would take the rest of the day to climb.

"Carl, guess you heard they've bugged out, if they were ever here at all. Can we break radio silence to find out what in the hell they want us to do now?"

"Not a chance," the pilot answered. "We're strictly non-communicado unless it's a mayday."

"Well, what the hell are we supposed to do?"

"That's not in my job description, Sarge. I'm just the bus driver."

"Great." He watched as his men surrounded the smaller formation and began clambering through the huge boulders. He nudged Johnson on the arm with the back of his hand and shook his head. "They're not in there." He stabbed a finger toward the towering rockface. "If I was gonna hide, I'd hide up there somewhere."

"We don't have the gear to climb that, Sarge. You think a blind civilian and his sidepiece scaled that rock face?" He shook his head, answering his own question. "No fucking way, man. Not a chance."

Malika lay still on the small outcropping and peered through the binoculars, refusing to yield to the sun beating down on her back. Andrew's "feeling" had been correct and although tired, they'd climbed most of the way up the formation. They spent the night huddled in a small crevasse with no food and very little water.

"They have searched the small pillar and are gathered in the shade."

Andrew shrugged. "I doubt they will bother to climb up here."

"What if they do?" she asked nervously.

"Then we might as well have got a good sleep in the tent."

Malika turned her head. "This is not a funny time for jokes, Andrew."

Andrew smiled. *"Au Contraire,* my sweet. If they find us, we might not have a reason to laugh again anytime soon."

"But they are American, like you. Surely, they will not hurt us."

"That's not what I'm worried about. I would suppose their orders are to collect me and return to base A.S.A.P."

"But not me?" she asked, her shoulders slumping.

Andrew shook his head, the weight of her voice settling on him like a wet blanket. He sat in a sliver of shade wishing things were different.

He didn't fully understand why the United States Army would bother with finding him, but they were. So far, he'd killed Souter, escaped a base of coalition forces, killed Ross and his co-pilot, four of Abdullah's guards, and two alleged British agents, but none of those should concern the U.S. government, outside the slight political scene it may have caused.

There was no way they would know about Souter and probably didn't know about the helicopter. If they did, they'd assume it crashed. Those were all Facility men. The four guards were Abdullah's men, so they wouldn't care about them. The two agents though, may be the source of the attention. Malika said that they looked like him, meaning Caucasian, so they weren't locals. Was that it? Were they really British? If so, they definitely worked for the Facility, not MI-6.

He'd laid awake until the sun began to climb in the sky trying to figure it out but was no closer now than he was hours ago. None of it made sense, but then again things had stopped making sense long before the helicopter came racing across the desert toward them.

"They are using the glasses to look for us," Malika said.

"Why don't you come and sit in the shade with me? There is nothing we can do now but wait. If they climb up here, we're done for anyway. Does it matter if we know they're coming?"

Malika sighed, then slid back from the edge of the cliff. She sat beside him wiping sweat from her face.

"If they come to take you, I think you should go."

"Do you really?" Andrew asked with a smile.

"I do. You are blind. You can get medical help in America that might help you."

"And then what?"

"I don't know," Malika answered, her voice faltering slightly.

"Then it's settled. They'll never climb up here anyway, so it's a moot point."

"I don't know moot, but your life would be better if you go home."

"Awfully magnanimous of you, but I think I'll hang around a bit longer." Andrew slid his arm around Malika and pulled her to him.

"Thank you," she said after a moment's silence. "You are a good man to me, Andrew."

"Likewise, my dear." Andrew laughed as the sound of the rotor blades below them grew louder. "Sounds like they're leaving."

"Good riddance."

Malika squeezed back into the fissure behind one of the jagged rocks and Andrew joined her.

"Be nice if they left us some water," he said as the sound of the helicopter thundered in his ears.

"It would be better if they left us alone."

"Yes," he agreed, his face close to Malika's ear as the aircraft began to circle the rock formation. "But we both know we haven't seen the last of them." She turned to look at him as the wind ripped at her hair. A sad smile slipped across her lips.

"You are a very good man, Andrew." She took his face in her hands and kissed his lips gently. "Please do not hate me."

With her back wedged against the solid rock of the formation, she slid her hands to his chest and pushed with all the strength she could muster. Caught off guard, Andrew staggered back trying to find his balance. He stumbled once, but his heel struck the edge of a rock and he fell backward, arms flailing, onto the open ledge.

"Are you crazy?" he yelled, scrambling to his feet as the sound of the helicopter grew louder drowning out his own voice. He extended an arm to the rock face and tried to find cover.

"Go home!" she yelled. The sound of the rotors echoed against the formation, coming from every direction.

Andrew staggered toward the crevasse, toward Malika.

Malika looked past him to the edge of the rock face waiting for the helicopter to appear. She wiped a tear from her cheek.

"Go home!" Malika yelled. "It will be better for you."

"No." Andrew grabbed her wrists as she tried to push him away. He pulled her to him and wrapped his arms around her tightly. "No," he said again into her ear.

Tears began to stream down her cheeks as Andrew held her body against him. She saw the movement of the helicopter's rotors as they cleared the edge of the rock and her heart stopped in her chest. Sobs wracked her body as the thought of losing him swept over her like a hot desert wind.

When the fuselage of the aircraft cleared the cliffside, it had already turned away from them.

She stroked the back of his head as they both sank to the ground. "I'm sorry," she said.

"It's okay," he said, burying his face in her hair. "It's okay."

Andrew held her tight against him, feeling the force of her sobs against his chest. She just wanted him to be safe, to be home and far away from all the danger this land had to offer him. But just like her, going home wasn't possible anymore. Things had changed and there was no going back.

Twelve

The scorching air slipped into Andrew's lungs with each breath, drying his body from the inside out. With each hot wind that swept across the sand, the scent of Malika's body met his face. She was hot and sweating profusely, but it dried quickly, leaving her with a musky, spice-like odor. Her respirations were up, her breaths coming in quick, raspy pants. She was dehydrated, probably badly, and the water was gone.

The decision to press on, into the heat of the day now felt like a foolish one. With each step they took, hope of finding shelter faded beneath the unrelenting sun.

To her credit, Malika kept a steady pace across the uneven sand. An ominous silence grew between them with each degree of heat, forcing them both to preserve what little energy they had left. He followed, lost in his thoughts and second-guessing himself.

The decision to abandon the camp and sneak away in the middle of the night was his. Despite Malika's protest, he persisted and won. The hope of fooling the Army by leaving their shelter behind was a mistake. That was abundantly clear now. What did it matter if they got away only to die in the desert? His arrogance had taken them out of the frying pan and into the furnace.

Because of him, Malika was going to die.

Malika, he thought, as the faintest of smiles came to his dry lips. What an amazing woman. She learned English from watching television and was brave enough to stab her abusive husband. There was no other woman like her in the world, he was sure, and he'd led her out into the desert toward a slow, painful death.

Andrew tried to clear his throat in hopes of bringing some moisture to his dry mouth, but all that came out was more hot air. He ran a leathery tongue across his cracked lips, finding no relief there either. He'd allowed his body to sweat profusely for short periods twice already to lower his body temperature, but it was creeping up again and he was becoming dehydrated himself.

"Do you want to stop?" he asked, his voice horse and scratchy.

"I do not know what to do," she said, almost in a whisper, then stopped. She turned to look at Andrew. "Do you think we will die here today?"

Andrew shrugged weakly and shook his head. "I don't know." He cleared his throat again. "I may have underestimated the effects of the desert."

"Perhaps," Malika agreed as she scanned the area, a hand shielding her eyes from the sun.

"I guess," Andrew said, bent over with his hands on his knees to alleviate the weight of the pack. They'd abandoned some of their weaponry, but he'd taken on most of their supplies, easing the walk for Malika. "The question is do we die walking or die sitting?"

"I prefer to not die at all."

Andrew smiled. "That makes two of us." He blew out a weary breath and stood up. "Lead on, beautiful."

Continuing their slow progression, he wondered how much longer Malika would last. Without his ability to preserve bodily fluid, she was sweating a lot. She had drunk the last of the water hours ago at his insistence, but it wasn't enough and they both knew it. The few swallows of tepid water might have bought her another hour, two at the most.

What would he do if she collapsed? There would be nothing he could do for her. Could he leave her in the desert to die alone? Was his desire for revenge so strong; so all-consuming that he would leave a woman he cared for to die slowly? Alone.

The Facility was still there. Still doing the same things they'd always done. Could he allow them to continue; to do the same thing to someone else that they'd done to him?

He decided that he'd sit with her until she died, then bury her body in the sand to protect it from scavengers. If there was a way, he'd mark it in hopes of retrieving it later for a proper burial. He owed her that much.

Andrew's fatigued brain switched gears, showing him an image of Savon. His white hair was neatly styled and combed from right to left. Perfectly trimmed above his tanned, hairless body as he stood naked before him, fully aroused. Savon's smooth face wore a smirk as he stared at him.

"You knew better, Doctor," Savon told him.

"Go to hell!" he had screamed, fighting his restraints. "I'll kill you!"

Savon's cold hand touched his face gently. "It's a pity, really." He stepped back and nodded to the men waiting nearby. They moved in quickly and subdued him, shoving his head into a vice-like device mounted on the wall. One of them held him while the other cranked it quickly, immobilizing his head.

Savon watched as the eyelid speculums were put into place. Each side of the device held one eye, cupping the edges of his eyelids, and pulling them open.

"You're crazy!" Andrew cried.

The smirk returned to Savon's face as he gave his men another nod. They exited through a door and returned a moment later, each holding the arm of a struggling woman.

Andrew's heart sank when he saw his wife. Somewhere deep inside he'd hoped that Savon would allow them to leave. Terror filled his chest as he began to put the pieces of the puzzle together and he began to plead for mercy.

Samantha tried to run to him but one of the men grabbed a hand full of hair and snatched her back.

"Let her go, Savon, please. Let my family go and I will come back to work. I'll do anything."

Savon's smile widened. "You see, Doctor, the problem is that you've already shown where your loyalties lie." He turned and looked at Samantha. "In a way, I'm glad you did. I'll have to admit that I've had an impure thought or two about your little wife."

"I'm begging you," Andrew pleaded as the men wrestled Samantha closer to Savon. They held her arms, forcing her to stand before him.

"Please, don't do this, please," she begged, crying.

"Savon, I swear! Please. Anything!"

Savon tore the silk night shirt that Samantha wore, revealing her breasts. Cupping them in his hands he lifted them slightly, feeling the weight.

"Very nice," he whispered. Turning, he looked at Andrew and smiled again as he clenched Samantha's breasts in his fists. Samantha screamed in pain as his fingernails dug into her flesh.

"Andrew," she cried. "Do something. Andrew!"

"Andrew!" Malika yelled, staggering back to him. "Andrew!"

"What?" he asked, shaking the image out of his head.

"I hear something."

Andrew rubbed his forehead and ran his fingers over the bandage, still struggling against the pain of the memories.

"Don't you hear it?"

Andrew nodded. He should have heard the sound long before Malika but, lost in the horror of the memory, he'd missed it.

"Should we hide?' she asked.

Andrew shook his head. "If there was anywhere to hide, we'd already be in it." He motioned for her to join him. When she did, he embraced her and pressed his lips against hers.

The noise grew slowly louder, becoming the sound of a helicopter. It had been tracking East before making a sharp left turn and heading straight for them.

"If they shoot us, then we will die together," Malika said.

"If they do it might be the most humane thing the U.S Army has ever done." Malika's scent was strong, but not unpleasant. It was a scent that he wanted in his mind if this was truly to be their last few minutes on Earth.

The sound of the rotors became deafening as the helicopter approached, blowing sand along the dunes in every direction. Andrew did his best to calm his heart rate but found it difficult. The physical exhaustion and dehydration were making any attempt at concentration next to impossible. He finally gave up and let his body do what it wanted.

He held Malika and enjoyed the feel of her arms around him as they waited, together, for whatever end the helicopter would bring.

"It was a good run," he said into her ear. "Thank you."

Malika raised her head from his chest enough to kiss his lips. "I am happy to die with you."

The helicopter's approach slowed as it drew closer. When a hundred meters away it turned slightly, and the side door slid back. A soldier stood behind a fifty-caliber machine gun mount, training the gun on them. The soldier looked away, into the cabin of the aircraft, and gave a hand signal. He nodded, then turned his dark face shield back to them. As he stared down at the two lovers a grin slid across his lips.

Another soldier approached the open door carrying a large canvas bundle strapped tightly into a square block. He looked at them and shook his head before tossing the package out the door. He watched it tumble through the air and land on the sand. Turning to the machine gunner, he made a slicing motion across his throat and then hauled the door closed. The helicopter turned and departed quickly.

"What happened?" Malika asked.

"I don't know," Andrew said, his hands still around her waist. "Can you still see them?"

"Yes, they are flying away, but they left something!" she said, her voice suddenly excited. "Maybe water."

Andrew dropped to his knees with a sigh as she pulled free of his arms. He shrugged the pack off and sat back against his heels. He didn't want to hope that the U.S. Army had left them food and water, but he couldn't help himself. If they did, there was hope. If not, neither of them would live to see nightfall.

He smiled at the sound of Malika's happiness. She was speaking quickly in Arabic, tossing in enough English words to tell him that there was water and food inside the package.

Malika staggered back to him and fell to her knees on the hot sand. "Much water to drink, but it tastes like goat piss."

Andrew took the flask from her and drank deeply. The briny fluid washed over his dry mouth, finding every crack in his tongue and setting it afire. He swished the liquid around in his mouth and swallowed.

"It's an electrolyte solution. Better than water for rehydrating you."

"Well, I have never been so happy to drink such bad water."

Andrew took another long swallow. "We shouldn't drink too much at once. We'll puke and it won't help things a bit."

Malika stole another long drink and closed the lid on her flask. "Come. Let us see what else they have left. Praise be to God, we are spared."

Andrew awoke with pains in his stomach. The cool air streaming in both open ends of the small tent told him that the sun had yet to rise. Malika's warm body felt good against his chest, lending him a smile, but it faded quickly.

Rolling onto his back, he sat up and felt for the flask. After several long swallows, he crawled to the edge of the tent and stood. The sand beneath his bare feet had cooled considerably, telling him that it was early morning.

The wind rolled silently across the desert and greeted him as he stifled a yawn. Bright green arrows undulated through the darkness of his mind, rising and falling with the uneven landscape.

His mind wouldn't allow him the peace that Malika felt, nor would it afford him the restful sleep he knew he needed. The past few days had taken a toll on him, both mentally and physically. The electrolyte drink was well on its way to rehydrating him and the MREs had fed him, but neither satisfied the indecision that worried his mind.

He was conflicted.

Malika had tried to reveal him to the Army helicopter while they were hiding on the rock tower, albeit for good reasons. She wanted him to be safe; to return to America where he could be looked after.

Although it had been for noble reasons, he wondered how she really saw him. Deep down did she think of him as a cripple? Handicapped? Or did she love him so much that she only wanted to save him from the possibility of being killed by Savon's men?

Andrew rubbed his face and scratched his beard with both hands. Then there was the situation with the aid drop. Why would the U.S. Army go out of its way to drop an aid package for him? They'd already raided their camp. Why were they devoting so many resources to one man? Yes, he was an American citizen. His presence would surely cause some consternation back home, but the life or death of one man would be easily dismissed in the news cycle.

His hand went to the breast pocket of his shirt. The letter was still there. Malika had read it to him in the last rays of the day's sun. Some Colonel had "ordered" him to proceed north by northwest for seventy-five miles to the "permanent coalition encampment" for processing as a displaced American citizen. They had been provided with enough food and water for three days. They also informed them that there would be no other aid. This was a one-time deal. Take it or leave it.

Andrew shook his head and drew in a long breath of dry air. He didn't like it at all. He wasn't in the army, nor was he violating any laws. He'd gotten a work visa to enter Saudi Arabia when he went to work for the Facility. Of course that would probably be revoked by now, so maybe he was breaking a law or two. Still, why would they care if he died in the desert?

He grimaced as another cramp wracked his stomach. Either the electrolyte solution or the salt capsules they'd both taken to help replenish their body wasn't sitting well. As the cramp passed, Andrew dismissed it.

Dinking so much of the concentrated solution on an empty stomach hadn't been smart. The Meals Ready to Eat, or MREs as the army called them, weren't much better either.

A hand went to the letter in his pocket. Taking it out, he unfolded it. Laying it in his palm, he ran a finger across the subtle indentations made by the typewriter. His mind followed the letters, putting them with what Malika had read to him. When he finished, his fingers dropped down to a new line a few spaces from the body of the letter. There was a single line of text that he couldn't make out. There were nineteen distinct words that Malika had left off. There was a long sentence and a very short one containing only three words.

What could they have said? Why didn't she read it to him? They would know that he was blind and that she'd be the one reading the letter. Were they orders of some sort?

Andrew sighed as he faced the desert, allowing the cool wind to blow over him, not wanting to believe what his mind was telling him.

Shaking his head, he folded the letter and slid it back in his pocket. What did they say? Was Malika working with the Americans? If she was, it might explain some things. But why?

He shook his head and crawled back into the tent, dusting the sand from his bare feet at the entrance. He spread a blanket over Malika and gently crawled beneath it with her. A low moan came from the darkness as she pushed her back against him. A warm hand took his and wrapped it around her chest, holding it tightly to her body.

He felt his heartrate climb slightly as he settled in beside her, smiling. There was no denying that he had strong feelings for her, though it felt completely different than when he was with Samantha. So much of the love he felt in his college days had turned out to be lust and desire. Samantha was a beautiful young woman with an amazing body. He wanted to be with her, but also be seen with her. In the small, private medical school he'd attended the only thing that trumped being a shit-hot doctor was banging the girl that everyone else wanted.

This was different. He'd never seen Malika's face, but he knew she was beautiful in so many ways. Her strength and courage made her attractive. She was exotic; unlike any woman he'd ever met. She was a strong, independent woman who had chosen to be with him when it would have been easier for her to leave him.

Though his mind still badgered him with questions, he decided not to dwell on them right now. Just a few hours ago they were very near death and had gotten a reprieve. There was nothing he could do now.

It's just the dehydration, he told himself. And the stress. You're not thinking clearly. Don't make a mountain out of a molehill.

The tension slowly began to seep from his body as he settled beside Malika. It didn't matter why the army had dropped the water. All that mattered was that they weren't going to die. Not tonight anyway

Lying in the darkness next to Malika, he listened to the steady rhythm of her breathing until it coaxed his tired body back into a deep sleep.

"Have you made a decision?" Malika asked Andrew, shoving the tent into her pack.

"Is there an option?"

"The letter from the army..." Malika's voice trailed off, swept away by a gust of wind.

"I'm sure you know, but I am not in the United States Army. I appreciate the food and water, but I don't have to follow orders."

"Did you not consider it?" she asked as she heaved the pack onto her back.

"Not even for a minute." Andrew slung three of the quart-sized flasks around his neck and slid his arm through the cord. He loaded his own pack onto his back and then shouldered the M-16.

He stood, listening to the wind and Malika's silence. "Look, I know you're worried about me going back to the Facility. To be honest, I am too, but I have to do this."

"For what?" Malika asked. "For who? For your dead wife? Your son?"

"Does it matter?"

"Yes. It matters to me." Malika stomped across the sand and laid her hand on his chest. "Andrew, I am sorry for what they did to you. They deserve to die a thousand horrible deaths, but I do not think you can bring this about."

Andrew stood in silence, absorbing the pleading of her voice. He'd spent so many hours thinking about his revenge; about wiping that smug look off Savon's face. Every day he was left to stagger around the

Facility, every hour he spent wandering the desert had been devoted to one mission. Every cold, hungry night had been spent plotting revenge on him.

"I love you, Andrew. I have come to know this. Because I love you, I say this is a foolish thing. They will kill you. They will kill us both."

"You don't have to come."

"Am I to just walk away? To leave you in the desert?"

"Malika," Andrew cradled her face in his hand. "You are an amazing woman and there is nothing more I would like than to spend the rest of my life growing old with you."

She took his hand and kissed the palm. "Let us do that, together."

"We can't." Andrew pulled his hand from hers. "They will not allow it. Don't you see that? Those agents were probably his agents. You don't understand this man. He's unlike anyone you've ever met."

"All countries have men like this."

"Maybe men just as crazy, but not with his resources. Alain Savon is not just a maniac. He's a maniac with millions of dollars at his disposal, billions maybe." Andrew shook his head in frustration. "They took my family, my freedom. They invaded my body and stole my eyes. They've left me with a lifetime of nightmares already.

They will look for us and they will find us. Then, they will torture, rape, and kill you in front of me and then lock me away to relive it for the rest of my life. The only way I will ever have any peace is if I know he is dead."

"You do not know this. Those agents could have been sent from a dozen places; a hundred. You do not know how this country is. There are spies and agents and soldiers and bad men everywhere. My country has been at war my whole life. People bomb and kill and shoot everyone. There is no one to be trusted."

"My point exactly."

"What do you say?"

"Nothing." Andrew waved his hands dismissively. "Just that people will know us, and they will tell, for a price. We will never be safe."

"This is not what you mean." She grabbed his arm as he tried to walk past. "Do you say that you care for me, but you do not trust me?"

"No." Andrew turned and faced her. "I don't know anything. I do care for you, Malika. Probably more than I even realize."

"But do you trust me?"

Andrew lifted his hands and let them drop. "Look. We're still tired and dehydrated. I didn't sleep well until late in the night. I have a lot on my mind."

"And I do not?"

"I know you do. Look, I'm sorry. Okay. I do trust you."

"You sound like the ass of a mule."

"What does that even mean?"

"It means I do not believe you. If you want to go to this place and have us both die, then we will go. It does not matter to me. Wherever I go I am a dead woman anyway." She pushed past him and started walking.

"That is not the direction." Andrew called. "We need to go more due west."

"I do not have a compass."

"Turn to your left a little then." Andrew began walking, following the sounds of her angry strides. "Do you intend to walk so fast? There are still a few hours of sun left. We should take it easy."

"If you are in a hurry to die then let us get it over with."

Andrew pushed the straps of the pack off his shoulders and let it drop to the ground. He was ready for a rest and a meal. Keeping up with Malika's torrid pace across the desert sand was difficult. Doing it in silence was miserable.

She spoke only a few words to him since they left camp late in the afternoon, and it was now close to midnight. They'd covered roughly eighteen miles and his back ached from hauling the pack up and down the dunes.

He lifted the canteen to his lips and swallowed the tepid solution eagerly. It tasted of salt and vitamins, but he was glad to have it.

Screwing the metal cap back on, he asked Malika if he could help with anything.

"I am capable of preparing food. Perhaps you would rather do it, so I do not poison you."

"Really? That's how you're going to be?"

"I behave the way I am treated, Doctor."

Andrew sighed and shook his head. "I said I trust you."

"And I said that I do not believe you."

Andrew sat on the sand and leaned on the pack he'd been carrying, crossing his legs at the ankles. "Well, actually you said I sound like the ass of a mule."

Malika grunted, mumbling in Arabic under her breath.

"I'm sorry." Andrew laid back and interlaced his fingers behind his head. "What do you want me to say?"

"I cannot tell you what to say." Malika walked up to Andrew and placed an MRE on his lap.

Moving quickly, Andrew leaned forward and grabbed her wrist. "I'm sorry. Can't we even talk about it?"

"What is there to say?"

"I don't know." Andrew put the meal aside and stood. "You tell me."

"Why do you not trust me?" she asked. "Because I am Yemini? Because I am ignorant? Because I come from a small village? A woman? Why?" Malika snatched her hand from his and strode away.

"This is why," Andrew said removing the letter from his breast pocket. He unfolded it and held it before him in a fist. "What does it say?"

"I told you what it said. I told you that I do not read English good, but I did my best."

"I know you said you read it, but it's a typed letter. Probably typed on an old army-issued typewriter. Every keystroke leaves a slight indentation on the paper. I felt it last night when I couldn't sleep. There is more on this letter than you said."

"That?" she asked, her voice catching slightly. "That is why you do not trust me?"

"I just want to know what it says, Malika." Her breath caught in her throat. "Please," he said, his voice softer now.

"The letter says everything that I told you. But you are right, there is more." Malika wiped a tear from her cheek. "I should have told you. I am sorry."

Andrew went to the sound of her voice, his anger lost on the wind. "What does it say?"

"You must know this?"

"Yes."

"Very well. It says 'If you are the native female traveling with Doctor Harkins, we make no offer of asylum. Do not ask.' Are you happy now? Now we both know what your people think of me."

Andrew reached out and found her, pulling her to him. Her body tensed, resisting momentarily, but finally allowed him to embrace her.

"Freaking assholes," he muttered. "I'm so sorry."

"This this how they see me? How they see us all?" she asked quietly.

"We're in Saudi now and so is the camp. I'm guessing the locals don't like your people."

"They do not *know* my people. That is why it is so easy to destroy us. In the west, the Yemeni people are slaughtered fighting bombs with rocks and sticks. And here, your American soldiers would have you leave me in the desert to die like a dog."

"I'm sorry." Andrew stroked her hair as she lay against his chest.

"How can people be this way to others? Are we so far apart? So different?"

Andrew shook his head, searching for an answer he didn't have. "I don't know."

"If you were to go to the soldiers, I was going to sneak away in the night when we got close enough to the base that you could find it alone."

He sighed. "Well, looks like I made the right decision."

"You have made a fool's decision, Andrew."

"I think we've clearly established that I am a fool, and a donkey's ass."

"Perhaps just a fool." Her smile faded. "I know that you are afraid. Not only of the bad men you feel you must fight."

"I'm more afraid of losing you than fighting them."

"Then we are together. I have fought many bad men, but I have loved only one."

"He was a lucky guy."

Malika shook her head, a dry smile on her lips. "Do all Americans make jokes so much at bad times?"

"Not really. Just the ruggedly handsome ones."

Malika put his arms around her waist. "No more jokes. Stop talking and kiss me."

Thirteen

Malika stood atop the dune, shielding her eyes from the sun as she stared toward the eastern horizon. The wind had picked up considerably since midday when it woke her buffeting the walls of their tent. There was no sign of a storm, but that was no guarantee one wouldn't come.

She shook her head. Something bad was on its way.

Lifting the binoculars to her eyes, she scanned the dry wadi she and Andrew had passed through just before dawn. She then swept her view across the sand until she faced west. Sand spread out before her all the way to the horizon, creating a pale ocean.

Her lips parted in a smile when she saw the clump of dark green vegetation less than two kilometers away. It would be nice to bathe in a pool and finally clean herself. Dropping the binoculars to her chest, she hurried down the side of the dune toward the small gravel plain at its feet.

"Andrew," she said. "There is a wahah."

"A what?" he asked, sitting up quickly, expecting trouble.

"A pool, a wahah. How you say, oasis?"

"Really?" Andrew smiled. "Awesome. Where?"

"A few kilometers away. To the west."

Andrew nodded. "That has to be it. That's the one."

"This is good, no?" Malika asked.

He grabbed her cheeks, pulled her to him, and kissed her lips. "It is wonderful."

"Come."

Malika led Andrew up the dune and fell to her knees. "It is not big. About half a kilometer long, but there are trees and plants. I cannot tell if there are others there."

"We should wait until it's dark before we go, just in case. We are not very far from the Facility. There were a few people who use it from time to time."

"Yes, perhaps..." Malika said as her smile faded. "...that is best."

Andrew turned his face toward the sun. "It will be dark in a few hours. We should start packing and eat so we can set out when the sun goes down."

Malika stopped suddenly when the beam of her flashlight fell on the bloated corpse.

"I'm guessing you found the body," Andrew said, stopping just behind her.

Malika turned her back on the scene with her hand clasped over her nose and mouth. Andrew followed her back to the edge of the desert.

"I told you there would be a body."

"You said that it was months old." She took a few more steps into the sand. "That thing looks like it is only weeks old."

"I told you I killed a man here, and that there would probably be a body. I didn't expect Savon and his group would care enough to come to get him. Guess I was right."

"Yes. You were right."

Andrew joined her, wrapping one arm around her shoulders. "I know it's unpleasant, but I need you to examine the scene; to figure out if any bodily fluids have contaminated the pool. We need the water." Andrew gave her a squeeze. "And a bath would do us both some good."

Malika shook her head. "I still smell it from here."

"I know, but we need the water."

Malika sighed heavily and shook her head. "I know this."

"If I could do it myself I would."

"I know this too, yet it is me that will see this dead man." Malika clamped one hand over her mouth and carefully followed the beam of light back through the undergrowth of desert palms. As she broke into the clearing, she stopped again, scanning the area around the body,

188

careful not to shine the light directly on the swarm of flies that covered the discolored face of what was left of Daniel Souter.

"The most important thing to look at is the area between the body and the pool. Check the sand good for dark areas that might have leeched into the water."

"I do not see anything," she said through her hand. "The sand around him is very dark, but that is all."

"Good," Andrew said. "The water should be fine. Good thing it doesn't rain much this time of year."

"Yes," Malika said flatly, pushing past Andrew. Once out in the desert and upwind of the body, she bent and put her hands on her knees. She wretched twice and vomited on the sand. She moaned and kicked sand over the mess, covering the remains of the MRE and the tiny microchip without noticing.

"Thank you," he said, putting a hand on her back. "I know it was unpleasant."

"Unpleasant?" she asked over her shoulder. "That is more than unpleasant for so many reasons."

"I know," Andrew said, guilt hanging in his voice. He wanted to explain that he was pressed for time; that he wasn't equipped to dig a grave. That he never planned on anyone else seeing what he'd done, much less anyone he cared about. He wanted to say all these things, but he didn't.

"I cannot sleep here tonight. I will have bad dreams. And the smell is very bad."

"Okay, fair enough. We can fill our flasks and wash up. Then we'll go."

Malika looked back into the darkened oasis and shook her head. When she looked back at Andrew, her brow furrowed.

"How did you kill him?" she asked quietly, pushing a stray lock of hair from her face.

"I hit him with a big rock. Why? Does it matter?"

"I don't know." Malika pulled free of his hand and took a few steps into the desert.

Andrew paused for a moment, then went after her. "You realize that I had to. Don't you?"

Malika shrugged, her back to Andrew. "It is bad to see a person that has..." she trailed off as a gust of wind tore at her hair. "Do you think the two agents look like this one?

"If someone didn't come for them, they probably will."

"It is strange to see someone that has not been buried. Their souls must be lost."

"I don't think old Souter had one. He wasn't a pleasant man in the least."

"I am sure, but it is not our place to judge him in death."

"Do you wish that he'd killed me? Because one of us was going to die." Andrew approached her from behind, putting his hands on her shoulders. "Do you think I wanted to kill him?"

"He worked for the place you hate. You want to kill that man. Did you not want to kill this one as well?"

"Does it matter?"

Malika sighed. "It should, but it does not. I know you said he was a bad man, but are not we all bad people to someone?"

Andrew shrugged. "I suppose you're right. It depends on what book you're reading, I guess."

Malika shook her head. "I have seen dead men before. I have watched men die. I stabbed my husband to death, but I did not see them after. They were not left to rot out in the open."

"You'll forgive me for not giving him a proper Christian burial, but I don't think he was a Christian anyway, or Muslim, or anything else for that matter."

Malika shook her head and sighed as she looked at the man she loved. "It was so bad to see."

Andrew pulled her to him and stroked her hair. "I know," he sighed. "Look, I'm not proud of the way things have happened. I'm not a killer; some wild assassin. Before I came here, I was a surgeon. I had a great life. Nice home, great job. I was a freaking star at the hospital. At least I thought I was. I helped people. I made people's lives better."

He sighed over her shoulder as another gust of wind blew in his face. "I never intended to kill anyone. I used to help people. I was a good guy…" He paused for a moment, examining his own words. He *was* a good guy, but what was he now?

Malika hugged him. "The enemies in our hearts can be easily defeated. It is the enemies in our minds that we lose to."

Andrew grimaced as he embraced her. There were at least five bodies in his wake, not counting any of the guards he might have personally killed, and of course, Malika's own father.

How did it all come to this? he asked himself. Six, maybe eight, lives taken by his own hands. Hands that were always meant to save lives. Hands that held his newborn son. Hands that slid a diamond ring on Samantha's smooth, demure finger. Hands that he used to clasp before him in prayer, at least occasionally.

Andrew pushed the thoughts away. The past was irrelevant now. He wasn't at his fancy hospital or in his nice home. He was in the desert and had work to do. "We better do what we have to do and get a camp set up." He lifted his face to the east as a steady wind blew through his hair. "Is it just me or has the wind been picking up lately?"

"It is not you. I too have noticed this."

"Will there be a storm?"

"I do not know, but we will soon." She stared across the darkened land. "Let us pray not."

Wind buffeted the side of the tent with a steady stream of punches that strained the thin fiberglass poles supporting the fabric. The high-pitched sound of sand being whipped across the rayon screamed of impending trouble, making sleep almost impossible.

The dawn brought stronger winds and the winds brought more airborne sand. They set up the tent in the shallow dip of two adjoining dunes with hopes of sparing themselves the worst of the gusts, which continued to increase in speed and frequency. Travel today would be out of the question, a fact that was both troubling and reassuring. They couldn't go far, but neither could anyone from Savon's group. They were close to the Facility, he knew, but finding it would take some work.

Andrew rolled onto his back, allowing his arm to fall over the space where Malika should have been lying. It was empty, just as he knew it would be. His internal clock had begun to count when she got up and left the tent almost twenty minutes ago. At first, he thought that she was going to relieve herself but as time passed her absence became more concerning.

A quick check of the small tent told him that the only thing missing was the small pack of personal items she always carried. All the water flasks were accounted for, so she was coming back. But what would keep her out in such bad conditions?

Andrew sat up with a heavy moan. Drumming his fingers on his thigh, he sat and listened to the howl of the wind. It would take a lot to keep a person out in such drastic conditions. He considered the possibility that Malika was taking care of some female issues. Under normal circumstances, he could smell the subtle difference in pheromones a woman put off during her monthly cycle, but these weren't normal conditions.

It was possible. The wind gusted again, slamming against the side of the tent, and reigniting his doubt. Pushing a hand through his hair, he sighed heavily. He told himself that she hadn't done anything to earn his mistrust, that she'd put herself in danger right beside him. Still, his mind persisted. What would keep her out in a wind like this?

Crawling to the edge of the tent, he poked his head outside and was met with a face full of stinging sand. He clambered out of the tent, clearing the sand from his face and beard only to collect more than he cleared.

Outside of the safe confines of the tent, there was nothing but the high-pitched wail of the wind as it swept past his ears in a steady blow. Finding anyone in these conditions would be impossible, especially for a man who couldn't see. He staggered around the tent and urinated with his back to the wind.

Once finished, he cupped his hands around his mouth and called out for Malika. He listened for a reply but only heard the scream of the wind. He tried again, getting the same result. Shaking his head, he staggered back to the tent and crawled inside.

He was halfway through his meal of a power bar and lukewarm water when Malika crawled back into the tent.

"Where were you?" he asked.

"I could not sleep so I looked around." Malika opened one of the flasks and had a long drink. "You are worried?"

Andrew shrugged. "I just didn't know where you'd gone to. I called for you."

"The wind is high," she said, removing her headdress and shaking the sand out of it. "I could not have heard you if you were beside me."

Andrew chewed the last bite of the bland food and washed it down with water. "Did you find anything?"

"I do not know. I think I may have seen something to the west. A few kilometers away, maybe more. It is hard to tell with all the sand in the air."

"Do these things last long?" he asked. "These sand storms."

Malika laughed. "This is not a sandstorm. It is just high winds. I hope that it does not become a storm, but I fear that it will. Soon."

"What do we do if it does?"

"There is nothing we can do. It is best to be inside a strong place."

"I'm guessing this tent doesn't qualify as a sturdy building."

"No. It does not."

"Well, I guess we're screwed if it gets worse." Andrew scratched his beard, dislodging more sand.

"One can survive a sandstorm, but it is not pleasant. We could be buried alive and choke to death. I do not know. It depends on the storm."

"What choice do we have? The only sturdy structure for a hundred miles is the Facility, which I doubt we could find even if we wanted to. And to be honest, I'd rather take my chances out here."

"You have never been in a sandstorm."

Andrew shook his head. "We don't get those in Pennsylvania."

"It is a horrible thing. You cannot see. The sun is completely gone. The sand hurts when it hits you. Your eyes will fill with sand, your ears, your mouth. It is difficult to breathe."

"What are you saying?"

"I am preparing you for what may come. It is not easy."

"You mentioned that." Andrew took another drink from the flask. His mouth suddenly felt dry. There was no choice to make. They would have to ride the storm out in the tent and hope for the best.

Malika wiped her eyes, clearing sand out of the left one. She rubbed it between her fingers before flicking it away.

"What if he went back to the oasis?" Andrew suggested. "The trees and undergrowth surely will help to shield us."

"If we were there now it would be a good thing. But it is a day's walk from here, maybe more in these conditions. We would never make it. If we were caught without even the tent, we would surely be killed."

"What do we do?" Andrew asked.

"When I was looking, I found a small rock mound and nothing else. There is nowhere to hide. These hills will block the direct wind from us, but they too will be blown into the air if the storm is powerful enough, but it is all we have."

"So we just stay put?"

"We have no choice." As if on cue the wind gusted against the side of the tent, bowing it inward. It swirled into the open end, dumping a layer of sand over everything in the tent, including them. "I'm afraid it is already too late, if even we had a place to go."

Moving quickly, Malika shoved their packs to one end of the tent to form a short wall. Grabbing the rifles, she stabbed the barrels into the bottom of the tent and wedged their butts against the packs. Grabbing Andrew, she pulled him into the lee behind the packs and laid down beside him.

"This is the best we can do. Hold onto the packs so they do not blow away or become lost."

Andrew could barely hear her over the roar of the wind, but he figured it out quickly when Malika pushed his hands through the harness on the pack. Prone on the floor of the tent, he tucked his face into the crook of his arm and waited for the worst.

Tucked in close to Malika, he could feel her heart pounding. She was scared, and so was he. If her mouth hadn't been against his ear, it would have been impossible to hear her say that she loved him over the wind, now one continuous roar.

The low half-circle tent shook violently as the wind beat against it, trying to rip it from the ground. He heard Malika's voice but couldn't hear what she was saying.

"What?" he screamed, raising his face from the shelter of his arm. Sand pelted him from every direction, flying into his ears and mouth. He buried his face again without getting a reply.

As the storm fell on them, the intensity of the winds rose well beyond anything he'd imagined. Suddenly, there was weight upon his back. Releasing the pack, he put an arm around Malika just as the tent began to bow in on them. Sand was washing across his body like waves in an ocean, snaking its way into his ears, his mouth. The air was hot and full of dust making it harder to breathe. His body coughed involuntarily, and he drew in a mouthful of sand. More sand filtered in with each movement.

A sharp snapping noise sliced through the roar of the wind as the thin fiberglass supports finally succumbed to the sand. It collapsed on them at once, burying them beneath the sand.

"We have to get from under this!" Malika yelled into his ear as she struggled beside him.

Andrew got his hands beneath him and pushed upward against the heavy load. Sand streamed down around his neck and filled the back of his shirt as he lifted the top of the tent. Malika's body slithered past him toward the edge of the tent, then he followed.

Nothing in his life could have prepared for the hell that awaited him outside the tent. Hot sand inundated him instantly, obliterating any of the senses he relied on. The only sound was the roar of the wind. The only smell was of hot sand. There was no sense of direction to be had, no sun or shade. There was only sand and wind, pain, and fear.

He cried out for Malika, but his mouth was suddenly full of sand. Waving his arms before him, he tried to walk, but the wind and the sand was like a wall. He slipped and went tumbling. Clawing the ground as he fell returned only fistfuls of hot, fine sand.

In the chaos, he heard something that might have been Malika's voice, but couldn't be sure. He tried to stand but was pushed backwards. Losing his footing on the shifting sand, he tumbled further down the slope.

When he finally came to a stop, he called out again for Malika, but heard nothing but the all-consuming roar of the storm. He crawled toward where the voice might have been, but it was useless. The wind battered his body filling every pocket, every orifice with sand until he collapsed.

He coughed to clear his lungs, but it was a vain effort. Every breath brought a new wave of pain until his lungs burned. Finally, out of desperation, he hid his face in the crook of his arm and laid still, allowing the sand to pile all around him. He was at the mercy of the storm. There was nothing else he could do.

Andrew moaned into the crook of his arm as he thought of Malika suffering the same fate as him. There was no way to know where she was, or if she was even still alive. In the storm there was nothing. No East. No West. Only wind and sand and both were furious.

"I'm sorry," he moaned into the crook of his arm. The only reply that came was from the storm as it raged overhead in one loud, all-encompassing primal scream that drowned out everything else in the world.

Fourteen

Pain in her left arm pulled Malika toward a gentle consciousness. Her heavy eyelids opened only a sliver, allowing a view of the I.V. port. She stared at it questioningly for a moment then followed the thin tubing along the bed and up to a bag hanging on a metal pole.

The medical terminology on the bag meant nothing to her, except that it was in English. Hospital, she thought hazily. That's good. She closed her eyes again and began to drift back toward sleep.

In the darkness of her mind, memories began to take shape. There was a storm. The winds were higher than she'd ever known. She was trapped. They were trapped in the storm.

She gasped, jolted from her stupor by the memory of the sandstorm. She looked down at the light blue hospital gown covering her body with alarm. Everything was gone. The pack, their guns, everything. All gone. She was defenseless and had no clue where she was.

The memory of getting separated from Andrew swam out of the haze that filled her mind. She called to him, but the wind and the storm enveloped her. She searched in the storm until her eyes filled with sand. Once blinded, she began to crawl, still calling for him, but never found him.

The memory of her lungs becoming clogged by the dust made her cough. She took a deep breath of clean, filtered air and coughed again. Her lungs still felt heavy but at least she could breathe.

Putting a hand on the bed to steady herself, she found sand on the crisp sheets and sighed tiredly. She wanted to sleep so badly but knew she couldn't.

Looking around the room, she found only beige walls that were bare except for a few paper signs held up with clear tape. The closest to her was a fire evacuation map, next to it was a sign reminding people to "wash in-wash out" with a picture of a pair of soapy hands beneath a running faucet. Across the room, a small alcove held a sink but no mirror. A roll of paper towels hung on the wall next to it. Just beyond that was a door with the silhouette of a man and a woman within a small black sign. A bathroom.

Her eyes moved to a small, metal, rolling stool beneath a similarly plain shelf that could be used as a desk. There was no other furniture in the small room except for the bed she currently sat on. The room had no windows and only one large, wooden door.

She rubbed her eyes and removed a few grains of sand from the corners of each. She was in a hospital, but where? Was this the Facility that Andrew talked about? Andrew! Her heart leapt into her throat as her mind wound its way back to him. Where was he? Was he alive? Did he survive the storm? Did they find him as well?

She stood on uneasy legs and walked the length of the tubing and came back to the bed. She looked around nervously, fear rising in her chest. There was nothing in the room that could be used as a weapon if she needed one.

She went to the metal pole connected to the bed that supported the I.V. bag. She worked it back and forth with the hope of freeing it. It gave slightly but did not come free. Looking at the connection, she found three rivets holding it in place.

She removed the bag from the pole and tossed it on the bed, then removed the port from her arm. Taking up a position at the end of the bed, she grasped it with both hands and pulled on the pole. It bent toward her with a groan but held. Working it back and forth, she kept an eye on the door. Pushing, then pulling on the pole repeatedly, she finally broke it free.

Smiling triumphantly, she held the pole in her hands. It was hollow and light, but it would serve as a good club. Laying it on the bed, she went to the desk and kneeled before it, examining the stool.

When the door suddenly opened, she shoved the stool towards it and scurried back around the bed. Grabbing the I.V. pole, she stood with it before her, her bare feet planted firmly against an assault. She was ready to fight.

The door stopped momentarily when it struck the stool, then opened slowly. Malika surveyed the man cautiously as he stepped through the crack in the door, accompanied by a woman in pale blue scrubs, clutching a clipboard to her chest.

The white lab coat he wore hung open, revealing a pair of khaki slacks and a collared, dark green shirt. A stethoscope hung loosely around his neck.

The look of surprise in his piercing blue eyes turned quickly to empathy as he surveyed the scene. He offered her a warm smile. "It's okay," he said, holding his hands before him. "No one's going to hurt you."

Malika lowered the pole to her waist but didn't relax. "Who are you? Where am I?"

"It's okay," the man said again. "We're here to help you." He stepped further into the room and allowed the nurse space to join him. "I'm Doctor Alain Savon, this is Amaya Cohen, she is a registered nurse. We're here to help you."

Malika looked from the doctor, with his white hair and tanned skin, to the darker-complected woman beside him, then back to the doctor. He met her gaze with a warm, welcoming smile and a reassuring nod.

"Savon?" Malika asked. The makeshift weapon in her hands slowly crept higher.

"Yes, Doctor Alain Savon. I'm the head of medical studies here."

"And where is here?" Malika asked.

"My dear, you are at the Al Saadian Biotechnical Research Facility and a guest of Mohammad bin Saadian, Crown Prince of Arabia. I serve at his pleasure, as we all do."

Malika eyed him suspiciously. "How did I get here? Where are my things?"

"I will be happy to answer all of your questions, but may I begin my examination?"

"I am fine. I would like answers to my questions."

The doctor shrugged as he crossed the room. He sat on the edge of the bed, casually brushing sand onto the floor. "A team of doctors was returning from a medical jaunt. As part of our agreement with the prince, we provide periodic medical visits to several local villages in the area. They noticed the dust storm coming and were racing back here when they saw you. The driver said he almost ran over you in the chaos. You were barely breathing, raving uncontrollably, and covered in sand."

"They brought you here and we began a long and tedious process of restoring you back to health." He looked briefly at the nurse then back to Malika. "And from the looks of things we did a good job of it."

"Where is Andrew?"

"Andrew? We found no one else. Was there someone with you?" The doctor stood, exchanging a nervous look with the nurse.

"Yes. A man. His name is Andrew." she almost spoke his last name but decided not to. "He is Andrew, and I was his guide."

"Good lord." The doctor turned to the nurse. "Alert the crew that someone else is out there, start the search where they found her. Hurry. Go!"

The nurse darted out of the room without saying a word.

"I'm so sorry. In the confusion of the storm the team found you and rushed back here. It was a very dangerous situation, as I'm sure you're aware of."

"Yes, I know." Malika lowered her weapon, allowing the top end to rest on the floor. "The storm took us by surprise."

"Didn't you hear any of the reports on the radio? They said it was one of the worst storms on record. Whole villages were buried."

"Our radio was broken," she lied.

"It's been days and we've still not dug out completely. We're operating now on generator back up power. Our solar arrays were heavily damaged."

"Days?"

"I'm afraid so. We had to keep you heavily sedated until we were sure you were going to be able to breathe on your own. You were intubated for quite a while."

"That is what is wrong with me? Medicines?" she asked.

Alain smiled. "That is what saved you. You were very near death when we found you."

"I am aware of that."

"I feel sorry for you two. It must have been very difficult and very frightening."

"It was. We had a tent, but it collapsed beneath the weight of the sand. Then we got separated."

"That is unfortunate. I'm sorry."

"Will they find him?" Malika asked, her thoughts now on Andrew.

"I don't know. For now let's remain optimistic, shall we? He may have found a cave or a place to shelter."

"I hope so."

"You survived, didn't you? I don't see why he might not have." The doctor motioned her over then patted the bed. "Either way you need to be examined. I've been very concerned about pneumonia with all the sand you inhaled."

"I am fine. I would rather wait until we find Andrew."

"Andrew?" the doctor asked. "Do you mean Doctor Andrew Harkins?"

"Perhaps. Perhaps not. Why do you ask?"

The doctor sighed heavily and massaged the bridge of his nose with his thumb and index finger. "Because I know him."

"Yes," Malika replied. "He told me all about you." She lifted the pole again.

"Oh, I wouldn't be surprised if he did." He looked up at Malika, his face now a mask of sadness. "Andy isn't well and hasn't been well for quite a while now."

"What do you mean?"

"Andy came here five, maybe six years ago. He had an exemplary resume. Almost too good to be true. He graduated at the top of his class, took a job at Mercy-General just outside of Philadelphia in the United States. Rave reviews from his superiors and co-workers. Steady home life. He was married with a son in kindergarten. He was smart and good looking. He had everything. The world on a string, so to speak."

Malika watched the doctor shake his head. So far everything he said was true, or at least matched when Andrew had told her.

"When we looked at him, on paper, he was perfect."

"On paper?"

"Yes, his dossier was immaculate, as I've said. Not even so much as a parking ticket. We flew him here and met with him. He checked all the boxes, said all the right things, did all the right things. So we offered him a job in our program."

"Yes. He spoke of your program."

The doctor shook his head again, offering another sad smile. "Our program here is very complicated work, but basically, we do research. We run experiments in the lab and look for cures for some of the worst diseases known to man. Ebola is our main concern right now. You've undoubtably heard of the outbreak in sub-Saharan Africa? Kenya has been stricken very badly."

"I have not heard, nor do I want to hear. I am from a small village. There is enough there to worry about."

The doctor nodded knowingly. "Several life-saving vaccines were discovered in this very lab. We serve as the de facto humanitarian arm of Prince Mohammad bin Salam. He is a very generous man."

"Perhaps, but what does any of this have to do with Andrew?"

"Ah, yes. Andy. Please forgive my rambling. Andy was a gifted surgeon. His duties here were more of a secondary line of innovation. He was in our bio-engineering department. He worked on the integration of ocular prosthetic devices."

"What does that mean?" Malika lowered the weapon again.

"I'm sure you've seen people who have lost limbs, yes?"

"Too many. My country has been at war my whole life."

"You are Yemeni?"

"I am from the village of Sayf Alsalam. My father was Abd-El-Kader."

"Tragic," he said shaking his head. "Yemen is such a beautiful country."

"On that we can agree." Malika relaxed her stance slightly. "I have seen many people who have been hurt or crippled in war."

"Well, Andy was working on better integrating prosthesis to the human body. In his instance, helping to restore sight. Quite genius, really. Our hope is to make a seamless transition from human to prosthesis in hopes of allowing people to lead richer, fuller lives after catastrophic injuries that result in loss of sight. Giving a man the ability to walk again or returning the ability to use a prosthetic arm to hug his children is wonderful. But restoring sight to the blind. Ahh. That would be our gift to all of humanity."

"Very noble."

"Won't you please join me?" The doctor patted the bed beside him.

Malika took a few tentative steps forward but stopped when the doctor stood.

"No worries, my dear, I'm just giving you room. The doctor usually stands, and the patient usually sits." A broad smile revealed his perfect teeth. "Please, you've nothing to worry about. You can even keep your...weapon."

Malika brought the pole with her. Leaning it against the wall, she sat on the edge of the bed and watched the doctor remove the stethoscope from around his neck.

"Do you mind?" he asked as he slipped the ports into his ears. He kept his eyes on hers as he rubbed the bell of the stethoscope against the palm of his hand. "These things are always so cold."

She nodded slightly but remained tense; ready to fend off an attack.

"Deep breath," he said, pressing it to her chest.

Malika complied and allowed him to listen to her lungs.

"Andy was truly gifted. He's a remarkable doctor."

"I did not know he was a doctor," Malika lied.

"He was. Now, deep breath." He moved the stethoscope to her back. "I worry about him. I do so hope they find him in time."

"As do I."

"If you don't mind me asking," the doctor moved his stethoscope to her back and asked her to take a deep breath. "How well do you know Andy?"

"Not well. He is blind, so I was his aide. His guide."

Savon stepped back from Malika and looked her in her eyes. "That's good. I really shouldn't be telling you this, but he's not my patient, per sea, so I will. Andy has syphilis."

"Syphilis?" Malika asked, eyeing the doctor with disbelief.

Savon took in the surprised look on her face and nodded. "Have you two been intimate?" he asked quietly as he hung the stethoscope around his neck.

"What? No." Malika shifted her weight on the bed. "I was his guide, not his wife."

Savon nodded. "Good. That's good." He pulled the stool over with his foot and sat on it. "Because if you had, you would almost certainly have it as well. It's bad, but we do have treatments."

Malika looked at the man before her. He seemed to be a caring, competent doctor; everything that Andrew said he wasn't. He didn't look like the monster Andrew described. On the contrary, he was quite handsome.

"Do you know what Syphilis is, ugh- I don't believe I even know your name."

"It's Malika."

"Good. Malika. That's a pretty name. It means 'queen' in your language, doesn't it? Quite fitting if you ask me."

Malika smiled. "My father always said it means princess, but it can also mean queen."

"Yes. I suppose so." Savon smiled. "I'm afraid that the prognosis is rather grim for Andy, however. I can print you out some information on it when we're back up to full power, but it is a nasty disease."

"It is gotten by laying with someone who has it, no?"

"There are other ways to contract it, but that is the most common." The doctor sighed and slumped on the stool. Picking absently at his manicured thumb nail. "We give thorough physical examinations to all our employees before they are allowed on campus. We are certain that neither he nor his wife had it when they got here."

"Could he have gotten it another way? Some accident?"

"It is possible, yes. If Andy came in direct contact with an open sore, maybe."

"Then that may be an explanation. Or his wife."

"All good theories. You are as smart as you are beautiful if you don't mind me saying so."

"Thank you," Malika said, smiling again as she dropped her gaze to her hands.

"But we looked into every angle. What we have here is considered a closed facility. It is necessary to do some of the research we do, you understand. We limit the number of people who come in and go out. It's all in the contract that our employees sign." The doctor stood. Going to the sink, he began washing his hands.

"Being a closed facility, any contagious situation is top priority. When Andy first began presenting symptoms, naturally we were concerned. We approached him about it, and he denied everything. He said he was just tired from working long hours. We were very worried."

Malika sat on the edge of the bed, suddenly invested in the conversation.

"As Andy was unwilling to consent to further tests and treatments, we went to his wife. She did test positive for syphilis, but she was at an earlier stage than Andy. She didn't have any symptoms yet. And his son was clear. Through whatever way he contracted it, he passed it to his wife, presumably through intercourse." Savon finished washing his hands and leaned against the sink as he dried them on a paper towel.

"Giving Andy the benefit of the doubt, the other doctors checked every village in the area. There were several men who also had the disease in various stages."

"Men?" Malika asked, her eyes wide in disbelief.

"Yes. But none of them had been treated by Andy, or anyone else for that matter. Men can deny their own medical symptoms for a long time, unfortunately. We don't like to admit when we're wrong, or sick."

Malika nodded in agreement.

"Our investigation did uncover a young woman who was in the later stages of the disease. Poor thing. We tried to get the village chieftain to allow us to treat her, but he wouldn't hear of it."

"What happened to the girl?"

"She was stoned to death for being a whore." Savon watched the surprise on Malika's face turn to outrage. "We did everything we could to save her. It was unfortunate, really, but our hands were tied."

"Yes. Many women find life to be 'unfortunate'."

"I've upset you," Savon crossed the room and put a hand on Malika's shoulder. "I just wanted to be forthcoming with you."

"I am fine, doctor. I thank you for telling me."

"There is more to tell, but I don't want to tire you. You've been through enough already." Savon turned to leave but Malika grabbed his arm.

"I am fine. Please, tell me the rest."

Savon pursed his lips as he stared into Malika's pleading eyes. "It can wait."

"No. Tell me, please."

Savon sighed and sat back down on the stool. "I will, but when I'm finished you must promise me that you will allow the nurse to put your I.V. back in. You are still dehydrated, and we've been giving you medicine to prevent pneumonia."

"I will agree."

"Okay. Well, the path of the contagion was apparent. Andy contracted it from the girl, by what means we can't speculate, but then he passed it to his wife. Her treatment was going well, until Andy found out. He was outraged at her and at us. Over the next few days he became increasingly agitated and withdrawn. I hated to see him like that." Savon shook his head, his face downcast.

"I believe he developed cerebral syphilis."

206

"What is that?" Malika asked.

"That's a later stage of the same disease. It begins attacking the nervous system. The brain. Andy began saying things that didn't make sense. He swore we were out to get him; that everyone was against him, even his own family. He accused his wife of having affairs. He became violent with a nurse. After that, my superiors demanded we send him out for treatment."

Savon leaned forward, resting his elbows on his knees, and looked down at his hands with a heavy sigh. "I just think that if I would have done more; handled things differently..." His words trailed off as he wiped a tear from the corner of his eye.

"I considered Andy a friend. We worked very closely on many projects. I respected him as a doctor and as a person. He was a good man; a good husband; a good father."

"What happened?" Malika asked.

"After the incident with the nurse, he barricaded himself in his living quarters. I don't really know what happened, but by the time security got to them he'd slit the throats of his wife and son and was in the process of gouging his own eyes out with his wife's nail file." Savon sighed again and ran both hands through his white hair, spun on the stool and stood. Going to the sink, he splashed water on his face and took several moments to compose himself before turning to face Malika again.

Malika recoiled slightly, wondering how it could be possible that the man she knew and loved could be capable of such things. Andrew had told her about his wife's murder at the hands of this very man, but that now seemed difficult to believe.

"I know this is a lot to process, and I am truly sorry."

Malika studied the grief on the man's face and shook her head. She wanted to believe both men but wondered if the truth lay between each of their stories.

"I am suddenly very tired," she said. "I think I would like to lie down." Malika leaned back on the bed. "Tell your nurse she can do what she needs to do."

"I am sorry." Savon crossed the room and laid a hand on Malika's arm. "I hope we can find him. If he's alive we can treat him, if he isn't..." Savon closed his eyes and shook his head. "No. We will find him, God willing." He patted Malika's arm and walked slowly out of the room.

Malika looked up at the plain white ceiling searching for answers. Why would the doctor lie? Why would Andrew? What if she had syphilis? That would tell her all she needed to know. She and Andrew had been together several times. If he had syphilis, she would have it as well.

"Yes," she whispered aloud. That was the cornerstone of Doctor Savon's whole tale. That would tell her who to believe.

A soft knock came at the door as it opened slowly. "Feeling better?" the nurse asked, poking her head inside.

"Yes, come in please. I must apologize for the way I acted. I must have seemed to be a crazy person."

"That's quite all right," the nurse said with a smile. "I imagine if I'd been out in that storm, I would probably be a little edgy myself." She crossed the room rolling a portable I.V. pole behind her.

"Was it a very bad storm?" Malika asked.

"Oh yes. It's the first one I've ever seen. I was freaking out. We lost the main power." The nurse shuttered. "And the sound of the wind. It was really something."

Malika nodded her agreement but said nothing as she watched the woman begin unpacking a new I.V. port.

"Little stick," she said and pushed the needle into Malika's vein. "There we go."

"You are good," she said, looking at the nurse's gentle features. "How long have you been a nurse?"

"Ten years," she answered. "I've been here four." She taped the port to Malika's arm and prepared a new bag of fluids.

"Do you like it here?"

"I do. Sometimes at first it bothered me. Being a closed facility and all. But you get used to it. I've got another year on my contract, and I haven't decided if I'm staying or not?"

"You can leave?"

"We can," Amaya answered with a laugh. "When your contract is up." She continued talking as she worked. "I've got four in. I gotta tell you though, I'll miss the money."

"The pay is much?"

"They pay very well. But the thing is that everything you need is here, so you really don't spend any of it. If you finish your contract and leave, you pretty much take five years' salary with you. Pretty sweet nest egg."

Malika nodded, watching the nurse attach the I.V. line to the port in her arm. "What is the medicine?"

"Just hydration fluids mostly. A few electrolyte balancers and some potassium. I have a dose of antibiotics that I'll have to put in through the port. The doctors ordered them to stave off pneumonia."

"Pneumonia? In the summer?"

The nurse smiled knowingly. "You inhaled a lot of dust and debris out there. Really no telling what. When you get those foreign bodies in your lungs, your body doesn't like it. It'll try to coat it with mucus to protect your lungs and eventually you end up with pneumonia." She patted Malika's leg. "It's just a precaution. If things look okay in a day or two, we can discontinue it."

"A day or two?" Malika asked. "How long do I have to stay?"

"Well," Amaya finished adjusting the flow valve on the tubing and looked at Malika. "You don't have to stay, but we're about a million miles from anywhere and we're still digging out from the storm. The plan was to transport you wherever you needed to go, but that won't happen for a while."

"So I could leave?"

"Yes, you could, but you'd have to walk. We don't even have a camel available." The nurse laughed loudly, proud of her own joke.

Malika settled back into the bed, resigning herself to the treatment. She did feel tired, and hungry.

"Can I get you anything?" Amaya asked as she cleaned the bed, stuffing the packaging into her pocket.

"I would like some food. I am hungry."

"Anything in particular? Doc said to make you as comfortable as possible."

"Some bread and cheese will be fine. Perhaps some fruit." Malika paused before deciding to ask her next question. "Do you like Doctor Savon?"

"Oh yes," she replied enthusiastically. "He's the best. He is incredibly smart. The best doctor I've ever worked with. And not hard on the eyes either, if you know what I mean."

Malika smiled with the nurse. It wasn't untrue.

"Don't you worry. I guarantee you that you're in the best place within a couple thousand miles. This place is top shelf all the way. You're in good hands."

"Uh," Malika began, catching the nurse as she opened the door. "What about tests. Medical tests?"

"Anything specific?"

"I don't know." Malika sighed and looked down at her hands, suddenly embarrassed. "I might need a test for syphilis."

The smile vanished from Amaya's face, her jaw drooping with her shoulders. "Oh sweetie," she said sadly. She walked back to the bed and patted Malika's arm. "Don't you worry about anything. I'll take care of everything."

Fifteen

Alain Savon walked down the same hallway he'd navigated a thousand times, but today his step had an extra spring in in. He shrugged the lab coat off his shoulders and handed it to Bailey. His new chief of security was following him closely.

"How long has he been awake?" Savon asked, not bothering to look at his companion.

"Almost two hours, sir. He's been raving like a lunatic since he woke up."

A crooked smile slid across Savon's face as he stopped suddenly in front of a metal door. "Good. I thought he might die and rob us of the pleasure of his company. The program running?"

"Yessir. Just like you wanted." Bailey pressed his thumb to a black screen next to the door and it came to life. He quickly entered a few commands and nodded. "It went silent ten minutes ago, sir."

"Good." Savon nodded as he rolled up the sleeves of his shirt. "That's all, Bailey."

"But sir, don't you want me to—"

"That is all." Savon looked over at his employee, causing him to shrink back a step. He turned back to the door and his smile returned. Bailey apologized and retreated a few steps.

Savon entered his personal code into the keyboard at the bottom of the screen. As soon as the seal on the door breached, he was greeted by a chorus of desperate, angry screams. The light from the hallway stretched into the darkened room, framing his shadow in a long rectangle of light on the floor.

He peered into the darkness, knowing who was there. Extending his right hand without looking he flipped the switch on the wall, flooding the room with light.

Savon stood in silence, surveying the man across the room. Dressed in dirty, olive-colored pants and a lighter green shirt, the man could have passed for a member of the countless village militias in the area. His hair was much longer than when he'd seen him last, and he had a full beard, but there was no doubt that it was Andrew Harkins. The man was curled into a fetal position, his hands clasped tightly over his ears.

Alain Savon's smile widened.

Since he'd awakened, Andy had been subjected to the voices of his wife and son. Intimate conversations, sexual adventures, and mundane complaint sessions that Samantha had registered were on the menu. Every moment of their private lives had been secretly recorded just in case a situation arose. A situation like this one.

"Welcome home, Doctor." Andrew tentatively pulled his hands from his ears and turned his head toward his voice.

"You!" Andrew growled. He leaped from the floor and ran toward Savon with his arms extended, his hands twisted into claws.

Savon stood motionless, his hands clasped behind his back, as Andrew sprinted toward him. His eyes followed Andrew when the restraints attached to his ankle reached their limits and sent him sprawling to the floor. Staring down at the man struggling against the restraint, Savon shook his head and sighed.

"Doctor Harkins, please, let me help you."

"I'll kill you, you crazy bastard! Where is she?" Andrew lunged at him again, pulling against the restraints.

"Who, Samantha? You know good and well where she is, Andy."

"You killed her, you maniac! And I'm going to kill you."

Savon sighed and shook his head. "Andy, I'm your friend. You are sick. Let us help you."

Andrew clenched his fists, his breath coming in angry pants. "I don't know what sort of game you're playing, but I'm not going to be part of it. You know who I'm talking about. Where is she?"

"Your traveling companion? Why would I know where she is?"

"Because you took her. She has to be here because I looked for her. I would have found her." Andrew pushed himself up from the floor.

"Do you mean in the storm? You and she were out in the worst sandstorm in recent history, and you blame me for what may have happened to her. You mean, you- a blind man- would have found someone in hundreds of square miles of desert. I don't think so, Andy. It's time you started taking responsibility for your own actions."

"Shut your lying mouth, you sorry excuse for a human being. You piece of crap. You know what happened. You have her and you're going to use her to get to me."

"Andy, look. Let us treat you. You have syphilis, cerebral syphilis to be exact. You're not thinking clearly. I don't blame you, Andy. You couldn't help it."

"So you think I'm just going to believe you, Savon? I know you. I know the head games you like to play. So what now? You try to convince me that you didn't rape and kill Samantha? That you didn't turn a maniac lose on my son. Is that it?" Andrew lunged at him but fell well short. "If you don't kill me right now, I will get free of this cable, and I'll kill you with my bare hands."

"Andy, we will have to treat you forcibly. It's for your own good, and that of the rest of the facility. You're sick. The storm might have been the best thing that happened to you. Now the board can declare a state of emergency and we can treat you. I just wish you had complied earlier. A lot of people could have been saved. Especially Samantha. Such a sweet woman. And your precious son."

Andrew's body began to shake as his anger boiled over. "You keep telling yourself that, Savon. You're forgetting that I'm not one of your yes men. I know you're full of crap and I'm going to do something about it." Andrew made another lunge at Savon but fell short and toppled to the floor.

He lay on the cold tile telling himself to calm down; that Savon was playing a game with him, and he was making it easy. There was no doubt that he also had Malika. The only unknown was what plan his sick mind had cooked up for them.

"You leave me no choice, my friend. I'm sorry it has come to this." Savon stepped closer, his eyes locked on Andrew's. "I'm doing this for the man that you once were, Andy. The man you are now is not the real you. I want my friend back."

"I was never your friend, Alain. I always knew you were a nutcase. You walk around and try to fool people, but I know. I've seen you at your worst. You are a tiny little man with a big ego. I won't play your game."

"There is no game, Andy." Savon flashed a grin as he knelt in front of Andrew. "Calling it a game would imply that there is a chance that you might win."

The two men stared into each other's eyes in an unblinking stare for a long time. Both knew the other was a formidable opponent. Both determined with a resolve that far surpassed an average man. They both knew that ultimately a showdown would happen, but neither was sure that they'd win.

Savon finally stood and went to the door. Sparing Andrew a last look as he lay on the floor, he flipped off the lights and closed the door behind him, sinking the room back into darkness.

Baily looked at him questioningly. "More?"

"Yes, Bailey. More. Give him two more hours and then an hour of complete silence. Repeat the cycle until further notice."

"Yessir." Baily began programming the keypad next to the door.

"No food or water until I say, and I'm sure it goes without saying, but no one goes in or out except me."

"Yessir. That's what I figured."

Savon paused, staring at his head of security for a moment, then walked away.

Malika woke suddenly, jolted from sleep by a vision of the dead body she'd seen in the desert oasis. She shook her head to clear it of the image, but it persisted. In the dream the empty eye sockets were pools of maggots, working and wriggling as they fed on the carrion. The man's face, covered in purple splotches, turned to look at her as the light from her flashlight fell on him. Maggots spilled onto the ground and began crawling toward her, leaving trails in the sand behind them.

A shudder ran through her as she sat up. Her hands washed over the hospital gown, finding it wet with sweat. She'd never had a dream so vivid, so real. It wasn't possible, but somehow, she could smell the corpse in the air around her.

Closing her eyes, she took a deep breath to calm herself. When she opened her eyes, she felt a little better. Looking around the hospital room reassured her that it had just been a dream.

A small light built into the base of the wall lit the room enough for her to see that things were just as she'd left them. The stool was still perched just in front of the door as a makeshift alarm system.

Looking down at the I.V. tubing, she reversed the steps the nurse had taken to attach it, leaving only the port taped to her arm. Going to the wall, she searched for the light switch. She found it by the door and the two recessed panels in the ceiling flickered briefly, then flooded the room with fluorescent light.

After a quick trip to the bathroom, she returned to the bed and sat on the edge. Her thoughts went immediately to Andrew. There was no way to know if he was alive or dead unless someone told her. She shook her head, not wanting to believe he was dead. He couldn't be dead.

If he were, she wouldn't have to consider anything that Doctor Savon had told her about him. She wouldn't ask and wouldn't listen to anything else about him, preserving the memories she had now.

Was it even possible that someone could be so deranged, she wondered? No. Savon was lying. He had to be. Andrew was smart and loving, and gentle.

Okay, maybe not gentle, she thought as the vision of the body in the desert returned. But that was self-defense, wasn't it? Andrew told her that the man had a gun and was going to take him back... "here" she said, finishing her thought aloud.

She pushed a hand through her hair and looked at the door. There didn't appear to be a lock on it, and they *did* say she could leave any time she wanted. But what would happen if she tried?

She went to the door, pushing the stool away with her bare foot. The metal knob turned easily in her hand, but she paused before opening the door, wondering if there would be a guard. If there was a guard, that too would answer a lot of questions.

She pulled on the heavy wooden door and felt it swing easily toward her. Peeping through the opening, she saw no guard. Emboldened, she opened the door wider and poked her head into the hallway.

The hall was dim, lit by the same lights at the base of the walls as her room. Positioned at regular intervals on both walls, they created alternating pockets of light and shadow down the length of the hallway in both directions.

To her left she found a long corridor that led to another wooden door like the one in her hand. The door at the end of the hallway had a yellow sign on it that read THIS IS A BIO SECURE AREA in large green letters. The smooth, white walls leading to it were interrupted by two more doors like hers. One door faced the other on opposite sides of the hall.

To her right she found a similar scene. The sign on the door at the end of the hall was different. The sign on that door read: THIS DOOR IS TO BE CLOSED AND LOCKED AT ALL TIMES. On the wall next to that door was a small black screen.

Malika stepped one foot into the hallway, looking around nervously. Finally, sure that she was alone, she stepped into the hallway and allowed the door to close behind her.

From here she could see an opening on the same wall as her door. She took a few cautious steps toward it and discovered an adjoining hallway that ran alongside her room. She approached the opening, keeping close to the wall. At the end of the wall, she peeped around the corner and found another hallway that looked just like the one she was in. This hall led to another hall that ran parallel to this one.

"*Mutaha,*" she whispered, using the Arabic word for maze. She made the turn, then stopped and ducked back around the corner. She leaned against the wall. After a moment of indecision, she stepped into the hallway and began making her way toward another intersection. Halfway down, she found a wooden door like the others, but this one had a window. Thin wire formed a grid between the glass but didn't obstruct her view. She cupped her hands around her face and peered into the opening.

Outside, a faint light fell on what must have been a courtyard, now buried under drifts of sand. The tops of four benches struck up from the drifts like grave markers. A fountain sat at the center of the benches inundated by sand; its water shut off. Beyond the courtyard dark shapes loomed in the shadows. Other buildings, though they were dark and windowless.

Her hand went to the door handle, but found it locked. She leaned close to the glass and looked down. Sand was piled against the door halfway to the glass. Malika shrugged. Locking the door suddenly made sense, especially in a medical research facility. A few grains of sand could probably cause a lot of problems in a place like this.

Pressing onward, Malika made her way further down the hall. On the interior wall, she passed another door. There was another dark screen on the wall beside it and above that a small black sign that identified it as a CONTAMINATION ROOM in white letters. Malika shrugged, not knowing what a containment room was or what they did in one.

As she approached the intersection, she made up her mind to go no further. It was early in the morning and people would surely begin to come to work in these locked rooms soon. She did, however, want to see what was around the corner.

She stopped suddenly as the sound of approaching footfalls came to her from the adjoining hallway. She gasped quietly, her heart leaping into her throat. She looked around for a place to hide but found nothing but an empty hallway. Turning back the way she'd come, she decided against trying to make it back to her room. It would take a full-on sprint to make it back to the corner before the person passed by and saw her. Her running down the hall would look suspicious. The fact that she was wearing a hospital gown would make it embarrassing as well.

She bit a thumbnail as the footfalls drew closer. With no other options, she decided to play it off as an innocent morning stroll. After all, hadn't Savon said she was free to leave whenever she wanted? If she were free to leave, she was free to roam as well.

As the sound of the footsteps approached the intersection, she smoothed the front of her gown and walked right into the hallway, colliding with the man hard enough to stagger them both.

"Whoa," he said with a laugh, moving quickly to put a hand on her back to prevent a fall. "Are you okay?"

"I'm fine," Malika said, her cheeks flushing against her will as she recognized Alain Savon. He was close enough for her to smell the light scent of his cologne. His eyes were bright and cheerful as they stared at her.

Malika cleared her throat and straightened her gown, admonishing herself for the momentary attraction that washed over her. "I'm sorry. I just got bored and couldn't sleep."

"Don't apologize. It was my fault, I'm sure. I tend to walk fast." He made a circular motion with his index finger alongside his temple. "I get things working up here and I just forget about everything else."

"Sometimes walking helps one to think."

Savon nodded. "That it does. I think fast and walk fast, I guess." He smiled, keeping his hand on the small of her back. "Is there anything you need? Coffee, tea, breakfast?"

Malika put a hand on her stomach. "I could use some tea and a bite to eat."

Savon stepped back and looked over Malika. "How about we find you something more fitting to wear, and some slippers."

Malika looked down at her bare toes and laughed. "I think I would like that. May I have my old clothes?"

"I'm sure they have them in the laundry, but they're probably not washed yet. It's not one of the priority areas."

"Priority?" Malika asked.

"Yes, the storm wreaked havoc on us. At one point we lost all but critical power. Maintenance has been working diligently to get full power restored. We're at about fifty percent now, so we have devoted most of that power to creature comforts like the cooling system, the kitchen, and the water pumps. We employ quite a few people, some of whom have families here. We wanted to restore as much normalcy for them as possible."

Malika nodded. It made sense. "If it's not a lot of trouble, anything but this will do." She tugged at the edges of the gown. It ended just past the knee, a length she wasn't comfortable with.

"They aren't very flattering, but I must confess that you make the gown look better than most." Savon smiled at her as his hand fished a cell phone from the pocket of his khaki slacks. He typed on it for a moment, then slid it back into his pocket.

"Amaya will be here shortly with some clothes for you. It might end up being just scrubs, but they will be better than a gown." He extended a hand down the hallway she'd just traveled. "May we?"

Malika started walking beside him as he headed toward her room, scolding herself for being so compliant. "What do you do in these locked rooms?" she asked.

"They are different labs. Up here on the right is the prosthesis lab I told you about. The doors are locked because of infection control. Every day those scientists work to better integrate mechanical prosthesis with the human body."

"Like a robot arm?"

Savon chuckled. "Actually, you're closer than you know." They stopped outside the lab doors and took her by the wrist. "Imagine if you or someone you love lost their hand." He flexed her arm with his other hand. "The movement will be limited by any current prosthesis. Mostly just up and down, and a little rotational control. Hand sensory is non-existent. That's what we want to change."

Malika could feel her heart speed up as Savon manipulated her arm. His hands were warm and strong, but also gentle. Her cheeks were getting warm and flushed and she slowly became aware of the smile on her own lips.

"We are currently working on a hand sensory mechanism that will more closely resemble the human hand than anything currently available anywhere in the world." Savon held her hand up to shoulder height, matching the tips of her fingers with his own. He pushed and released each of her fingertips one by one, allowing Malika to return the pressure he applied.

"There are hundreds of nerve endings in each fingertip, Malika. Returning the ability to touch, to feel, is life-altering."

Malika nodded as she looked into his eyes while he spoke. His tanned skin, snow-white hair, and deep blue eyes were in such stark contrast to each other that they must either look comical, or incredibly handsome to everyone he met. Coupled with his voice, deep and authoritative; knowledgeable, but not condescending, she thought it was more often the latter. Doctor Alain Savon probably wasn't lacking for admirers.

Savon cleared his throat and stepped back from Malika, letting her arm fall limply to her side. "But I could go on and on about this stuff. I'm quite sure I've bored you to death."

"No, you have not. I have seen many people who would benefit from these devices. I hope you make them available to places like my country." Malika stood tall again, recovering from her temporary swoon.

"I'm quite sure we will." Savon paused and looked at her. "I was wondering..." He shook his head and gave a dismissive wave. "No, never mind."

"What?" Malika asked, intrigued.

"After you've changed, I was wondering if you would do me the pleasure of having breakfast with me."

"I am hungry," Malika said with a shrug.

"Very well then, Amaya will escort you to the cafeteria when you are ready."

"Thank you."

Savon motioned her down the hall toward her room and they began walking again. "I'm just a doctor at heart," he began. "I love bioengineering. That's what it's called. But it is an expensive process. That lab we just passed cost us almost twenty million dollars to set up and we've barely produced two prototypes. I'm afraid any meaningful return on this investment is unlikely."

"What about the Crown Prince?" Malika asked, prodding just a bit. "You do serve at his pleasure, no?"

"That we do. He has been extremely generous, but even he has his limits. Everything I have is tied up in this place. That's how much I believe in it. Everything I own is here."

"You live here?"

"I do. As a matter of fact, I haven't left the grounds in nearly ten years." Savon stopped when they came to Malika's door.

"Well then, perhaps you should consider a vacation." She looked him in the eyes and gave him a sly smile. "Is there an American saying about too much work?"

"Ah, yes. All work and no play make Jack a dull boy." Savon smiled at her. "Good thing I'm not American then." He shook his head and gave an incredulous grunt. "They can be an exasperating bunch sometimes, can't they?"

"Who, Americans?"

"Yes. I have employed many throughout the years and I find them a little exhausting, really."

"I would not know. I have met only one." She arched one eyebrow slightly then stepped into her room, closing the door behind her.

Savon's eyes widened, surprised by Malika's comment. He stared at the closed door, nodding as a smile slid across his lips. "Indeed," he said aloud.

Malika fell against the door and breathed a sigh of relief. It was easy to see how Alain Savon could manipulate people. There was a way about him that made you want to please him.

She sighed and scolded herself again. She wasn't here to flirt with Savon. She told herself that it was only to discover the truth, but that didn't mean she could not enjoy it.

Malika took a deep breath and wiped her sweaty palms on the front of the gown. She intentionally turned her thoughts away from Alain Savon to Andrew Harkins and guilt began to tug at her. He could be lost in the desert again, no water, no food, no idea where he was. Her heart sank as she thought of him. He could be searching for her now, while she was enjoying the company of his sworn enemy.

Andrew was good man who loved her. When she told him the story of how she killed her husband, he did not blame her. He operated on her father because she wanted him to. When she came to him in the night, he rose up and met her eagerly. He didn't care that she wasn't a virgin; that the flower of her youth had passed. When she'd failed him in the desert by allowing herself to be drugged and captured, he didn't shame her. All he wanted was to love her and keep her safe.

Malika sighed heavily and went to lie down on the bed, feeling tired again. The weight of her foolishness fell on her like a heavy cloak. She'd known Andrew much longer than she'd known Alain Savon. She had spent practically every waking hour together since they met. When they were together, she felt sure of her feelings, but in Savon's presence, she reacted like a silly schoolgirl. If she believed Andrew in the desert, why would she question him now?

Savon was undeniably handsome, obviously very smart, and quite sophisticated. Andrew was also very smart, and handsome in his own way. He was strong and resilient and said he loved her.

But does he really?

Malika grunted angrily and pushed the thoughts of Savon from her head. She couldn't allow herself to be swept away by the man's looks and charming talk. A devil can also talk sweetly when he wants something from you, she thought. She had to continue to believe that

Andrew was alive and what he told her about Savon was true until she found out otherwise.

The nurse told her it would take two days to get the results back from the blood sample taken last night. She had to trust Andrew until then. The results of the test would tell her which man was telling the truth.

Andrew sat on the floor with his elbows propped on his knees and held his head. The voices of his wife and son came at him from the darkness in hushed whispers. He'd diminished his auditory levels drastically but dared not shut them down completely. Doing so would spare him the torture of their pained cries, but it would also leave him vulnerable to an attack from Savon.

"Daddy, why aren't there any trees around here?"

Andrew raised his head as Lane's voice flooded the room. Hearing his voice again swelled his heart with equal parts joy and pain.

"We're in a desert, son. There aren't any trees in the desert," his own voice explained.

"Why not?" Lane asked innocently.

"It's much too dry for most trees here. There are some, in areas where there is water underground."

"Like an oasis?" Lane asked, his tiny voice sounding pleased.

"Exactly."

"I kinda wish they had a few trees here, so you could build a tree house like back home."

Andrew's heart sank.

"Do you not like it here, sweetie?" his voice asked.

"I don't know. It's just different. I like the sand."

"Plenty of sand for your construction machines."

Silence fell on the room again, leaving Andrew to his memories. He sighed and put a hand to the ragged bandage around his eyes. He sobbed, but his dehydrated body could spare no tears.

"I'm sorry, sweetie," he said as guilt swamped him. "I'm so sorry."

Andrew drew in a deep breath and did his best to push the memories out of his mind. There was nothing he could do to bring Samantha and Lane back, but if he had any chance of saving Malika, or avenging his family, he would have to pull himself together.

Physically, he was nearing the danger zone. He was hungry, but not starving yet. His body was dehydrated, but he had another day before he had to worry. His lungs were heavy, and he'd coughed up thick phlegm that tasted gritty in his mouth several times. He was running a low-grade temp, probably the early stages of aspiration pneumonia, but there was nothing he could do about that. Most of his energy was devoted to clearing his lungs and maintaining brain function. There wasn't enough to take care of everything at once.

The sounds of his family were being blasted into the room at measured intervals, leaving him only one hour out of three to sleep. It was the perfect sequence to interrupt his neurotransmitters, making rational thought more difficult as time passed. The mixture of painful screams and pleading coupled with the simple, innocent conversations were intended to keep him in emotional turmoil, intensifying the effect of the lack of REM sleep.

Savon was a master of torture and he had months to plan his revenge. There was little doubt that he'd unleash everything in his considerable arsenal to make Andrew's life a living hell until he bored with the game and killed him.

Andrew drew in a deep breath and blew it out slowly as he began to rebuild his mental state. It would take all his abilities to combat the assault, but it was the only chance he and Malika had.

Reaching down, he found the restraint that kept him tethered to the eyelet recessed in the floor. It was made of a series of tiny wires wrapped into a one eighth-inch cord covered by a thin film of plastic. It was the sort of lead that big dogs were tied to when the owner didn't want to use a chain. It was connected to his foot with a device like a handcuff, but he couldn't find any opening for a key.

He pinched the cord with the thumb and forefinger of each hand and began working it back and forth. It would be impossible to break as one cord, but if he could get the individual strand to break one by one, he might have a chance.

Sitting in silence, working the wire with his hands, Andrew's memory dredged up a pleasant memory from his childhood to combat the psychological warfare Savon was waging on him.

His little league baseball coach called timeout during a game and rallied the whole team around him at the pitcher's mound. They were getting killed, but he was still coaching. Coach King, in his early fifties with a pot belly and gray beard looked at each kid and smiled.

"I ain't going to lie men, we're getting beat, but it ain't over yet. I want each one of you to know this, if I see any one of you not giving everything you got to win this game, you'll be riding pine the rest of the season. Don't quit. Don't ever quit on me and I won't ever quit on you. I'm still going to coach. All I ask is you keep playing hard. A man is never beat until he gives up. You got that?"

Andrew smiled at the memory. They lost the game, and a lot of other games, but not one player ever gave up. No one quit.

He didn't have much of a chance, but it was still a chance.

A chance was all he needed.

Sixteen

Malika's eyes darted back and forth across the paper. Most of the medical jargon escaped her, but she gleaned enough information to know that the doctor was right about the effects of syphilis.

She tossed the papers onto the bed with a sigh. If Andrew did have untreated syphilis that had attacked his nervous system, he could suffer from paranoia, mood swings, and personality changes, but was that the case? She could wrap wounds and help people, but she was no doctor. She had no frame of reference.

The memory of a young soldier returned to her. Growing up, the boy had always been adventurous and brave, often besting the other boys in wrestling matches. When he was old enough, at the age of fourteen, he was allowed to join a local militia and fight for what he believed in.

The boy they dumped at the edge of their village just six months later was a shell of the one she knew. He was timid and shy, and very nervous. He stayed to himself and rarely spoke to anyone. Some of the younger kids made a game of sneaking up on him and yelling loudly. The soldier's shrieks and attempts to cover himself always brought laughter from the kids as they ran away.

No one ever knew what trauma he had been through or what he had seen, but he came back broken. Physically he was fine, mentally he was beyond repair. Eventually the boy threw himself off a mountain to quieten his demons.

She never understood how he'd changed so much, but the complexities of the human mind were far beyond her reach. But could she have been with Andrew for so many days and not recognized any symptoms? How could she have been intimate with him without noticing any of the rashes or sores that the papers spoke of?

Part of her wanted to hate him for giving her a disease, but the part that loved him knew that if what Alain Savon said was true, he would not have been able to help it. He wouldn't believe he was sick. He would be like the boy she once knew.

If Andrew really believed what he was saying, she would have been easy to convince. Was his story so believable because it was Andrew's own reality? Was his mind broken beyond repair? Was Alain Savon his demon, and this place his mountain to leap from?

She rubbed the headache forming at her temples. They never made love in the daytime hours, and when they did it was only sex. She couldn't remember ever touching him where the sores were likely to be. It was at least *possible* that he could have had it and she would have never considered it. Why would she even think of such a thing about him?

He could also heal himself quickly. Could he mask the sores and not realize what they were? Did a part of him know, but refuse to believe the truth? Could he block something like that out of his mind completely?

Malika stood and walked to the end of the room and back. Returning to the desk, she poured herself a glass of water and drank it in long gulps. Staring at the glass, she rubbed the condensation with her thumb. Could all of it have simply been the delusion of a man driven mad by a sickening disease contracted from a whore?

Shaking her head, she sat the glass down and fell back onto the bed. Running contrary to her heart, her mind began to point out situations that bolstered the idea that Andrew had cerebral syphilis. Twice he had acted paranoid, questioning her loyalty to him. Her mind went back to the letter contained in the aid drop. He'd spent all day thinking that she was lying about what it said. She had, of course, left off the last embarrassing part that instructed him to "leave the native girl behind," but he hadn't even given her the benefit of asking.

He was also suspicious when she urged him to go home. She didn't want him to go. She just didn't want him to come to this place and get himself killed. The truth was that despite his abilities, he was blind. The desert was no place for him. She loved him, yes, but that also meant wanting what was best for him, not her. However, if he returned to America, they'd surely discover his disease. Could that be his reason for not returning?

Everything that she'd seen here told her that this place was just a secure hospital setting; nothing at all like the dungeon that Andrew had painted it to be. There were no prisoners, no unwilling test subjects being dragged, kicking and screaming, into the labs for experiments. Doctor Savon seemed anything but a monster. Andrew's passionate hatred for the hospital was beginning to look like an unhealthy fixation.

The version of the story told by Alain Savon sounded more plausible than Andrew's horror story. Viewing the lab through Andrew's eyes made it easy to hate. She'd imagined dark corridors and hunched doctors in bloody coats. In real life it was what she assumed a modern laboratory should look like, not that she'd ever seen one in person.

She buried her face in her hands, lost in confusion. None of the countless scenarios she'd run through in her mind ever reached any conclusions she could feel certain of. There were still too many unknowns for her to even begin deciding how she felt.

Her thoughts returned to the breakfast she'd shared with Alain. He was positively charming, complementing her so casually that it felt natural; like she'd known him for years. He spoke confidently about running the lab and about his work, and humbly about his youth in Johannesburg, South Africa. He listened intently when she spoke of her village and commended her for being such a strong woman in a country where women were largely suppressed.

He'd said that women like her were going to change the world. It was high praise for a woman who currently had nothing to her name, or even a place to call home.

Sitting up, she ran a hand through her hair and massaged the back of her neck. It was hard to imagine that just a few short months ago she was living a simple life in a small village. That life felt a thousand miles and a thousand years from where she now sat. Everything in her life had changed and she couldn't escape the sense of floating. She had no roots, no friends, no family. She had nothing but Andrew and his quest for revenge, and now that too seemed lost.

A soft knock at her door pulled her from her thoughts. "Come in."

Amaya opened the door slowly, entering headfirst. "Good afternoon," she began, a thin smile on her lips. "How are we doing?"

Malika shrugged but said nothing.

"I see you've been reading the information we printed for you. Good. That's good."

"Perhaps it is good. Perhaps not. I do not know. There is much that I do not understand."

"Yeah, I know what you mean. The doctor said you two had breakfast and that your spirits were up some. That's good."

Malika opened her mouth to speak but said nothing, opting instead to simply shrug. If she started talking, she'd burst into tears, and she didn't want the nurse to see her cry.

The smile left Amaya's face as she looked at Malika. She joined her on the bed, putting a hand on her arm. "Honey, we got the test results back."

Malika's stomach knotted as she stared into the somber eyes of the nurse sitting beside her.

"I'm so sorry. The results are positive."

Malika closed her eyes as she drew in a deep breath and held it. She blew it out slowly and opened her eyes. "Are you sure?"

"It's common practice to do a double-blind test. That means that two people check the test independently. Both came back positive. I'm sorry." Amaya rubbed Malika's back as tears welled up in her eyes.

"It is just so..." Malika didn't know how to finish her sentence. "I do not know what to say."

"It is not good news. Remember though, we can treat it."

"It is not that I have it, but how I came to have it."

"I know, sweetie. Sometimes we get the answers we don't want."

Malika nodded absently, her mind reeling. "I think I would like to be alone for a while."

Amaya rubbed her back again and sighed. "I'll be back to check on you later. Okay? The sooner we start the meds the better."

Malika nodded as she thumbed a tear from her cheek.

Amaya got up and left the room, closing the door quietly behind her.

Malika buried her face in her hands as sobs wracked her body. One of the questions that had been plaguing her mind had been answered, but it wasn't the answer she was hoping for.

Andrew wiped his bloody fingers on his pants leg and leaned back against the wall. He was getting tired. Days without food or water on top of the mental torture were beginning to affect him more than he expected. Externally he allowed his body to continue its work on the cable while internally he fought the pneumonia forming in his lungs.

The labor of his breathing and coldness in his extremities told him that the oxygen saturation in his blood was down, a common effect of the pneumonia. It would continue to worsen the longer he waited. Eventually, he would be too weak to do anything but lie on the floor.

The thought of Malika being tortured the way Samantha had been plagued him, leaving him wishing several times that he was dead in the desert. With Samantha, he didn't know what he was getting into. Bringing Malika here had been a mistake. It would have been better for her to be alive and hate him, than what she was being subjected to at the hands of Savon.

He drew in a deep breath and blew it out slowly. Calming his mind, he forced himself to continue his mental tour of the Facility. He visited practically every inch of the place during his years working here, including Savon's personal living quarters. After his sight was taken from him, he'd been allowed to roam the facility unhindered. Savon thought he'd rendered him moot and wanted him to be an example to anyone else who might be considering stepping out of line. He walked the halls, his tortured mind not allowing him sleep, for months while he plotted his revenge.

Andrew bent forward, sliding his hand along the floor until he found the tether's connection. His fingers slid up the length and found the protruding wires, flinching as they stabbed into his fingertips.

Gripping it with his thumb and forefingers again, he began bending the wire back and forth in a monotonous cycle. As each wire broke it freed up the cord to be bent a little further. He sat on the floor and worked the cord while his mind planned his escape route. Overhead the incessant buzzing of the florescent lights came to life followed by the sound of Samantha and Lane laughing playfully.

Another tiny wire snapped, stabbing into the tip of his thumb. Andrew smiled. He was half-way through.

Malika stood under the water in the tiny shower, allowing the spray to hit her face. Crying had left her eyes puffy and her cheeks sticky with salt. She hadn't had a proper bath with soap and shampoo in ages and it felt good to be clean.

Bowing her head, she rested it against the wall, allowed the water to hit her shoulders and run down her back. She moaned quietly as her mind took her back to the first time she saw Andrew. He looked so helpless and lost sitting under that tree. Somehow, she just knew he needed her. The other women wanted to leave him, but they all had husbands.

She turned the shower off and bent to wring the water from her hair, catching sight of the ring of sand around the drain. She sighed and shook her head. The sand reminded her of the storm, and the storm reminded her of Andrew.

For the first time in her life she felt completely helpless. As a child her father had protected her. When she grew up, she protected herself in the ways he taught her. She'd gotten used to fending for herself, and even took care of a few of the village orphans. But in the storm, she panicked and was separated from the one person who would have tried to save her.

Was that it? she wondered as she toweled her hair. Did she fall for him because no one else wanted her? Did he need her, or did she need him?

As she dried herself, her mind drifted to the first time Andrew kissed her. There was something in that kiss other than simple lust, and more than some mental misfunction. Even if he were suffering some delusion, that kiss was more real than any she ever had. When they made love, he wasn't making love to his dead wife, he was making love to her. He wanted her. Her. It was so wonderful to finally be wanted; to be cared for; to be loved.

Malika pressed the towel to her eyes, determined not to cry again. She held it there and took several breaths through it until the wave of sadness passed. He couldn't be gone. Andrew was the most amazing man she ever known, blind or not. She couldn't give up the hope that he was still out there, alive. If he were, he would find her. If he didn't, she would have to find him. If he did have this disease, she would help him.

Walking out of the bathroom, wrapped in a towel, her eyes went immediately to the red garment folded neatly on her bed. She looked suspiciously at the door and found the stool tucked beneath the desk beside her bed. The fact that someone had entered her room while she was showering was disconcerting. She made a mental note to be more diligent about installing her makeshift alarm.

Malika picked up the garment and allowed it to fall to its full length. Holding it up, she gawked questioningly at the dress and shook her head. It was an evening dress, and judging by the size, it would be rather snug on her. When she tossed the dress back on the bed, a small note fluttered onto the floor.

Clutching her towel, she picked it up.

I hope you don't think me presumptuous, but I took the liberty of picking out a dress for you. I hoped you would wear it tonight and do me the honor of joining me for dinner. Amaya will be able to assist you with anything you might need. Dinner is at seven.

With all sincerity,

Alain

Malika reread the note several times, her anger growing with each. What did he think she was, some whore to be dressed up and brought to his bed? She shook her head and grabbed the scrubs she'd been wearing all day. She dressed quickly and read the note again before wadding it up and throwing it across the room.

"Oh, you're done. Good."

Malika turned as Amaya entered the room, this time without knocking.

"I have finished with the bath. Yes."

"Is everything okay?"

"It is not." Malika grabbed the dress from the bed and held it up before Amaya.

"What is this?" she asked.

"It's a dress, dear," Amaya said with a shrug.

"I see that it is a dress. It is a whore's dress. And this." She looked for the note but couldn't find it. "Dinner alone with Doctor Savon?"

"Okay, calm down. I see you're upset. He asked me to deliver these things to you. He didn't mean to disrespect you, I'm sure. He said you asked for better clothes."

"I am not a whore."

"I'm sure no one thinks you are, but you weren't exactly wearing a burka when they found you. It's a nice dress. I'm sure it is a simple misunderstanding."

"Perhaps for you. Not for me. I will wear this until my clothes are cleaned. Please let the doctor know that I will be eating alone tonight. And that I plan to leave soon."

"Don't do that. You still need more treatments for the... you know."

Malika crossed her arms with a huff. She hadn't considered that. According to their own tests she had syphilis. Surely the doctor wouldn't want to sleep with her now.

"Very well. I will stay until my treatments are finished. But I would still like to eat alone. Here, if I may." Malika looked down at her hands, hoping to hide her embarrassment. The fact that she had syphilis would certainly mark her as untouchable to any man who knew.

"You can do whatever you like dear. I'll make sure you have a full meal. Will there be anything else?"

"No," Malika answered, most of her steam now gone. "Thank you." Malika closed her eyes and shook her head. "I am sorry. Please let the doctor know that I thank him for the offer, but I do not feel well."

Amaya paused at the door and smiled back at her. "I will. You get some rest. I'll bring your medicine at mealtime."

Malika let out a frustrated sigh and tossed the dress onto the bed. Being here, without Andrew, and not knowing if he was dead or alive was becoming too much to bear. With each passing hour, unease grew within her chest. Sleep brought unpleasant dreams, the rich food gave her stomach aches, and she couldn't keep her thoughts organized. Her heart longed to be in the desert with Andrew, away from everyone else in the world. She just wanted the whole ordeal to be over.

Sitting down hard on the bed, she picked up the towel. She pressed it to her face and began to cry again.

Andrew sat perfectly still, his auditory acuity on alert, and waited. The tour of the room had given him the information that he needed. As he suspected, he was in the containment room. Besides the labs and Savon's living quarters, it was the most secure room at the Facility, with its own power, ventilation, and sound system. Once locked, it could only be accessed by Savon's own personal code.

When the lock deactivated on the door, Andrew smiled. It would be now or never. He wouldn't get a second chance.

Alain Savon walked into the room, his footfalls mixing with the faint sound of the camera system switching on with a single, soft, beep. Their interactions were being filmed for some reason, but he couldn't figure out why. He'd given up trying to figure out Savon's degenerate mind a long time ago.

"Well, well, well. You seem quite content."

Andrew sat perfectly still as the sound of the door re-engaging behind Savon echoed throughout the empty room.

"Giving me the cold shoulder, huh?" Savon asked with a laugh. "Or are you doing that thing where you shut down?"

Again, Andrew gave no sigh that he was aware of Savon's presence. He listened to the echoes of Savon's voice; to the sounds his slacks made as he walked; to the thump of his hard-soled shoes on the tiled floor. He listened and waited.

Savon took a few steps into the room, careful to keep out of reach of the tether. "I know that we haven't always agreed, Andy, but you have to admit that you need help. I am willing to give you that help."

Savon sighed as he stared at Andrew sitting cross-legged near the back of the room. "The smell in here is getting worse. Fortunately for you, we have gained clearance to treat you. You won't have to wallow in your own filth much longer."

Walking along the front wall of the room, Savon kept his eyes on Andrew. He pursed his lips and shook his head, disappointed in the lack of response. Watching him struggle like a dog on a chain had been more fun that hr expected.

"Bailey is preparing the sedation. We're going to have to dart you like a wild animal. Are you happy that it's come to this?" He paused but got no answer. "After you are sedated, we will transport you to the hospital wing. Of course, you will have to remain in restraints until the treatments have begun to work and you've come back to your senses."

Savon paced the length of the room, his hands clasped behind his back, as he talked. "I do have some news for you that might bring you out of your stupor. After the storm subsided, a team went out and searched for your friend." Savon paused, watching Andrew intently.

Andrew's heartrate quickened slightly, but he steadied it. He would only get one chance to escape and if Malika were still alive, he would have to make it count.

"You're quite good at that, Andy. I know your heart rate sped up a little, and rightly so. She is quite a beautiful woman. Quite beautiful indeed." A dirty grin slipped across Savon's face as he watched Andrew.

"She was nearly dead when we found her, thanks to you. What the hell were you thinking? You've been quite reckless, Andy." Savon resumed his pacing. "Reckless and brutal, even for you. Oh yes, I've heard some nasty rumors about you and your friend."

Andrew sat motionless. He didn't care about anything Savon said except for Malika's condition. A heavy weight lifted from him. She was alive. Her being here wasn't the best situation, but at least she was alive.

"First of all, we know that you two were lovers. And secondly, we know you have been traveling all over the region with your little desert flower." Savon stopped pacing abruptly. "Daniel Souter, dead. Two Canadian agents, dead. Four Yemeni security guards, dead. A helicopter pilot and co-pilot, dead. Oh, and let's not forget about the old man in the village. Also dead. The body count is piling up. Including your wife and son, that brings your body count to an even dozen. And that's just the ones we've been able to attribute directly to you and your friend."

Savon's jaw clenched as he stared at Andrew. The ember of his frustration was growing. He'd hoped for some reaction. Anger, surprise, anything. He got nothing but an unflinching audience.

"I've been in touch with the Saudi government, Andrew. It seems that they want you two as well. See, they want to behead both of you. Sometimes in these border regions it's hard to tell where you are, or where you murder people. Isn't it? Luckily, they had someone like me and my security team to tell them all about the murder of your family.

"Of course, I worked out a deal with them. Given the fallout from the storm, they agreed to allow me to keep you both for an indefinite amount of time. When I'm ready I will turn Malika over to them to have her pretty little head loped off. Would you like it as a present? Or is the other end more necessary for your needs?"

Savon brought his hands in front of him and wiped them together as if cleaning dirt from his palms. "Naturally, they won't concern themselves with what condition she'll be in," he said with a chuckle, "That's the fun part."

Andrew sprung from the floor and sprinted toward Savon.

A smile slid across Savon's face as he watched Andrew react, happy to have finally broken through his defenses.

He was still smiling when Andrew's hands closed around his throat. The collision drove both men against the wall next to the door. A grunt escaped Savon as the back of his head slammed into the wall.

Andrew hands gripped Savon's throat, ignoring the impact. A second later he felt something hard and stiff lash him across the back. For an instant he thought someone else was in the room, but then the end of the restraint fell across his shoulder.

Savon clawed at his hands, struggling for breath. He pushed his body to the left then to the right along the wall, but Andrew's strength was greater than he anticipated. He kicked out repeatedly, trying desperately to free himself, but was blocked each time. His fingers found Andrew's hands, clawing at them franticly.

Andrew felt each of Savon's muscles as it tensed, allowing him to anticipate his next move. Months of pent-up rage held Savon's throat in a vice despite his struggles, fueled by unmitigated fear.

Savon finally landed a blow, punching Andrew in the stomach. The blow caught him directly under the solar plexus, knocking the air from his lungs. Andrew groaned as his breath escaped him, barely side stepping a second punch. With his left hand firmly clenched on Savon's throat, he delivered a punch of his own. His fist landed solidly in the middle of Savon's chest.

Savon clawed desperately at Andrew's grip with one hand while his other flailed wildly, landing blows along Andrew's shoulder and upper chest. He was running out of air and getting weaker by the second. His throat hurt like hell and his lungs were on fire. Raking his fingers over Andrew's face and down his neck, he found the end of the tether and grabbed it.

Kicking out to distract Andrew, he drove the jagged end of the tether into the side of his neck. He yanked it downward, opening a series of deep gouges in Andrew's skin.

Andrew growled in pain and punched Savon in the face. Seizing the moment of confusion it delivered, he found Savon's hand clenched around the tether and squeezed it in his own.

For a moment, the two men were frozen in a stalemate, but as Savon's strength faded with his lack of oxygen, Andrew began to gain the advantage. Both fists, and the ragged end of the tether inched toward Savon's face.

The sound of Savon's ragged, gurgling breath filled Andrew's ears. How long had he dreamed of this moment? How many times had he thought of killing this very man? Within a minute, two at the most, it would be over. Savon would be dead.

Savon's eyes stared at the jagged tangle of bloody wires as they inched toward his face. No. His eyes. The pain of his burning lungs gave way to an explosion of pain in his neck as Andrew's thumb found his esophagus and began to squeeze.

Savon's arm suddenly went limp, overpowered. He managed to turn his face enough to avoid the brunt of the wires. The end of the restraint drug across his left cheek and slammed into the wall. He grunted in pain but continued to fight, driving a knee into Andrew's crotch.

Andrew dropped the cord as the pain exploded up through his stomach and spread to his whole body. He bent in agony and was met by Savon's fist as it slammed into his chin. His hand slipped from Savon's throat as he staggered backward.

He threw his arms up to deflect an assault, but none came. The only sound besides his own labored breaths was Savon's irregular footsteps as he staggered out of the room. A moment later the sound of a siren drowned everything else out.

The door was already half closed by the time Andrew started toward it, barely squeezing out as the gap narrowed. He let out a sigh of relief, but quickly realized that the end of the tether was caught. He wrapped it around his hand and began yanking. Valuable seconds were being wasted that he hadn't planned for.

He put his foot against the wall and strained against the mechanical door. Security would be on scene within three minutes of the alarm sounding and he'd already wasted thirty seconds.

He sat down and put both feet against the door, hoping that he wasn't too exhausted to free himself. He let out a long groan, pushing his body to its limits as he forced his muscles to react beyond their limits.

The cord began to slip through his fists as he pulled. "No," he cried through clenched teeth, tightening his grip. The cable released suddenly, sending him sprawling on the floor, gasping for air. He quickly gathered the cord and staggered down the hall on legs that could barely support him.

When Malika opened the door to her room, the sound of the siren increased dramatically. She stepped into the hallway, nearly colliding with a man rushing to get somewhere else.

"What's going on?" she asked, taking a few steps after him. She watched the man rush around the corner and a second later two more men appeared, rushing in her direction. Both men wore the same khaki slacks as everyone else, but their olive shirts had "security" printed on the left breast pocket.

"That's her," one of them said, pointing in her direction.

Malika ran back to her door and slipped inside. She pushed the door but was unable to close it. The man who had pointed at her had his foot against it.

"You need to come with us," he said as they pushed into her room.

"What's going on?" she asked, taking a cautious step back.

The two men took up positions on either side of her. A quick glance at the guns on their hips and the stern looks on their faces told her she didn't have a choice. She did not resist as each man took an arm and ushered her out of the room.

Malika questioned them as they whisked her down one hallway then the next, but they didn't answer. Everyone they passed gave them a wide berth, despite being in a hurry themselves. When the frantic pace finally stopped, they were in an elevator.

Malika snatched free of the men and turned to face them. "I have been nice so far, but I want to know what is going on?"

"Ma'am. There's been a security breach. We were instructed to get you and bring you to a secure location."

"What kind of security breach?"

"I don't know, ma'am."

"Where is this secure location?" Malika felt the elevator going up.

"You're safe now."

When the doors to the elevator opened, the men escorted Malika out the doors and to the end of a short hall where two heavily armed guards awaited. The four men nodded, then the first two spun and headed back to the elevator.

"Ma'am," the guard on her right said with a nod and a smile. He pressed a button next to the door and said, "She's here, sir," into the intercom.

"Good. Send her in."

Hearing Savon's voice, she gave the guards a puzzled look as the door opened. The guard who had announced her arrival motioned with his hand for her to enter the room. She complied hesitantly.

She entered the expansive room and was greeted by a sweeping view of the desert through a wall of glass. The scene was breathtaking, but when she came to the end of a short wall, her mouth fell open slightly. The room was larger than most people's houses and furnished more eloquently than she would have ever imagined. It was better suited for a king's palace than a laboratory in the desert. She'd thought Abdullah's opulence was gluttonous, but it paled in comparison.

"Please, do come in."

Malika jumped, the voice snatching her from her awe of the room. She looked to her right and found Savon standing next to a mahogany cabinet holding a crystal tumbler half filled with a dark liquor.

"Please, make yourself comfortable. I'm sorry, but I have some matters to attend to." Savon turned to face her, revealing the bloody scratches on his face and the dark bruising on his neck.

Malika gasped, mumbling in Arabic as she went to him. "What has happened?"

Savon shook his head and finished his drink in two gulps. "We've had a security breach. I asked that you be brought here so that you will be safe."

"Me? Why would I not be..." She let her voice trail off as Savon's expression answered her question. "Andrew is here?" she asked, clutching her hands before her.

"Very much so, and in quite good health, apparently. At least physically."

"He did this to you?" she asked, crossing the room. She tried to examine the wounds, but Savon looked away.

"He did." Savon wiped a smear of blood from his face with the back of his hand. "It's superficial. I wanted to make sure you were safe before I summoned the doctor." He downed the drink in one gulp.

"Why would he do this to you?" Malika asked, the shock of Savon's condition subsiding.

"I've told you he is not well." Savon poured himself another drink. He cleared his throat and shook his head. "There is a reason that my team couldn't find him in the desert, Malika. He was already here." He turned up the glass and drank half the liquor before looking into her eyes. "Perhaps that's why you were separated in the storm."

Malika pursed her lips, considering her words wisely. "It is easy to be separated in a storm like that."

"True," Savon agreed with a shrug. "But it was also an opportunity to leave you behind."

"I'm sure he would have looked for me."

Savon shrugged again. His expression told her that he thought her a fool. "Look, Malika, Andy isn't well. He came here to kill me because he blames me for his family's death."

"Why would he do that? Why? It does not make sense."

"Because he has gone mad. He's delusional. It makes sense to him because he's lost his mind." He drank from his glass and sat it down hard on the counter, walking away from her. "He doesn't want to accept the truth. The truth that he killed his own family. I own this place. I'm the authority figure. He blames me because this is my lab. I brought him here." Savon walked to the intercom on the wall when it buzzed and answered the call.

"Doctor Thorsby," came the guard's voice.

"Send him in." Savon pressed a button to unlock the door and looked back at Malika.

A short, chubby man in a white lab coat entered and went straight for Savon, ignoring her completely. When Savon sat in a chair, the doctor opened the small bag he brought with him and went to work.

"I cannot believe such things. The man I know could not do these things."

Savon sighed. "Malika, I know it is hard to believe, but it's true. Andy isn't well. The human brain, when ravaged by such a vicious disease, is capable of anything. Surely, you've seen people go senile with old age, or people gone mad before. It's actually not that uncommon."

"Actually," Doctor Thorsby began as he cleaned Savon's neck, "Many people in this part of the world are stricken with various psychoses that are attributed to demonic possession. Usually. they are simple labeled as witches or heretics and come to an unfortunate end."

"But they are *majnun*..." she waved a hand in circles beside her head as she struggled to find the English word. "Lunatic. Andrew has not behaved like this." He was smart and resourceful, not a raving mad man.

Savon sighed and shook his head. "Malika, I want you to watch some film footage. If you have any doubts about what I'm telling you, this should erase them. You don't have to believe me, but maybe you will believe your own eyes."

Seventeen

"Okay, come on out before you suffocate." Nicodem Peterson released the pressure plate on the back of the old wardrobe and stepped back. He was an old man with very few friends, but Andrew Harkins was one of them. He'd gotten used to being alone since the fire that burned his face and scorched his eyes shut. Part of him was thankful for the blindness because it prevented him from seeing his own face in the mirror. He didn't know how he looked, but a lifetime of comments from unkind people had told him all he needed to know.

The small door opened in the back of Peterson's armoire and fresh air flooded into the small false back where Andrew had spent the last six hours. Luckily, he'd been able to sleep, allowing his body to begin to heal. He climbed out slowly, flexing and stretching his aching muscles as he did.

"Well, Peterson, looks like your papa's old wardrobe did it again," Andrew said, referencing the fact that Peterson's parents had used the armoire to hide Polish Jews from Hitler in route to smuggling them out of the country during World War Two.

Peterson smiled a crooked smile. Bringing the armoire had been his one condition for taking the job here so many years ago. "I think he'd be happy. One tyrant or another, he keeps thwarting them."

"That he does, buddy." Andrew grabbed Peterson and embraced him. "I'll admit it was a little unnerving hiding in there with all those explosives."

Peterson chuckled. "I guess it was. You were still safer in there than out here when those goons came by."

"I heard. They sounded as pleasant as ever," Andrew joked.

"Yeah," Peterson said with a grunt. "Nice as a cat with turpentine on its butt."

"You're a wonderful person." Andrew coughed and into a napkin. The phlegm he produced was full of sand.

"Did you get the bleeding stopped okay?"

"I did," Andrew answered, gingerly touching the side of his neck.

"You need more water?"

Andrew shook his head. "I will, but time is of the essence. We better get to it. You got the stuff?"

"Yeah, I got it. I've had it." Peterson sighed, turning away from Andrew. He hobbled over to a chest of drawers and kneeled. He produced a thin box from the bottom drawer. "You know, the whole time I was working on this I wondered if you'd ever use it. I guess deep down I knew you'd come back or else I would have quit on it."

He stood on unsteady legs and laid the box on the dresser, opening it gently. "Pull us up two chairs. This will take a bit and I don't know if my old legs will hold out that long."

Andrew made his way out of the room and returned a moment later with two wooden chairs. By the time he got back several textured sheets of latex were spread across the top of the dresser. They'd concocted a plan that would allow Andrew to get Savon alone, but he'd decided to escape instead. He was glad his friend hadn't given up on him, as they'd just started the disguise.

"I did my best, but I was just going by feel."

Andrew allowed his hand to gently wash over the silicone, feeling the lines and crevasses that mimicked Peterson's face. He paused for a moment and sighed.

"It's okay," Peterson said quietly. "I know how badly I look."

"It's not that. I just..." Andrew trailed off, not knowing what to say. He was friends with Peterson before he lost his sight and knew what he looked like, but now felt guilty asking the man to replicate his own face in silicone gel. How many hours had he spent feeling his own deformity to replicate it? How much personal pain had he endured?

"Just sit down. You owe me no explanation." Peterson ran his hands across Andrew's face. "Yeesh, you went and got hairy in the desert."

"Better to blend in."

"I guess, but we gotta get rid of it. All of it." Peterson found a pair of scissors on the dresser. "Sweet Mary, how did you get so hairy?"

"I'm a man of many talents," Andrew said with a smile.

"I hope holding still is one of them," Peterson said. He grabbed a lump of hair and deftly cropped it close to Andrew's skin.

Malika watched the collection of videos while the doctor bandaged Savon's face, then watched them again when he excused himself to shower and change clothes. She could not believe her own eyes. The footage was clear and focused, showing every conversation that Savon had with Andrew, right up until the last attack.

She backed the footage up with the remote he'd left her, stopping on one image. Shot from above and directly behind Savon, Andrew was sprinting toward the camera, his face frozen in a savage growl. His hands were extended toward the camera, his fingers curled into claws. She stared at the screen wondering who that man was. There was an anger, a savagery, that she'd never seen in him.

"If you think it's hard to look at now, you should see it coming straight at you."

Malika jumped, dropping the remote. "You startled me." She looked over her shoulder as Savon reentered the room.

"I'm sorry." Alain rounded the sofa and sat down, now wearing a bandage on his cheek.

"Are you well?" she asked, looking at the bruises on his neck. They were darker now that they had been when she first came to his quarters.

"I'll heal." Savon cleared his throat. "The doctor wants to run some tests after the alert is over. It's routine I suppose." He crossed his legs at the knee and nodded at the image frozen on the television screen. "Hard to believe, isn't it?"

Malika turned back to the screen with a sigh. "It does not look like the man I know."

"I know," Savon said with a sigh. "Me either. I worked with Andy for years. We ate countless meals together. We drank together. We were friends. It's very hard for me to see him like this."

Savon shook his head, his eyes locked on the screen.

Malika stared at the man beside her, reading his face. His eyes were narrowed slightly, and his lips were pressed firmly together in a dismayed frown. There was a genuine sadness in his features, and maybe a little fear as well.

"You know, the human mind is an amazing thing. Capable of more interactions in a second than any computer in the world. Creating electronic impulses from tissue and fluid and controlling every aspect of our existence. It's incredibly resilient, and amazingly fragile at the same time. There are still more unsolved mysteries about the human brain that there is in all of space. Fascinating."

"There are things we are not meant to understand, Doctor."

"I guess you're right." Savon's fingers danced along his bandage. "I just hope they can find Andrew and sedate him quickly. The sooner we start the treatments, the less likelihood of long-term damage."

"Can a disease really cause all this?" Malika asked, reminding herself that the same disease was running through her own veins now.

"If left untreated, yes." Savon stood and went to the liquor cabinet. "You know, Henry the eighth was said to have syphilis." He paused as he looked at the ceiling thoughtfully. "Or was it George the fourth? Anyway, they say he was mad as a hatter by the time he died. Can you believe it, the King of England had syphilis?"

Malika shrugged but said nothing as she watched Savon pour scotch over the ice in a crystal tumbler. Her eyes followed him back to the sofa.

"I must apologize for my invitation the other day. I'm afraid you might have misunderstood my intent."

"It is fine. I'm sorry that I acted rudely to the nurse. I haven't felt well."

"I suppose not." Savon took a sip of the drink. "Getting caught in a raging dust storm and waking up in a strange place. Then finding out the man you've been sleeping with has syphilis, then finding out he's given it to you. That's quite a lot for anyone to fathom, even an exceptional woman like you."

Malika forced a smile. "Thank you. But I do apologize."

"No offence was taken, my dear. I am not a man easily offended." Savon stared into her eyes long enough to make her drop her gaze. "But I do appreciate a gem when I see one."

Malika offered another awkward smile then changed the subject. "Do you not have a tracking system or something to find him?" she asked, staring at the image of Andrew frozen on the screen before her.

Savon laughed. "This isn't television, my dear. And this isn't a jail. People come and go and want their privacy at times. Especially the ones whose spouses are here."

Malika began chewing on her thumb nail as her eyes washed over the image on the screen. Could Andrew be so savage? So crazy?

"Look, Malika, I'm going to come out and say this. It is imperative that you be onboard with us in having Andrew get the help he needs. This is all the disease ravaging his central nervous system. I know you don't understand the neuroscience of it all, but I do. The man needs help before he hurts anyone else, or himself."

"Yes, I know. I'm just very confused."

"I know," Savon said, placing a hand on Malika's back. "It isn't easy to admit that the man you love is crazy from syphilis and that he's given it to you."

Malika's head jerked around. "I was his guide."

Savon smiled. "Must you keep up the pretense? He has syphilis, now you have it. Did he rape you?"

"No,"

"Did you come in contact with any open sores?"

"No."

"Then there is only one way left."

Malika dropped her gaze to her hands as she picked at a thumbnail. It was humiliating to have to admit that she'd slept with a man who wasn't her husband. If this had happened in her village, she'd surely be stoned to death as a whore.

"Look," Savon slid closer to her on the couch. "I'm not from the same religious group as you are. I don't find it a big deal that a woman has needs and wants. People crave intimacy, even if they aren't married."

Malika grunted, her eyes still on the screen, but said nothing.

"You are merely a woman, Malika. A beautiful woman, yes, but still a woman. We all have needs and desires. I do not judge you for that."

"Thank you, Doctor." She slid a hand alongside her face, shielding the shameful flush of her cheeks from him.

"I'm not going to lie," Savon reached out and gently moved her hand. He lifted her face to his and offered a smile. "It's easy to see why any man would fall for you. You are simply stunning."

Malika ran a hand through her hair and flashed an anxious smile before looking away. "Thank you. You are very kind to say so." She pulled back enough to signal that she was uncomfortable with his touch. Savon retracted his hand with a heavy sigh.

"I'm not going to say I'm not disappointed, but you obviously have feelings for Andy."

Malika nodded. "I do, even now."

"If you do then you must help us. That may be the only hope of returning Andy to the man he was. Will you help us?"

Malika sighed. "What can I do?"

"He's fixated on you. I hate to tell you this, but he called you Samantha several times in our interviews. I had them edited out to spare you, but you need to know what we're dealing with. The disease, coupled with the dehydration and physical stress he's been under has twisted his sense of reality."

"He didn't act deranged or crazy. Not the man I knew."

"Don't you see? The man you know doesn't even exist!" Savon stood and went to the windows. "The man he became out there in the desert isn't the mild-mannered surgeon that I knew for years. Andy was as timid and docile as they come." Savon took a long drink from the glass in his hand. "Hell, his wife even complained to some of the other women that his lovemaking was so gentle that she couldn't even enjoy it. The word was that she stopped sleeping with him because it wasn't worth the bother."

Malika tensed at the mention of Andrew making love to another woman. Andrew's efforts with her had been anything but timid and shy.

"Andrew—"

"That, see," Savon said, cutting her off as he turned to face her. "Everyone around here knew him as Andy. Out there somewhere Andy went away, and Andrew showed up. He made himself into another person. The Andy I know couldn't hurt a fly much less do all the things the reports say Andrew did."

"Reports?" Malika asked.

Savon smiled. "I am in a position to find things out my dear. People tell me things, in exchange for other things. My gratitude is very valuable out here in the middle of nowhere."

"Everything we did was in self-defense."

"Calm down," Savon patted the air in front of him. "I'm not saying it wasn't. All I'm saying is that the man I know, Andy Harkins, M.D., couldn't do any of those things."

Savon took a sip of his drink and shook his head. "Andy spent most of his life studying and working in labs and hospitals. He's a genius, but to be honest, he's kind of a nerd. He's definitely not some heroic figure who could defend you, or even himself for that matter."

Malika sank back into the couch and rubbed her temples. An ache was forming deep inside her head. Everything Savon was saying made perfect sense but then again, she believed everything Andrew told her too.

"Andrew said you hurt people." Malika stared at Savon, judging his response, but he simply leveled his gaze at her and shrugged.

"I'm a scientist and a businessman. I probably hurt some people's feelings. I do like to win negotiations, but that is about the extent of my ruthlessness." His hand went to the bandage on his cheek. "I wish I was more like he said I was, maybe I wouldn't be wearing this."

It made sense that any average man in good health would be able to overpower a man who'd been wandering the desert for days, after surviving a sandstorm no less. Savon wasn't a big man, but his frame looked solid. He should have been able to easily subdue Andrew in his weakened state.

Malika's eyes went to the image on the screen. Andrew was suffering from something, but what? "You have to promise that you won't hurt him," she finally said.

Savon rejoined her on the sofa. "Malika, all I want to do is save my friend from himself. That's what I've been trying to do for months."

"I have a question." Malika sighed and looked at Savon. "When he has recovered from the treatments and return to the way he was, will he remember anything that happened in the desert?"

"You mean do I think he'll remember you?"

Malika shrugged and nodded sheepishly. She drew in a breath and held it, unsure if she wanted to know the answer.

"To be honest I don't know. My medical training tells me that he won't remember much at all."

Malika put a hand to her mouth to cover the gasp she hadn't expected. She wanted to be alone. She was going to cry and didn't want Savon to see her. "May I return to my room?"

"I'm sorry, but it's not safe just now. I have several guest rooms you can choose from."

"Very well," she replied begrudgingly. "I will do anything you ask to help Andrew, but right now I want to lie down."

"I will get everything in order. You rest and I will take care of everything." Savon stood and led her to a door that opened off the main room. "You will have the suite all to yourself, I promise. The door even has a lock on the inside if you'd like to use it."

"Thank you very much, Doctor." Malika walked into the room, going straight to the bed. Savon watched her for a moment then pulled the door closed. It had barely latched when a thin smile broke out on his face.

"That should do it." Peterson sat back in his chair with a tired sigh.

Andrew's hands went to his face, searching it carefully with his fingertips. The uneven surface and scar tissue of his new face felt real, but there was no way to know how it looked.

"I did the best I could with the coloring," Peterson said, as if reading his mind. "I think you'll be okay if it's off some. Nobody looks at an old blind man very hard, especially if his face could make you lose your lunch."

"Stop. That's not true."

"How the hell would you know? You're as blind as I am."

"I wasn't always. And I never lost my lunch once."

"Well, it is what it is, old friend. I've done what I can, now it's up to you." Peterson handed Andrew his cane. "Use it in good health."

"How can I ever thank you, Peterson?"

"When you kill that crazy bastard, they'll probably shut this place down. Tell 'em to come get me. If they can find me, send me home. I'm so damned tired of sand I could spit." Peterson laughed, putting his weight on Andrew's shoulder to help himself up. When he was upright, he slapped Andrew on the back. "Now get the hell outta here before you get us both killed."

Andrew shrugged on Peterson's old green cardigan sweater and smoothed the gray wig atop his head as he walked toward the door.

"The key is confidence, Andrew." Peterson stopped in the middle of the room. "I haven't mellowed any while you've been gone. Give 'em hell."

Andrew smiled. His old friend's laugh was full of life, genuine. "Thanks again. I couldn't do this without you."

"If you're waiting for me to kiss you goodbye, you'll be here a while," Peterson said with another laugh.

Andrew opened the door and stepped into the hallway. Haunching over his cane, he took the first tentative steps as Doctor Nickodem Peterson. He hadn't gone far when his first test arrived.

"Coming by, Doc."

Andrew hugged the wall as three members of the security detail hurried past. He was about to breathe a sigh of relief when he heard them stop a few feet in front of them.

"Did you sign the log?" one of them asked.

"Shit. I thought you did?" another added.

"I know I didn't. Better go back and sign it. The boss will have our asses."

Andrew tensed as they three men neared him again, approaching from the front.

"You're Peterson, aren't you?" one of them asked, stopping in front of him.

"Yeah, what if I am?" Andrew replied, mimicking his friend's voice as best he could.

"Has your living quarters been searched?"

"Hell yes. Some brutes tossed the place over an hour ago. You wanna have another go at it?"

"C'mon. All the living quarters have been searched," another man said from behind Andrew.

"Maybe you want to help an old man clean the mess you made. That'd be nice."

"You're supposed to stay in your quarters during the alert," the man in front of him said.

"Savon summoned me. I'd be glad to go take a nap if you'll tell him for me," Andrew replied with a hoarse laugh.

"Go ahead then."

When the man joined his team, Andrew breathed a sigh of relief. Either the coloring on his disguise was close, or Peterson was right about people not wanting to look at him too closely. He shook his head and tottered off down the hallway, careful to walk as slowly as he could despite his mind's insistence that time was of the essence.

Savon stood, one hand resting on the glass, and looked out over the desert. His mind raced with scenarios and hopeful outcomes. The girl was finally convinced that Andrew Harkins was crazy from syphilis and that she had it as well. That was good, but he wasn't convinced how strong her determination was. If Andrew somehow showed up here, she would surely falter in her resolve. That would be a problem.

Andrew would rightly assume that he would bring her here. This was his fortress, impenetrable unless you were buzzed inside. The button on the wall looked like a simple buzzer to allow entry, but it was a fingerprint reader. If anyone but him pressed it, they receive a rather nasty shock that would render them unconscious, if it didn't kill them outright. This was the most secure site in the whole facility for a reason.

He smiled, imagining the tortured look on Andrew's face when Malika told him that Savon is right; that he should accept the treatments for syphilis; that he is crazy. The betrayal would be the sweetest revenge he could have. Then the security team could forcibly contain him, and he'd spend the rest of his miserable life in chains. There would be no further escape.

He briefly toyed with the idea of keeping Malika as his personal pet. She was an attractive woman, and her body was stout and full. It would be nice to have her, but the danger was too great. But, he thought, if he could turn her and eventually fool her into giving herself to him willingly, it would elevate Andrew's torture. It would be his ultimate victory.

Savon chuckled at the prospect, but he knew it would never work. It would be too much of a liability. He'd have to kill her, but maybe after a bit of fun. She'd put up a good fight. Taking her by force would be very satisfying. It had been a long time since he'd had such a spirited woman. Breaking her would be an adventure.

His hand went to his face and the smile faded from his lips. Andrew had scarred him because he had underestimated him, assuming that his jaunt through the desert would have weakened him. It wouldn't happen again. The best thing might be to simply kill them both and be done with the whole matter.

No, he thought. It would end Andrew's suffering too quickly. He had to break him too; reduce his arrogance to a sniveling pile of useless human flesh.

His jaw clenched as he recalled Andrew's disobedience. He'd been so damned self-righteous, calling him a "Godless bastard" in front of a whole team of scientists. Andrew had humiliated him in front of his subordinates. No, killing him was too easy. Andrew Harkins had to suffer. He and everyone else had to know that he had bent to the will of Alain Savon.

Andrew Harkins was a bully and would pay just like all the other bullies he'd encountered in his life had paid.

Eighteen

Andrew slowly made his way toward the men standing guard at the elevator. Half slumped and breathing heavily, he stopped and leaned on his cane.

"Well," he said.

"Well, what? Nobody's going up without authorization."

Andrew straightened slightly, turning his face to the guard on the right. "Listen, young man. I'm one of the foremost scientists in the eastern hemisphere in the field of synthetic positronic intelligence. I need to see Savon's stupid ass and I need to see it now. This alert is interfering with my work." Andrew made a move toward the button beyond the man.

"Hold it, old timer," the man said, putting up a hand to block him. "I don't care if you're the Queen of Sheba, you're not getting up without Savon's personal authorization."

Andrew sighed. "If I were you, son, I'd move my hand and let me pass."

The two men shared a laugh. "Well, we're not moving. Get authorization and we'll carry you up the stairs." Both men laughed again.

"You get your rocks off bullying an old man? Is that what you like? You sniveling punk."

The guard on the right stepped forward and gave him a gently nudge on the shoulder. "Go back to your quarters and have a nap, pops."

"He's a cantankerous old coot, ain't he?" the other added, laughing.

Andrew reclaimed the step he'd lost and waited. When the weight of a hand fell on his right shoulder, it lent him the perfect reference of the man's position.

He grabbed it and quickly spun the man around, shoving him into the other guard. One man fell to the floor, but the one he pushed caught himself on the wall.

"You're screwed now, old man."

Andrew brought his cane up and caught the man in the throat just as the second guard got to his feet.

"What the—"

He never got the chance to finish his sentence as Andrew swung the cane, hitting him across the temple. He assumed a defensive position and listened. The guard on his left was unconscious. The other was on his knees, gasping for air. He turned to him and poked his back with the cane.

"Go to your quarters now and ice that. It's imperative you keep the swelling down. If you waste time reporting this to Savon, you might lose your ability to speak forever." Andrew found the button and pushed it. When the door opened, he walked onto the elevator not bothering with the pretense of being Peterson. As the doors closed, he heard footfalls running away from the elevator and smiled. A man's loyalty was only as deep as his willingness for self-sacrifice.

Andrew took a deep breath and leaned against the back of the elevator to regroup. He resumed the position and demeanor of an old man as the elevator began to crawl upwards. When the doors opened again one floor up, he was leaning on his cane.

"Is this the right floor?" he said, muttering to himself. "Of course it is. There're only two floors. Yes, yes. It's the place."

The two guards exchanged puzzled looks as they watched the old man hobble toward them.

"Hello?" Andrew called out. "Is anyone there?"

"Sir, I think you must be lost."

Andrew turned toward the voice. "Who are you?" he asked. "I'm Doctor Peterson."

"How did you get up here?" the second guard asked.

"I took the damned elevator. Didn't you just see me get off?"

The younger voice of the two laughed. "Sir, you can't be here now. We're on lock down and this area is off limits."

"I'm looking for Doctor Savon. Is he here?"

"Sir, you can't be here. There's been a security breach. Here, I'll help you back to the elevator."

"A security breach? Heavens. What happened?"

"That's none of your concern but you have to vacate the area. Now."

The younger guard stepped forward and placed a gentle hand on Andrew's shoulder. "Sir, I'll help you back to the elevator."

Andrew turned and accepted the man's help as they both walked down the short hallway. As he stepped onto the elevator, Andrew thanked the young man.

"I'm afraid I can't see how to operate this thing. I'm blind, you know." Andrew lifted his face to the young man, drawing a slight moan. The disguise was well made.

"Here, I'll help you." The guard stepped onto the elevator to push the button.

Andrew twisted the curved handle of the cane and detached it, revealing a three-inch blade. He grabbed the guard by the hair and pulled him to the side, behind the narrow wall next to the door and out of view of his companion.

"I can slit your throat with a flick of my wrist, but I don't want to. Tell your buddy you're riding down with me." When he hesitated, Andrew pushed the blade against his skin. "Do it now. Please, don't make me kill you."

"Hey, man," the guard called. "I'm going to ride the old coot down to make sure he doesn't hurt himself."

"Whatever." Four hours of standing watch had taken the zeal out of them both.

"Look," Andrew said as the doors closed. "I don't have a problem with you. You seem like a good kid. When these doors open you simply get off and walk away. I know you guys live on the east side of the building. Go to your quarters. Everything will be fine."

"Fine by me. I'm tired of this gig anyway. I'm not getting paid enough for this crap."

"If it's any consolation, you wouldn't have a job much longer anyway."

When the elevator doors opened, the young man did as instructed, and the doors closed again without incident. Andrew replaced the blade and reassumed his disguise. The elevator stopped with a bump and a slight buzzing sound. A light over the door warned that it was about to open. Andrew prepared himself for a fight.

He pushed himself off the wall with a grunt and walked casually toward the guard, leaning heavily on his cane for support.

"What the hell?" the guard asked as he approached Andrew. "Where the hell is Nel—"

Andrew brought the cane up hard and fast, driving it into his crotch. He followed the sound of the grunt as the man bent, hitting him across the back of the head. The next sound Andrew heard was the guard collapsing onto the floor.

Andrew stepped around the body and went to the door. His hand found the buzzer and pressed it.

"Yes," came Bailey's voice.

"Doctor Peterson to see Mister Savon," Andrew said in a deep voice. He hoped to sound like the guard, or that Savon paid so little attention to them that he wouldn't notice.

In the room Savon looked up from his position on the couch next to Malika, who had given up on sleep and rejoined the group in the main room.

"What the heck does he want?" Savon asked, his response measured in Malika's company. He stood and went to the intercom. "Send him away. We're on lock down. He shouldn't be out of his quarters. Send him away."

"Yessir. But he says he has news on the doctor."

Savon exchanged a puzzled look with Bailey. "He can tell us now."

"Savon?" Andrew asked, now using Peterson's voice. "That you?"

258

"Yes, it's me, Peterson. What do you want?" Savon got up and went to the intercom. "Tell me what you want to tell me and one of the guards will escort you back to your quarters, Doctor."

"I know where your man is."

Savon's brow went up. "Do you? Pray tell, Peterson. Where is he?"

"I'm not telling you over this contraption. If I sell a man out, I want to do it face to face. And I have a price."

"Very well. Just a moment." Savon turned from the intercom and pointed at Bailey. "You get over there with that machine gun you've been carrying around all day. If this is a trick and things go south, shoot whoever comes through that door."

"What is happening?" Malika asked as she stood. "What is going on?"

Savon went to her and put his hands on her shoulders. "This might be a trick. It might be Andy. If he's made it this far, he's made it through four armed guards, maybe even killed them. We will do our best to take him peacefully, but if we can't..." he trailed off. "You should go back into your room. I'll call you when all is clear." He hurried Malika across the room and into the bedroom.

Savon pointed to Bailey as he closed the door behind Malika. "Get on your radio and get some more guards up here." He crossed the room and stood by the intercom, waiting for Bailey to finish his call.

"You still there, Doctor Peterson?"

"I'm here. How long are you going to leave me standing here. You ain't gotta tidy the place just for me."

"Okay, I'm buzzing you in now." Savon nodded to his head of security and pressed the button. Both men readied their guns, expecting Andrew to come screaming into the room.

From his position, Savon couldn't see the door, but he saw Bailey relax his weapon as soon as the door opened. He waited as the sound of shuffling feet and the thump of a cane made their way down the short foyer.

"Peterson?" Savon asked. "What the hell are you doing here?"

"I've already told you. I know where your man is hiding."

"And how would you know that old man?" Bailey asked.

"Because I hid him."

"So why are you telling us now?" Bailey asked, approaching him casually. "You two were thick as thieves."

"I want something in return."

"And what would that be?" Savon asked smugly. "At your age?"

"That's just it." Andrew leaned against the wall. "I'm old and I don't have many years left. I have kids and grandkids, great grandkids I've never met. I want out, Savon. Send me back to Poland. Send me home."

"I thought you two were fast friends," Savon said as he tucked the gun into the back of his waistband.

"We are. That's why he came to me for help." Andrew sighed. "I know I probably look like the ass end of a mule for doing this, but I don't wanna die in this God-forsaken desert. I want to see my homeland and die there. Is that too much to ask?"

"No, not really. I don't suppose it is."

"Good, then give me your word that you'll take me home and I'll tell you everything."

"You have my word." Savon crossed the room to the liquor cabinet and crossed his arms, watching the man from across the room. "You will be taken home on the next flight out of here."

Andrew smiled and nodded. "Thank you." To his left a door opened, but he pretended not to hear. It had to be Malika. Savon would bring her here. It had to be her.

"Where is he?" Savon asked.

"In my quarters."

Bailey shook his head. "Nice try, old man. All living quarters have been searched thoroughly."

"You're an idiot, Bailey. My family has been hiding people for longer than you've been alive. My grandfather hid Jews from Nazi thugs for years. Hiding a man from your paid goons was child's play."

"Then why don't you enlighten us to his whereabouts," Savon said, growing irritated with the exchange.

"In the bedroom of my quarters is an armoire. If you press the top left corner in just the right spot, a door will open. It's not a lot of space, but it's big enough for a half-starved man to hide." The door to his left opened further. The squeak of the hinges was loud enough for everyone to hear.

Andrew's heart began to race when Malika's scent reached him. She'd bathed in a gentle soap, washed her hair, and brushed her teeth in a mint flavored toothpaste, but the underlying smell was undoubtably hers.

"Excuse me, sir. I didn't know you were there," Andrew said as he took a few shuffling steps away from Malika.

Savon looked at Bailey and motioned with his head toward the door. He buzzed him out and motioned for Malika to join him. She complied only partially, coming to the center of the room, but kept her eyes on the old man now bent over his cane.

"What a lovely scent. Is there a lady present?" Andrew asked.

"That's none of your business—"

"Yes," Malika replied, cutting Savon off.

"You smell heavenly, ma'am. If you'll forgive me for saying so."

"Thank you. It is very kind of you."

"Come over here, please." Savon opened his palm to Malika, motioning her toward him.

"Worried I'm going to steal your native girl, Savon?" Andrew let out a coarse laugh. "I beg your forgiveness, ma'am, for my crude language."

"Do not worry about me," Malika said, eyeing the old man suspiciously.

Andrew turned to Savon. "I don't want to be here when you bring him in. I want to leave."

"Conscience bothering you, Peterson?" Savon asked with a chuckle.

"No, but yours should bother you."

"Whatever do you mean?" Savon asked, forcing a smile for Malika.

"I know what you did to Doctor Harkins in the containment room, how you tortured him."

"Containment room? Malika asked. Her brow furrowed as she studied the strange old man. Hadn't she seen a sign on one of the doors?

Savon chuckled, shaking his head. "He must be confused. He's an old man," Savon said to Malika with a shrug. "If you want your plane ticket, Peterson, maybe you should go now. Quietly."

Andrew tracked Savon's voice and the echo of his hard-soled shoes as he approached.

"Get stuffed, you murderous bastard," Andrew said as he turned toward the door.

Savon approached him from behind, grabbing his left arm. Andrew spun quickly, catching Savon by surprise, and drove the end of the cane into his stomach. Air rushing out of Savon's lungs in an audible grunt. Malika gasped in shock somewhere behind him.

Andrew wheeled and swung the cane again, but Savon reacted quickly enough to only catch a glancing blow to his hip. Groping blindly with his left hand, Andrew found Savon again and hit him across the back with the cane. The blow landed solidly across his spine and Savon fell to the floor with a shriek of pain.

Andrew moved forward, hoping to put his weight on top of Savon, but his feet suddenly flew from beneath him. He grabbed the arm of the chair on his way down, but still hit the floor hard.

Ignoring the pain, he scrambled to his feet and lurched toward the sound of Savon's heavy breathing.

Pain exploded in his right cheek as Savon's fist slammed into his face, rocking him backwards and tearing one of the latex panels on his cheek.

"Stop!" Malika screamed.

Savon landed another punch into Andrew's stomach before he backed off.

"What is this? You fight an old man?" Malika cried.

"Shut up, you stupid bitch!"

Andrew launched himself at the sound of Savon's voice, catching him around the waist and driving him into the armored glass of the windows. A loud grunt escaped him as Andrew drove his shoulder into the man's chest.

Savon clenched his fists together and slammed them onto Andrew's back twice. As Andrew's grip faltered, Savon punched him in the ribs and shoved him to the side. Now free, he took a few cautious steps back and reached for his gun.

"Looking for this?" Malika asked, holding the gun that had fallen out of his waistband when the men hit the glass.

"No, Malika, you don't understand." Savon took a tentative step toward her but stopped when she raised her aim to his head. "This man is mad, don't you see?"

Andrew pulled himself up onto a padded chair arm. "Shoot him, Malika! Do it!"

"Andrew?" Malika asked, recognizing the voice.

"See, I told you he was mad." Savon began to ease slowly toward the door buzzer, sure that Bailey's men would have searched the room and would be back by now.

"Don't let him press that button," Andrew warned. "This room with be full of guards and we'll both be as good as dead."

"What is going on here?" she asked, looking back and forth between the men.

"He's crazy, remember. The sickness. Just look at him. Look at what he's done to get in here to me."

"Malika, sweetie, don't believe him. Anything he's told you is a lie. I've been here as long as you have. He's had me locked in a room, starving me. Playing tapes of my family over and over to drive me crazy."

When Malika looked back at Savon, he'd taken a few more steps toward the buzzer. "Not another step! Do not make me shoot you."

"Malika, why would I make any of this up? Why?"

"He's a liar!" Andrew yelled. "Malika, it's me." His fingers found the loose edges of the latex mask and pulled most of it from the right side of his face.

"Look around, Malika. I have money, power, influence. I can have anything my heart desires. Why would I go through the trouble to be bothered with a mad man? Ask yourself that."

"Malika don't listen to him. He's a psychopath. He enjoys watching people suffer."

Malika raised the gun and pointed it at Savon as she stared at Andrew, his face still partially covered with the mask of Nickodem Peterson's burned face.

"Why did you do this?" she asked. "This disguise?"

"It was the only way I could get in here. I know him. I knew he'd bring you here." Andrew held out a hand to Malika. "You gotta trust me."

Savon laughed. "Trust? Like you trusted her?"

Malika looked back and forth between the men. When she looked back to Savon he was almost in reach of the button. She fired two shots at the wall. The first missed, but the second hit the panel just beneath the button. It erupted in a shower of sparks, driving Savon back.

"I said do not open that door."

"Okay. Hey, just calm down. You're forgetting who the good guy is here."

"Good guy?" Andrew laughed. "Malika. I might not have acted like it sometimes, but deep down I always trusted you. I never left you."

"He left you to die in the desert. He left you so he could come here and live out his fantasy of killing me. He left you to die."

Malika pursed her lips, fighting back the tears welling in her eyes. "Andrew. What is going on? He said you have a disease from laying with a whore."

"What? That's crazy. I haven't left this place since I got here."

"He said that is what made you crazy, so you kill your wife and son."

"Malika don't believe him. Deep down I don't think you do. I didn't kill Samantha and Lane. He did. I told you. He's made all this up to turn you against me."

"I do not know what to think."

"Malika, sweetie, I'm not crazy from anything but hatred. I should have never brought you here, put you in this position. I'm sorry."

"Andrew?"

"I love you, Malika. I do."

Taking advantage of the momentary lapse in her attention, Savon launched himself at Malika. His body collided with hers, sending them both sprawling behind the counter that defined the small kitchenette from the main room. The gun fired, striking the ceiling as Savon wrestled it out of her hands.

He staggered to his feet and hauled her up by her hair. She struggled until he placed the barrel of the gun against her temple. "You stupid bitch!" He released her hair and put one arm around her neck, holding her against him.

"Stop or I'll kill her," he said, stopping Andrew's charge.

"You two fools deserve each other."

Savon drug Malika across the kitchen. He went framed artwork on the wall and flipped it with the tip of his gun. The picture swung open on hinges to reveal another keypad. He pressed two buttons, then brought the barrel to Malika's temple again.

"I was planning on killing you, my sweet, and leaving him to suffer for the rest of his life. Now, I guess I'll kill him and let you suffer."

A squelch came from the speaker in the hidden keypad and the room filled with the unmistakable sound of a helicopter in flight. "Go ahead, Boss."

"Get your ass back here. Now!"

"Roger that. There's nothing to see out here anyway."

"Land on the roof of my quarters," Savon barked over his shoulder.

"Sir, I don't think that structure is suited for—"

"Just do it!" Savon ordered.

"Roger that. Returning to base. ETA seven minutes."

Savon looked at Andrew and smiled. "I gotta say, Doctor, you surprised me. You know Peterson is going to die for this."

Andrew stood motionless, smiling as he looked toward Savon's voice. "It was his plan, not mine."

"What plan?" Savon asked.

"Any minute now, you'll find out. I don't think you'll like it."

The guards knocked on the door to Nickodem Peterson's living quarters once, then kicked it in. Men rushed through the door; guns drawn. After clearing the living room quickly, they made the turn down the hallway and burst into his bedroom.

"What the hell?" Bailey asked, finding Doctor Peterson lying on his bed, holding a black and white picture of an old man. "What the hell's going on Peterson?"

"Just taking a nap," he replied with a smile.

Beasley produced a radio from his belt and held it to his mouth as he stared at the old man.

"Boss, there's something happening. Peterson is here in his quarters. I don't know who that is there." Beasley looked at his radio when no reply came. "Damn."

He sent two of the guards back to Savon's quarters then turned his attention back to the armoire.

Two men snatched the doors open and yanked the clothes from their hangers. Beasley reached forward and depressed the pressure switch while the other guards trained their weapons into the armoire.

The sound of Nickodem Peterson's laughter filled the room an instant before being silenced by the explosion.

"That plan," Andrew said as a rumble swept through the facility.

"You're crazier than I thought," Savon said. "You'd kill everybody here just to get me?"

"They'll have time to get out." Andrew took a step toward Savon. "You see, Malika, this place is powered by gigantic solar panels. All that power is directed into huge banks of batteries."

Savon backed away, dragging Malika with him as Andrew stepped toward him.

"Wanna guess where that bank of batteries is?" Andrew asked and took another step toward Savon.

"You want me to blow her head off? Take another step." Savon pulled Malika toward a narrow hallway off the kitchenette that led to another door. "When I get to the roof, I'll let her go."

"Nobody believes that. Do you, Malika?"

"I do not," she said through clenched teeth as she struggled against Savon's grip. He hit her on the side of the face with the pistol then shoved it hard against her temple. "Don't be stupid. I'm not one of your sweaty camel jockeys. I'll blow your head off and never think twice about it."

"Hit her again and you'll have to kill us both right now," Andrew sad as he continued, matching Savon's progress. "If I were you, Alain, I'd let her go and make a sprint for the roof. Those batteries could blow any second."

Savon fired a shot at Andrew but missed badly, his aim thrown off by Malika's struggles. "I don't mind killing the both of you, but the girl will get it first."

Andrew stood again after ducking Savon's shot. "Those battery banks are located directly under Peterson's bedroom. He used to complain that the damned humming sound kept him up at night."

"You were a fool for coming back here," Savon said with a laugh. At the end of the hallway he opened a door and drug Malika through it, closing it behind him.

Andrew ran to the door and swung it open, ducking as a bullet whizzed over his head. Crouching at the base of the steps, he counted Savon's footsteps up the metal staircase.

When it was clear, he crawled up the first flight of steps and paused. A door opened above him, then another shot rang out in the stairway, ricocheting off the metal railing. He ducked again and waited for the door to close before hurrying up the steps. Savon was headed for the roof.

Andrew pushed the door open a few inches, only to be driven to his knees as a shot struck inches from his head. He pushed against the heavy metal door again, more cautiously this time.

"You can't get away!" Andrew yelled.

Savon's answer was another shot at the door. This one hitting high on the metal with a loud crack.

"Just let her go, you maniac. Save yourself." Another shot struck the door as Andrew crouched, listening. Wind sailed across the rooftop, creating a barrage of sounds as it passed the various pipes and vents. An air conditioner unit started up, adding to the riot of noise.

Andrew took a deep breath and calmed his mind despite the urgency of the situation. If he charged Savon he'd get shot before he even got close. He had to have better situational awareness if there was a prayer of saving Malika, but time was running out.

He focused on the air conditioner. The motor ran with efficiency despite the handful of loose sand that hung in the air within it, trapped by the vortex of the fan blades. The mechanism spun on the ball bearing housing, pushing the blades that chopped the air with a steady rhythm. The exhaust was forced through a metal grid, making a distinctive high-pitched whine as it passed each of the thin wires making up the grid. The unit was about twelve feet away, near the center of the roof.

Releasing from his intense focus, Andrew heard Malika's voice speaking in Arabic. They were near the front of the building, overlooking Savon's expansive balcony. In the distance a helicopter's blades beat the air with a familiar thump. It was getting closer.

Andrew leapt from his crouch and sprinted toward the air conditioner unit. He misjudged the position slightly and slammed a shoulder into the back edge of the housing as he dove for cover. The blow spun him around behind the unit and out of Savon's sight.

With his pain receptors shut down only a dull ache managed to get through, telling Andrew of his bruised shoulder as he crawled alongside the unit. He accessed the situation again by honing on the sounds one by one, like switching channels on the radio.

A steady stream of Arabic alerted him to Malika's presence. Andrew smiled. He didn't know what she was saying, but it didn't matter. She knew he'd need help finding her amid all the noise and the sound and pitch of her native tongue was a perfect beacon.

Switching to the helicopter, he put it less than a mile away. It was approaching from the east at a high rate of speed. By now Savon could see his escape route and would be getting anxious.

Another, more distant sound caught his attention momentarily. He was trying to decide if it was an echo from the helicopter bouncing back at him from the opposite direction when Malika screamed, drawing his attention back to her. He listened for her voice, but she'd gone quiet. The sound of their clothes flapping in the breeze came to him, but nothing else.

"Whatever you do, Malika, don't get on that helicopter," Andrew pleaded aloud as he inched forward. If she did, she'd probably never be seen again. Not alive anyway. Andrew considered his options but found only one. He had to rush Savon and hopefully free Malika before they got on the helicopter. It was a foolish plan, but as Malika had told him many times, he was a fool.

When the wind from the helicopter blades began to buffet the rooftop Andrew used the sound to paint a more perfect picture of the situation. The air moved across the concrete roof in undulating waves that he could see in his mind. Unlike the wind, they swept in all directions equally, reacting to obstacles in their path. They bounced off the knee-high wall that surrounded the roof and fell back on themselves, sliced through a grate, bent around pipes. In the midst of the wind, he saw a disruption in the steady sound of the propwash as a shape moved along the roof. With each foot the aircraft descended toward them, his vision became clearer and clearer. In his mind he could see the vectors made by the wind, and the position of the interruptions.

As the helicopter's skids neared the roof, Malika cried out for Andrew. It was his last chance. It was now or never.

He sprung from behind the unit and raced toward the helicopter. Savon, busy forcing a struggling woman into the craft, didn't see him emerge from his hiding spot.

Half-way to the helicopter, someone screamed Savon's name and a second later a shot rang out. His left shoulder erupted in pain, and he was knocked back by the force of the shot. Malika screamed his name. The propellers continued their monotonous thump.

He hit the ground hard, and his hand immediately went to the wound. Warm blood covered his fingers as he clutched his shoulder. He accessed his bodily functions again and tried to shut down the pain receptors. He managed to get the pain down to a level that just hurt like hell, then flooded the area with clotting agents to stop the bleeding.

In the helicopter, Malika lashed out at Savon. She attacked his face with a series of punches and scratches. "I'll kill you!" she yelled.

Savon swung the gun, hitting her with a back hand that sent her tumbling to the floor. He delivered a swift kick to her ribs then turned to the pilot. "Let's go!" he screamed. The new pilot sat in stunned silence until Savon pointed the gun at him. "Go!"

The helicopter began to lift slowly but tilted suddenly to the right. Savon was thrown against the wall as Malika crawled hurriedly toward the open doorway. Nearing the exit, she could see Andrew struggling to stand and called out to him.

Savon grabbed Malika by her ankles and hauled her back inside the craft as it sat down hard on the roof. He stomped her between the shoulder blades and pushed her to the floor. Leaning forward as he put his weight on her, he put the gun against the pilots' helmet. "One more stunt like that and I'll blow your fucking brains all over that window. Got it."

The pilot raised his hands in surrender then resumed the controls as another rumble shook the building. The helicopter rose slowly off the roof as a massive explosion rocked the far end of the complex, sending a fireball skyward.

"What the hell is going on?" the pilot asked.

"Just shut up and get us out of here."

Now on his feet, Andrew ran toward the sound of the helicopter. A shot struck the roof to his left, showering him with shrapnel as the bullet exploded on contact with the concrete. Unfazed, he was in a full sprint now, determined to reach Malika before she disappeared forever.

Another shot struck the roof, but it landed behind him. His internal map screamed at him that he was running out of time and out of rooftop. The helicopter was rising quickly and drifting over the edge of the building.

Running at full speed, Andrew reached out, finding nothing but air. The helicopter was airborne. The sound suddenly shifted as the steady beat of the blades began to fall from the roof top to the balcony below. It was moving away from the building.

Out of options, Andrew ran to the edge of the roof at a full sprint. His foot found the short knee wall and he propelled himself through the air toward the sound of the helicopter. Extending his arms, he prepared to grab whatever part of the helicopter he touched.

One second of flight turned into two, then three, and Andrew felt the arc of his jump reach its zenith then begin to fall. He'd missed. Flailing his arms as he fell through the air, he heard the helicopter's blades briefly reflect off the perimeter wall, then fade as it headed out across the desert.

Preparing himself for an impact, Andrew covered his head with his arms and tried to get his feet under him. He landed on Savon's massive wooden table, breaking it in half as he tumbled into the glass partition that served as a railing.

He growled in pain as he scrambled to his knees. The sound of the helicopter was fading fast.

"No," he cried as his head slumped forward. "No." His head swooned, then his body gave way, sending him crashing to the base of the railing in a heap.

"Oh shit." The pilot stared through the windscreen as four dark spots appeared on the horizon. "Boss, you better see this."

Savon leaned forward between the seats and stared at the scene. "Turn around. Lose them."

271

"It's not a car chase. Where the hell am I supposed to go? We've got a thousand miles of open desert."

"Well you better do something fast."

The four black dots on the horizon were now four Apache helicopters heading straight at them.

"Do something!" Savon demanded. "Shoot them down."

"What? Are you crazy? Those are Apache Longbows. They could have already shot us out of the sky." The pilot turned the helicopter sharply away from the oncoming aircraft and accelerated.

"They'll be on us in ninety seconds, Ben," the co-pilot said flatly. "Not a chance."

Savon shoved the gun toward his visor. "You two better make a chance happen then."

"What the hell do you want me to do? This rust bucket is nearly thirty years old. Even brand new it couldn't outrun them."

"One minute," the co-pilot announced.

Savon looked around the cabin anxiously. "This can't be happening."

"They're here," the co-pilot announced as the helicopters split up, taking up positions behind the Blackhawk. The two outer aircraft moved up quickly until they were on either side of them.

Savon grabbed Malika from the floor and hauled her up. Holding her around the neck, he pushed the door open on his side of the aircraft. He waved the gun at the nearest Apache and then put it to Malika's head.

"Unidentified Blackhawk turn your craft around and return to your original location. You are ordered to land. Return to your original location and land your aircraft."

"I can't," the pilot answered into his mic. "I am going to decrease speed, maintain my present course."

"Unidentified Blackhawk aircraft do not continue. Decrease speed and vector to zero-four-zero to return to your previous location."

"Tell them I'll kill her!" Savon yelled. "Tell them!"

"I'm sure you can see in my open doorway, starboard side, that I am under duress. I am under duress."

"Unidentified Blackhawk, understood. You must return to your previous location. You are under the orders of the United States Marine Core and the Government of Saudi Arabia to cease your escape attempt. You must either land your craft or return to your previous location."

"I cannot. I am decreasing speed to hover."

"No!" Savon screamed. "Keep going."

"I can't. Don't you know what we're up against here?" The pilot looked around at the pistol pointed at his head. "Look, either I get shot by you or shot by them. I'd rather get shot with your fucking nine mil than a sidewinder missile."

The pilot decreased speed and held the craft in a hover, watching as the four helicopters surrounded them. He looked through his windshield. The pilot in front of them stared back at him through a dark visor.

"Unidentified Blackhawk, you will land the aircraft, or you will be fired upon."

"I am under duress. I repeat, I am at gunpoint to stay aloft."

"Unidentified Blackhawk, you will land your aircraft, or you will be fired upon."

"Oh shit, Ben. I don't wanna go out like this. I didn't sign up for this."

"I never wanted to be here in the first place."

The pilot looked through the windshield and raised his palms in surrender. The opposing pilot twirled his finger in the air in front of him then stabbed it downward.

Ben raised his palms to the pilot staring back at him, signaling that there was nothing he could do. He dropped his hands and looked over at his co-pilot. "Oh well," he said. "Nice knowing ya."

Nineteen

Andrew pulled himself to his feet against the railing, his left arm clutched closely to his torso. His whole body hurt, but it paled in comparison to the sinking feeling in his chest. He'd failed. Savon had gotten away, and Malika was gone forever. All because of him.

He leaned on the rail, absently listening to the sounds of the people evacuating the building. Hearing the fire alarm for the first time, his mind began to grope for some semblance of a plan. Most of the people here had been roped into working for Savon, just like him. They were scientists and doctors and stood no chance against a man like Savon.

"Damn," he grunted and spat over the rail. Malika was gone, but the people below still might need him. Many of them were probably hurt by Peterson's makeshift bomb. He was still a doctor and had an obligation to help, even if all he wanted to do was curl into a ball and die. Staggering along the balcony, his left arm clutched to his chest, he checked each of the towering glass doors.

When the last one resisted his pull, he leaned against it and sighed tiredly. His body was in agony and his strength was gone. He just wanted to sleep for a very long time. The people below would have to make do without him.

When his knees began to weaken, he did nothing to stop them. His body needed rest and medical attention. There was nothing else he could do. He slid down the glass and sat on the expensive terra-cotta tile as his chin dropped to his chest. It was over. Nothing else mattered.

"Think it'll work?"

Ben shrugged. "We'll see. Hold on." Ben threw the Blackhawk into a rapid descent, tossing Malika and Savon upward in the back of the craft. He then leaned it into a hard, right bank, flying under the Apache stationed beside him. The helicopter took evasive action, then fell into pursuit formation behind them as they headed back to the Facility.

"Are you crazy?" Savon yelled, shoving the gun against the pilot's neck. "I should kill you now."

"Do it, you dipshit, and we all plunge into the sand. That what you want?"

Savon's expression eased as he accepted the rationale. "Get us the hell out of here then." He turned to leave, then put the gun against the pilot's head again. "If you ever talk to me that way again, I will kill you. It won't matter where we are."

"I'm doing my best to not get us shot down. That'll have to do."

Andrew raised his head slowly. His brow furrowed as the faint sound of approaching helicopters fell on his ears. Cocking his head, he listened intently, blocking out the sounds of the fire alarm and the circus of noise as his one-time co-workers evacuated the building. The helicopters were definitely coming toward him and moving fast.

He got to his knees and hauled his weary body up from the floor. Staggering to the railing, he stared over the wall and into the desert. The lead helicopter sounded a lot like Savon's Blackhawk, but it wasn't alone. There were at least two more following. No, he corrected himself. There were four and they were different from the Blackhawk. Andrew shook his head and fought the smile that wanted to come to his lips as a glimmer of hope returned.

Alain Savon shook his head as he stared down at Malika's limp form on the floor of the helicopter. He saw now how foolish it had been to try to use her to get back at Andrew. Too many variables always foiled a good plan. What a shame, he thought as his eyes washed over her body, I didn't even get a chance to have her.

"Hi, honey. We're home."

Savon jumped, snatched out of his thoughts by the pilot's sudden outburst. He spared the girl one last glance, then stood. She would have to wait until he had more time.

He pushed his head into the cockpit, watching as they neared the facility he'd built in the desert. A plume of dark smoke rose from behind it, ruining the view he always enjoyed. His shiny jewel, his oasis in the sand, was ruined and Andrew Harkins was to blame. The name resonated in his mind. Andrew Harkins. He'd done this. He'd ruined everything, and for what? Some misguided sense of morality?

"Look, on the balcony." Savon pointed to his residence as they drew closer to the facility. "That's him. Shoot that son of a bitch! At least I'll know he's dead."

"Are you crazy? If we fire, they'll blow us out of the sky."

"Do it!" Savon demanded as he grabbed for the stick controller. "Shoot him, damned you." He flipped the weapons system on and grabbed at the stick again. "Do it."

Ben fought for control of the aircraft while the co-pilot switched the weapons system off.

Savon turned and fired a shot into the side of the co-pilot's neck, splattering the side window with blood. His body slumped forward, falling against the side of the craft.

"What the hell? You're fucking crazy!" Ben managed to slow the craft while fighting for control with Savon. Another loud report filled the cabin and his arm exploded in pain.

Savon quickly flipped the weapons on and used both hands to fight for the controls. He got his finger around the trigger and began firing the fifty-caliber gun mounted beneath the nose of the aircraft. His eyes widened with excitement as the glass panels along his balcony began to explode into shards of glass. The sun reflected beautifully off them as they shattered, flying in every direction.

If nothing else came of this whole fiasco, he'd know that Andrew Harkins was dead, and at his own hand.

The gun beneath the Blackhawk began to spin, producing a loud whirring noise an instant before the fifty-caliber bullets began to fly. It wasn't much time, but it was enough for Andrew to start running.

Multiple projectiles flew at him, screaming through the air with a loud whistle. He was already running when the first glass panel exploded behind him. Shielding his face with one hand from the shower of broken glass, he ran along the balcony as each panel exploded next to him, barely managing to escape their reach.

His body, almost spent, responded to the massive dose of adrenaline and endorphins that propelled him along the balcony with little sense of his position. The only thing that mattered now was avoiding being cut to ribbons by the bullets.

His knees struck the end railing in full stride as the last door panel exploded beside him. Andrew tumbled over the rail and landed on his back on the sand one story below. A cascade of broken glass rained down on him as the arc of bullets pitched upward suddenly and came to a stop.

He rolled onto his side with a groan and shook the glass fragments from his face. Forcing his reluctant body to react, he crawled to cover at the base of the wall. Everything that had hurt before hurt more now and it was getting harder to breathe. The new pain in his ribs told him that he'd broken at least one of them in the fall.

Hugging the smooth stone wall, he limped to the corner of the building. The helicopter was still aloft just outside the wall, but it sounded like it was having trouble. The motors sputtered once, then again before coming down on the sand hard outside the compound.

There were other helicopters in the air, but there was no way to tell who they were. All he could do was hope that somehow, they were good guys. So far there hadn't been an explosion from the Blackhawk that went down. If Malika were in it, she could still be alive.

He started toward the crash site, quickly becoming aware that he was not alone. The already panicked employees who had evacuated the building scattered when the shooting started. Now they were filtering back out into the courtyard to avoid the crashed helicopter. He was suddenly surrounded by people that he might or might not be able to trust.

"Doctor Peterson?" The female voice came from his left. "Thank God you're okay. We feared the worst. Praise the Lord, you made it out."

Andrew's memory spat out a name. "Susan?" he asked.

A soft hand came to rest on his back. "I'm just so thankful to be alive."

A vague memory of the woman swam forward in his jumbled mind. She was a middle-aged woman who worked in the genetics lab on the other end of the facility. Samantha had once called her a tight ass, the reason for which he couldn't remember and didn't waste time trying.

"Your face," she gasped.

"I don't have time to explain, Susan, help me to the gate. Hurry. It's very important."

"Anything." She increased the pressure on his back. "Coming through," she said, almost pleading with the group of people in front of her.

"Get the hell out of the way!" Andrew yelled as they waded through the quickly growing crowd. "Get back! Stay away from the helicopter. It might explode and kill us all."

"Doctor Peterson!" Susan gasped.

Andrew reached out and grabbed her shoulder. "Get me to the damned helicopter!"

Susan pushed her way through the people, many of which had filed out the gate to look at the carnage and were now streaming back in to take shelter from the possible explosion behind the perimeter wall. Andrew clutched the blouse at the base of Susan's back and prodded her forward.

"There," she said, coming to an abrupt stop. "Fifty yards straight ahead."

Andrew released her and rushed past.

Andrew's outstretched hand fell on the hot metal of the helicopter's fuselage. It was tilted to the side on top of one crumpled skid. The pained moans of an injured man leaked from the craft.

He called out to Malika, but the pilot answered.

"Ronald's dead. That crazy bastard, Savon, shot him."

"Where's the girl?" Andrew screamed.

"She was in the back with Savon. I don't know about her, but I saw him running away. He just left us all here to die, the son of a bitch."

Andrew hoisted himself into the damaged craft, groaning as the pain in his shoulder and ribs reignited. The fuselage of the helicopter was littered with broken equipment and the smell of fuel was thick in the air. There wasn't much time left.

"We gotta get outta here. This thing's going to blow the hell up, man."

Andrew violently shrugged the hands off his shoulder. "Do you see the girl?"

"There, in the back." The pilot pushed past him, headed to the back of the craft. He returned dragging a body through the debris. "I got her. Come on. Now!"

Andrew helped the pilot evacuate Malika, then hopped down from the helicopter.

The pilot, injured himself, managed to carry Malika a few feet before falling to his knees and dropping her onto the ground.

Andrew fell beside Malika and lifted her upper body off the sand, cradling her in his arms as the pilot staggered away.

"I'm so sorry," he whispered, his face buried in her hair as he hugged her body to him.

Urgent voices suddenly surrounded them, drowning out the chatter from the retreating crowd. The chaos transformed into a series of loud, commanding shouts. Hands were all over him, hoisting him off the sand. He struggled against them, clinging to Malika's limp form, but he was no match for the strong hands holding him.

Andrew's head began to swoon as the voices faded in and out. He could feel himself falling but was powerless to stop it. His body was spent by the time he escaped the isolation room, his endurance was at its end. His body, no longer responding to his commands, began shutting down.

The last words he heard as he felt his body being drug along the sand by two very strong hands was a man yelling orders for someone to "Bring the body."

Twenty

Andrew turned his clean-shaven face to the ocean breeze and took in a deep breath of sea air. The crispness of it filled his lungs, giving him a new appreciation for fresh air and healthy lungs.

Below him, past the tropical growth that covered the hillside separating his villa from the beach, the Mediterranean rolled gently onto the sand. These early morning hours, before the clamor of beach goers and tourists, were quickly becoming his favorite time of day.

He adjusted the dark sunglasses on his face and reached for the table next to him. His hand found the small tape recorder and picked it up. He sighed heavily and switched it on.

"Nickodem Peterson is a hero, just like his father, and grandfather. He risked, and ultimately sacrificed, his life to stop a tyrant. Alain Savon's reach wasn't as wide as Hitler's, but it was as thorough and as savage. He was a man that had to be stopped and I could never have done that without his sacrifice.

"The things that happened in the desert should never been allowed to happen. The pursuit of medical advancement is a noble endeavor, but not if you must break the first rule of medicine, do no harm.

"What happened in the Facility did much harm. My life has been changed forever and I doubt if I will ever fully recover." He switched the recorder off with a sigh.

In exchange for immunity, Andrew had agreed to recount everything that had happened at the Facility and in the desert. Reliving it, he realized how improbably it all had been; how unbelievable it was for a blind man to do the things he did. He wouldn't believe it himself, if he hadn't experienced it.

Alain Savon had taken so much from him and the fact that he somehow "escaped" angered him to the core of his being. He would never be completely comfortable again, but that was his new life. Fear and apprehension would always be in the back of his mind. Savon was a mad man who belonged behind bars for the rest of his life, but like so many others in his position, justice would be delayed.

The old adages of "international incident" and "governmental acquiescence," along with the desire not to "embarrass the Royal Family" had allowed Savon to end up a "guest" of the Saudi government, with all assurances that he would be "contained." It all stank of corruption and indifference, but there was nothing to be done about it. This was the way of such things.

Countless countries, including the United States had purchased technology refined at the Facility, some of it his own, and people with more power than he wanted it to be kept quiet. No one would ever know exactly what went on in the middle of the Saudi desert except him and whomever heard his recordings. The number would probably be very low.

Andrew sighed. Maybe it was for the best. His hands weren't exactly clean either. He'd been in some ethically questionable situations himself and would have to live with that knowledge. The only solace to be had was in the hope that maybe he'd contributed something good to humanity that would help more people than he hurt. In the end that was all anyone could hope for.

As the breeze gusted, blowing across his neatly trimmed hair, it brought a thin smile to his face.

The words of an old song came to mind about the ocean being a desert in disguise. Maybe, he thought, but some disguises worked better than others. There were things he'd miss about the desert, but he never wanted to go back again. His new life would be what he made it. It was better to leave the past in the past and let the words on the recording speak for themselves.

He switched the recorder back on. "I have suffered further than a man should for his weaknesses," he began. "I have lost people that I love, I have lost my sight, I have lost friends, and I will live the rest of my life knowing that it was my decision to join the Facility that brought it all about. The world is a better place because of people like

Nickodem Peterson and Malika Kader. They are the ones who really stopped Alain Savon. The things they did, the sacrifices they made are as heroic as any other in the service to mankind. Neither of them will ever be famous nor receive any medals, but they should.

"I suffer no delusion that justice will ever find him, for men like Alain Savon seem to move outside the lines of justice and retribution. All I ask, no, all I beg is that he not be allowed to reopen another facility somewhere else in the world. But even on that I am doubtful. Some people never get what's coming to them, some people do. He's one of the ones that don't.

"That's it. That's all I've got to say. I am obligated to recount my memories of what happened, but I don't intend to spend the rest of my life reliving them. You've given me six months in this house. I hope not to meet any of you again. When that six months is up you will find a key under the mat and an empty house. Do not look for me. You will not find me."

Andrew switched the tape recorder off and held it against his lips as he allowed himself to experience the moment of sorrow. He could push it away by flooding his brain with dopamine, but he wanted to feel this one.

Dropping the recorder to the Spanish tile that covered the table next to him with a heavy sigh, he picked up his cup of coffee and settled into the chair, losing himself in the sounds of the ocean.

A hand touched his shoulder and he stiffened.

"How are you this morning?"

A smile slid across his lips as he recognized the voice. "Strangely content."

"Is that a good thing, or a bad thing?"

Andrew took the hand in his and turned in his chair to face the voice. Pulling Malika closer, he kissed her lips then hauled her into his lap.

"It is a wonderful thing." Her laugh lit up his face.

"What would you like to do this morning?" she asked.

"I don't know. You feel up to exploring the beach?"

She kissed him again and smiled. "As long you do not pull me in the water again."

"Promise."

"I mean it, Andrew. You know I cannot swim."

Andrew laughed. "Okay, okay. I promise."

Malika stood from his lap and took his hand, leading him toward the back door to the small villa they shared.

"Come, we must get dressed."

Andrew slapped her on the bottom as they entered the house. "Maybe we'll go to the beach later."

"Perhaps," she said with a laugh, "We will go tomorrow."